RON STOOD MOTIONLESS LISTENING

when he realized that Kristy was not upstairs at all, but was standing in the far corner of the room. Suddenly, as though flicked off by an unseen finger, the stereo died, leaving the room in silence.

"Yes. You can talk to me," said Kristy, standing in front of the stereo. Her voice was soft, almost a whisper. "Yes, now I can hear you! Oh, yes," Kristy shrilled. "Yes, I will. Sometime soon. I will."

"Kristy," Chandal scolded, "stop that!"

"No, no, no!" Kristy screamed and stamped her feet. "Leave me alone, goddammit!" With shrill laughter, she began scratching herself, lifting her dress above her waist.

"Kristy, honey, are you all right?" cried Ron, rushing to his daughter. Kristy appeared not to understand and mumbled over and over, "She likes me . . . she likes me," until the murmur became lower and lower, then a whisper that died away . . .

Books by Ken Eulo

The Brownstone
The Bloodstone
The Deathstone

Published by POCKET BOOKS

THE
DEATHSTONE

KEN EULO

PUBLISHED BY POCKET BOOKS NEW YORK

This novel is a work of fiction. Names, characters, places and incidents are either the product of the author's imagination or are used fictitiously. Any resemblance to actual events or locales or persons, living or dead, is entirely coincidental.

Another *Original* publication of POCKET BOOKS

POCKET BOOKS, a Simon & Schuster division of
GULF & WESTERN CORPORATION
1230 Avenue of the Americas, New York, N.Y. 10020

Copyright © 1982 by Ken Eulo

ISBN: 0-671-45285-1

First Pocket Books printing November, 1982

10 9 8 7 6 5 4 3 2 1

POCKET and colophon are registered trademarks
of Simon & Schuster.

Printed in the U.S.A.

For our firstborn, Kenneth,
a special light whom we all love

PROLOGUE

1299 A.D.
Rottingen, France

THE EXCITEMENT WAS INFECTIOUS. EVEN THE BLAZE OF THE SUN fracturing the twisted rooftops at so many different levels could not diminish the suspense. The sounds in the square rose, the mingling and slowly loudening voices of people, the blacksmith's hammer smashing against white-hot iron, the noise of hooves and wheels on cobblestones, the street howls from peddlers: "Rags and bones! Rags and bones!" Then a competitive cry: "Dog skin . . . human hair! Dog skin . . . human hair!"

Chickens and pigs clucked, rooted, grunted and pecked among heaps of straw and slop, getting in everyone's way though no one noticed or cared. Soot and ash settled over landscape and invaded human orifices. There was a paroxysm of coughs; then silence. All at once, in that choke-filled, excrement-ridden atmosphere—the time had come.

Now a tide of people squeezed through the gate and followed a well-worn path leading up the side of the mountain. The horseman sat astride his animal and ordered the people to clear the way. People grumbled.

"Stand aside!" he ordered, forcing the huge sweating side of the animal against the crowd. "Scum! Stand aside!"

Most of them had come from far away to witness the spectacle. They did not welcome the delay. Many would have to remain on the road all afternoon to ensure getting home before nightfall. Besides, they had made the journey in joy; their hearts were always full when they watched the soldiers putting witches to death.

1

Further on, the procession had already stopped. The captain wiped beads of sweat from his brow and shielded his eyes against the harsh glare of the sun. He peered down the rocky hill and waited.

A stranger could not mistake the fact that this was a place of death, because five upright beams stood naked against the sky. Sometimes there were more, but there were never less than five.

For a long time people stood aside, wide eyed like children, comfortable with their lice and smoky smell and dirty hands and faces. They drank wine and ale, laughed, while the young ones babbled questions. Dice were thrown and plaintive songs were bawled in high humor. Death was cheap. It came, it went. There were always dead beggars to be seen along the roads. Rarely did anyone pause. Sickness and fever were a way of life.

Still the sun rose higher in the sky. Soldiers dozed on the jagged rocks. Below the rocks, beggars scrambled among the people begging for a molded crust of bread which might otherwise be discarded.

"Here, eat this!" a woman screamed with laughter and lifted her dress above her waist. The beggar was instantly shoved aside and from everywhere eager hands reached out to ravish the whore. Today there was no charge. Fornication was a favorite pastime before and after an execution.

Others stood aside in small gatherings and discussed their favorite death. They had seen death by spear, stoning, quartering by horses, strangulation, drowning, burning—still crucifixion was preferred. Other methods, the majority agreed after some pleasurable deliberation, were all too quick. Hardly worth the journey.

"Crucify them!" someone shouted. A chant quickly began. "Crucify them! Crucify them!" Behind the cries, hot sticky fingers lustfully probed between the whore's wanton legs.

Abruptly a moan escaped the crowd as five women appeared at the foot of the hill. The captain rose in his saddle and stared down through a remorselessly sunny landscape. Each woman carried a huge piece of timber on her right shoulder. It was ritually prescribed that each would carry her own crosspiece.

Barely in view, one of the women stumbled and almost

collapsed. Her knees bent; then, by effort, they straightened. A rousing cheer went up from the crowd—they were primed to see blood.

"Crucify them!" the crowd hissed. "Crucify them!"

The ragged band of women started their climb up the mountain. They moved slowly, breasts partially exposed, legs and arms bruised from where the soldiers had taken pleasure in beating them. Each step brought with it a sharp pain as the jagged rocks cut deep into the balls of their bare feet. A whip was used to keep them moving.

Along the sides of the path people argued the guilt or innocence of one of the women who had been popular at the inn. "A good whore put to waste," grumbled a voice. A fight suddenly broke out and soldiers sprang forth with spears to quell the disturbance.

Now the walk to the cross was half-finished. The spectators were not so numerous on the hill, because this was a restricted area. Only the Town Elders were afforded the privilege of making this final climb. Still, those who were there spat at the women, hurled stones, laughing and shouting: "Go to hell where you belong! Die!" Others shouted: "Bitch-witch, Bitch-witch," in a sort of sing-song chant. Under the law, sympathy toward the accused was forbidden.

All at once, from between the tightly pressed crowd, a little girl clawed herself free. Her eyes were transfixed on her mother. Tears coursed down her cheeks. Mutely her mother stopped and held out her free hand to her child. Blood ran down the woman's arm and drew up into a small puddle in the palm of her hand.

Other women, seeing this, began to sob and found it exceedingly difficult to bear the sight of her, this broken woman who was about to have nails driven through her wrists and feet.

"Stupid bitch!" scowled an angry husband. "Do you want them to see you? Accuse you?" The old woman quickly dabbed her eyes and laughed.

"Momma!" screamed the child and darted for her mother's outstretched hand.

"Hold, child!" the soldier ordered and forced her back into the crowd. "Momma! Momma!" the child screamed. She thrashed out violently, trying to free herself. The soldier held

3

his grasp. She clawed at his hands, chest, her eyes swollen, one hand desperately reaching out to her mother.

The woman begged her child not to grieve, and her covert glance into the crowd warned a friend to shield her daughter from as much of what lay ahead as possible. Do you understand me? she asked silently. DO YOU UNDERSTAND ME?

A softer eye contact. Please.

"Move it, slut!" The soldier stuck his spear into the soft flesh of her back and pushed. The woman lurched forward, a tiny trickle of blood flowing from her fresh wound. Glancing back for the last time, she watched her daughter break free of the soldier and disappear into the crowd. It had been a poor sort of farewell.

The woman moved on. The minutes passed slowly and yet too quickly. There was the longing to go rapidly toward the inevitable conclusion; the longing for the humiliation to cease. And yet, the desire for life to go on even in its worst agony.

From time to time she peered into the crowd and could see her daughter frantically pushing between people, trying to get a last look at her. The child appeared confused and frightened and shook so violently that it seemed she could scarcely stand. She wailed, "Momma! Momma!," while with an elaborate show of disdain, people cleared their throats and spat upon her. Several men took hold of the child and spun her around, while others picked up stones. A sound went through the air as though a herd of animals had suddenly stampeded. The crowd was getting restless. Soldiers jumped to their feet in alarm. The mountain rumbled as people stamped the ground with their feet and smashed rocks together, tapping out the passage of time, tapping the slow cadence of a dead march.

Now, at the top, a hush fell over the crowd. Excitedly they pressed in upon the soldiers and, with a muttering of curiosity, smiled their idiot grins.

A young soldier broke ranks and came across the rocks to where the captain sat astride his horse. He leered senselessly, conspiratorially. "We are ready," he whispered and pointed in the direction of the women.

"Indeed," the captain scoffed and shifted the weight of his

4

lumbering body in the saddle. The horse shifted its hind legs with the redistribution of power. "Whoa," the captain soothed. "Easy . . ."

His body bent forward slightly as he stroked the suppleness of the animal's neck. From the corner of his eye he caught sight of the women's faces. All but one were weeping. But then, he mused, her child had done enough weeping for both of them. His eyes met the flat gaze of the woman. Although he was not interested in the confrontation, he did not feel the inclination to avert his eyes. Her face was sunken, the deep wrinkles of her brow full of sweat. Her expression remained that of stone. Yet in her eyes there was a kind of triumph, the triumph of an unconquered spirit and the superior will of an avenging angel.

Nervously he scratched the black stubble of his bearded face. It required a degree of courage, indeed passion, to do what he was about to do. He waited a moment longer.

The crowd stirred.

"Let it be done!" his voice suddenly boomed. "Let it be . . . done." His voice trailed away. The soldiers moved in quickly and began to strip the women naked. The nudity added shame to the proceedings and, at the same time, exposed the women to the millions of insects of the air. The vultures would come after the crucified were dead. The crowd roared its approval. The crucifixion had begun.

The sun dipped behind a cluster of clouds for a moment, causing the crowd to gaze upward. Below the mountain, the leaves of the trees and the flowers moved in a soft breeze. Lizards darted swiftly among the rocks and down into the dark crevices below.

Abruptly the sun reappeared. Cheers, yells, as all refocused their attention on the women. Screams now: "Sow! Witch-bitch! Burn them! Fuck them first! Fuck them!"

But still the little girl who huddled feverishly against the rocks would not take her eyes from her mother, from the soldiers who fondled her, mocked her. The child's eyes burned with sorrow. And something else. Hatred. Deeply felt, seething hatred.

"Let's see your heathen god save you now!" the soldier snarled as he tore the last bit of clothing from her body.

"If she believes in the devil," another guard shouted, "then let him rise up from these stones and save her!" Other soldiers joined in the taunting.

Once they had completely stripped the woman naked, a cloth was wound between her loins and between her thighs with the loose end tucked in at the back. Her clothing, along with that of the others accused, was tossed onto a pile of wood and set afire.

A sharp crackling noise filled the air. Smoke swirled cocoonlike into the sky, mixing with a malevolent, hissing chant, "Burn, burn, burn . . ."

The child watched as her mother was brought swiftly to the ground. As soon as she fell, the beam was forced up tight against the back of her neck. The woman gave no resistance and said nothing. Even when her body hit the ground hard, she withstood the pain in silence.

Once begun, the business at hand was done effortlessly and efficiently. The woman's left hand was held flat against the board. Staring up at the soldier's face she wondered if she could withstand the torture. She couldn't. With a sharp blow, the first square-cut iron nail was driven into the woman's wrist. Her long agonized wail rose quickly in the noonday air. The soldier wiped a splattering of blood from his face, then moved to the other side of the woman's body to the other wrist.

Rivulets of blood flowed freely over the rocks now, making their serpentine way into dark crevices of stone to where lizards dwelt, where nightmares were conjured, where lamentations and suffering were buried for centuries, set free now by the oozing scarlet liquid that softly, silently, reawakened their powers and stained all flowers a bloody red.

The child's eyes swelled with tears. Her body trembled, shook—the hammer was brought down again. Hatred. She would not forget her hatred. Another forceful thud as the hammer struck iron. *I shall remember,* she said . . . *I shall remember,* she thought . . . *I shall remember!* she screamed.

With the last thud of the hammer, the child turned away. Her mother had been crucified. She would remember.

ONE

FIRST STEPS

ONE

Father, the root of this little white flower
Among the stones has the taste of blood.
Something is very strange on the hill today.
The sun fades and reptiles are everywhere.
But do not run away, because . . .

THE HOUSE WAS SMALL. RESTRICTED. A SPANISH-MOORISH stucco dotted with palms in the Hollywood Hills section of Los Angeles. On either side were other such dwellings; to the rear, the abandoned estate of Huntington Hartford and, beyond, the precipitous clambering of hills. But in the early evening of July 18, the house looked festive. At approximately 6:20 P.M., Ron Talon glanced into the hall mirror, ran his hand indifferently through his hair, then turned to open the front door. Kristy, his six-year-old, was upstairs in her bedroom getting dressed; his wife Chandal was on the terrace making a last minute check of the food and drink. It was to be just another informal poolside gathering on an indolent Sunday night.

Ron's hand stopped just short of the doorknob. He had heard a sharp, brittle sound from above. It came from Kristy's room.

He paused to listen.

The sound was odd. Almost rhythmical. Now louder, faster. Then the sound abruptly ceased. Ron glimpsed his image in the mirror. And then it happened. It was something that had started with the first hot days of summer. Colors seemed to suddenly fade, and with the dulling of his perception, there came an overwhelming feeling of loneliness.

During these moments that seemed to be coming more frequently these days, he had the disturbing feeling that time had somehow eluded him, and that he had become lost in the scheme of things. He felt awkward sitting at his desk or discussing business with a client over lunch—even walking into his own kitchen in the evening. The simple act of eating dinner had become a chore.

Chandal slid open the terrace door and stuck her head inquiringly in his direction. He tried to smile and, as always lately, he groped for something he needed to tell her. Something half-remembered, just out of reach. Even now, as the warm colors of her existence flooded the living room, the words once again eluded him.

"Ron, someone's at the door."

"Do you think they'd go away if we didn't answer?"

"Probably forever." Chandal nodded as the doorbell rang twice more, its chimes sounding angry under the persistent finger.

"I'm coming, for God's sake," he said and opened the door.

"Ron!" Pamela shrieked, throwing out her arms. She was upon him now, her skeletal limbs poised like ropes in the air above his shoulders. He did not know if she wished to embrace him or to strangle him.

She embraced him. "God, it's nice to see you again!"

"Where's, uh, Stuart?" he asked, connecting with the name at the last possible instant. He thought: Some friends. I don't even know their names.

"Isn't he here yet?" she was asking.

"No. You're the first."

"How original of me!" She took him by the arm. "Well, let's have a drink, shall we? Then we'll sit down to a nice long chat."

Pamela exchanged hellos with Chandal, insisted on pouring her own drink—a stiff one—then immediately migrated back into the living room. With a double scotch in one hand and a ferociously puffed cigarette in the other, she settled too close to Ron on the couch, chattering her way to a nonstop insistence of how wonderful life was, how free she felt: "My God, like a woman out of prison." Her smile stretching ever wider until it seemed certain to snap like an overextended rubber band. "Please," she groaned, still smiling, "if the economy gets any worse, I'll have to drain my pool!" The notion made her roar with a laughter that gave way to panting.

Very funny, Ron thought and wondered if Pamela knew the real reason for the party that night. For Ron, it was a bit of a smoke screen. A way of pretending that his talent agency hadn't gone into a recession. Yet, despite bad times, Ron refused to let go. He told himself it was the business he was in. Being a theatrical agent, even in the best times, was like grabbing hold of a red-hot comet's tail. That stung, brought blisters, but was infinitely better than what was happening now.

The writers and directors strike had all but shut Hollywood down. Most of his clients were on the unemployment line. Still, he had managed to keep a full staff at the office, but exactly how long he could hang on was another question. No work, no commissions. It was that simple.

"You know," Pamela sighed, a little drunk already, a little more honest, "I never knew middle age was going to be this rough."

"What?"

"Menopause, Ron, darling. I'm going through menopause. Don't look at me like that. It's really a terrible thing." She shook her head, lighted another cigarette from the tip of the first, and said: "Stuart and I are getting a divorce."

Instantly, Ron was sympathetic. He was always sympathetic to other people's problems. More so than to his own. "Jesus, Pam—I had no idea."

"I know," she replied. "Neither did I. But then that's always the way of things in Hollywood, isn't it? Under every table you can find a married man fingering his latest broad. Best kept secrets, that sort of thing. Well," she said raising her glass, "to my divorce!"

Instinctively, Ron took a healthy drink from his glass. Then

11

a moment's hesitation. Abruptly, he glanced up to the ceiling. There it was again. An odd scraping sound. Like the sound of furniture being moved.

What's going on up there?

He wondered if he should investigate. But then, after listening for a moment, he rejected the idea. Kristy was probably still upstairs fooling around. Besides, whatever it was, it had stopped.

Ron turned suddenly when he felt Pamela's body press closer to his. With a childlike gesture, she laid her head on his shoulder. He could see she was about to cry. Oh, Christ, what if she becomes hysterical? he asked himself with alarm. Then he heard her soft voice in his ear. "You've got to tell me the truth, Ron. Tell me right this minute, was I really a bad wife to that bastard?"

At that point, the doorbell rang. Ron offered a silent prayer of thanksgiving as he excused himself and, with a sigh of profound relief, moved away to greet his next guest. Almost before he had closed the door, the doorbell rang again. The parade of guests continued uninterrupted. There were embraces and kisses, the latter always delicately smacked into air just missing the recipient's cheek so as not to disturb the cosmetics. Soon the room was full of young theatrical types; with subdued Kenny Rogers on the stereo and joints being passed around. There were six actors, two directors, one TV writer, a producer, two lawyers, a tax consultant and an assortment of wives and escorts. Mimi Halpern, Ron's assistant and the agency's primary asset, arrived last with Dwayne Clark in tow. Dwayne was a singer, career on the skids, and enough sadness in his black eyes to kill you.

"What's this?" Ron asked as Dwayne left Mimi's side. "Part of your Mother Earth sympathy package?"

"Sympathy, my royal caboose," she retorted lasciviously, then assumed a conspiratorial tone. "Have you ever seen a face that beautiful?" she whispered. "He looks like Adonis in black curls with a Kirk Douglas chin."

Chandal caught the exchange and grinned. "My husband is cuter."

"Not through the chin, he isn't," Mimi said decisively.

Chandal hesitated, but only for an instant. "Let's talk

about it, shall we?" She good-naturedly hooked her arm through Mimi's and the two women moved away demurely, hips swaying slightly to two separate rhythms.

Ron exchanged a whimsical glance with his wife as she looked back over her shoulder, then watched as she and Mimi disappeared onto the terrace. Dressed in a sheer green blouse and a pair of designer jeans, Chandal looked younger than her thirty-six years. She was wearing the diamond earrings Ron had given her for their first anniversary.

Then Chandal had scarcely been a year separated from something worse than a breakdown. Tonight there were seven years piled between her and a best-forgotten past. And still sometimes Ron worried. Even now, as sensational as she looked, he imagined there was a degree of tension in the faint line between her eyes. The thought had crept into his mind unbidden; a sudden twinge like a nudge in the ribs, and was quickly replaced by a small, scolding voice saying, Forget it. The past is buried. Forget it.

Two bourbons later he decided that the party was going well. Some of the guests were scattered about the terrace helping themselves to drinks, cheese and melon; others hung inside the glass doors enjoying the conditioned air while indulging in small clusters of conversation. By this time, Ron was feeling reasonably sociable. So socialize, he told himself. By Christ, boy—socialize.

After several false starts, he began drifting from one group to another, picking up bits of useless information. Where and how to put his money into tax shelters. Real estate holdings. Donations to the Actors' Fund, various travel costs, monthly expense write-offs. He wondered if anyone knew how broke he really was.

"The total operating cost of the Falcon comes to around $230,000 a year, while the total operating cost of a Lear jet runs about $140,000 a year . . ."

"Is that a fact?" Ron murmured moving on.

In the corner, Chandal was handing Kristy a glass of ginger ale. Kristy smiled, holding onto the glass with both hands and Ron felt the same mesmerization he often felt when looking at his daughter. He thought he had never seen such a face—not just the beauty of the features—but the repose, the level stare into space that seemed to bounce off an unseen object and project itself back into her sapphire eyes so that she was quietly merged with her own person and had little connection with the rest of the room.

"Ron," breathed an oldish character actress now leaning heavily on his arm. "I hope you don't think I'm doing anything wrong. I just felt in the mood to come over here and give you a hug." Her breath was wretched with drink and cigarettes; her mouth sloppy, smeared with lipstick and smiling. "Do you mind?"

It was a challenge of sorts, Ron decided, to him or to herself. Looking at her kindly, he knew she could not pull it off. She was embarrassed by her age. It was right there in her cruel hurt eyes. But she dared to hug him anyway and then ran from the room crying.

Ron glanced at Kristy and was relieved she hadn't seemed to notice the brief encounter. With her favorite doll hung flaccidly over one arm, her attention had remained fixed on her glass of soda.

"Oh, hell," the producer was saying over to Ron's right. "Death doesn't matter. It doesn't matter one goddamn. That's just the way I feel about it."

"He's just saying that because he wants to get to me," said his wife who was short and shapeless.

"No," the man insisted. "That's just how I feel about it."

Ron found himself entering the conversation with some interest. "Do you believe in life after death?" he murmured smiling a little.

The producer said promptly, "Hell, no! I believe when you go, you're gone, just like that. Hell, what difference does it make?"

"In other words," his wife added bitterly, "I haven't made his life mean anything to him. That's what he's trying to tell me. He doesn't care if he drops dead tonight."

"You really don't care," Ron asked, "if you drop dead—"

"That's because of me," the producer's wife interrupted.

"It doesn't have a thing in this world to do with her."

"You see, he won't even give me the importance of hating me. He doesn't care anything about me one way or the other. And we've been married thirty years. Oh, God, I've wasted thirty years of my life on him."

"So your wife doesn't have anything to do with your lack of interest in life?" Ron couldn't resist asking.

"Hell, no."

"Does she make you happy?"

"If she didn't, I wouldn't be with her."

Ron smiled sardonically to the producer's wife. "Well, there's some kind of a compliment for you, I suppose. But still, I think the best thing for you would be if your husband dropped dead tonight. He won't care and you'll be better off."

There was a sudden hush in the small circle as Ron wandered off in some confusion. He had no idea how he had come to say such a thing, only that when talking to a jackass one tended to bray somewhat in response. He was quickly swept into another circle.

"Why the long face?" The voice was tender, effeminate. A slender masculine hand laid itself briefly on Ron's wrist. No offense intended, the touch said. Just in case.

Wordlessly, Ron laid his hand on the young actor's shoulder and turned away to his own inner confusion. He felt swallowed up, desperate. Who—were—these—people? he wondered. More to the point, who was he? Ron was having a hard time recognizing himself this evening.

Dropping onto the couch, he continued to keep an eye on Chandal. His sweating palm beaded the tall cool tumbler. He tipped it and the soft bourbon slipped down his gullet and flowered upward into a smile which grew on his lips.

"How you doing, Ron?" Mark Russell sat down beside him. As his accountant, Mark knew full well how he was doing.

"Lousy."

"Business is shit, right?"

"Right."

Russell aimed his smile at Chandal and waved her over with that goddamn good-willed gesture of his.

"Feeling tight, Russell?" Chandal dropped onto the couch.

Russell sat between them smiling like a friendly maniac. "Right. Tight. Ron tells me you're heading for the poorhouse."

"He did, did he? Well, we're just taking a busman's tour by

the poorhouse, so to speak. Looking it over once to see if we like it."

Russell grunted with laughter, his belly capturing the sound and honing it to a rumble.

Chandal put her hands to her temples, smoothed back her hair, and with obvious effort tried to remain calm. She had just the beginnings of a headache. No big deal, nothing even to mention, but she kept nervously massaging her temples. Of course, Ron noticed it. After all these years, the headaches were the one danger sign. The headaches that occasionally worsened into migraines. During those times—it could be several hours or several days—Chandal would lie in a darkened room and no medication could lessen the pain that squeezed her skull, worked through her body until there was only the pain. Nothing else. Until the flashes of memory were so vivid as to seem real. Memories of a bloodstone pendant that seemed to sparkle with blood. Memories even further back. The brownstone in New York City as it burned. The two old women who had died. The Krispin sisters. Yes, finally Magdalen and Elizabeth Krispin were both dead. Two old women who had tried to rob a young woman of her youth. What did it all add up to? Only that Chandal had once been welded to evil and . . .

Careful, Ron warned himself. *You're on thin ice here.* He quickly took another drink. The mahogany-colored liquor went down like fire this time, catching at his throat, then burning its way into the pit of his stomach. Now he tried desperately to look outward from himself, to evade the onslaught of memories that threatened to push forward through the front of his skull. Again he attempted the ritual of oblivion in tipping, drinking, but still memories came, filling the last reaches of his consciousness and then spilling over.

Evil in the form of Elizabeth Krispin. Even now he could see the old woman, not whole, but as she had spoken to him through Chandal's lips. As she had looked at him through Chandal's eyes. So long ago and yet the old woman's image remained crystal clear in his mind.

Somehow, those days spent at the carriage house in New York City seven years ago would not leave him alone. Perhaps it was Chandal's reluctance to speak about it. There

16

were so many things he wanted to know. How had it all begun? Suddenly one thought loomed large in his confusion: the danger had been real. He could still feel the power of the bloodstone pendant Chandal had worn around her neck. Elizabeth Krispin's pendant. And the sparks that flickered from it, flashing in a dark place.

Something had happened. Something bad. Why wouldn't Chandal speak of it? Even after all these years, she still wouldn't allow Ron to discuss it. Elizabeth Krispin and Chandal had been one. Everything Ron had done in New York had hung on an old woman's breath. Until *finally*—she was gone.

"What now?" Ron had asked.

"Well, she remembers now," Doctor Luther had replied. "She's recaptured that part of time which was lost. Who knows at what cost of anguish—but in my view, she was prepared to pay it."

Ron had hesitated. "Do you think there's a chance—just a chance, that maybe she didn't imagine it?"

"No," said Doctor Luther. "It was all in Chandal's mind. The possession, the old woman—all imagined. Now that she is better, she will come to see that. Chandal will be coming home from the hospital tomorrow. She's going to need all the help she can get. Believe me, after enough time has passed, everything will work itself out. Things will return to normal."

"There's something I need to ask you."

Dr. Luther smiled. "I think I know."

"What would you say?"

"I say for your sake, be very careful. For her sake I say, go to her. Marry her. It's what she needs most."

"I suppose you know what I'll do."

"Sentimentalist that I am, I'm very glad. I hope you'll both be very happy. I think you will."

Now Ron could feel the color drain from his face. Party noise continued to eddy around him. He forced past his confusion and smiled.

Russell was talking again, laughing and carrying on about the economy. He knew Russell was patting him on the back; and he knew also that the smile had gone from his face, for

Russell was saying, "Oh, hell, Ron, don't take it so hard. As soon as the strike is over things will pick up. They always do."

Ron attempted to drink again and found his glass empty. This negative note started a strange and unfamiliar ache which had been hidden in the far recesses of his being, somewhere under scores of past days and nights, crawling to the surface, an ache that oozed upward and formed a pocket of despair at the bottom of his empty glass.

He breathed deeply, then glanced involuntarily at the wedding ring on his finger and, turning it once around slowly, looked up at Russell. Quietly, like a concerned parent, Russell asked: "Ron, are you all right?"

"Sure. Everything is just fine. Fine," Ron said and rose solidly to his feet.

"Where are you going?" queried Russell.

"To get another drink," Ron replied intently. "Del, would you care for another?"

Chandal shook her head. "Maybe later."

Confidently Ron made his way over to the bar. He was drunk. That was it. He was cockeyed drunk. He was shit-faced! A sudden uncontrollable smile fixed itself on his lips. To hell with business, to hell with the past, just step right up, folks, and call me Ronny—hallelujah—amen.

Pushing through a press of bodies he brushed against a curving thigh, and he caught in his nostrils the sweet odor of familiar perfume. Laughing slightly, he turned to face Cleo Talise, one of his supposed hotshot clients, worth $100,000 per film and all the time her value skyrocketing. The only problem was that Ron had not yet landed her a contract.

"Hello, Ron, darling," she cooed.

Ron nodded. "What's this I hear you were as loose as a goose at LaCasa Spinoza last night."

Cleo reddened. "What the hell do you mean?"

Ron grinned, knowing she knew full well what he meant: that she had been at LaCasa acting as loose as a goose. In the nude with a guy and a girl and that somebody had taken pictures. But, of course, in reality it was none of his business and he could already read in Cleo's pea-green eyes that she would be out agent shopping before the last clamoring of his hangover had subsided in the morning.

Ron shrugged. "Sorry, I guess it's . . ."

"None of your goddamn business, right!" Cleo sauntered off as simultaneously the room seemed to grow quiet.

Bemused, Ron smiled. Then in the pause which followed, he heard it again. He stood motionless, listening. What was that? His eyes arched upward to the ceiling. A fluttering of sorts, like bird wings. The flutter was followed by a loud, dull thud. Then a scraping, clawing sound.

What the hell was Kristy doing up there!

Once more, there was a flapping of wings.

Ron turned and started for the stairs. He stopped suddenly when he realized that Kristy was not upstairs at all, but was standing in the far corner of the room, her eyes blazing with a remote light. So powerful was her gaze that conversation had died around her. Suddenly, as though it had been flicked off by an unseen finger, even the stereo died, leaving the room in total silence.

"What's wrong?" Russell asked, appearing at Ron's elbow.

"Damned if I know. A loose wire, I guess."

Kristy's gaze remained fixed as Ron moved her aside. "Excuse me, sweetheart. Let daddy have a look." He checked the on-off switch. It was still on. He checked the plugs in the back of the unit. Okay there too. He began to trace a wire across the room as Russell followed another wire up and over the bookshelf.

"Yes. You can talk to me," said Kristy standing again in front of the stereo. Her voice was soft, almost a whisper, masking her excitement. "Yes, now I can hear you! Oh, yes . . ."

Ron looked to Russell, who, he knew, was staring at Kristy. In fact, the entire room was staring at Kristy. Other guests had begun to filter in from the terrace. Expressionless as statues, they formed a double line in front of the glass doors. Irritated as much by their silence as by their damn gaping, Ron snapped: "Okay, gang, it's party time. We'll have the problem fixed in a minute. Kristy, please get away from the stereo."

Kristy did not move.

Chandal rose from the couch. "Kristy, come away from there, sweetheart. Your father is trying to fix it."

19

"Oh, yes!" Kristy shrilled. "Yes, I will. Sometime soon. I will!" She listened intently, gave a serious nod, then whispered: "Soon."

"Kristy," Chandal scolded. "I said stop that!"

"No, no, no!" Kristy screamed and stamped her feet. "Leave me alone, goddammit!" Eyes sparkling, she turned again to speak to the dead stereo. "Oh, I'm glad! Yes, I will. I promise."

There was a momentary silence. Ron turned to stare at his guests with barely concealed astonishment. There was no sign of amusement on their faces, only a slight expression of disdain tinged with embarrassment as they glanced briefly at Kristy, then back to Chandal.

"Maybe she hears static or something," offered Russell.

"I guess," Ron replied and moved closer.

Kristy jumped back with a start. With shrill laughter, she began scratching herself, lifting her dress above her waist and pressing it against her breast. A murmur traveled through the room. Under her dress she was completely naked.

"Jesus," cried Ron, rushing to his daughter. "Kristy, honey, are you all right? Here, let me help you." He pulled her dress down, at the same time holding onto her hands.

"She's funny, Daddy! So funny!"

"Come on, sweetheart." Ron took Kristy by the hand and tried leading her away.

"No, Daddy—she wants to talk with me!" There was a murmur of voices in the room as she tried to break free of Ron's grasp.

"Kristy, please . . ." He turned and began to apologize silently to his guests.

"Well, it's about that time . . ." he heard Russell say.

"No, no, please stay," Chandal protested, turning to face the room fully. "Ron will be back in a few minutes."

Ron dragged Kristy into the hallway, saying: "Want to be carried?" And without waiting for an answer, he raised her in his arms until she sat upon his shoulders.

Up there, holding tightly to his neck, she whispered: "The little girl on the radio likes me."

"Yes? Who is she?"

"Oh, just a little girl—far away. Real far. She likes me, Daddy. Isn't that nice?"

"Who is she?" Ron asked repeatedly, but Kristy appeared not to understand and mumbled over and over again, "She likes me . . . she likes me," until the murmur became lower and lower, then a whisper that died away as Ron opened her bedroom door.

TWO

IN THE DEAD LIGHT OF DUSK, KRISTY'S ROOM LOOKED BARREN and unreal. For some time, she had had a problem sleeping at night, convinced there were strangers in her room. But the problem had been solved with the addition of a night light and the removal of an offending coat rack. When draped with coats and hats, Ron had suddenly realized, the coat rack bore a certain human resemblance. Other things also had been removed from the room: a set of large Maurice Sendak posters, an ornate mirror over her dresser, and most of the toys from off the bookshelves. Finally the nightmares had stopped, but only after the room had been almost stripped bare. Now all that remained was a single bed, a small rocking chair, a dresser, and little else.

"Hang on," Ron said, reaching over to turn on the light.

Kristy groaned playfully, shifted herself to one side, then straightened. She leaned forward and smiled. There was no confusion, only intensity in her gaze. He hurriedly placed his hands on her waist, lifted her from his shoulders; his back ached when he released her onto the floor.

"Now, young lady," Ron said, "just who is this girl you heard on the radio?"

Again she said the little girl far away. Ron shook his head. There was no point in continuing. He did not know why he had bothered to question her in the first place. Children have these imaginings every day. What the hell was all the fuss about?

"I'm sleepy, Daddy."

"I know, sweetheart." Ron touched his palm to her forehead. "Kristy, are you all right? Is something wrong?"

"No, Daddy. I'm sleepy." Her eyes had already begun to droop.

"Then let's get you brushed up and into bed. Okay?"

"All right," she yawned and moved away toward the bathroom, a little girl of six with tired eyes, wearing a yellow summer dress with white lace trim. On her feet were brown patent leather shoes, scuffed in the front and worn at the heels. Childishly, she rubbed her eyes with her fists. She entered the bathroom but did not flick on the light. She turned then to stare back into the bedroom. Her face remained lost in the shadows. Only the underside of her eyes and mouth remained lighted. With lips pursed in a rigid black line, her face bore a look of grief.

"Kristy? What is it?" Ron could feel the chill of the room now. Felt the sweat roll down from the back of his neck, struck suddenly by the cold air. Still the child did not move. "Kristy," Ron breathed, "what are you doing?"

"Daddy?"

"Yes?"

"When are we going on our vacation?" Her voice came as a soft murmur, a sound outward and beyond rather than something from her own body. Then she lowered her head, almost ashamed to have mentioned the unmentionable.

"Kristy," Ron said softly, "we've already discussed it. We can't take a vacation this year. Try to understand, all right?"

"But Mommy said we would." Anxiously she stepped from the bathroom.

"She did? When?"

"Yesterday. She said—"

"No vacation this year. Now that's final." Ron tried to force the point with a stern look.

Kristy stood very still. Her eyes were wide. For an instant Ron thought she was going to say something. But abruptly he saw her change her mind. Secret knowledge was written plainly upon her face. Then he saw in her eyes a sudden fluttering of wings, flight.

She ran from the room. The bathroom door closed behind her with a dull thud. It only took a few minutes for her to emerge from the bathroom scrubbed and clean. At first Ron thought he had imagined it, but after a second glance he realized he hadn't been mistaken—Kristy was smiling.

In part, he was fascinated by all this. Was Kristy manipulating him? If so, she was doing a damn good job. Her subtle change of mood had completely thrown him off balance. But also it was frightening. The three-to-seven age group Spock talked about was obviously a delusion: in Kristy's case at any rate. A six-year-old child should not know the subtle art of persuasion. Yet, it appeared she had already graduated with honors.

Ron helped her into her pajamas, and had barely tucked her into bed, when she solemnly began discussing places such as the Grand Canyon and the cavern in the mountains where Butch Cassidy and the Hole in the Wall Gang hid out.

"And where they have flower wars and dancing jackals," she added with eager eyes.

Ron laughed. "Dancing jackals?"

"With teeth that bite."

"Who's been telling you such things?"

"I've seen them."

"When?"

"At night. Around my bed."

"You were just dreaming."

"Nooo, I wasn't," she said and sank further under the covers.

For a moment Ron experienced a flash of guilt and, turning away, began to chastise himself for reading her all those bedtime stories. They all seemed to be filled with horror and always ended so damn sadly. When he was a little boy, didn't the stories have to do with love and a purer sort of adventure —even when the dragons were killed, he didn't remember them bleeding over the pages. But maybe they had. Probably he had simply forgotten the blood letting. The Grimm Brothers had been grim for many years, after all.

"Kristy, about the vacation . . ." he said and turned to face her.

Kristy was sound asleep. Dreaming, no doubt, he reasoned, and watched his shadow pass over her lovely face. He kissed her forehead. "Kristy," he whispered, "do you really dream of dancing jackals?" Then, smiling a little because he saw she was smiling a little, he said: "That's right, sweetheart, sleep." For a time he waited, listening to her soft, shallow breathing. Beside her on the same pillow was a china

23

doll face framed in yellow curls. The doll's eyes were open, walled back in her head. Her lips were open in a slight smile, showing two small teeth. A blond, china-faced, talking doll, Ron mused. Perhaps that was it. He reached over and flicked out the light.

Then, no color, not a tint, and no fear either. Only darkness.

THREE

"ARE YOU KIDDING?" CHANDAL DROPPED HER HAIRBRUSH ON the dresser.

Ron stood hunched in the doorway, smoking. "Not at all. I just don't think it's anything to get so excited about."

"Oh, well, pardon me." Chandal gazed into the mirror stormily meeting her own icy blue eyes.

"Can we talk about this rationally?"

"If you can, I can. I say we should let her see a doctor. The sooner the better."

"Christ!"

"Look who's being rational." Tears welled up suddenly. Angry tears. "Ron, you saw them. The way they all looked at her. Her actions caused a mass departure. When have we ever had a party break up this early? Dwayne and Mimi left without even saying good night."

"There's nothing wrong with her!" Ron said fighting back his own temper. "So she hears voices," he said in a softer tone. He was pleading now. "She's only six years old, for Chrissakes. Come on, sweetheart. So she has an imaginary playmate. So what? Let's forget it. All right?"

"Whatever you say," Chandal flung back at him.

Ron watched as she began to remove her clothes. She unzipped her jeans and slithered out of them, then crossing her arms in front of her, took hold of her blouse and, yanking it over her head, slipped out of it in a single gesture. She was not wearing a bra, only a pair of thinly laced panties. Ron's eyes lingered on her nakedness, her tight buttocks, the fullness of her breasts. Slowly he moved behind her and slipped his arms around her waist. "You smell good," he said nuzzling her neck. "I love the smell of you."

"Don't, Ron." Chandal tried to wriggle from his grasp.

"Why?"

"Kristy is . . ."

"Asleep."

"Please, Ron . . ." She squirmed free and moved to the bed.

"Okay, okay. I hadn't realized you were so upset about this."

"Well, I'm not. See." She mocked a smile. "It's forgotten. Now let's get some sleep. I have to be up early in the morning." Chandal slipped into bed and wiggled deep under the covers seeming to burrow herself into a self-imposed hole of isolation.

"Hon?" He leaned over her in the bed. "Are you all right?"

She looked up at him. "Of course I'm all right."

He smiled. "I'll be with you in a minute."

"Whenever," she said and rolled over to face the wall.

Hesitantly, almost reluctantly, Ron sat down on the edge of the bed. Forgotten, my ass, he said to himself. Then he studied his reflection in the mirror set into the back of the closet door. His eyes, bloodshot and slightly drunk, seemed more solemn than he would have imagined. He felt a sort of anxiety now as his mind struggled to put things into perspective. Kristy's behavior tonight was no big deal, he decided conclusively. Although Chandal was making something of it.

By tomorrow or next week, whenever the next smallest incident occurred, she would insist on going the shrink route. Ron didn't need and, certainly, couldn't afford that particular solution. Psychiatrists, he had told himself for so long, were a thing of the past for his family and—reluctantly, he finished the thought—he would feel a very personal sense of failure if his six-year-old daughter had to begin visiting a psychiatrist who would look to Chandal and him, no doubt, for his answers. Neglect, permissiveness, oedipal complexes. Ron knew most of the words from friends who had their whole families in analysis or therapy. Not Kristy. Not now. When all the child needed was a little extra attention.

"Del?"

"Humm?"

"Have you thought about the vacation?"

"What!" she said. She was sitting up in bed now. "What?"

He turned and stared at her through a mist of alcohol. "About the vacation. Remember? The month of August. We decided it was time we had—"

"But I thought you said we couldn't afford it?"

He shrugged. "Maybe yes, maybe no."

"The entire month?"

"Why not?"

"August?"

"A good month."

Unconsciously he had already made the decision. A smile hovered on his lips. "Would you like that?"

"Seriously?" she said. She was propped on her elbows, looking at him in profile.

He was just about to say: "Of course, I'm serious," but stopped himself. Once he had said yes—it was yes. Chandal was like that. Once something had been set, it was set. There was no changing it. He stared glumly ahead, inhaled deeply, and saw in the mirror the reflection of the glowing red tip of his cigarette. It was the dead quiet part of the night. The time when people went mad with the pull of the moon. The time when hospital corridors were empty places, echoing pain. I'm losing my mind, he thought with mirthful acceptance.

"Think about it before saying yes," she said, moving closer. "Whatever you decide will be fine with me."

In the dim light as soft as melted amber, Ron felt the warm length of her thigh pressed against his body. There was so much he wanted to say to her. To ask her. Did she still dream? After all these years, did she still think of the past? He gazed obliquely at her now and found it strange that he could go that far back in time and at the same time could see himself sitting next to her in a room that seemed to be growing darker. Or was it his thoughts that were growing darker?

Shadows shifted and the unnatural thud of his heart beat on as some deep part of him kept pondering an unseen world that was not beautiful, not pleasant, not warm, not large, not small, not of this earth. Yet it had been part of his life.

Now, following her gaze, he leaned back and stared up into her face. He kept his head that way for several moments, before saying: "You're right. I really should think about it." His remark seemed to draw no response.

He rose quickly to his feet. Taking a final, deep drag from his cigarette, he crushed it into the ashtray, then turned to look down at her. A sheaf of hair had fallen over her eye and she tossed it back with a quick movement of her head.

The sheet entangled between her leg seemed an ancient style of costume, he thought vaguely. Something Greek, possibly, or perhaps a simplistic ritual of dress. For an instant he pictured a vestal virgin filling her lamp with oil, then the image receded and he found himself utterly alone.

He suddenly wanted to reach out and hold her closely; wanted her to wrap him tightly in her arms, crush him, tell him that everything was going to be all right. That things, all things, were going to be okay. The impulse was so strong, so compelling, yet he stood motionless, his hands now fists held rigidly by his sides.

"I love you, Del," he said and, without waiting for a reply, turned and left the room.

FOUR

LATER THAT NIGHT HE HAD A DREAM, OR DID HE IMAGINE IT while he was awake? He knelt at the base of a great stone. It was the core of the universe that wound upward from below, the roughness of its broad surface twisting and turning, until finally it formed the highest spire of a great cathedral.

Squat in the darkness, head hung, someone whispered: *"The stone around which moving is done."* Then the clandestine sobbing. A soft sound—nothing tangible, yet it seemed the weeping of many. Ron listened with his eyes down, looking at the still smoldering ash that coated the rock-layered floor. He bit his lip and gazed upward. He prayed.

High above, through the transparent skin of the steeple, he could see the sky splattered with stars. Frozen, suspended—

they hung there tossing back tiny spearpoints of dazzling light; and beyond their glitter . . . another light. So soft, no movement at all. Then something began to happen. Something Ron could not fathom. A sudden flash, an explosion as one of the stars shot downward, huge and liquified, like a droplet of blazing water flicked from the finger of God, and crashed into the steeple roof; the cathedral exploded in a burst of flames and began to dissolve.

People were running now, screaming, clawing to get out. Too late. Much too late. Ron knew that—that it was all too late. The flames were everywhere, licking, spitting—and as they scorched each person, one by one, the people began to dissolve. Now the heavens were filled with tiny human flesh-sparks of light, drifting into the darkness above, as if their time on earth had ended—as if God, scornful, hateful, had withdrawn their right to exist, saying, No, you have betrayed me and now you must die.

Ron felt himself fall backward, felt hands seize him, manipulate his body until he was stretched out on a cold slab of marble.

He lay absolutely still. For an instant it seemed to him that he lay in a patch of light, something close to a spotlight. Through it he could see shadows in a susurrant cluster. Then fanning out, they moved toward him from the outer edges.

Then the house might have caved in for he was fully awake, his head stuffed into the pillow, his hands gripping the edge of the bed.

"No! It's not true!" he pleaded.

"What's not?" Chandal mumbled. He had awakened her, but that was not particularly unusual. He often talked in his sleep, and she often answered him.

"Nothing." He stared at her blankly and tried not to release the pent up breath held midway in his chest. For a moment he thought he was still dreaming. Then he noticed his trousers thrown over the back of the chair, the digital clock on the nightstand.

Chandal smacked the pillow with her fist and rolled over to face the wall. "Oh," she murmured and was instantly asleep.

Hesitantly, almost timidly, Ron breathed and waited for the dream to drift away into the darker recesses of his mind.

"Del?" he whispered. He paused, hoping she would answer. But he continued to lie there silently, his face twisted into an expression of bewilderment, which was habitual with him when he was disappointed. Sleeping people made rotten company.

He swung his legs out of the bed and lighted a cigarette. He sat in the dark smoking. He inhaled deeply, let the smoke roll around inside his head, then pressed it through his nostrils. Off in the corner, the air conditioner hummed to itself gently. It was almost below the limit of hearing—a normal room sound, yet quite unmistakable and quite irritating.

Fragments of the dream flashed in his mind. A shooting star, people weeping, a huge stone. The stone around which moving is done. He shivered. As comfortable as the room was, he felt chilled. He was probably coming down with a cold. Always, midsummer, he would catch a goddamn cold. He turned to glance at the clock. It was 2:35 A.M.

For a moment, he had the annoying sensation he had forgotten something, then with a sense of relief, he remembered. The vacation. What about the vacation?

FIVE

THE NEXT MORNING, BLEARY-EYED AND HAGGARD, HE WAS STILL thinking about it. Defeated at smiling, he frowned, took a cigarette from its pack and lighted it. Through the pale swirl of smoke he saw Mimi's face peering at him from the outer office. She quickly began shuffling papers around on her desk.

Ron grimaced and, shaking his head, spun his chair around and faced the window.

A moment of relief came as a huge bounteous light in the bosom of the thin white clouds above. The knots loosened; he opened up, sank deeper into his chair, the glass of the window creating an illusion, the smoke inside and the clouds outside appearing as one. He glimpsed a hard sharp region of his mind like a lone flicker of a comet, and held there, suspended. Kristy. He could not get his daughter out of his mind; her unfathomable face haunted him.

He sat in quiet amazement as he watched her face appear in the glass; a young girl's face, no longer a baby. No, not a baby at all but his growing daughter, whom he now saw before him in a multitude of images. Images that spun around in his mind's eye, then dovetailed.

God, she's beautiful! the nurse had gasped. Yes, indeed—she's beautiful. The doctor, laughing, laid the child on Chandal's stomach. No, Ron wanted to protest. Not beautiful at all. All wet and wrinkled and unformed . . . But, oh God—yes, she's beautiful. Happy birthday to you, Happy birthday to you, Happy birthday, dear Kristy . . . her skin pale and creamy now, her features delicate and her hair thick and black. God, those eyes, Del! Look at those eyes! Enormous deep-blue irises, inky black lashes, so thick as to seem double-fringed, creating an impression that they had been lined in black by an expert makeup artist. But it was the expression in them that created the final bit of mesmerization —some kind of smoldering fire that must be an illusion, for what child would ever . . .

It was hard for Ron to think now; his thoughts were tiny slivers of rippling light against the window pane, and he seemed to sag under the effort of two simultaneous and contrary actions, retention and evaluation, both of them beyond him at this moment.

His eyes cleared, Kristy's image faded, and he turned again to face his desk. He was instantly aware that Mimi was covertly watching him. Snuffing his cigarette, he watched her watching him in silence, unsmiling. Beyond their eyes the noon traffic began to squeeze into the city.

"All right," he finally bellowed. "What's next?"

"Lunch. My treat."

"Right."

Landell's was a good restaurant. Small enough so that one received personal service. Large enough so that one didn't have to speak with the waiters. So while Ron and Mimi ate at their usual table, Ron made only one comment; that he suddenly felt like he'd fallen into a black hole. Then he found a dark spot on the tablecloth and kept his eyes lowered.

"I've read about black holes," Mimi said helpfully.

"They're rethinking the whole theory about the creation of the earth. Just because of black holes."

"Jesus," Ron said weakly. "Why is that?"

"Because now they're saying they aren't black holes. They're nothing. Just void. A bottomless, empty nothingness. And somehow or the other—I don't understand it—that affects the whole concept of how the earth was created."

"Mimi," Ron said sarcastically, "I want to thank you. You've cheered me up enormously. I'm leaving now to get looped. Not sloppy drunk. Just a little looped. I'll pick up my car later."

"By the way," Mimi said and stopped.

"What?"

"Nothing."

"No, it's something or you wouldn't have stopped like that."

"Tarasco called," Mimi said. "From the Sinclair. He said Dwayne Clark hasn't filled the room worth a damn. He's opting out on the last half of the commitment."

Ron felt the veins of his eyes constrict as murder rushed through his blood. "He's a lying, no-good son of a bitch. Call him and tell him I said that. Tell him I was there a week ago and the goddamn room was packed."

"Paper," Mimi said. "He said he's been papering the place ever since Dwayne opened to those rotten reviews. You want me to call him anyway?"

Ron hesitated, feeling his senses smart with the all too familiar fear. The way business was lately, there was no point in agitating one of the few contacts who still gave some of his clients work. Although he knew damn well that Dwayne Clark was filling that room. He knew paper when he saw it. Tarasco had probably fallen under the charms of another young female singer.

"Forget it," he said, not looking at Mimi. "Call Dwayne." He knew it was a call he should make himself, but he couldn't face the man's disappointment. He shuddered to think of that sadness.

"I'll call him," Mimi said softly. "Go on home. Skip the booze. I'll see you tomorrow."

Ron nodded. "Are you and Dwayne . . ."

"Yeah," she smiled.

"I'm glad." Ron paused for a moment, then turned and passed quickly through the tables. After a slight, sociable nod to the maitre d', he punched his way into the sunlight.

Twenty minutes later he found himself loitering along Sunset Boulevard, eating chocolate Häagen-Dazs out of a cup and peering into travel agency windows. London, impossible. He figured he could afford to fly approximately halfway over the Atlantic. Mexico, too close and too dull. Kristy would be highly indignant if the decision was to be Mexico. Forget New York. Forget Hawaii, New Orleans, forget flying anywhere, he finished, his eyes on the colorful poster that promised to take you away for only $600 per person.

A flicker of relief spasmed in his belly and he was forced to acknowledge that he was damned glad not to be flying anywhere. It was a secret phobia he'd developed, starting God knew when, but fairly recently, he believed. Flying had never bothered him, but now all of a sudden it did.

It wasn't the idea of dying. It was the idea of falling to earth inside of millions of pounds of heavy metal. Of knowing at some point or the other you were going to crash, that there was nothing you could do about it and that, Jesus Christ, you had better be saying good-bye to your wife and daughter who were also going down in the big bird in the sky.

Yes, he was just as glad he had decided he couldn't afford to fly.

That left him with Kristy's not-so-terrific plan. A car trip through the Old West. Thousands of miles of wandering desert and plains through sweltering heat. In a flurry of masochistic pleasure, he decided he'd do it.

The last spoonful of Häagen-Dazs burned ice cold against the pit of his stomach. He shivered. To counteract the sensation, he conjured a mental image of the Painted Desert smoldering hot before his gaze.

He nodded then. It was a mental agreement with himself, a sort of handshaking ceremony.

The thing that amazed him was how comfortable he felt in the decision. Even though he was sure to regret it long hot hours from home, at the moment he felt rather triumphant. It was a curious reaction because a long car trip wasn't his style at all. Not at all. Yet he simply could not change his mind.

SIX

RON SPENT THE NEXT FEW WEEKS BROWSING LEISURELY OVER
literature pertaining to the Old West. It was as though an
unseen pressure had removed itself, leaving him at last able to
relax. During the days he managed to get in some tennis.
Evenings Chandal and he ate simple healthy dinners. Grilled
steak, baked potatoes and plenty of green salad. After dinner
they merely talked over brandy. Endless, easy talk that
always ended with enthusiastic chatter about the upcoming
vacation. They were incredibly happy.

"I don't suppose," Ron said one night across the table,
"that you ever think much about having another child?"

"Well, no," Chandal answered doubtfully.

Ron said no more about the subject that night. But the next
night he did; and on the next night, while dining out, after
drinking his fair share of wine and after he had acknowledged
that he was a little soused, he said: "Baby time!" Then
grinned like a gargoyle. A wise ass gargoyle.

"You *are* pie-eyed, aren't you?"

"And feeling sexy."

"These things aren't mutually exclusive."

"You've been pondering these matters?"

"I believe—"

"It's time to go."

"Is that a memorandum of intent?"

"Uh-huh."

Leaving the restaurant Ron slipped his arm around Chandal's shoulder. It felt good. The evening air had cooled some
and the moon shone bright between the branches of the palm
trees lining the drive. A chorus of insects sang in the
darkness, reminding Ron of July nights from his childhood. It
was a warm memory.

It had been weeks since Chandal and he had made love. He
could not imagine how they had allowed all that time to go by

33

without coming together physically. Incredible, he mused, and glimpsed Chandal's legs briefly as she entered the car. He felt a tremor of desire, the suddenly quick heartbeat. When all was said and done, Ron still found Chandal a very exciting looking woman to be married to.

"Ironic, isn't it?" asked Ron, starting the engine.

"What is?"

"That we—" He stopped himself. "Forget it."

"No, I want to know." Chandal looked at him questioningly.

"Forget it," he said and pulled away from the drive and accelerated toward home.

When they entered the house, they found the babysitter standing frozen in the hallway. She drew back, then gasped: "Oh, thank God you're home! Kristy . . . Kristy is . . ." Her eyes bored into Ron's eyes. Terror engulfed him immediately.

Ron couldn't feel his legs. But they moved. He was in the hallway, then up the stairs. He knew nothing except he had to reach his daughter. He found Kristy sitting motionless in her rocking chair.

"Kristy, are you all right? Kristy?"

Chandal was beside him. Holding his arm. Saying something. Ron quickly picked Kristy up in his arms. She looked pale. Her eyes were dulled and sluggish and her movement passive, almost as if she were in a trance. "But then who would be Queen?" she murmured and her eyes closed.

"Del, call the doctor. Hurry!"

The rest of the evening passed in a series of painful lulls and confusion. The doctor's examination was tediously slow. Ron stood frustrated in the corner of the room with his arm around Chandal. He could feel that her body was trembling. "She's going to be okay, Del." He hugged her closer to him and they continued to await the doctor's pronouncement in silence; always more and more fearful, glancing nervously at Kristy, then to the doctor, who finally said: "She has the flu. Pretty bad case of it, I'd say." He turned then, and smiled. "But she is going to be all right."

"Thank God," Ron breathed and Chandal began to cry.

In the morning the bathroom stank of vomit. Ron had been up most of the night, helping Chandal care for Kristy. He had a headache, his stomach was sour, and the sourness had begun to flood his entire body. He felt poisoned. Even the saliva in his mouth had thickened from the fear. A fear worse than anything he had known since Kristy's birth. And he had the thought: people take such a risk when they have children. They take the risk that if anything happens to them, they simply won't be able to go on.

He could feel the inward flinching at the thought and then he pushed past it and he was all right. He took an Alka-Seltzer, spent some time in the bedroom, then went looking for Chandal. She was standing by the kitchen window watching the children play in the next yard. As he moved closer, he realized the window was closed, yet he could hear the children's voices distinctly.

There was a small hallway in the rear corner of the room. He went to it and saw the back door, with the pane of glass nearest the top smashed and lying in fragments on the floor.

"Del? How did it happen?"

"I don't know," she said without looking at him. "I don't know," she repeated.

He met Chandal's eyes—vast and blue in her white face—and was able to smile reassuringly. "Hey, she's okay, you know. That kid's tough."

"Tough," Chandal repeated and left the room.

The next few days passed quickly, with Kristy growing stronger, until finally she arose one morning, jumped from her bed and ate a large breakfast. After that, she disappeared into the garden to play.

"Two more days," Ron said, sipping his coffee.

"What?" Chandal had been watching Kristy play out back.

"We leave for vacation Monday. Finally!"

"I don't know," Chandal said. "Do you think Kristy is up to it?"

"Of course. Look at her out there." Ron knew what Chandal was feeling; he felt it too. Yet, for the first time in days he also felt positive about something. Really sure. He felt omnipotent at the prospect of his new calling. Adventure. It was what they both needed. Though he still dreaded the driving part of the vacation, he knew he would be happier on the road than sitting around the office waiting for the boom to be lowered. If his agency was going to go under, he wanted to be well away from it when it sank to the bottom.

"The question," he said whimsically, "is whether or not we should ever come back again. With that kind of jump on our creditors, maybe we should just disappear into the setting sun."

"Are we in that much trouble?"

"Maybe. Maybe not."

When Chandal spoke again, her voice was remote. "We could put off the trip if you like." She shrugged. "I know you're worried about the agency, and—"

"Hey, we've been all through that."

"I know," Chandal said, staring at nothing. "But, if—"

"Del, stop worrying. You'll see, once we're away from here, everything will look different." He got up suddenly, took Chandal by the waist. "Del, face it. It's about time we said to hell with everything and everybody and enjoyed ourselves." Gently, persuasively, he added: "I know I'm ready to."

Chandal looked into his eyes and smiled. "You're a very courageous person in your own way," she said thoughtfully. Then she reached up and kissed him, a warm kiss, a kiss for the long journey ahead.

SEVEN

THE DAY CLOSED IN, AND DIED THAT NIGHT, LIKE A FLOWER LEFT to wither in a current of hot air. Another moon turned in the sky and then another; in the full moon of vacation eve Ron wondered if he hadn't been possessed even to consider such a vacation. When Kristy had come up with the idea, it had caught him off-balance, tickled him somewhat. Now it filled him with dread.

He took a deep shuddering breath and began to strip off his clothing. Whenever he felt despondent he always seemed to gravitate toward the shower. Lately, he'd become a fervent shower taker. He liked his showers long, hot and steamy.

The brisk spray punched holes into his flesh and began to

draw the tension from his body one drop at a time. When he stepped out, his anxiety had evaporated, his vision had cleared. Toweling off, he moved to the steamed-over medicine cabinet. He looked at himself cautiously in the circular design he'd rubbed onto the glass. He nodded approvingly.

If he wanted to be a nitpicker, he could still detect a slight restlessness in his eyes, a faint frown on his lips, just the merest sag of skin under his chin, but all and all, he was relieved that he wasn't looking at a stranger. It was him all right. Good old Ron Talon, smiling now and thinking about the vacation.

It would solve a myriad of small problems. Four weeks alone together. No pot-smoking parties, no uncomfortable silences, just—please, God—a whole new outlook on life.

Confidently now, he squeezed toothpaste onto the brush, watched the green snake slither across bristle, then humming silently to himself, he began running a last minute checklist through his mind.

When finally he emerged from the bathroom, some sense of order, however minimal, had been achieved. Making his way into bed, he discovered that Chandal had already fallen asleep.

So that was it, then. He rolled over on his side and forced his mind to shut down. It was an effort, the struggle for sleep only helping to keep him awake. But he kept at it. Slowly his limbs became heavy. He raised his right hand over his thigh, his belly, his chest. He stopped and touched the soft folds of skin over his fingertips. Then he felt himself drift with the weight of his hand on his chest. Before he fell asleep, he felt the same odd sensation that he always felt just before going under. It was a brief quivering in his neck that ran slowly upward, upward, until . . .

This time, the dream was in technicolor. It was the first time in his life he'd dreamt in color. It swooped in on him quickly, like a sudden rush of water being forced through a tube. Then curling in against his nostrils there came a vapor, silent and colorless, pressing with a gentle insistence, and he knew his dreams were no longer safe.

It was testimony to the demons' poor taste that they would attack him in his bed, in his subconscious, but then that was demons for you. He forced himself to relax and resisted being afraid to sleep. If nothing else, he would show the demons a bit of class.

He could feel the pull of the dream now, drawing him deeper into its spell. Seducing him in a way. Sighing, he sank a level deeper into sleep. He knew his way this time. There was the stone, grey blending into black, which became the sky over the steeple. Stars blew by, silver and icy cold. Now the explosion—water like blood. Cries from the people. Their blood? His blood? He couldn't be sure.

He trembled as his body was placed on cold marble. Looking up, he saw snow melting from mountains, sliding toward him in an avalanche of mixing colors—reds, greens, blues, all falling into the valley where he lay waiting in the center of moans, screams.

Abruptly, the technicolor snow disappeared.

Now lying drenched in his own cold sweat, he was aware of something else. Something too confusing for him to understand. He visualized human images in twisted, distorted poses, hands that reached out to fondle him, dark seductive creatures wandering up from the mist, sucking his tongue, caressing his penis, forcing their breasts against his mouth, their crimson nipples as pointed as steel spikes. Incredible, crazy, mixed-up images that left him exhausted and spent, and staring at the goddamn floor like he was doing now.

He blinked incredulously. When had he wakened? He had no memory of opening his eyes, of reaching for and lighting a cigarette. And yet here he sat on the edge of the bed drawing in smoke. He wondered if perhaps he wasn't on the verge of a breakdown. Not a serious breakdown, he reassured himself. More of a pressure explosion that had to do with a business that was doing lousy, a house that was not only "rustic" but falling apart around him, and the fact that his attitude stank. All the time negative lately. Summer felt like a curse. His Sunset Strip office had been an expensive mistake and he had eaten the wrong flavor of Danish for breakfast that morning.

With a sense of anger, he stubbed his cigarette in the ashtray on the floor. He could feel tension lingering in the small of his back, the nape of his neck, below his skull. And finally there was nothing he could do but to get up, slip on his robe, pace the room, and walk over the the window to gaze into the sweet curtain of darkness.

The night was bright under a clear moon, and the surface of the pool's water flashed like mercury. The moon had risen over the back of the garden wall. He stared at it with upturned face. If he could only fly, he thought, rise up and soar and dart through the air like a wild bird until his muscles relaxed and his mind was swept smooth, wiped clean as a slate, stilled.

"Ron?" Chandal's muffled voice rose from the pillow.

"Yes."

"Are you okay?"

"Yes."

"Anything the matter?"

"Nothing," Ron sighed. "Go back to sleep, sweetheart. We have to get an early start in the morning."

"Okay. Are you sure you're all right?"

Ron nodded. "Positive. I'll be there in a minute."

They remained facing each other in the gloomy silence of the bedroom, and then both moved, Chandal to the corner of the bed where she fell back to sleep almost immediately, and Ron to the bedroom door.

He stopped in the hallway to peek into Kristy's room. He could hear her move in her bed, and as he listened he could see her small back expand and contract as she breathed deeply. The day's activities had worn her out, Ron thought, unduly so.

Without thinking, he reached in and turned on the light—which Chandal had strictly forbidden—and tiptoed over to the bed. Kristy remained asleep, her mouth open. Ron looked at her for a long time. Then, with trembling hands, he reached out and pulled the covers up over her body. With his heart pounding in his chest, he kissed her forehead.

He found himself strangely comforted by that simple action.

After closing Kristy's door slightly, he made his way downstairs to the living room, where he stopped for an instant to glance at his surroundings. A tidy world, everything immaculate. He sniffed. The room smelled of lemon oil.

Mechanically he slid open the glass doors leading to the

patio and pool area. The air was filled with the faint buzz of insects and something else. Something too silent, too calm to quite understand.

The day had been long, hard and hot; that was the best way to put it. The only way to put it.

He breathed deeply, but the air was dull, too sluggish to revitalize him. The ripple of water was inviting. He imagined himself plunged into its coolness, somehow cleansed. Cleansed of what? he thought and walked barefoot to the edge of the pool. So long as he kept moving he would be all right. To keep moving, that was the secret. To live as freely as an animal, close to the gut, day by day by day.

Without further thought, he unfastened his robe and let it drop to the ground. For an instant, he stood stark naked, his lean body shimmering against the dark night lit by the luminous glow of the moon, then dove suddenly, his arms slicing cleanly through the water, his body sharp and free. Free, he thought exultantly, swimming the pool lengthwise until he had lapped it several times. Still he swam faster, his breath coming in short gasps, his arms flying out in front of him; moving, he had to keep moving . . .

"I've read about black holes," Mimi said in his ear. "They're nothing. Nothing," she whispered. "Just void. A bottomless, empty nothingness. And that affects . . . how the earth was created, you know."

He turned and started to swim back. The cold was getting to him in a way he didn't like. With a sense of panic, he felt the walls of his chest press in upon him. His body seemed to be sinking. He began to choke, fighting for each tortured breath.

Groping like a blind man, he sought to reach the edge of the pool. Now he knew he wasn't going to make it. Give up, he told himself. You've had it. Rest now. Let yourself go, sleep . . . let yourself sleep . . .

Ron stopped suddenly, confused, and found himself standing in the shallow end of the pool feeling the coolness of water streaming down from his hair, hearing the dead silence of the night. Droplets of water rolled down his face.

He stood still, his mouth agape, and let the drops flood his eyes. Light sprang up and pierced the darkness like a sudden heat entering a chilled room. At first the light appeared as a solid mass, then quickly separated into two small dots before his eyes. But when he wiped the water away, he realized that they were more than mere dots.

Near the edge of the walkway, two bright patches of light moved, uncertain shapes against the garden wall. They flashed before his eyes, now brighter, now dimmer, until they shimmered away, leaving behind an especially concentrated darkness. He felt his heart hammering in his chest. What the hell was that? he wondered . . . then caught sight of two figures standing beside the garden wall—the figures of two small children.

The boy stood still, half grinning, with his hands folded in prayer. The girl, thin framed, dressed in dirty, ragged clothing, raised her hands in the air as though beckoning to him. The child's fingers were long and extended with sharp nails protruding from their tips, all of which appeared to be transparent. She smiled and moved closer.

"Daddy?" Kristy stepped suddenly from the darkness.

"What?" Ron spun around.

"I'm thirsty. May I have a glass of soda?"

When Ron glanced back into the garden the children had vanished.

"May I, Daddy?"

Kristy was standing at the edge of the pool in her pink and white pajamas. Ron could tell she hardly saw him because she couldn't quite get her eyes open. He regarded her sleep-puffed, shapeless mouth and thought: Just like her father. It was a habit of his to constantly look for similarities between Kristy and himself. Almost as though he were trying to prove something.

"And what are you doing up at this hour?" Ron stepped quickly from the pool and wrapped himself in his robe.

"My room is too hot. I'm thirsty."

"You couldn't get a glass of water yourself?"

"I want soda."

"I don't think . . ."

"Daddy!" she whined.

He glanced again at the garden wall. He was uncertain whether his eyes had ever been open. Or maybe he had suffered a sort of mini-blackout in reverse. Bright lights instead of dark spots before his eyes.

In the kitchen he lifted the Coke bottle from the refrigerator, then placed the glass on the counter and filled it with soda. The soda rose rapidly in the glass and splashed over the rim onto his hand.

"Here," he said and dried his hands. Kristy drank greedily at first, then began to slow. Ron regarded the kitchen wallpaper, which was covered with pictures of an ancient stag hunt and which was starting to show signs of wear. How often, how many days now had Chandal been after him to have it replaced? Two weeks. Three? Or had it been months? He sighed. As soon as they got back from their vacation, he'd take care of it.

"I'm hungry," Kristy said, her big eyes peering over the rim of the glass.

"Kristy, it's three-thirty in the morning."

"I can't sleep when I'm hungry," she whispered solemnly.

Ron's wink accepted the conspiracy. Instantly he began fumbling through the cabinet, searching for brownies. In mid-action he stopped, having distinctly remembered eating them himself. Sheepishly he closed the door and stared at the bread box. "How about . . ."

With a slice of raisin bread in her hand, Kristy sat at the table and began to chew. There was a slice of raisin bread for Ron also, smeared with butter. And a cup of coffee.

He ate slowly, while she took quick bites, all the while holding the bread close to her mouth.

"Kristy?"

"Yes."

"When . . . when you came into the garden. Did you see anyone out there?"

"You. You were there."

"No, I mean other people. Children."

"Nooo," Kristy laughed. "That's silly."

Ron nodded. "Yeah. Silly."

They were silent then, because neither seemed to have an answer. Ron considered the possibility that perhaps he had picked up Kristy's image standing beside the pool. His vision blurred when he rubbed his eyes. He saw double. All perfectly normal. Yet he couldn't help feeling there was still something he wasn't quite able to grasp.

"Good night, Daddy."

"Night, sweetheart." He looked up just as Kristy cleared the kitchen door. "Hey, hey—not so fast. Back."

Kristy turned slowly and shuffled to the table. Ron smiled, pushing loose black curls away from her eyes. "I love you, stinker."

Kristy lowered her head in a sudden flush of embarrassment. "I love you too," she muttered.

"Kiss, please."

Kristy looked up, her face having burst open into a magnificent glow. She puckered her lips and placed a kiss sloppily on Ron's cheek.

"Good," Ron said softly. "Now you, young lady, must get some sleep."

"Okay."

Ron kissed her gently on the forehead. "Good night, sweetheart."

"Night, Dad."

Ron watched as she scrambled from the room, almost running into the refrigerator on the way out. "And don't tell your mother about the eating tonight!" he hollered after her.

"I won't."

He listened to Kristy's footsteps hurry away up the stairs, until they became lost in the soft hallway carpeting above. It wasn't until he had heard her door close that he actually found himself acknowledging the acute loneliness he now felt, and the small fragments in his unconscious, the distorted but familiar pictures, which seemed to hover over him like scavenger birds.

Yes, sir. This sure has been one hell of a night.

He finished his coffee quickly. Then stood and tested his legs. There was a spot just below his right knee that felt as though it had been freshly bruised. He was surprised to see several deep gashes along the bottom of his shin. A faint line of weariness pulled at his mouth as he watched the blood clot at the thin edges of each gash. Christ, he never remembered doing that, but then again, he wasn't remembering much of anything these days.

43

Sometime later, he climbed into bed, rolled over on his back and closed his eyes. He would try to go again to where stars burned like fire, where God had neither compassion, nor mercy, but how, or even why, he did not know.

Curiously enough, there were no stars this time. No great stones clinging to heaven. No spectacles. There was only a riddle. Something about a well and a bell—he heard the ringing, felt himself falling—a small descent, nothing to be worried about. Not yet, at any rate.

He dozed and saw Kristy's face. Then Kristy's face became Chandal's face. So much alike, and yet so different. So incredibly different.

But then Kristy was his child too, wasn't she? A combination of both of them. And something else. Motion. Grappling motion. Always moving, changing shape, growing, growing, growing . . .

EIGHT

"COME IN," WHISPERED THE STONECUTTER'S WIFE. IT WAS NOT an invitation, but an order.

The old man shuffled past her, his face appearing mothlike in the flickering light of her candle. He breathed deeply, in a steady, unbroken rhythm. Today his breathing was more regular than usual, somehow healthier, and she thought he might sleep well tonight.

"Do you have it?" she asked.

The old man's face flushed proudly as he handed over a crisp twice-folded piece of paper. There was a brief pause as they gazed at each other across the flame. Now the old man's face was unsure, as if he were about to apologize for not getting there sooner. The old woman remained stiff, unyielding.

Abruptly, she broke open the red seal on the paper and read the name that was written there. Then she jerked her head up, her gaze as hectic as the old man's. She nodded.

44

Head bowed in respect, the man withdrew. The house fell silent as the stonecutter's wife peered from the lace curtains in the living room. She watched his shadowy figure hurry away down the twisted path. Her thin lips, smeared with a touch of lipstick that only accentuated the gray folds of her face, parted to reveal tiny white teeth, perfect and sharp.

My husband will be pleased, she thought with a chuckle. Very pleased.

Moments later, the woman descended the basement stairs. She stopped to gaze at the vast room that seemed to embrace her. A touch of mirth clung to her lips. Above, along the edges of the high ceiling, shadows gathered into darkness, smoky and impenetrable; along the walls and floor was only a murky half-light, more yellowish than gray, a light that seemed born of its own volition. Outside the basement door, it was black night, but inside it was merely dusk.

Even at that hour, the coolest part of the night, the motionless air was faintly heated. She passed swiftly through an archway into another room where the Ruling Elders sat waiting. Seated in a position of honor was her husband. The paper was quickly passed among them. Approval was signified by the casting of smooth stones into a basin of liquid. The vote was unanimous. All eyes turned to the altar.

The altar was illumined by four black candles, reeking of the sickening sweet odor of bitumen, and by the faint flicker of light that crept its way under the door and shimmered like gold dust upon the floor. The silence was broken by the sudden harsh blasphemy that spewed forth from the young priest dressed in his mock costume, marked with an inverse cross. His words were spoken slowly, deliberately, with a sneer.

With great ceremony, an animal was selected. Tonight it was a white angora cat, whose limpid eyes gazed trustingly into the eyes of the priest.

The knife flashed with a swift light; a moment more and the fresh blood gushed into the sacramental cup from the gaping throat of the cat lying fettered there, as the film of death closed over its agonized eyes.

The stonecutter was the first to drink.

All at once the basement door was flung open, and a blast

of cool air rushed through the room. Figures had begun to descend the stairs. Everything stopped then, became perfectly motionless.

Her children. They had come to her at last.

And the stonecutter's wife smiled as her husband slowly raised the golden chalice to his lips and drank deeply.

NINE

RON'S EYES FLICKERED OPEN AND HE WAS INSTANTLY AWARE OF three simultaneous phenomena: Chandal was still lying asleep beside him; the TV set in the living room wasn't on, which meant Kristy was also still asleep; and last night's demons were gone. Burned away by the sun, blocked out by the sure thought that it was going to be a great day. He allowed a thin smile to tug at his lips. It had been weeks since he had experienced such a moment of complete and utter calm.

Out of chaos there had come order. He started to wake Chandal and then thought better of it. Just for a minute or so he wanted to cling to the light, heady sensation that now occupied his mind.

He lay still and closed his eyes. He could see the world spread out before him like a Triple-A travel map. In his mind's eye, he buzzed competently along, avoiding the detours, and favoring the bypasses. He could see the whole country spread out three thousand miles to the east of him, and the whole Pacific Ocean three thousand miles to the west of him; and it all looked so goddamn magnificent. Sparkling clear and endless.

He laughed, tossed over on his side, and watched last night's anxiety disappear immediately before his eyes in an azure flash. Finished. He fell back into a soundless, bottomless sleep almost instantly.

Outside, the day continued to lighten by small degrees.

He awoke a half hour later to the muffled disembodied voice of the local meteorologist. ". . . temperatures in the mid-eighties along the coast and ninety inland . . . bright and sunny . . . winds out of the south at five knots . . ." A small click and the voice ceased. Ron drew a luxurious breath, rolled over, and opened his eyes. Chandal's hand slid from the clock radio.

"Morning, honey." He yawned.

Chandal smiled lazily.

"How do you feel?" Ron asked snuggling against her side. He slid his arm across her thin rib cage to hug her.

"Good day for a vacation," she said sleepily.

"That's not what I asked you." He leaned over and kissed the vein of her neck. Her arm came around his head, holding it there, her long fingers playing with his hair. "What I asked you—" he looked up at her, "was . . . how do you feel?"

"Hummm." She smiled her second smile of the morning.

"Romantic?" he murmured.

"Is that the way most people begin a vacation?"

He touched the tip of his finger to the tip of her nose, ran it down to draw an O around the lushness of her soft lips. "We're not most people," he whispered and kissed the sleep from her eyes and from her mouth, passionate kisses that seemed to surge from desire left unattended for too many days. She must have felt it, because she pressed her body flush against his and began to rub her knee gently between his legs. He immediately felt the surge.

"Ronald!" she shrilled playfully. "I'm shocked."

He took hold of her just as playfully and nuzzled her breasts. Then their mouths were together again, hands and arms touching, something deep within each of them breaking suddenly through muscle and skin and bone to come together in an intense, slow, tender, sensually magnificent love dance.

They made love without restraint, holding nothing back, having suddenly rediscovered the secret of total abandonment.

They remained locked in each other's arms for a long time, feeling everything, saying nothing—allowing the moment to speak for itself. It all had been so natural, that was the wonder of it. So natural and so unexpected that it was impossible to know what the beginning had been—physical or spiritual—and once begun what boundary had been crossed. Only that some boundary had been crossed and that somehow a blending of spirit and flesh had been achieved.

Sunlight flooded the room now as Chandal disengaged herself from Ron's arms and stepped naked into the bright glow of a July morning. He quickly reached out and clasped her hand and tried to lure her back to bed. She smiled, leaning over to kiss him. "Love you," she breathed.

"Love you too," he said, squeezing soft flesh.

Abruptly she pulled away from his playful hands and slipped into her robe. "I'm onto you," she said and then switched to her early morning Army sergeant routine: "Kristy, come on—up. Get up, get up! The great day has finally arrived. Everybody up!"

Lying at peace, Ron watched Chandal brush through her hair and shake it out. It fell in soft waves across her face, obscuring her profile as she placed the brush on the dresser. Sun rays filtering in from the window waltzed through her hair, creating a myriad of highlights that rippled and danced over her soft skin. Rusty colors like the autumns of his youth.

The image carried with it an atmosphere of peace as strong as the fragrance of the burning of fall leaves behind his aunt's house, golden and yellow and red; Ron could see himself coming down across the woods, forever a small boy, with spruce pitch stuck in his mouth and a triumphant gap-tooth smile; he saw it and breathed it, his eyes smiled peace.

"I never saw anything so beautiful in my life," he said musingly.

"As what?" she mumbled and began to gather her hair, sweeping it up and away from her face. The gesture was deceptively simple, the sudden upsweep of hair accentuating her high cheekbones, showing off the elegance of her long slender neck. "What's beautiful?"

"You are," he said honestly.

"How can you still be that much in love after seven years?" she murmured, pleased.

"Well, I . . . Jesus, you know . . ."

"You're pretty gorgeous yourself," she grinned and popped out the doorway, leaving him to grope for the words that should have been easy to say and yet had remained inexplicably out of reach.

Ron lay in bed a while longer, marveling at how Chandal could leave a bed as smoothly as a porpoise sliding through soft swells. As for Ron, he took murderous pleasure in struggling up from the mattress, each part of his body finding courage at different intervals. He finally drew a cautious breath and leaped.

He stopped in front of the mirror. Christ. He looked haggard, with dark circles under his eyes, the eyes themselves narrow slits.

Forty . . . and today I look fifty. How the hell could he feel so good and look so lousy?

Chandal and Kristy were both dressed and seated at the kitchen table having their breakfast when Ron, still in his bathrobe, stumbled into the kitchen.

"You both dressed already?" he said peering into the refrigerator.

"Listen, Kristy and I are the quick ones in the family," Chandal said.

Kristy scolded, "That's right, Daddy. You're always so slow."

"Don't be so smug, either of you," he said, poking around between the bottles.

"What are you looking for?"

"Orange juice."

"Green container."

"Last week it was red."

"Last week I didn't have tomato juice, this week I have. Tomato juice always goes in the red." Chandal rose and carried her plate to the dishwasher. "How do you want your eggs?"

"Don't."

"Want eggs?"

"Correct," he said and swallowed the last of the orange juice straight from the green container. "What I want is to shave, shower and be on the road by—" He glanced at his watch. "Nine o'clock."

"Kristy, got to hurry." Chandal began clearing dishes.

Ron scooped up the morning paper and headed for the bathroom. He shaved slowly, meticulously, taking brief glimpses at the headlines.

"By the way." Chandal popped her head into the bathroom.

"Humm?"

"Did you happen to see those lights last night?"

Ron tensed and took his time before responding. "When?"

"While you took your little dip."

"You were watching me?"

"Of course. Pretty sexy, if you ask me." She reached out with her finger and removed a glob of shaving cream from the corner of his mouth.

She paused. "Did you?"

"What?"

"Happen to see those strange lights?"

"No," he lied. Then wondered why he had.

"Oh, well—" She disappeared down the hallway, adding: "The suitcases are just about ready to go."

Ten minutes later, Ron stepped from the shower and groped blindly for a towel. He wiped soap from his eyes, but couldn't wipe away the nibbling in the back of his skull. He hadn't been wrong. The lights had been there. So what? The hell with it. He had made up his mind not to think about last night. He would have all he could do to get his dragging ass through the day.

He threw the towel aside and opened his eyes. He could see nothing in the steam-choked bathroom. Then a slight fluttering overhead. He listened. The fluttering was followed by a sharp, dull thud. A moment later, he felt the air move against his face, and something came to stand in front of him. "Chandal?" He stretched out his hand.

There was nothing.

He reached further, and this time he touched it. Now he was seized with vertigo and apprehension; his heart seemed to flutter, jolted him with an unlikely pain on the left side. More of the same when he took a deep breath. He gripped the towel rack as the light appeared before his eyes, and the child—like a floodlight had suddenly been let loose on her. He called out, "Del . . ." but it came out too weakly to be heard. His eyes were fixed on the child, and through the glare he could see the smile on the little girl's face, the glow in her eyes as she reached out to take hold of him.

Impulsively he raised one hand, letting the tips of his fingers pass lightly over the child's warm flesh. Immediately, he could feel a strange sensation passing through him. He lifted his other hand and slowly started to bring the child to him. Her fingers took hold. Restful, so suddenly restful, no sound, no movement, just the touching. Then a quiet hum that lasted for a moment until it was broken by the sound of his own heartbeat. He tried to fight the wave of dizziness that had come over him, to step back, and thought: *I'm not going to make it.* And still someone whispered, *"Rest."*

He felt the floor going out from under him and his own weight forcing him down. He cried, "Chandal!" even more urgently, the sound of his voice rumbling off the walls. He raised his eyes, strained to see through the blur of light, searching for the little girl; above, around—where was she?

He turned, startled, and waited for the room to work itself into clear vision: the mirror, the sink, the bathtub, all of them thinly veiled with steam; and with relief, with overwhelming relief, the space directly in front of him which was now empty.

"Yes?" Chandal asked, opening the bathroom door. Steam swirled quickly into the hallway. She waited for him to say something. He stood silent, saying nothing, perspiration dripping from his naked body.

"Mommy, can I . . ." Kristy stopped outside the door and stared up at her father. Quickly, Ron covered himself with the towel.

"Please," he murmured, "get her away from the door."

"Kristy, how many times . . ."

"Mommy, I can't find Jennifer."

"Well, she has to be . . ."

"Get her out of here!" Ron screamed.

Chandal turned to stare at him. "All right, Ron. Take it easy." Quickly she ushered Kristy away and closed the door.

Ron dropped on the edge of the tub, his heart still pounding. Through the flesh-wracking thuds, he could hear Chandal apologizing to Kristy for him. Then the house suddenly fell silent. There was no sound whatever; the house could have been perched on an invisible mountaintop in space. Then, far off but clear, he heard Kristy crying.

Chandal slipped quietly back into the bathroom and shut the door behind her. Slowly she inched forward and sat beside Ron on the edge of the tub. She took hold of his hand. "You all right?" she asked.

"Christ, I don't know. I really don't know." But as absurd as the thought was, Ron reasoned in silence, it was possible, really possible, that he *was* on the verge of a breakdown. What else could explain it? No matter how steamy the room was, and airless, and suffocating, however tired he was, he couldn't have fallen asleep, not on his feet, not that suddenly and completely. What in the hell had happened to him?

"Hey!" Chandal raised his hand and pressed it gently to her lips. "We love you, you know."

Ron shook his head.

"Forget it, okay? Kristy will. She always does. That's what the next four weeks are supposed to be about. Take some time off. Relax. We need it—all of us."

"I know, but—"

"Enough." Chandal rose and glanced at herself in the mirror. With a flick of her hand she brushed recalcitrant strands of hair from her forehead. "All right," she said. "Now tell me what it was all about."

"What *what* was about?"

"Your calling me in here in the first place."

"It wouldn't make any sense to you."

"It never does. But try me."

Ron frowned. "It's those goddamn lights you saw last night. I—"

"The Palmer kids," Chandal interrupted. "Kristy said they sneak into our garden all the time. To take little swims. At night they use the lanterns from their garage. I knew those were no ordinary lights."

"Del . . . it was three-thirty in the morning."

"So. The Palmers are crazy, you know that. Hey, come on, come on. It's almost nine o'clock." She kissed him on the temple and was gone from the room before he could respond.

Ron slipped on his robe, sitting at the edge of the tub. His body felt drained. The same kind of sensation as he sometimes experienced at his health club when stepping from the steam room. He looked at his leg. One of the small gashes from last night had opened up and a slight trickle of blood flowed down over his foot. He flexed his hands. His fingers felt sprained from a struggle. Struggle? *With what?*

For a brief moment, he had the feeling of not being able to

tell whether he was awake or not. Then it passed. Kristy. He had to apologize to Kristy. But how, that was the question. He never was much good with apologies. Slowly he tightened the robe around his still moist body and left the room.

TEN

"AND KRISTY . . . ?" CHANDAL ASKED QUIETLY.

Ron had somehow avoided Kristy until Chandal had literally brought them together in the hallway, and the embrace was, for Ron, a mild and pleasant relief.

"Do you forgive me?" Ron asked.

"Yes, Daddy," she said and wasted no time in making a hasty retreat to the living room, where she immediately became absorbed in playing with her collection of miniature toys.

"She won't forget it, Del," Ron said somberly. "She'll remember."

"I told you, Ron, that's ridiculous."

"Goddamn it, it's not!" he insisted. "Jesus. Did you see her? The hatred—I could see it in her eyes."

"That's all in your mind."

"No. It is not in my mind, Del." He pressed his fingertips to the center of his forehead with painful reflection. A distant look grew steadily in his eyes.

"Hey." Chandal shook his arm. "Sometimes you're worse than a child yourself. You just don't know when to get off of it." She smiled. "Peace?"

Ron shrugged. "I guess."

"Promise?"

"Yeah."

"Look," she said, tightening her hand on his arm for emphasis, "I don't want to begin our vacation this way. Ron, please. We've worked so hard for this. Don't spoil it now."

Ron nodded. "I wouldn't do anything to wreck your vacation. You know that."

"Our vacation, Ron."

"Okay," he smiled. "Our vacation then."

"How are you doing with the suitcases?"

"Everything's in the car."

"Good. I'd better check all the windows again, just to be sure."

"Go ahead," he said and watched her scamper up the stairs. Dressed in blue jeans, a pale green tee shirt, a gingham shirt over it, and sneakers, she looked like a child herself, Ron mused. He shook his head. *All of us children, I guess.*

He hesitated a moment, then lighted a cigarette and walked quietly into the kitchen. Heavy clouds had begun to drift across the sky; it was as though the house was all at once covered with fur. The light in the kitchen was frosted and brittle.

He moved closer to the window and gazed at the Palmers' house next door. A familiar Hollywood scene: fancily balustraded frontside with palms lining the drive; Jacuzzi, wet bar, poolside lifestyle to the rear. In between, wallboard that leaked like tissue paper with the first good winter rain.

Ron looked at the house for a long moment, then turned away. He tried to coordinate his thoughts. He was still unable to believe that it was Ned Palmer's daughter he had seen in his garden last night. They had a pool of their own, didn't they? What would they be doing sneaking into his garden for a swim? It just didn't make sense.

Blankly, he looked at his watch. The last thing he had any desire to do that particular moment was to keep mentally abusing himself that way. The pace of his heart quickened as he climbed the stairs. At the top he paused to light another cigarette.

"Do you have to smoke?" Chandal asked and ducked into the bedroom.

"Why?" he hollered after her. "Is it going to stunt my growth?"

"Daddy?" Kristy appeared at the foot of the stairs.

"Humm?"

"She's gone!" Kristy stopped midway between the dining room and the kitchen, dropped her head as though someone had struck a sharp blow to the back of her neck, then turned slowly to gaze up at him.

Ron had seen that look before. It was a game they played. At first, Ron had found the game amusing. Lately, it had become a mild source of irritation. The game was always played in the same fashion. Kristy would throw away her favorite doll. Then she would claim to have lost it. Everyone was then supposed to look for it. Sometimes the doll was found in minutes, other times an hour or so went by before the doll was found. After playing the game numerous times, Ron decided to ask a friend—a lay analyst—about it. The woman had merely shrugged. "That one is easy," she said. "Kristy is trying to overcome her fear of rejection."

Rejection? Had Ron and Chandal rejected her in any way? Perhaps they had. But then again, perhaps they hadn't. Children were funny that way. And Kristy wasn't any different. Besides being extremely beautiful, she was also highly imaginative, more so than most children her age. And more times than not, her imagination would get the better of her.

Still, as a theatrical agent, Ron had seen what could happen when one let down one's guard, forgot what was real and what was make believe. Catastrophe. Erosion of family life. The loss of everything that meant anything. He had seen wives replaced by mistresses who became wives only to be replaced themselves by mistresses. He had seen beautiful children sold to the highest bidder. He had seen ideals reduced to the most vulgar denominator.

Well, it was not going to happen to him. Not to his wife, his child; not to Ron himself. He descended the steps quickly.

"Honey, do you need the doll? There'll be so much for you to see and do, you won't . . ."

"I can't go without the doll."

"Honey . . . ?" Ron said patiently.

Still Kristy hesitated. In that moment, that precise moment, Ron was starting to have serious doubts about the whole thing. It was true that his time was his own; he kept no scheduled hours but worked as he chose. It was also true, however, that he had been forced to work most of the time, leaving little time to spend with Kristy. But to suddenly take a four-week vacation at this time was, perhaps, a bit extreme.

Kristy now lay face down on the living room rug, her arms plunged under the sofa, her feet scrambling to push her still further. "I have her! She's here!" Kristy squealed and pulled into view the lost doll.

"Well, good," Ron said, and wondered how on earth such a matronly doll could become so indispensable to a little girl. Not a Barbie doll with an immense glamorous wardrobe or a baby doll, cuddly and cute, but this hard, plastic-bodied, stiff-wigged, china-faced doll which had become Kristy's best friend and imaginary playmate. Sometimes they would even have loud vicious arguments, with Kristy doing both voices. Once Kristy had ordered "Jennifer" shut into the basement closet only to wake Ron up in the middle of the night: "Daddy, Jennifer's scared. You have to get her. Jennifer's afraid to stay down there."

Casually, Kristy now picked herself up from the floor, Jennifer held upside down by one hard plastic leg, and threw the doll into the toy box. "Okay, I'm ready."

"Did you go to the bathroom?"

"I don't have to go."

"Go to the bathroom." Ron picked up the toy box with one hand and the suitcase at the door with the other. "I want to be on the road in five minutes. Chandal?" he bellowed.

Chandal emerged from the bedroom, blue flight bag over her shoulder, purse dangling from her hand.

"What's that?" Ron demanded suspiciously. "Is that another ditty bag? I told you only one damned ditty bag—that plastic bag that I packed an hour ago."

"This is just more or less a purse," she said descending the stairs.

"Then what's that in your hand, for God's sake?"

"It's—ah, it fits into the flight bag. I've got everything in there—cards, peanut butter and crackers, pencils, crossword puzzles . . ."

"Did you go to the bathroom?" Ron interrupted.

"I don't have to," Chandal said cramming her purse into the center compartment of the flight bag. The zipper refused to budge.

"Go to the bathroom," Ron ordered grimly. "I want to be on the road in five minutes."

"But—"

"Hurry up, Mommy." Kristy dashed from powder room to front door where she collected her red patent leather pocket book, crayons and two coloring books and disappeared into the car before Ron could mention that he had already packed crayons, magic markers, coloring books, artist's pads and construction paper into the toy box.

Twenty minutes later, they were on the road, better time than Ron had expected to make. "Women," he thought affectionately and noticed he had an ache in his lower back.

TWO

GETTING THERE

ONE

Father, the root of this little pink flower
Among the stones has the taste of blood.
And reptiles are everywhere. Here's one in
My hand, Father, look; And there is one on
Your arm. But do not run away, because . . .

TO THREE RACES AND TWELVE GENERATIONS, THROUGH ALL ITS
many names, it has been known simply as the valley. It is
blazingly hot by day, cool by night. In its abysmal depths
whole mountains contract and expand. Everything changes
shape constantly in its shifting light. And all these mutations
of form, these permutations of substance, are suffused with
infinite variations of color, color brought to life by its power.
Never static, never still, it is inconstant as the passing
moment, and yet durable as time. It is its people's way into
the nebulous past, into the apocalyptic future.

And who are these people who choose to live under an
umbrella of stone? Farming men, mostly, generations of
them, who walk two or three miles in the dark, after twelve
hours' toil in the fields. Some of these men cannot read or
write. Some, if a stranger is present, can adopt a clever
disguise of intelligence. Some cannot.

And some who can, will not. For there is a darker side to
the people of the valley which cuts them off from the rest of
the world. A nexus of superstition and hatred that has been

61

passed down through the ages like a barbed-wired fence that stretches from here to the moon.

Progress has brought little change to the life in the valley. Farmhouses built hundreds of years ago, when walls were made from rough-cut pine and birch, now have modern windows and doors, a few fancy lighting fixtures and TV antennas on their roofs. Horses have been replaced by tractors and automobiles. Narrow roads have been widened a little, some tarred over, most still in poor condition. A few new stores, a new library and school, a new single-decker bus paid for by the Elders to bring the kids back home in the evening. Still, these are the subtle disguises which conceal the old ways and the superstition that lives on as before.

To the north and south lay the hills. To the east, a steep-walled canyon that connects with smaller canyons, all forming a network of crevices that seem to hem the valley in on all sides. On the edge of the western slope rests a great stone. Even in summer the stone seems to cast a shadow over the valley, robbing it of warmth.

So the outside world tends to pass the valley by. And the people of the valley, either from hatred or fear, prefer to stay within the rocky boundaries of their own choosing, to be born there, schooled there, wed there and buried there. It is said that anyone in the valley can find a family connection somewhere between any two individuals in the area. Some say that the people of the valley have married their own for too many years. It can be seen in the wild remoteness of their eyes.

The children are generally told what will be expected of them when they are between six and ten, whenever they seem capable of understanding. No matter how well the matter has been explained to them, there are always a handful who feel sickened by the idea. They feel anger, disgust, outrage, despite all the explanations. But the terms are strict and absolute, and eventually most children bend under the will of the Elders. Those who don't, well . . .

They go on. They leave the valley, they walk ahead into the unknown world beyond, and if they are lucky, very lucky, they do not come back.

TWO

THE MOUNTAINS JUST SOUTH OF SALT LAKE CITY WERE DEAD silent except for the rustle of scurrying lizards and the sound of wind on stone—still a fit place for scavenger birds.

To the west, over jagged ridges of rocks and peaks, thin white clouds drifted against a cobalt horizon; to the east, the mountains stood purple in wine-colored infinity. Nothing was visible except the land—no stock, no dwellings, nor man.

"Do you see it, Dad?" Kristy wailed. "Do you?"

"No, but we'll find it." Ron's eyes flickered to the rearview mirror. Kristy's eyes loomed out at him. For the first time in days she was excited about something. Really excited. New Mexico, Kansas and Nebraska had bored her. The Black Hills of South Dakota frightened her. Wyoming put her to sleep. Ron had placed his hopes on Salt Lake City. A complete bust. But suddenly, out of nowhere, Kristy had found something to have captured her imagination.

"How far do you think?" Chandal hesitated, leaning on the overnight bag that separated her from her husband.

"Until the next bathroom," Ron filled in knowledgeably. "I don't know. Maybe twenty miles, maybe a thousand. I'd say let's stop, but we're in lizard heaven. I mean, you wouldn't like to go over there by that brush, would you?"

Chandal shuddered as a lizard lifted its primitive head. "Keep driving."

"Right."

At the detour sign, Ron turned the dusty blue station wagon off the main highway onto a narrow asphalt road that shimmered with vapor and sunlight.

On either side, vast splotches of thorned brush, scrub oak, aspen and red pine spread across the desolate land, and the road seemed endless. Ron drove the car flat-out for a ways, then slowed. He winced a little. The road wasn't any great shakes. The country was suffering from softening of the arteries.

"Hold on," he said, too late. Kristy had already been jolted backward and slid down between the seats onto the hard floor, between the cooler and the collection of plants Chandal had amassed along the way.

"Are you all right?" Chandal asked. The wind from the open window caught her fine brown hair and swept it neatly to one side as she turned to stretch over the back of the seat.

Kristy had already regained her balance.

Chandal reached out and pushed loose strands of black hair away from the child's sweating face. "She's so hot. Let's stop for a minute, Ron."

"Just a few more miles. I know the damn thing is around here somewhere. We saw it, right? So it's got to be here." Ron slowed the car and peered out. The sun was hot and fierce. There was no shade or shelter in sight—one spot was as unrelenting as another.

"Maybe that's it, Ron." Chandal leaned against the dashboard and pointed straight ahead.

Kristy practically climbed into the front seat in anticipation.

"No, that's not it. Too small," Ron said. "It was bigger, wasn't it, Kristy? Different shape entirely."

"No, Mom. That's not it! That's not it!" she wailed.

"Hush up, we'll find it." Chandal shifted restlessly, fidgeted.

"Your mother's right, Kristy. Relax."

"All right."

Then a small sideways glance from Chandal, followed by, "Let's stop for a few minutes, okay? Then I'll drive for awhile."

"We're supposed to change every hundred miles."

"What difference does it make? Fifty—a hundred."

Ron slowed down again, glanced into the rearview mirror, then hit the accelerator.

"Ron, you really should slow down."

"I'm only doing fifty-five."

"Sixty—then twenty. When you realize you're doing twenty—you speed up again. You're not consistent. Think about your driving."

"But it's around here somewhere. Kristy wants to see it."

"Maybe the detour has turned us around. It could be anywhere."

"I know where it is," Kristy chimed in.

Ron turned to face her. "You do? Where?"

Kristy did not answer him. Merely smiled.

"Watch out!" screamed Chandal.

From the corner of his eye he saw it. A large boulder sliding down into the roadway. He never slackened speed. His hands jerked the wheel; the car skidded across the road with a howl of rubber, back end swinging. Ron gripped the wheel tightly, shoved the accelerator to the floor.

A metallic twang mixed with a crash as the car was hit in the rear by the rock. The vehicle bounced and leaped off the road, onto another road made not for cars but for livestock. Ahead there was a sharp turn. Ron swerved the car around the bend and slammed on the brakes. The vehicle bucked and sputtered to a dead halt.

It took Ron a few seconds to understand that the car had stopped, and that everyone seemed to be in one piece. Chandal clung to the dashboard, not moving. Confused, Ron turned. Where was Kristy? A sudden swirl of dust and heat made it difficult to breathe.

"Kristy, are you all right?"

"Yes, Daddy," she said and began to whimper.

"Del?"

"Christ," she breathed and seemed to collapse with the sudden release of breath.

Ron did not move for a moment. Then, like a volcanic crater, he began venting steam. "Goddamn it!" he shouted. "Son of a bitch! GODDAMN SON OF—"

"Ron . . ."

"Right," he said and flung open the car door. He clambered out, his voice trailing off when he found his feet touching hard earth. He was standing, he was moving, everything was going to be all right.

He stood alone behind the passenger's side of the car. Through the rear glass he watched Chandal reach back and wipe Kristy's face with a handkerchief. "Is she all right?" he hollered.

"I think so."

Shaking his head, he examined the damage. The back end of the car was dented, but not badly. The bumper had been crushed and the rear tire was flat. Other than that, the car seemed fine.

"How bad is it?" Chandal asked, leaning out the car window.

"A flat."

"That's it?"

"A few dents. Nothing serious."

Ron lifted the spare from the back of the wagon and began to change the tire. He remembered what a great adventure the vacation had promised to be. But even Kristy had lost her enthusiasm. Somehow the hot summer days had blended into hot summer nights, and then into hot summer days again, and there had come to be a feeling of monotony about it all. It was partly because of money, Ron thought for the fiftieth time, lowering the car off the jack. Of course, it hadn't helped either that the car's air conditioner had broken down somewhere outside of Rapid City, South Dakota. He had stopped several times to get it repaired, but had always been told it would take days to fix. So they had driven on.

"Oh, Jesus!" he wailed.

"What is it?" Chandal wailed back.

"The spare. It hardly has enough air in it. The damn thing is almost flat. I can't believe this," he said flicking large beads of sweat away from his brow. He looked as though he had just stepped out of his swimming pool. "Damn," he muttered, then thought: It was time to stop anyway. But he did not laugh at his own humor. Who could laugh? The temperature had to be well over a hundred degrees with no shade in sight.

"What do we do now?"

"I don't know," he said and climbed the leeward side of a small hill, man and temper stewing in the fierce heat, and at the top he stopped. He looked in all directions, seeing nothing but more hills, and after that a hundred more, all higher and steeper than the one before. Like a machine who had run out of fuel, he dropped dejected onto a rock. The silence was deafening.

"Daddy?" Kristy poked her head out of the window.

"What?"

"There's a gas station, Daddy. Just ahead."

"Sure. And my ass chews bubble gum!"

"Ron, cut that out!" Chandal scowled.

"Sorry."

"Just over the next hill, Mom. There's a gas station."

"How do you know that?" asked Chandal.

"I saw it," Kristy said. "When we were at the top."

Ron stood and looked around automatically; there was no gas station to be seen. "She must have been seeing things." He dropped again onto the rock. Had he known that traversing the rocky wasteland was going to be like this, he gladly would have stayed at home. Suddenly all he wanted to do was to bury himself in the midst of some teeming metropolis. He was obsessed with the desire for traffic and buildings and masses of people, clients screaming at him over the telephone, air-conditioned offices and tall frosted glasses of rum topped with cool crisp pieces of pineapple.

Ron settled back now, clasped his hands on his stomach as he closed his eyes; he blew a loud sigh through his lips. He began to drift. After a moment he heard the car door close, heard Chandal say, "Kristy, you stay here," then pictured her inching forward. He felt her shadow pass over him.

"What are we going to do?" she asked.

He opened one eye and peered. "Melt."

"Seriously."

He sat up. "Oh, I'm serious. I can feel it. I'm melting!"

"Maybe Kristy did see a gas station. It's worth a try."

Abruptly he stood up, his frown clearing into a smile rapidly like dissolving clouds. "Always the optimist, ah? Well, it's worth a try. Let's go." Doubtful, yet with his fingers crossed, he backed the car up the narrow road, spun around onto the main road and headed east.

Almost before Ron brought the station wagon to a dust-spraying stop in front of the General Store and Station, Chandal had Kristy by the hand, had the car door open and was out and heading for the second of the two doors marked Men and Women. Ron hunched over the wheel, his jaw set in stone. He still could not believe it. Kristy had been right.

When he next looked up, he found himself being stared at—a primeval weather-worn face out of the Dark Ages gazing at him with intense indifference.

"Can I help you?" the man asked. His breath struck Ron full in the face, smelling of cheap booze.

Ron stared in disbelief. At first he wasn't so much frightened as he was confused. The leather-faced apparition peering at him through the window was holding a rifle, for Chrissakes. Two barrels with a heavy wooden stock. Ron had never actually come face to face with a shotgun before, but he was positive he was looking at one now.

"Sorry," the man said and laughed. "Just got back from hunting." He lowered his weapon to the ground. "You hunt?" he asked.

Ron said, "No."

"Afraid of getting shot, I bet." The man chuckled.

"I guess."

"Hell, just hang a sign around yourself saying: "Don't Shoot! I'm A Man!"

"I'll have to remember that."

"Your back tire's going flat."

"I know."

"Got a spare?"

"That is the spare."

"Oh, hell." The man inched back some, squatted down and inspected the tire. "On vacation, are you?"

"Yes." Ron stepped from the car.

"Well, a person can learn a lot traveling the country." He rose and kicked the tire. "Plenty to see if you keep your eyes open."

"What do you think?"

"About what?"

"The tire."

"Shot." His eyes flicked at Ron, his mouth forming a wry grin. Still staring, he explained that the gas station was closed. He'd gone out of business a year or so ago, when the new highway came through. He'd been unable to sell. Now his brother and he made a small earning, not a living, from the General Store. But the gas station, yes, the gas station had gone out of business. "However," he added, "I'll be glad to pump some air in that tire for you. That should at least get you to Brackston."

"Where?" asked Ron.

"You'll have to go to Brackston." His voice had a friendly tone to it now.

"How far?"

Beyond the two dusty gas pumps the man moved, bending, reaching. "Not far at all," he answered lightly, returning to the car with an antiquated tire pump in his hand. He dropped to a crouched position and fastened the valve. "You're lucky I still have this old pump. Probably save your ass," he said, his hands now moving with a steady motion as he forced air into the tire.

"I appreciate it," Ron said.

The man grinned. "Who knows, you might turn out to be Howard Hughes." He laughed. "No, sir—Brackston isn't far at all. You go straight ahead about two miles. Then take the first left you come to. Another mile or so you're over the top. You'll strike another road there."

"A road up there!" Ron exclaimed incredulously.

"The old mining road."

Ron strained his eyes into the distant sunlight.

"You can't miss it," the man wheezed. "It runs straight as a stick along the top ridge till it meets the wall. Careful, though, it ain't much of a wall there. Turn left and hold till you come to the large stone on the left side . . ."

"Stone?"

"Looks like a damn creature of sorts. Can't miss it. Turn left again and a little ways on is Brackston. They'll fix you right up."

"Brackston," Ron mumbled and reached up on the dash for the map.

"You won't find it on the map," the man chuckled. "There's dozens of towns like it, thousands of people like them in Brackston—want their privacy. Fine people though. Always willing to help a stranger." The man stepped back from the car and kicked the tire. "There you go. It should get you there."

"Thanks. How much?"

"Hell, buy me a beer. That'll do it."

Without pausing he ambled across the flat gravel drive to the General Store. Sharp sunlight drew a pen-and-ink outline of the building whose rustic facade sat flush up against the mountainside. The roof sagged on one side and the tiny bells above the screen door chimed as they stepped into the interior.

"Name's Hadley," the man said, placing his shotgun down on the counter. "Frank Hadley."

"Oh. Ron Talon."

"Well, browse around. I'll get the beers."

He quickly disappeared into the back room.

The inside of the store was almost without light. Its one window had been plastered over with a large Coke sign. Only a small shaft of sunlight fell in the doorway and slowly fanned out to revolve about the room. Patches of dirty floor showed here and there, between rows of shelves stuffed with tourist come-ons.

In the far niche in the wall stood a large wooden Indian. Ron hadn't seen one of those in years. The dark, muddy brown figure appeared to be watching Ron as much as he was watching him. His painted tiny-dot eyes peered from his dusty face with disturbing intensity. Curious, Ron moved closer. It was then he noticed a long table running the full length of the room.

Upon the table rested elaborately carved stone figures. A grotesque figure of a dancing monkey. Another figure in a squat position, head hung. Ron squinted at the hunched figure. If he could believe his eyes, a human pelt dangled from its waist.

Further down Ron stared at a group of masks, human size, their mouths twisted into distorted smiles. Beyond the masks, other works done in turquoise. A turquoise snake, teeth protruding from the jaws of its two heads. The lines of the snake were delicate, crisp.

"Sweet Jesus," Ron breathed and stepped back. It may have been the angle at which he looked at it, an unfamiliar angle, the snake was actually braced upright against the wall, or it may have been the light. Whatever the reason, the piece seemed to shimmer with life—not like a real snake, but like some unknown ancient reptile from another time. Even the scales, winding gracefully up its neck, appeared to expand and contract with life's breath.

Ron's heartbeat quickened. The snake had started to move

now, coiling out slowly in waves, its bulging eyes widening, blurry and unfocused. All at once its mouth curled back, laughing. An ugly laughing snake.

"Isn't this place great?"

"What!" Ron started.

Chandal, her eyes lost to shadows, smiled. "I just think this place is fantastic."

"I—I didn't hear you come in," he said remembering to breathe. His eyes darted to the bells over the screen door.

"I'm the sneaky type." Slowly she stepped into the light. "Were you able to get the tire fixed?"

"No. No, they don't—"

"Here we are!" Frank Hadley emerged from the back room like a ghost carrying three bottles of beer. He found his way across the room and pointed with his nose. "The glasses are behind the counter."

Ron glanced down at the snake. An oddity of illusion, he guessed. "By the way," he said, moving behind the counter. "That stone we've been looking for. It's up there."

"How do you know?" Chandal asked.

"Mr. Hadley just mentioned it," Ron said, placing three glasses in a neat row.

"Oh, hell—the stone is famous." Hadley moved around to the other side of the counter, past the screen door, and for a moment the sun fell over his face like warm milk. "About the only thing around here that is." He popped a bottlecap. "Had a woman once, got on TV doing her bird imitations. The Carson Show, I think. It was a long time ago. Other than that . . ."

Chandal was hardly listening. "These are interesting, aren't they." She stared curiously at a small group of masks.

"Those are carnival masks," Hadley said amiably, pouring the beer. "Do my best business this time of year. I sell lots of those."

"And these over here, what are they?" Chandal picked up a mask, placed it over her face, and turned to Ron. Her eyes instantly brought the mask alive. With snake-plaited hair and a nose pendant, the mask seemed threatening.

"The Goddess of Water," Hadley said, handing Ron his beer. "Damn scary if you ask me."

71

"Oh, I don't know." Chandal lowered the mask and studied it. "I think she's kind of cute. What do you think, Ron?"

Ron's remembrance of masks was restricted to the papier-mâché kind which, in his childhood, he had made in grade school. The poorly painted, stupid expression faces that made you laugh. But the mask Chandal held was quite different. There was a viciousness to it, a rage.

"Ron?" Chandal looked at him oddly. "What do you think?"

"Well, I wouldn't want to wake up one night and find her sleeping next to me, that's for sure."

"Oh, you." She turned smiling to accept a glass of beer from Hadley. "The trouble with him is he never was a good judge of beauty. I like her. I like her very much. She has a certain feminist look about her. The whole problem with the relationship between men and women, as far as I see it, is based on the assumption that women are delicate, sensitive creatures, easily tired, who must be feted, amused and protected. But this woman," she held up the mask, "this woman needs none of that. She is what she is. A woman. What all women should be." Chandal paused. "I'll take her!"

Ron nearly choked on his beer. "What?"

"How much is she?"

"Twenty dollars," Hadley said gleefully.

"For the Goddess of Water—she's worth it at twice the price."

"Del, do you really—"

"And a mate. We need a mate." Chandal hurried over to the table. "This one. What is this one?"

"Xipe Totec, the God of Spring."

"Friendly enough. Here, Ron—try it on."

"No, Del—I really . . ."

"All right. Later then." Chandal stood before him, calm and smiling, the very picture of a woman with a new lease on life.

"I'm taking them both," she said and moved to the cash register. "Forty dollars, is that right?"

Ron frowned. "Chandal, could I see you—"

"Oh, hell," Frank Hadley said hurriedly, "you can have them for thirty, seeing how you're buying two." He rang up the sale with the air of someone who has made his quota for the week. The two rapid puffs he gave to his unfiltered cigarette plainly celebrated a photo finish victory. Then, a little self-consciously, he began discussing the history relating to the masks as he made change.

Thirty dollars, Ron mused. For a set of useless masks. He glanced helplessly around the room, which had become dense with smoke and stank of beer. How did I get myself in such a place . . . he shook his head. Then, glancing through the screen door, he saw that the car was empty.

"Del?"

"Humm?"

"Where's Kristy?"

"Isn't she outside?"

Ron pushed the screen door open, the bells above chiming crisp and clear. "I don't see her."

"She's probably out back with my brother," Hadley said simply and pointed. "You want me to get her?"

"No. I'll find her."

Ron pushed open the back door, then stopped suddenly, looking dead ahead. Kristy was sitting on a wooden crate, her hands clinging to her doll as if she would fly away if she let go. Her eyes were desperately fixed on a large wire-mesh enclosure, not so much an enclosure, actually, as a cage.

A huge, flat-faced, balding man in denim shirt and trousers was bending over a separate, smaller cage that sat at Kristy's feet. Ron took a step forward and stopped when he saw that the man had taken a rabbit from the smaller cage and was letting Kristy nuzzle its soft fur. Kristy relaxed a little as the man placed the creature into her lap and she seemed to enjoy the rabbit; Ron supposed all kids were fascinated with animals.

Then it happened. So fast. Much too fast for Ron to react. The big guy took the squirming cottontail and dropped it into the fenced enclosure. Kristy's hands remained in her lap, in a cupped position, as if she were still holding onto the rabbit.

All Ron could do was to stare in dumb amazement as the rabbit went into a frenzy, as if struggling to escape from a trap. Ron's eyes quickly shifted to the far corner of the enclosure, drawn there by a sense that something had begun to move. He watched as the long, black snake leisurely uncoiled itself and glided forward. If ever death could be physically described, this was it: sleek, graceful, unrelenting as time itself.

Without warning the snake snapped, snapped again, a series of quick lunges, while the rabbit frantically leaped over the nightmare serpent that was trying to devour him. But it was as futile as trying to stop a flood. Already, the rabbit was tiring, dashing from one corner of the fence to the other, looking for a way out.

Eyes bulging, neck distended, the rattler's head once again whipped around to face its target. Ron knew the end was near. He imagined the rabbit knew it too.

Thumping bravely at the snake with both hind feet, the rabbit made one last attempt to free itself. The snake lunged twice more, its large, flat-scaled head came closer each time, until finally it darted downward, stabbing with dual fangs sharp as knives and twice as deadly. The rabbit staggered back from the force of the blow, spasmed; then, in a matter of seconds, fell on its back—dead.

"Goddamn it!" Ron screamed. "What the hell do you think you're doing?"

The man smiled. "Bet you never seen anything like that before."

"Kristy, are you all right?" Ron moved around to face her. Her eyes remained fixed on the snake with a childlike curiosity. Not fear, not confusion or puzzlement. Just simple curiosity. "Kristy?"

"Is the rabbit dead, Daddy?"

Ron took hold of her hand. "Come on."

"Is it, Daddy? Is he dead?"

Ron turned to glare at the man. He wanted to kill the stupid son of a bitch. Right then and there, if he'd had a gun, he would have shot the bastard dead.

"Don't worry," the man said. "The Lord saw fit to put His words into action. His way, don't you know?" He guffawed in a short loud burst, spitting tobacco juice onto the ground.

Over his shoulder, standing by the back door, Ron saw Chandal observing them. She was nodding and smiling; she waved. "Yoo hoo, Kristy. There you are!" she cried.

"Yeah," Ron mumbled. "Here she is. Let's get out of

here." With Kristy in hand, he retraced his steps through a labyrinth of junk, until he had reached the interior of the store.

"You know your brother is nuts, don't you!" Ron screamed at Hadley.

"Why? What happened?"

"Let's go, Del."

"Ron, what is it?" Chandal's eyes glanced off his and gazed confusedly at Frank Hadley.

"Never mind. Let's get out of here."

"Hey, what's wrong?" Hadley nervously stepped from behind the counter.

Ron didn't wait to explain. He stormed from the store, dragging Kristy with him. He heard Chandal struggling to keep up. Then the only sound was Ron muttering to himself and his car starting up. He jammed the car into drive and smashed his foot down on the accelerator. Through the rearview mirror, he watched the Hadley brothers disappear in a cloud of dust as he sped from the gravel drive.

THREE

THE ROAD WAS EMBLAZONED IN RED. IT WAS AS THOUGH SOME unseen god had used a magic marker to chart their course, much like a travel guide indicates a preferable route to be taken. They rode, as usual, with the windows down. Travel noises drowned out the radio which Ron angrily shut off. "Damn that air conditioner!" he said in a savage undertone that left little else to be said. They rattled on, Ron under visible strain. Now and again, he vented himself of random and inopportune thoughts. He could hardly hear his own mutterings. Once he spoke to Kristy whose face he had caught in the rearview mirror. "You know, don't you, that you are never to go anywhere, anywhere, with strangers. Next time, listen." Kristy made no response. Chandal suggested that they stay the night in Brackston, giving them all a

75

chance to calm down. There was a friendly note to her voice that gently reminded him this was supposed to be a pleasure trip.

Ron found the first road, turned left, and started the climb. "Let's see Brackston first," he said. "From the sound of it, they probably don't even have a motel. Look for yourself, the damn town isn't even on the map."

Ron came up over the top of the pass and instinctively slowed the car. There, rising before him were the most awesome mountains he had ever seen. The car took a gradual series of rises and descents, yet from below he had imagined the horizon was the same level in all directions.

"God in heaven," Chandal said simply, gazing from the window.

Abruptly Ron turned, his eyes drawn to a cluster of trees by the quick movement of bodies. There were at least six of them. Filthy things dressed in rags. Awful looking children with dirty hands and faces. He slowed the car and strained to get a better look. Some of the children were wearing sackclothes; others he realized now were naked.

"Del, look."

"What?"

"There in the trees. Children."

"Where?"

"There. Some of them are . . ." When he turned back, the children had vanished.

Chandal craned her neck. "I don't see anything."

Ron's attention was diverted as the road narrowed; it seemed hardly traveled but for an occasional farm wagon or tractor. A moment later the road dropped drastically and he began stomping on the brake pedal more than the accelerator. In the distance was a small opening in the mountain, barely large enough for a car to pass through. Chandal placed her arm over Ron's shoulder. "Can we get through there?"

"I think."

"Are you sure we took the right turn?"

"Christ, Del—I'm not sure of anything."

"The valley is up ahead," Kristy mumbled.

"What, hon?" Chandal turned.

"Nothing."

They came through the pass slowly, like a flock of lost sheep reluctant to finish their journey. Ron slowed the car to a stop as the valley suddenly sprang up before his eyes.

"Look, Daddy! There it is! We found it . . . we found it!"

The great stone clung to heaven for support. Twisted and gnarled, it rose above all things, the uppermost part crumbled away, leaving only two huge jagged edges that looked like the jaws of an alligator.

Kristy was in a state of exaltation close to ecstasy. "It's beautiful! Yes, yes, yes . . . beautiful!" She was out of the car now, running toward the stone.

"Kristy!" Ron shouted and Chandal said: "It's all right, I'll get her."

Ron hunched over the steering wheel and waited for the two girls to return. Standing at the foot of the stone, they looked like miniature toys. How high was the stone, he wondered. Fifty feet? A hundred? It was sure an impressive looking thing. The whole area surrounding the stone was a solid layer of hard chalk, dotted with dark, almost black foliage of trees that looked like—what? Not trees, actually, but . . . he couldn't put a name to it.

Directly ahead of the stone, the road dipped abruptly. Just before the descent was an old milestone with the inscription "2 miles to Brackston."

Once Chandal had Kristy safely back in the car, after having gone through one of the "Daddy-is-waiting" routines, she said: "The town is below. Over to the left." A tolling of a distant bell brought Ron around to gaze at the stone.

"Right," he said and let loose the emergency brake. Slowly they began their descent.

FOUR

The town eased up on them, one house at a time, until suddenly, almost without warning, they were in the midst of a strange conglomeration of buildings surrounding an enormous square. Like most small towns, Brackston was nothing more than a wide spot on the road. A mere dot in the center of mountainous country covering a vast area. It sat, serene in its isolation, as far from civilization as Genesis from Revelation.

It began with a main street of commerce, flowed lazily into the courthouse square, then drifted away into a few back streets lined with slatboard and stone houses and a few odd creations recently constructed. Most of the dwellings were unpainted and crude. Scattered here and there were several buildings two stories in height, bearing the appearance of having significant importance to the community.

Ron eased the car through the square and pointed it toward a weather-beaten Texaco sign at the other end of town. The bell of the village church struck twice more, then stopped. From deep within indigo shadows of doorways, eyes seemed to peer out. Mouths agape, no doubt, Ron mused. The town was just as he had pictured it; a self-proclaimed oasis huddled under sun and dust and flies.

A dog barked and was choked by the silence. Then loomed a group of elderly men, hats reared up on the backs of their heads. They stood, complacent in their honorable laziness, in front of the drugstore. Shooting the breeze, Ron guessed. Just smoking, spitting into the street, and discussing the weather, crops, people and . . .

An old woman dressed in black with a black headscarf crossed in front of the car, stopped suddenly to peer into the windshield. Her loose wrinkled lips drew back and she smiled. Ron waved her on. She nodded shyly; then hurriedly, respectfully, she crossed the street and disappeared into the grocery store.

"Be ready to slide down to the floor," Ron said.

"Why?"

"Because I have the strange feeling that any minute people are going to start shooting at us."

Chandal laughed and turned to Kristy. "Don't mind your father. He's joking."

Ron brought the car to a stop in front of the gas station. Joking? Maybe. But something here eluded him. "Wait here," he said, closing the car door. "This could take a few minutes. Then again, we may be here all day."

"Kristy and I will be across the street having a soda."

"All right," Ron said, barely listening; he was peering through the dirt-encrusted window of the station. He saw a small dirty room. Empty. Tentatively, he followed the flag-stone path around the building to the work area. There was a car lift on either side, a horse trough set in the middle, and a heavy wooden door to the rear.

Bare to the waist, an ageless man in denim trousers bent to pick up a shirt from the edge of a water barrel. His back and shoulders were wet; water dripped from his flowing mop of hair. He had just drawn the shirt over his head when he wheeled around to confront Ron. His was a strange, remote, pale face. So pale it might have been bleached; skin, hair, eyes were all of albino pallor. He had eyebrows and lashes, but they were visible only from certain angles; what Ron saw was bones of eye sockets, red-veined lids and deep-set colorless eyes.

"I never heard you come up behind me," he said, just missing eye contact with Ron.

"I'm sorry," Ron said.

"I thought I was alone."

"Your shirt."

"What?"

"You're buttoning it crooked."

The man glanced down, started over, buttoning it straight. Shaking his head, he moved forward to pick up his shoes. "Hot," he said and dropped onto a pile of old tires. "But the fishing was good though."

"What'd you catch?"

"A fair-size cat. Plenty for one man."

Ron watched his hands as he laced his shoes. Large, bony

hands, like his face, like his whole body, and they moved with the same awkwardness. Ron suddenly realized the awkwardness was partly caused by poor vision. Even as he watched, the man squinted down at his shoe, having as much trouble pulling the lace through the small round eye as a nearsighted woman has in threading a needle.

"Are you the owner?" Ron asked.

"Of what?"

"This station."

"Shoot, no," he said and straightened. "Work scares the hell out of me."

After a minute Ron asked, "Then you don't work here either?"

The man looked at him for a moment with an expression Ron could not fathom. "You don't know me?" the man inquired.

Ron chuckled. "No . . ."

"Sure you do. Everyone knows me. I'm Tyler Adam. Everyone knows . . ."

"TYLER!" a voice boomed.

Tyler Adam turned quickly to Ron and whispered, "You better look at me good," he said. "Remember me."

"Get the hell away from here, Tyler!" The rear door swung shut with a thud. "This isn't a public bath. Now get!"

Over his shoulder, Tyler mumbled again, "Remember me." It was uttered casually, as though an afterthought, and within seconds Ron had forgotten he'd said it.

"Matthew Todd's the name," said the man in the coveralls, wiping his hands with a rag. "Can I help you?" He was a tall husky man, barrel-chested, who obviously had once possessed great muscular strength. That power was apparently gone now, but age had not stooped him and his baked leathery face was still handsome.

"I sure hope so," Ron said and quickly spelled out the problem. Under the circumstances, he had managed to tell his tale of woe with placid, undeniable calm.

His calm shell developed a hairline crack when Matthew Todd said: "I'm afraid I can't help you. Today's Saturday. I'm about to close."

"Close?"

"All businesses in Brackston are about to close. Tonight's

the first night of carnival. Besides," he peered at Ron's car. "I don't have your tires in stock." He had the easy rambling air of a man who missed the seriousness of the problem because it wasn't his problem.

"Like I've said," he repeated, "I don't have your tires in stock. Those on the car won't go a hundred miles before they're flat again. No matter how well I patch them up. Hell, if you're not in a hurry, stay over until Monday. Monday my man goes to Salt Lake City for parts. He can pick up your tires then. In the meantime, there's the carnival. You sure as hell don't want to miss the carnival.

Ron knew, with terrible clarity, that the situation had become hopeless. He was overwhelmed at the prospect of staying in Brackston until Monday. Still he murmured, "Is there a hotel or motel in town?"

"Not a one. But Mrs. Taylor takes in boarders. She speaks six languages. You'll enjoy her company," he said as though any woman who spoke six languages was bound to be enjoyed.

From the corner of his eye, Ron watched Chandal and Kristy climb back into the car. They were both smiling.

"The big stone house on the edge of town," Todd said. He slid a steel gate across his front door and bolted it. "You can't miss it. Leave the car parked there. When the tires get here on Monday, I'll send my man over. Well, enjoy yourself," he said with surprising joviality and climbed into his pickup truck. A moment later he was gone.

Ron stood motionless, the swirling updraft of the truck cooling him slightly. The air was still then, and heavy, and smelled faintly chemical, the odor of gas or oil. A green flag hung limp on the side of the gas pump. No cars passed, no people milled about, no dogs barked. All was still.

"Well, anyway," Chandal said in a small voice, "we're having an adventure. Aren't we?"

"An adventure, right," Ron said with growing irritation, adding, "In the meantime, we're stuck in this damn place until Monday!"

He never slowed the car until he had reached the opposite end of town. There he stopped to obtain more specific directions and soon found himself on a one-lane country road. A sign to the left read: Private. The driveway curved between a row of trees, over a stone bridge and passed a small gate house. The gate was encrusted with rust and stood open. Ron's attention moved swiftly to the large stone house at the end of the drive.

The house stood on a slight incline and appeared to be carved from the mountain directly behind its massive facade. In the harsh light, the stonework of the house appeared dark gray and the roof black. It was only after Ron had driven closer that he realized the roof was a flaming red. He parked the car near the house and walked through the settling dust to the edge of the driveway.

Ahead of him was a small stone fence with a steel gate. Beyond was a stretch of undernourished grass, a few shade trees growing out of stony, arid ground. The windows were all closed and shaded. There was no sign of life and yet the house did not look deserted.

"Are you sure this is the house?" Chandal let the car door close behind her.

From behind the house a black dog, coarse-haired, curious, came toward Ron, then stopped, staring.

"Hello," Ron called out. "Mrs. Taylor?"

The dog came nearer, watching.

Ron inched forward and lifted the latch from the gate. From the corner of his eye he thought he saw someone peering from the top window of the house. Yet, when he looked closer, the window was empty.

He inched cautiously forward. He finally took a deep breath and rang the bell. It seemed a long time before anyone came. From time to time he glanced nervously over his shoulder and saw Chandal standing aside, apparently gazing into the mountains. What was she looking at? he wondered. Kristy's chin lay on the window frame, her eyes fixed curiously on her mother.

Finally the door opened and she was standing there.

A sophisticated woman of forty, sharp featured, with hair pulled severely back into a bun. She was slender and elegant, her face full of intelligence. Ron's eyes caught hers for a moment, then shifted to a starfish of diamonds pinned over her bosom on her lavender lace dress. "Hello," she said, displaying her smile generously.

"Hi, I'm . . ."

"Mr. Talon, I know. I've been expecting you."

"What?"

"Matthew called me as soon as he arrived home."

"I see."

"Please, come in."

Ron turned. "Del."

Kristy had already opened the car door and was on her way up the walk. Ron waited, watching Chandal. Although she moved toward the house now, she still seemed preoccupied with the mountains beyond. Absently she pulled the ribbon from her hair, allowing her hair to fall softly over her shoulders.

"What a pretty child," Mrs. Taylor said. She took Kristy by the hand and drew her invitingly into the house.

In a low voice, Ron said, "Del, do we really want to do this?"

Chandal nodded. "Yes," she said wearily. "Oh, dear God, yes."

They followed Mrs. Taylor into a vast anteroom and the still vaster hallway, the sound of their footsteps on the highly polished oak floorboards echoing off the walls and the distant ceiling. The floor sloped slightly as they neared the living room, then widened into an impressively carved staircase that spiraled upward to the second-floor landing.

More solid oak. More polish.

Passing over the threshold, Mrs. Taylor stepped aside, allowing Ron a view of the most awesome room he had ever seen. The ceiling was an elaborately painted Gothic mosaic of clamoring angels, the floor richly carpeted, over the center of which hung a magnificent chandelier. The walls were decorated with tapestries and paintings of Renoir, Degas, Cézanne, and, Ron guessed, several early Picassos. The scent of roses was everywhere, masses of them set about in porcelain bowls.

Chandal nudged Ron, whispering discreetly, "Can you believe this?" and Ron mumbled, "Jesus."

In the background, music, a soft interweaving of notes like the sound of water, and not unlike the room, blended with a fantastic garden which was more like a tropical jungle, or forest, in the prehistoric age of grand fern-forests when living creatures had scales for skin and had just discovered the subtle art of dry-land procreation.

Color: the room was flooded with it; the room breathed.

Ron fixedly stared at a massive tree-flower that suggested various organs of the human body. Beneath this exotic plant sat a petite woman who presided over a silver tea service. To her left, almost lost in another cluster of greenery, an elderly man was seated comfortably in a rocking chair.

"Mr. and Mrs. Talon, I'd like you to meet . . ."

"Carroll's the name. Isabelle Carroll," said the little woman who had suddenly risen to her feet behind the tea tray. There she stood, all five feet of her, thin-framed and frail, with light red spit-curls cascading over her delicate forehead. A tiny pair of glasses rested precariously on the bridge of her nose.

"And this is Alister, my husband," she said playing with a double strand of huge pearls that hid completely any crepy or loose skin that might hang about her neck.

Ron nodded. "How are you?"

"Never ask an old man how he is. He's liable to tell you."

"Now, Alister, behave," she smiled.

Ron kept his gaze fixed on the old man. Beneath highly lacquered silver hair he saw a bright, very clever face, a thin mouth, fluffy eyebrows, watery blue eyes, sharp and observant, and a slender neck above his open plaid shirt and vest.

"Please," Mrs. Taylor coaxed. "Won't you be seated."

Chandal quickly slid into a stuffed chair near the fireplace while Kristy selected a position on the piano bench. Ron remained standing.

"And you, young lady—" Isabelle was saying to Kristy. "How are you enjoying our little town so far?"

"It's all right."

"Oh, Alister. Isn't she exquisite? I've never seen such a beautiful child. She looks like a goddess. Doesn't she, Alister? Just like a goddess."

Isabelle went on talking, all the while smiling, maintaining eye contact, holding Kristy impaled. She quizzed her about her likes and dislikes and then pumped her about their vacation, after which she declared her own preference which was Europe.

She began making comparisons when Alister gave a significant dry cough and turned to Ron. "So you've come to the mountains looking for some good old-fashioned country values, is that it?" he asked.

"Something like that."

"To make contact with real people. Well, you've come to the right place. My wife, Isabelle—hell, she'll make you feel right at home. She's a one-woman welcoming committee all by herself. A real—"

"Damn it, Alister," his wife said. "You're always such a one to mock. With people getting lost all the time, how can it hurt to have someone around to help?"

"Does it happen often?" Ron asked.

"What's that?" Mrs. Taylor inquired.

"People getting lost?"

"Now and again . . ." Alister smiled. "Now and again."

Isabelle shrugged. "My husband is jealous because I've just been elected head of the Organizing Committee."

"Not at all, dear. I'm happy you can still be useful." He eyed Ron directly. "People usually wander out here wanting to see where it all began. Some stay, realizing all that fast living they're doing in the cities isn't getting them very far. Just into trouble."

"Oh, really?" Isabelle stuck her nose in the air. "Is that why you watch those Charlie's Angels running around half-naked every week? The man sits there and doesn't utter a word. Not a word. Just sits there and stares."

"And what do you expect me to do with legs like damn twigs. Do you expect me to start jogging?" he cried. "I'm just an old man now. All I can do is look. And—"

"Alister, hush up!" Isabelle's voice contracted with her hazel eyes.

"I haven't got the get up and go I used to. Nothing wrong with that." The old man lit a cigarette, located a flowerpot by his right elbow to flick the match into, and seemed to inflate a bit upon taking the first satisfying drag on his cigarette.

"Alister, you just—"

"It's all right, Isabelle," Mrs. Taylor said. "Ash is very good for plants."

"But he shouldn't—"

"I think, Isabelle," he said calmly, "you've said enough."

"Enough?"

"That's right. You're as windy as a fart today, my dear."

"I'm what?"

"Never mind," he said smiling.

"Well! If you imagine I'm amused, you're very much mistaken."

"Well, perhaps if you would be so kind as to pour me a little more wine, I'd—"

"No!" She stared at him now, openly hostile.

"If you don't," he said with a sly grin, "I will not let you kiss me."

"When you talk like that, I have no desire to kiss you." She turned abruptly to Mrs. Taylor. "Erica, I'm sorry. To all of you, my apologies. Come along, Alister."

The color in the woman's face ebbed as quickly as it had mounted. With a defiant little nod, she hurried from the room.

"Righteous indignation," Alister murmured. "You have just witnessed a splendid example of righteous indignation." He rose slowly to his feet, each part of his body arriving at the standing position at different intervals.

"Here," he said holding out his empty glass to Ron. "Keep an eye on this. If you should suddenly find it brimming with liquid, call me. I only live a few blocks over."

"Glad you came, Alister?" asked Mrs. Taylor.

He nodded.

"Next time I may have a surprise for you."

"At my age, I doubt it." With a slight wave of his hand, he disappeared from the room. "Don't bother to show me out," he hollered from the hallway. "I know my way." All paused as the front door closed with a dull thud.

"Interesting man, don't you think?"

"Yes," Chandal said. "Yes, he is."

"May I offer you a glass of wine?"

Chandal did not hesitate. "All right. Ron?"

"Just a little."

"And for Kristy, let us see." Mrs. Taylor paused. "How about . . . a Shirley Temple?"

Kristy smiled.

She was still smiling, at the same time slurping her drink loudly, when Ron began discussing the feasibility of staying with Mrs. Taylor until Monday, when the new tires would arrive, and the financial arrangements. Terms were arrived at. Chandal became enthusiastic; Ron wished he could be. God knew, he had reason to be. Mrs. Taylor had asked thirty dollars for the entire weekend and that included meals for all three of them. What he should do, he reasoned with some saving bit of humor, was spend the remainder of the vacation at Mrs. Taylor's house. Not much fun perhaps, but he couldn't afford fun. He could afford Mrs. Taylor's. Still he remained skeptical. The cool air within the house had revived him, as had the wine. But not enough. He stood ponderously by the fireplace and thought: No. There was no discord. But neither did it feel like home.

"I will enjoy so much having a child in the house again," Mrs. Taylor said, her red lips sparkling against her creamy complexion.

The last of the wine in Ron's glass disappeared down his throat. Chandal followed his lead.

Mrs. Taylor smiled, then laughed softly. "The young. Oh, how I envy the young. Their eyes. Eyes that see everything in a new light. Fresh, wondrous, before life has twisted and distorted their vision. Children see beyond our eyes, into another dimension. Only children really have the Seeing Eyes." She paused to look at Kristy. "Your daughter has Seeing Eyes. I noticed them as she came up the walk. Lovely eyes. Seeing Eyes," she said, her voice trailing away into a whisper.

There was a sudden stillness in the house high up on the hill.

In the utter silence, the woman in lavender rose to her feet. "Well," she said. "Shall I show you to your room?"

FIVE

SHE CONDUCTED THEM SLOWLY TO THE STAIRCASE, COVERTLY glancing at her image in one of the two huge mirrors that flanked either side of the hallway. She seemed pleased with what she saw. She walked straighter then and began leading the way up the stairs, the sound of harsh bird cries resounding from the garden below. She looked downward, pausing for a moment.

"You will find," she said, "that the house gets a bit chilly in the evening. I've placed extra blankets in your room and there is plenty of wood should you wish a fire. Nancy will help you with anything you need." After this announcement she sailed slowly up the stairs like a stately vessel on a calm sea. She filled in the ensuing silence by stating they would meet Nancy later.

"Nancy hasn't been feeling well, I'm afraid," she said. "But she will be here to help with dinner this evening."

Ron nodded.

As their curious little procession made its way along the second floor landing, the woman continued to make conversation. Simultaneously, wild ravenous cries of birds echoed from below. The sound came in even waves like a strange chant.

Ron's gaze passed quickly over a wolf's-head carving in stone. The head protruded from its pedestal base like a sentinel midway down the corridor. Beyond, other statues hovered in the shadows, their massive bodies and faces roughly carved and strategically placed.

The harsh sound of bird cries stopped suddenly.

Mrs. Taylor said: "I'm hopeful that you'll have an opportunity to meet my Aunt Beatrice during your brief visit with us. She doesn't get out much, and she so loves to meet new people." She turned then and opened a large oak door. "I believe the accommodations will be to your liking."

The room had been beautifully cleaned and graciously prepared, as though it had been prepared some time ago for guests who had never arrived. The bed was turned down, the linen everywhere was fresh and smelled of lavender. The furniture was old and ornate, pieces gathered with loving care through the years, perhaps purchased at various auction sales. An oak sideboard with a large hand-carved crystal mirror, scrolled-back matching chairs, a magnificent rosewood desk, dressing screen and brass four-poster bed with lace canopy. Orchid-colored drapes rose from the polished pegboard flooring and curved hugely into an arch above the bay window, which opened out onto a balcony. On the dresser, a fresh bouquet of roses.

Mrs. Taylor, in a subdued voice, said, "I hope you'll be comfortable here."

Chandal released her breath but did not release her hold on Ron's arm. "It's lovely," she breathed.

"It used to be brother's room," Mrs. Taylor said solemnly. "He wrote his first sonatas at that desk. Lovely work, really. I can't help believing it remains some of his finest work."

She paused momentarily, then opened a connecting door to reveal a large bathroom, another room actually with an oval window, that was perfectly appointed. "And your room, young lady," she said, "is right through this door." She opened yet another connecting door. "If you please."

Kristy stepped into the room slowly, then stopped. Ron could see that his daughter was impressed. Who wouldn't be? The room was almost identical to the first.

"If you should need me for anything," Mrs. Taylor said, "you'll find me in my room which is downstairs off the terrace. I prefer living below. Fewer stairs. And I do love my garden. Morning, noon, and night." She drew a deep breath and, with a gesture of eloquence, added: "I do so love a well-groomed garden. Perhaps you had noticed my Venus flytrap. Magnificent. Just a delight."

Kristy tugged on Chandal's arm. "What's that, Mommy?"

Mrs. Taylor smiled down at her. "It's an insectivorous plant, my dear. Yes, it feeds on insects. Later, if you like, I'll show you how it functions. Would you like that?"

"Oh, yes!" Kristy wailed, then glanced thoughtfully up at Ron. "Can I, Daddy?"

"Well . . ." Ron hesitated.

"Good." Mrs. Taylor dabbed her cheeks with a handkerchief which she had taken from her sleeve. The scent of lavender in the room immediately became stronger. "Now if you will excuse me, it is time for my nap. Just make yourselves comfortable. If you wish, you may see the rest of the house. All quite interesting." Slipping the handkerchief into her sleeve, she turned to Chandal. "Shall we say dinner at seven-thirty? Or is that too late?"

"No. No, that'll be fine."

She turned, then, and went silently from the room to the hallway, closing the door behind her. No sooner had the door closed and the sound of her steps disappeared, than Ron dropped wearily onto the bed. Instantly Chandal noticed the tense look on his face.

"Ron, what's wrong?"

"Nothing. Nothing at all," he said. "It's just not your typical Holiday Inn, that's all."

"Then that makes it a real nice surprise, doesn't it?"

"It's that, for sure." He gave the room a long, even glance, then fell back on the bed. "It's just not for me, I'm afraid."

Kristy's voice broke in. "Daddy, can I go look at the Venus flytrap?"

"Later, sweetheart."

"But, Mrs. Taylor—"

"Is taking a nap!" Ron snapped. He quickly raised up on his elbows. "Tell you what," he said. "Run down to the car and get your toy box and doll. When you come back, you and I will walk through the rooms of this ancient tomb and see what we can see. Would you like that?"

"Yes, Daddy."

"Good. Be careful on the stairs."

"I will," she said and left the room.

Chandal hestitated. "Well, as for me—I feel a whole lot better now that we're here."

"Better—how?"

"I don't know. Safer."

He laughed. "Because of all the show?"

"You think that's silly, don't you?"

"Maybe."

"My mother would have loved this house. She was always after my father to leave . . ." Chandal broke off.

Ron immediately sensed her tension. "Your mother was always after your father to leave New York." Ron paused. "New York, right?"

"Yes."

They were both silent for a moment. "Del?"

"Yes?"

"I was wondering, do you still . . . you know. Do you think about New York? The carriage house?"

"Ron, look!" Chandal moved quickly to the fireplace.

Carefully she lifted from the mantel a well-posed photograph exquisitely mounted on a mat of deep blue velvet, encased in aging, yellowing ivory. "Who do you suppose he is?"

Ron glanced at the face in the photograph. "Mrs. Taylor's brother, probably."

"Handsome enough."

"I guess. Del, about New York . . ."

Chandal made a gesture with her hand to stop him from speaking further. "As far as I'm concerned," she said, "New York is forgotten. The carriage house, the brownstone, it's all forgotten. I don't want you to mention it again. Ever."

It hardly came as a surprise to Ron; her reaction to the past had always been as violent as his own. Still he wished he could say to her what had constantly been on his mind lately. He wished he could say simply: Chandal, I'm trying to reach out to you, but I have forgotten how. Are you still you? If so, please listen. There was a time, a time long ago. Are you still back there . . . can you tell me that? Is the woman with the violet eyes still with you? "Chandal?"

"Yes?"

And he was surprised that he had actually spoken her name aloud. He laughed at last, a husky chuckle, and his brown eyes stared mischievously into hers. "Hey, come on," he said and took hold of her hand. "Let's investigate."

"What about Kristy?"

"She'll catch up. Let's go."

A few minutes later they were walking slowly through a vast room, counting windows. Twelve, each of them enormous and all oddly designed. At the far end of the great chamber was an immense fireplace with massive stone gargoyles supporting the mantelpiece. Ron sat on the window ledge that faced the mountains and surveyed the room. An emptiness of inconceivable grandeur.

"Why do I love this place?" Chandal breathed.

"I don't know. I hate it."

"You really do, don't you?"

"Yes."

"Why?"

Ron shrugged. "Because it's old, I guess. Imagine trying to heat the damn thing. I would end up cursing God every winter."

"No, it's so . . . elegant. Like a different age—it has style."

Chandal leaned her head against a carved stone pilaster and began to laugh, her laughter echoing in the huge chamber.

"What's so funny?" Ron asked.

"Oh, God, just think, if we hadn't gotten that flat, we wouldn't be here."

"And that's funny?"

"Oh, Ron, I love this place. I really do. And I thank you, sir, for bringing me here."

With a last soothing touch of her hand on Ron's face, she smiled wistfully and quit the room.

SIX

DINNER WAS NOT ALTOGETHER A SUCCESS. MRS. TAYLOR SOON exhausted her flow of small talk, and an uncomfortable silence fell upon the elite gathering around the table.

Ron ate lightly with no appetite, but through the blur of his taste buds he eventually became aware that the fish was especially good. He nibbled at it wondering why he was in no mood to eat, despite the excellence of the fare. Perhaps it was because he felt awkward around Mrs. Taylor.

It was Chandal who tried to be courteous and keep up their end of the conversation. "I noticed a picture upstairs on the mantel. Is it a picture of your brother?"

"Yes. My favorite. Although Clayton never cared much for the picture. He said it made him look existentialistic." She chuckled softly.

Chandal glanced at Ron, then back to Mrs. Taylor. "I'm afraid I don't quite understand."

"Well, he felt as though his features in that particular photograph looked like a series of trivial events in meaningless juxtaposition," she said. "Clayton became quite fond of that expression after that."

Ron suddenly realized who she was talking about, who her brother actually was. "Clayton Byron Taylor? The composer?"

"Yes. Do you know his work?"

"Yes, I do. I had no idea . . ." Ron suddenly felt like an ass. Here he was sitting down to dinner with the sister of one of the most famous composers of his time, and he hadn't even known. The fact that he had found her singularly uninteresting was a further blow to his self-esteem.

"You would like my brother, Mr. Talon. Like him very much. He is a man touched with a perceptive genius on the one hand and an almost consuming sensitivity on the other. His gifts of music to the world were and are most exquisite."

Ron's gaze shifted to Nancy, who had moved silently to Mrs. Taylor's elbow. She had paused momentarily to allow the woman to finish her thought before removing her dinner plate from the table.

"Thank you, Nancy. We'll have our coffee on the terrace. I believe the night is cool enough."

Nancy nodded. She was scrawny and stringy-legged, Ron observed. With long brown hair that flowed around her face like Spanish moss. Her dark eyes could, in an instant, become vague, as though someone had literally jammed a question mark into their placid depths. Ron's gaze followed her from the room.

"Poor child," Mrs. Taylor breathed. "Hasn't spoken a word since her mother's death."

"Oh?" Chandal encouraged.

"Horrible story, really. Nancy has never gotten over it. None of us have, actually." The woman let the subject dangle in the air for a moment to heighten the suspense. Then she went on to say that the woman had been murdered. Someone had hacked her head from her body with an axe. After which, they had tied her to a horse and sent her headless body galloping through the town.

"The man responsible was caught, naturally," she said with a sigh. "Punished severely. Some felt not severely enough."

"How dreadful," gasped Chandal.

Kristy asked, "Did they kill the man? The one who did that?"

Mrs. Taylor smiled. "In a way, yes." She turned to gaze intently into Chandal's eyes. "Well, would you care to stroll the terrace?"

"Yes," Ron said. "That would be nice."

"You all run along, then. I'll be with you in a moment."

"Can I see the Venus flytrap now?" Kristy asked.

"If you like. But first you and I will see what treat Nancy has conjured up in the way of dessert. Would that be fun?"

Kristy smiled. "Yes, I'd like that."

"Good. Come along then."

When they were alone, Chandal chortled behind her hand. "I would like to compliment you on your incredible knowledge of the music world."

"Did you know he was her brother?"

"No. But then I'm not a theatrical agent." She took his hand and gave it a comfortable squeeze. "Come on."

Arm in arm, they moved onto the terrace. The moon had come up out of the east, full and golden as a Florida orange, and turned the last of the lingering grey dusk to night. Chandal stood out in the open air and drained her glass. Ice clinked against her teeth.

"What are you thinking?" Ron asked, hovering in the archway.

"That it's a beautiful night. And . . . that I love this place."

"A bit artificial, if you ask me."

"Artificial. How?"

"The whole thing. Horror stories—she shouldn't have told that story. Not in front of Kristy."

"I thought you said this place was artificial? It sounded like the real thing to me."

Ron was stuck for a reply.

Beyond the terrace, down two shallow steps, lay a piece of level ground that stopped abruptly against the side of a stone wall. It was on this level ground that Mrs. Taylor's exotic garden began. A narrow walkway cut through the garden from end to end and at the farther point, where the wall began, stood an oddly shaped stone statue.

"Del?"

"Humm?"

"Have you noticed the statue over there?"

"Interesting, isn't it?"

"Also familiar."

"I don't understand."

"Back at the General Store this morning, I saw the same statue. Only a smaller version. Also the statues in the upstairs hallway. I wonder . . ."

"Thomas Wheatley," said Mrs. Taylor and Ron turned to find the woman standing behind him. "My uncle. He is a stonecutter. Aunt Beatrice likes to refer to him as a sculptor, but as you can see—the statues are quite crude. Alas, he keeps on trying."

Nancy stepped onto the terrace carrying a large silver tray and began setting coffee, sugar and creamer onto the white marble table. Kristy was not far behind her. Smiling, she held out a smaller tray of her own. "Look, Daddy. Cake."

"Petits fours, my dear. Petits fours."

"Petits fours," Kristy beamed.

Ron found that he enjoyed the cake more than the dinner.

After Nancy had poured Chandal a second cup of coffee, and after she had left the terrace, Chandal said: "Poor girl. Does she live alone now?"

Mrs. Taylor smiled. "It is customary in Brackston for the young men and women to live with their parents until they marry. She lives with her father. Nice man. Though I don't suspect she'll ever leave home. Not now. Oh, not because no one will have her. Plenty of young men have asked. But, well . . . there is a strong bond here between parents and children which persists through adolescence into maturity. Nancy very much adores her father."

"I see." Chandal settled back in her chair. Serenely, she let her eyes examine the garden.

Ron's gaze drifted with hers. Small birds of many colors were hovering overhead. A faint breeze stirred through the leaves of many trees, so that they rustled with a metallic sound indescribably soothing and peaceful. The bright moonglow, pure, dazzling and yet still soft, illumined a scene of paradisiacal perfection.

Chandal's face clouded as she said: "This is truly a beautiful night."

"You will find that life in Brackston moves at a gentle pace," Mrs. Taylor said. "Except, of course, during carnival time."

Chandal turned suddenly. "Is that what that noise is?"

"Yes. You can hear it?"

"Something. I can hear something."

Kristy's attention was riveted to Mrs. Taylor. "Carnival? Tonight?"

"Right now," Mrs. Taylor said. "Tonight is the first night of the Carnival of Summer. You should experience it. It's quite a sight to behold."

All eyes then turned to Ron.

"Oh, please, Daddy. Can we? Can we go?"

Kristy lifted her chin pleadingly into the moonlight and smiled, and Ron let his eyes linger on her pretty face for a moment. Eager eyes, he mused. Such eager eyes.

Suddenly he laughed.

SEVEN

SO THERE THEY STOOD, THE THREE OF THEM, BENEATH A BRIGHT-ly lit sky in late August.

The carnival grounds lay stretched out upon a huge field alongside Matthew Todd's gas station bathed in a profusion of blinking lights and neon signs, with a large string of bulbs across the entrance archway spelling out the word C-A-R-N-I-V-A-L. Floodlights poked holes in the sky above, along with the flashing hot lights of the Ferris wheel. The brightness formed a thin, smoky, faintly yellow cloud over the entire area. In the center of the field was a roller coaster with strands of lights outlining the dips and curves and a pavilion that seemed all but dark.

They hesitated at the entranceway jammed with people. It appeared as if all of Brackston had descended upon this one square stretch of earth. Children dodged in and out, their shrill cries blending with the music. Young and old couples sauntered along or stood at booths playing carnival games. A cacophony of sound fractured the night air: gongs, bells, rifle shots, calliope music, the roar of the roller coaster, screams, shrieks, laughter and the steady drone of human voices.

Chandal's face tightened as she said, "It's a little noisy."

"I never have liked carnivals," Ron said and glanced down at Kristy. She stood beside Chandal, her face pale in the garish light. She was staring around wide-eyed at all the activity.

"What do you want to do?" Ron asked.

Chandal looked around indecisively. "I'm not sure."

"Let's go home," Ron said and watched Kristy's bright blue eyes cloud and her round face collapse into disappointment. He stood still a moment, hands dug deep in his pockets and let his gaze travel beyond the wildness to where a row of tents lined the back part of the grounds.

"Tell you what," he said. "We'll take a walk over there. Seems to be livestock. Kristy, would you like that?"

Kristy sniffled and nodded her head.

Chandal hesitated for a moment, then, with a fatalistic shrug of the shoulders, said, "Why not."

With a loud clamor of bells that sent the jackals running into the night, the Carnival of Summer had come to the town of Brackston. The tent sparkled with flags. In the vast field beyond the town, people massed together: workmen, farmers, ranchers, quiet merry women carrying their babies, all chattering as they walked. In the center of the carnival, the music screamed louder, faster; people danced.

"Look." Kristy pointed at the sky. "Over there, a Ferris wheel!" Impatiently, she began to skip to and fro, pulling Chandal's arm until Chandal began to rock to the child's rhythm.

Chandal turned her head toward Ron and tried to smile.

"Kristy," Ron said. "Calm down."

The child suddenly broke from her mother's grasp.

"Oh," she cried, and ran toward a small brightly lighted stage near an open place where few people stood.

"Look," she called. "Oh, Mother, look."

On the bright stage, littered with cardboard cut-outs of trees, house and perfectly rounded sun, sat Punch and Judy.

They all watched as slowly the large puppets came to life. Daintily at first, Judy kissed Punch who grimaced, his short, thick-set, humpback shaking with agitation. Promptly he pulled out a handkerchief and began blowing his enormous hooked nose, his wide mouth and long chin forming a grotesque smile.

Ron felt himself begin to relax. As Punch honked derisively from his bulbous nose, Ron's chuckle joined the resounding laugh that encircled and embraced the stage. Chandal's shoulder under his arm rose and fell as she too began to laugh.

Judy, on the other hand, leaned over and began to weep convulsively.

Into an infinitesimal pause, Kristy inserted her clarion voice. "You've hurt her," she cried at Punch, her voice a pure, charged fury that ripped through space. "You've made her cry!"

"Hush, hon," Chandal said automatically, still smiling.

Ron was all at once roused by Kristy's harsh voice. Now, watching his daughter wring her hands with anger, he sensed with a speed that made understanding almost violent, what being an adult and what being a child meant. Vaguely uneasy, he watched the smug Punch reach down and bring forth a handful of popcorn, which he flung at Kristy.

Just as smugly, Judy reached down and brought forth a large stick. Ron could see Kristy's eyes light up.

"That's right," Kristy said. "Hit him. Hit him."

"Don't, Kristy." Ron placed his hands on her shoulders. Simultaneously Judy smashed the stick across Punch's head, her dark eyes glistening with delight as she glanced down at Kristy.

"Hit him again. Again!" Kristy shrieked. Judy lifted the stick, and the bewildered Punch looked out at Kristy pleadingly. "Again," whispered Kristy, "again." The second blow cracked across the puppet's head. He staggered back and began to wail.

Silently and unnoticed, a small knot of onlookers had gathered behind Ron, watching Judy beat Punch with the large wooden stick. Their presence distracted Ron, inciting him to push his body back some to gain room. All at once he felt hemmed in. Breathless. Blood rushed to his face. Furiously, he said, "Del, let's go!"

"No, Kristy and I want to see this," she said tonelessly.

"Don't be silly. Let's go!"

He felt Chandal draw away from him. He turned to stare at the crowd. Beneath their smiling, almost placid exterior, he knew there were dark twists in their minds. He knew they could go for years without showing their emotions and then . . . This is absurd, he thought. He forced himself to stand still and look with studied calm at the two puppets. Punch's head, which had been yellow, was now covered with a thin layer of . . . green? No, red. Surely not red. *For Chrissakes, he was staring at blood.*

"Kristy," he screamed and the scream stopped Judy's fling of her stick in mid-air. When Ron looked around he saw that the crowd was no longer smiling.

Noiselessly the curtain of the lighted stage dropped closed and people began drifting away. Ron listened intently to the wild broken cries of Punch behind the closed curtain. Then he turned to stare at Chandal.

"All right," she said smiling. "What's next?"

"I want some ice cream," Kristy chimed in.

"Ron?"

"What?" he gasped.

"Are you all right?"

He shook his head. "Tired," he said. "Very tired."

"We won't stay long," Chandal said. "Let's walk over to the Ferris wheel."

Ron paused for a moment, his eyes fixedly set on the grotesquely illustrated curtain on which was painted the famous Punch and Judy. Below Punch was written: "The devil take this woman!" Ron shrugged wearily without bothering to turn around. Now people were forming around him again for the next show.

"Ron, you coming?"

"Yeah," he breathed and popped a cigarette into his mouth. His lips drew tight as he inhaled deeply.

"Ah! Mr. Talon!" a voice boomed.

He turned and saw Isabelle Carroll heading straight for him. A will-of-the-wisp apparition, dressed in yellow flowered hat and silk dress, whose plump face was as smiling and soft as a marshmallow.

"A splendid evening!" she shrilled. "I'm so glad you could come. Where's your wife?" Chandal stepped beside Ron. "Ah, there you are."

Alister and another man came up behind Isabelle and immediately general introductions took place. "Sheriff, this is the young couple I've been telling you about. Mr. and Mrs. Talon—Sheriff Nash."

Nash, who appeared the gregarious kind, removed his hat and beamed at Ron. His light hair was almost white, his skin, which once must have been fair, was cracked and tanned by wind and sun, his lips were femininely soft, his chin lacked character. "Pleased to meet you," he said with no change of expression. "Always nice to have new people visit our town. Will you be with us long?"

Ron gave him a measured stare. "Well, actually," he remarked, "we're only here for the weekend."

Nash hastened to reply: "That's too bad. The carnival is just getting started."

Ron found himself explaining that they had planned to spend the last week of their vacation in San Francisco, and that it was only by accident that they had come to stay in Brackston at all.

"Well, we wouldn't want to spoil your vacation, would we, Isabelle? No need for that." He laughed shortly.

"Gracious, why are we all just standing about like a flock of silly geese? The dance is about to begin." She lavished a smile on Chandal. "And you will just love it, I can tell. You have a dancer's look about you. Doesn't she, Alister?"

Mr. Carroll's reply was inaudible. Isabelle winked at Ron, her smile becoming one of infinite charm. "And I do hope my first dance will be with you, Mr. Talon. Or may I call you Ron? Please, would you be so kind as to escort me?" Her insistent hand slipped around Ron's arm and began to tug gently.

Amid the terrific rumbling of the roller coaster and calliope music, the shouts and shrieks of young and old voices, amid laughter and singing and shouting, they arrived at the pavilion, along with scores of others, most old, some young, and still others younger.

"Everyone seems to be really involved in all this," Ron offered as they entered the huge hall.

"Ah, yes," Isabelle beamed. "The Carnival of Summer comes but once a year. People always like to make the most of it."

A great scurrying ensued: the men hastening to one side of the hall; the women, faces aglow like fireflies on a hot Fourth of July night, to the other side; the children to the rear, their chins propped on a wooden railing, their eyes big as eggs, all white with glinting yolks.

Grunting and swaying, the caller hog-footed his way onto a planked stage and grabbed for the microphone. Sticking his finger between his shirt collar and neck, he snapped his bow tie and shouted: "Here we go!"

The small four-piece band behind him readied their instruments. They were mostly farm types: suspendered overalls, plaid shirts and work boots, with short cropped hair and weather-beaten faces. Most of the men in the hall were similarly dressed. The women were dressed just as plainly. Most wore bonnets, others went hatless, their hair either in braids or pulled back into tightly fashioned buns.

Just now Ron felt embarrassed by it all. Embarrassed by the amused look Alister Carroll flashed his way. Turning, he saw that Chandal's gaze had fallen on him from across the hall; she gazed for a long moment, tiny dots of excitement igniting her eyes, and Ron suddenly felt a great distance between his wife and him, as though the hall was larger, much larger than its actual size, and that she was standing beyond his grasp, his reach, both mentally and emotionally.

Then up and away they all went. Ron was soon a link in a human chain that swayed around the floor, singing in a strange language while the bright-eyed caller shouted commands. It was all so confusing that Ron hardly realized it was Chandal who had taken his hand in the change. Before he could speak, he was swung around again and seized by the plump fingers of a laughing woman.

On they went, dancing, and whenever they stopped, their eyes and the intense energy in the air seemed to carry on their dancing. Only the state of stupor or insensibility could have created the notion that Ron intended to join the procession of dancers that now formed at the edge of the stage.

"Come on," Chandal shouted to Ron as she took hold of Kristy's hand. A sudden blast of fiddle strings and the plaintive hooting of voices sent the procession on its way, sauntering around the large hall like a snake gone berserk.

The procession had gone around the hall three times and was in full swing when someone placed a hand on Ron's shoulder. In the hot and heavy-footed atmosphere Ron straightened.

"What's the matter?" Sheriff Nash asked. "All that dancing get to you?"

"Killed me would be more accurate," Ron replied, wiping large beads of sweat from his brow.

"How about a cold beer?"

Ron's tongue contorted in his mouth. "Where?" he wheezed.

"Beer tent."

Ron glanced at Chandal and Kristy. "No, I don't . . ."

"It's no use arguing. I won't hear of it."

Nash quickly steered him toward the door where he instructed Alister to tell the ladies where they had gone. Alister's grin helped push Ron from the hall.

The dank ale-soaked warmth of the beer tent was an odd change from all the commotion that was going on outside. Twenty or more wooden tables with benches ran the length of the tent. At either end were large wooden kegs of beer, their taps spewing drink at a steady pace. Most of the occupants were men.

From the rear flap of the tent, a heavy whiff of animal life drifted in, mixing with the smell of tobacco and beer. A few boys, high school age, carried large pitchers of beer and undersized bowls of pretzels back and forth to the tables. Soft chatter accompanied their movement like water flowing from a tap.

Ron and the sheriff moved down the aisle, found an empty table, and sat. They were talking about Brackston.

"Social life is taken very seriously here," the sheriff explained. "Being a small community, we're all very close. Love of one's neighbor—this is the basic ideal here in Brackston. The idea of life as sacrifice. Mind you, we cherish our privacy. We don't go around sticking our noses into other people's business. Especially when it isn't wanted."

Ron watched as he drank off half a mug, wiped foam pleasurably from his lips, and said: "What we need is a little of this." He produced a brown paper bag wrapped snugly around a pint of bourbon. He spiked Ron's beer, then peppered his own.

"Here's to you," he said and drank.

Ron obediently followed his lead.

"So, you're in the theatrical business," the sheriff ventured.

"Yes."

"Bet you meet a lot of movie stars. That right? You meet movie stars?"

"Sometimes."

Now the sheriff's eyes became binoculars, tinted lenses, peering into Ron's mind, hopefully zeroing in on a stored up, well-remembered image that would satisfy his taste.

"Rachel Powers," he stammered. "Have you ever met her?"

Ron shook his head. "No, I can't say that I have."

The sheriff lapsed into silence, his binoculars trained on Ron steadily, relentlessly holding him in view as if studying him under a microscope. A few more swallows, then he said, "Well, I guess that's that."

"Yeah," said Ron, draining the last of his drink.

The sheriff's thin lips curled into a crooked smile. "Let's have another. I mean, we're committed. Right? There's no turning back now. What do you say?"

Ron did not accept or reject the idea. He did not even look up.

The sheriff ordered another round of beers, spiked them with bourbon, then sat back and said: "I'm going to tell you something about myself that you'll find hard to believe. I've never once," he said, "seen the world beyond the ridges. That's right. I've never once been out of Brackston."

He swallowed his beer in one gulp and put his glass down hard on the table. "Never wanted to either," he said. "That's why I was curious about Rachel Powers. Oh, Lord—she really does it for me. Know what I mean? She's really something. Whoo-ee!"

He closed his eyes then, and let his head fall back against the post. His face was flushed as he rolled his head from side to side, moaning with delight, caught by some emotional fantasy that he seemed helpless to articulate.

Taken aback, Ron sat hypnotized by the man's unexpected behavior.

The words were forming on Nash's lips now, a rambling description that rolled from his mouth. "Oh, Lord, oh," he chuckled. "She's got breasts like honied melons, you know. Ripe. Just ripe and round and delicious, so delicious . . . and those fucking legs of hers, they go right up to her ass without stopping. Whoo-ee!" He shook his head wildly, to let Ron know how he felt, to let him know there was no mistake, to show him how deep his lust ran.

All at once a high-pitched yelping of a dog emanated from behind the tent. "Shut up, goddamn it!" a voice boomed. A thud then, a sound like a boot kicking in a ribcage. More yelps, agonized cries of a wounded animal mixing with laughter.

Ron's heart started to pound. He glanced at the sheriff who still rested his head against the post, eyes closed. Other men in the tent stared at Ron now. Unsmilingly. He suddenly felt like a stranger who had walked uninvited but somehow expected into their home. The men stared at him a moment longer, then their eyes turned in on themselves. He tipped the mug to his lips and noticed that a young girl had materialized on his right.

She was wearing a pink off-the-shoulder blouse, a flimsy peasant skirt and flat white sandals with straps that wound around the calves of her legs. She wasn't very tall, but tall enough. Her soft red hair fell casually over her shoulders and stopped midway down her back. Her eyes, deep green; her face, freckled. A wide copper-studded leather belt wound tightly around her slim waist, dividing perfection from perfection. All of her—perfection. She wore a strange necklace with a heavy medallion that dangled between her not so large, but large enough, breasts.

She did not see Ron immediately. When she did, she smiled. Ron tried to appear nonchalant, as though his eyes had only just fallen upon her. But he strained with the attempt. Their eyes locked.

"Cynthia Harris—Ron Talon," a voice said.

Ron turned to stare at the sheriff who had come back to life with his eyes open and a fresh cigar stuffed between his soft lips.

"What is it you're looking for, Cindy?"

"My father," she said, keeping her eyes on Ron.

"Well, hell—that isn't him, now is it?"

"Have you seen him?"

"Just a minute ago. He and Todd were shooting the breeze behind the pavilion." He paused to roll his cigar between his fingers. "Hell, you know you're not supposed to be in here. Now get."

She hesitated. "I just finished cleaning the jailhouse."

"That's nice."

"I caught Martin looking at the papers on your desk again. I know you don't like him prying."

"What difference does it make? He can't read, now can he?"

"Not enough to count, I guess."

Nash's expression had changed to one of utter amusement. His features jovial. "You—you should know by now that Martin is a 'Good Old Darky.' And they're hard to find these days." He chewed thoughtfully on his cigar for a moment, then turned to Ron. "How do you feel about it, Ron? You feel them niggers have been treated badly all these years? I mean, do you feel there's a need for change?" He rubbed his jaw. "No, let me put it another way. If you discovered tomorrow you were black, would you feel a need for a change?"

Cynthia laughed. "Well, now, he's not all of a sudden going to turn black."

Nash had edged forward, perspiration glistening from his forehead. "Not all black. But maybe just part. Like a fifth. He discovers some deep part is black as coal all of a sudden. Would things still be right with you, Ron?"

Ron sat silent, petrified by the hatred that dripped from the sheriff's crooked mouth. He could feel the gooseflesh on his arms, and the chill that ran down his spine. Overwhelmed, he slumped back and said nothing.

"That's sure something to think about, isn't it?" Cynthia seemed entranced by the prospect.

Nash gestured toward the exit. "All right, Cindy. On your way. There's plenty to do outside without you hanging around the beer tent."

She shrugged. "Not really. The usual. Always the usual.

Why do we do it?" she asked. Ron could see she did not expect an answer, other than her own. "I guess . . ."

"Cynthia!" the sheriff barked.

"I'm going. I'm going."

She stirred, slowly made her way across the tent—a sea of eyes parted to accommodate her crossing—until she reached the exit, where she called out, "Tyler, leave that goddamn dog in peace!"

Then she was gone.

Instantly Ron felt Nash's collector's eyes bore into his soul. "Pretty girl," he said and Ron said, "Yes, she is."

Nash pushed another glass of beer across the table. "She's not Rachel Powers, but then who is? Her father is the schoolteacher here in Brackston. Came to us about three years ago. Right after he lost his wife. An accident or something outside of Kansas. Some say Lou was driving the car when it happened. They don't talk about it much. Then a little more than a year ago," Nash went on, "Cynthia came here to live with him. A mistake, I think."

"Why's that?"

Nash grinned broadly. "Because this isn't her home. She wasn't born here. Lou, he was born and raised here. We expected him to come home some day. Never expected her though." He chuckled. "It was quite a surprise, I'll tell you." He paused to chew on his cigar, then added: "So, what do you think of our carnival?"

Ron shifted uneasily on the bench. "To be perfectly honest with you, I find it a little too high spirited for my taste."

"Well, sure! That's the whole point. You've got to give the young ones a chance to get rid of all that tension. Nothing much to do around these parts. It's when nothing's provided for them they cause trouble. If you don't mind me saying so, Mr. Talon, I somehow get the impression you're not altogether happy with our community."

"Not at all," Ron said. "We just have a different idea about how to have a good time."

"We want some life in the town. New life. Nothing wrong with that."

"I didn't say there was."

Nash's bravado had begun to fade. "It's not good having people thinking the worst of their neighbors."

"I'm not your neighbor."

"No, I guess you aren't."

Ron had begun to lose himself in a reflective thought. Yesterday at this time he had been looking forward to the days ahead. He tried now to recall what it had been like yesterday, or this morning for that matter, what he felt, thought about, but he was unable to think of anything. Yes, he did remember, he recalled exactly his conversation with Chandal, their plans to drive on to San Francisco. We'll drive west, he had said. No, south, Chandal had insisted. Much more scenic. Then we'll drive west. But now it was as though the conversation had nothing to do with him.

Now he viewed himself with detachment. Some of it, he guessed, was due to the heat, and some of it to the strain of the trip. Then again, he and the sheriff had made a spectacular dent in the sheriff's bottle of bourbon, and he knew fuzzily that he'd done more than his fair share.

When he next looked up the sheriff was gone and he had the feeling he'd been gone for a long time. This seemed to be the night for losing track of people. The beer tent was by this time nearly empty.

He staggered to his feet and made his way precariously toward the exit. Throwing back the flap, he walked off into the night and veered toward the pavilion. He could barely see his way. Most of the lights were out now, and most of the grounds empty.

He walked like a drunk for the first few paces, but as he reached the pavilion he hastened his steps. Where the hell was everyone? All at once he caught the sound of footsteps behind him. He turned as the footsteps approached quickly, one by one, gathering in momentum, hurrying toward him. He squinted into the dull night lit only by the moon. There was no one there. Not even a shadow and yet the footsteps continued.

Trembling, he tried to call out but the words would not come. The steps were on top of him, loud crashing thuds that shook the ground. He caught his breath and felt a sudden gust of warm air. The footsteps passed him and were gone.

"Lose something?" a feminine voice asked, then laughed.

Ron turned and peered down at the heavily made-up oval of the upturned face and recognized Cynthia Harris. She took hold of his arm. "For a minute there I thought you were running away from me," she said.

"I was looking for my, ah . . . wife and daughter. I—I don't suppose you've seen them?"

Ron felt his body relax as he waited for the girl to speak. Her hand upon his arm had a calming effect, almost as though she had been sent into this world for the express purpose of calming men's souls. He made no effort to disguise his feelings, the night was too dark, and he was too drunk to do otherwise. For a long time, an eternity, he allowed her warming presence to wash over him. At the same time his sluggish brain tried to grasp the moment, tried to express his gratefulness, but his gut instinct told him to go with it, drift with it, and not think at all. He had been doing too much thinking lately.

Cynthia pointed into the darkness. "Back there," she said. "They are back there." She smiled and took hold of Ron's hand to help him along. They began to wander zigzag into a small area behind the pavilion. Shadows deepened as they passed under an archway and moved along the wall toward a small door at the farthest edge of the building.

For an instant a glimmer of understanding flashed into his mind, images flickered, and then they were gone. Something odd . . . But he could not focus on the significance of the images.

"Not far now," Cynthia told him. "Not far at all," she said, her voice not her normal tone, but a low gutteral drone. She opened the door slowly and they entered a room with arched ceiling and blue velvet curtains covering the walls. There were old chairs, a cabinet, and a chaise lounge.

Ron's eyes fixed on a narrow shaft of light that filtered in from a circular window and followed its beam across the room to where it stopped abruptly in the far corner.

"Nobody's here," he breathed.

Cynthia had begun uttering something, but Ron could not understand what she was saying. He strained, listening, trying to make out her words.

"Cynthia, where are we?"

"Don't you know?" she whispered and moved closer.

Ron glanced desperately around the room but couldn't

keep anything in focus long enough to identify it. "I'm drunk," he murmured and felt himself sinking.

"Yes, drunk," she said, touching his cheek with her warm fingertips. Seductively, she ran her tongue over his lips.

"What—what are you doing?" he whimpered, the liquor slushing around in his brain.

"Hush." Her mouth fell upon his, and the hands that had been pressed against his shoulders moved down, crept between his legs, then over the smooth roll and coil of his warm thigh muscles. She was all over him now, clinging to him, forcing her body against his. And slowly, as he swayed in slow rhythm back and forth, as she began to undo her dress, he sensed the danger of what was happening to him. He tried to fight against the odd dissolving of substance that had begun to take place within his body and simultaneously he had the strange sensation that he was going to sleep, that his eyes and mind were drifting away into the darkness.

"The stone around which moving is done," someone whispered.

Then the clandestine sobbing. A soft sound—nothing tangible, yet it seemed the weeping of many. The dream, that was it. That's what he had seen—the images in his dream.

Ron felt himself fall backward, felt hands seize him, manipulate his body until he was stretched out on a cold slab of marble. A sharp light was suddenly turned on him. Through it he could see shadowy figures in a susurrant cluster. Then fanning out, they moved toward him from the outer edges. Hands reached out to fondle him, dark seductive creatures sucked at his tongue, bit his lip, caressed his penis.

"No, no, NO!" he cried out. His arms flailed the air in front of him. Still they kept coming, forcing their breasts against his mouth, the crimson nipples as pointed as steel spikes. "No," he whimpered, his eyes flooded with tears.

Cynthia was kneeling astride him now, her thighs jerking convulsively, while the taut muscles of her vagina pulled and ripped at his penis. Through a thin yellowing haze he saw her death's-face smile leering at him, mocking him, the unbridled pleasure of the moment contorting her face like some wild beast whose readied orgasm was about to consume her.

Then something clicked, a distant shutter behind his eyes

flew open, and he felt the increased tempo of his heart, and felt, anew, a sickening despair. He screamed, the sound of his voice raising from the depths of memory, starting as an agitated murmur then building slowly and steadily on a current of thin air into a crescendo of pain, horror, and something else. Something beyond all description.

Yet, as the night turned in upon him like a velvet cape, he knew what that something was. Physical spiritual longing and lust.

"Lust," he murmured and felt his soul fly to the whispered summoning of a great dark god.

A violent shaking now as he was swept into a maelstrom, his breath cut off, and then the thin slivers of moonglow and consciousness of life were abruptly extinguished.

EIGHT

THE STONECUTTER THRUST HIS COPPER CHISEL INTO THE SLAB OF granite laid out before him. Sweat dripped from his sullen face in a steady stream. His eyes ached of a sudden glare as he raised his mallet. He marveled at the power which had been bestowed upon him. His heart beat faster as he brought down the mallet.

Shadows suddenly shifted, the moon dipped behind the mountains, and the town of Brackston sank into complete darkness. Below, in the black corridors, the halls beneath the stone, there were also crepitations of darkness, ferments, chemical nightmares of pitch blackness.

It was only the glare in the old man's eyes and the flame of a single squat candle that kept the blackness alive. And the old man knew this to be so. He knew that with each meticulous blow of his mallet—the night belonged to him. He was night. Eternally.

Now in the flickering light, his gaunt, wrinkled face flashed arrogancy, pride, and seemed the incarnation of Death. His long thin fingers loosened their grip on the chisel for a moment, and his eyes slowly, imperceptibly, became glazed with intense concentration.

He willed himself to recall the memories of torment he had suffered and the faces of his tormentors. He willed himself never to forget his father's face, a ghostly haze, hanging from the lowest bow of the highest tree. His body ached with a thousand wounds as he recalled his mother's body broken and beaten, her flesh covered with scabs of vile treatment. He himself had helped to put them there. Let me carve all this, he told himself, into the stone. Let me carve the names of those departed with the names of those among the living. Let suffering beget suffering. Let the future belong to us. Let this stone be our salvation. He paused to let the ghosts of his words sink deeper into his tortured, yet unrepentent, soul.

Without warning, he heard the clicking of footsteps. He turned swiftly around on his heels looking outward, his eyes staring wildly into the darkness.

In the flickering half-light he could make out his wife's face. The oil lamp shook in her trembling hand.

"May I enter?" asked his wife.

"Not yet," answered the stonecutter. "I have not finished."

His wife muttered to herself and, like a phantom, disappeared into the darkness beyond. Faint footsteps growing fainter, then silence. Total silence.

He nodded his farewell and smiled, the passageway ahead dimming as he looked away. He felt painfully alone, yet a smile hovered on his lips nonetheless.

Once again his eyes fixed upon the slab of stone before him. From the very bowels of the earth there came a distant sound. It was the sound of voices, human, not yet, but growing in numbers and strength. His energy had begun to wane badly. It frightened him. He wept.

With tears in his eyes, he raised his mallet high over his head, then brought it down hard. As his chisel cut deep into the stone, his head rolled from side to side, shaking in time with a mystic chant known only to himself. Intense joy magnified through tears shone on his face with each new thud of his mallet.

As he worked, the stonecutter remembered the tomb of the boy pharaoh Tutankhamen, which contained some of the rarest of stone carvings. He brought the mallet down again. From this ancient art of stonecutting, his people had learned how to survive. Just like the great pharaohs of Egypt, they would, within hollowed walls of stone, live on for all eternity.

The stonecutter paused, looked with satisfaction upon his work. Now that the name had been engraved, nothing—absolutely nothing—could change it.

THREE

MARDI GRAS

ONE

Father, the root of this little red flower
Among the stones has the taste of blood.
But I have something more strange to tell.
So leave the reptiles, Father dear, and
Listen. But do not run away, because . . .

RON AWOKE TO SEE FRAGMENTS OF WHITE FLUFF; EVANESCENT distillations. Gradually he realized they were the soft folds of the canopy that dwarfed his bed. He tried to move and it sent his head spinning. He lay still and waited; he was too heavy laden with sleep to do more.

There was not a sound to be heard anywhere in the house. Apparently there was no human astir. He made these notes indifferently, a bedridden ghost, a phantom of a man lying between reality and fantasy.

He relapsed into a doze. The air was fragrant with lilac and drowsy with the hum of bees. In the distance the sound of bells. Church bells. The booming voice of the Holy Ghost. He rolled over on his side, envisioning himself a vainglorious cock with a variegated harem of hens at his spurs sauntering through debris. Cynthia Harris was part of the harem.

Suddenly his sleeping world sprang wide awake.

The tall antique clock on the stair-landing struck the hour. Instantly he heard stealthy footsteps scurrying in the hallway, followed by a low exchange of voices. Confused, Ron expected Chandal to enter the room, bearing a cup of coffee and a mild reprimand. He waited. The footsteps moved away and began to descend the stairs.

"Del, is that you?" Ron called out. He pushed back the covers and lurched from the bed. His feet smacked the floor at the same instant the hammer crashed down inside his head. He staggered back and reached for the bedpost. Christ, what a hangover.

The front door closed with a sharp thud.

"Chandal?" he called out and staggered to the window. Beyond the lace curtains everything appeared to droop. In the distance solid-looking mountains reflected the blazing fire of the sun, its harsh red glare scorching the earth. Nothing was visible except the land. No stock, no dwellings, no man.

But in a moment, something was visible. Just below the balcony to his left. Three raggedly dressed children dashing for the trees. Ron watched as a small shapeless bundle was passed from one child to another, after which they all scattered in different directions; the boy now carrying the bundle running the fastest for the garden wall. He cleared the stone in one leap and disappeared. "It's them," Ron breathed. The same children he'd seen running in the hills yesterday. The thought stirred him fully awake and alert.

"Chandal!" he boomed and spun around to face the door. Where was she? "Kristy?"

He wrenched the door open with a grunt of pain.

Out of the green and brown wallpaper images materialized. Blurred. He had only managed a few steps before he stumbled clumsily back to the bed. A young girl's face was staring at him through the mist of fever, and his hand clenched the bedpost to steady himself.

For a while he did not move. He stared straight ahead, studying the odd floral pattern covering the walls like a jungle. Prehistoric. Lush. There was a ringing in his ears and he realized that it had been there all along, only he hadn't been aware of it.

It took him a few minutes before he could look back and remember with any continuity all that had happened last night. But certain things remained fixed in his memory. The sheriff's lustful eyes peering at him across the table, the hideous puppet show—dancing, he had been dancing, and . . . Oh, Christ—he hesitated before allowing himself to say the words—Cynthia Harris.

He knew that he had been with her. He remembered that much. He took another conscious-raising step forward. He had consumed more than his habitual amount of bourbon; this in addition to four, maybe five steins of beer. Furthermore, he had left the beer tent alone. Suddenly, out of the darkness, he had found Cynthia Harris standing there. A room. They had gone to a small room behind the pavilion looking for Chandal, hadn't they? What then? The dream—it had come to him again with predictable nauseating results.

It was difficult to say what had happened after that, not much point to it either. Except to say he was stunned, completely stunned by his behavior last night.

He rose slowly to his feet, a study in vagueness, until his eyes fixed on a small note propped on the dresser. The note was written in Chandal's meticulous handwriting, all the i's dotted and the t's crossed. He snatched it up and read:

Ron
You were asleep. I didn't want to wake you. Kristy and I have gone out for a while. Back soon. Del.

He read it twice, then stood for a moment staring into space, unsure of what to do next. Swiftly, drifting through a crack of consciousness, a tiny light visible so far, far away, so far in the past—the carriage house in New York. And a voice whispered: *"Do not forget it, because it is still with you."*
Whose voice?
His own.

Stepping from the shower, he toweled off quickly, then returned to the room and began to dress. He reached down for his jeans, slipped into them as rapidly as possible, as if clothing his naked body would armor the overwhelming vulnerability he now felt.

Brother, he thought, you've got a problem. Memory, he knew, was a tricky business. It throws up, when nudged, a scattered mass of sorted details, a looming event here and there, a sequence broken by years of forgetfulness, by blurs, confusion and darkness. Accuracy in recollection, at no time more necessary, at no time less certain.

Now the room—as he blinked—became drained of all color. A slight breeze caught the drapes off the balcony, fluttering them outward before they resumed their sedate vertical folds.

Closing the balcony door, he heard a strange sound from above. A scratching, sputtering sound. Then footsteps. Someone was walking in a room above his head.

When he stepped into the hallway, he noticed that the small door at the end of the corridor was open. He advanced slowly. Dust particles hung quiescent in shafts of light and whirled up as he approached.

The stairwell leading to the attic was empty. To the top was a door; it stood ajar. Slowly he started to climb; the stairs were narrow and deep. He glanced upward. Yes, a light was on up there.

"Hello?" he called out.

Nothing. Not a whisper of breath.

He cocked his head forward, having stopped to listen. Nothing . . . except a creaking board as he took the next step. "Anyone up there?"

He mounted the steps, one by one. He held onto the railing, and his palm was sweaty and slick. He reached the top and turned soundlessly to look around.

Before him stretched a narrow room that ran the full length of the house. There was no ceiling, except for a steep and slanted roof, all its rafters bare. The entire room was thick with dust. A glow shone overhead where a dim bulb dangled from its cord. It swayed back and forth casting light here, and then there. Portions of the room which had been nonexistent only seconds ago, had now come out from behind the clouds; now vanished.

"Hello. Anyone here?" He waited in silence.

There was no furniture, not even a trunk, only rows of deep-shadowed shelves to the rear of the room where the light did not reach.

Slowly, he reached over and tried the wall switch by the door, hoping for more light. But it had not given any. He flicked it again, still no added light.

Something brushed against his forehead. A cobweb, he thought, and he flicked his hand to brush it away, but it returned. He brushed again, turning his head to one side to avoid any further contact, and saw a pair of eyes glinting at him in the darkness beyond.

"Who's there?" he shrilled.

The eyes remained locked on his face. Now he realized there were many eyes staring at him. Dozens of them.

In a rush, without thinking, he moved closer. The dimmer portion of the room reached out to him. There, resting in thick dust and stifling heat were hundreds of dolls in mocked, grotesque imagery. Their dry painted faces struck by a strange enchantment beyond the touch of man. Wax-over-composition dolls; masked peg wooden dolls; wax-head dolls, all leering at him with their lifeless, frozen eyes.

He stood there flaccid; his face, his muscles, his whole body was softer, open to signals. He barely moved, barely breathed; it seemed their eyes were sending wordless tidings from an unnatural world.

Uncomfortably, he let his eyes drift from one shelf to the next, until he gazed fixedly on the last shelf, upon whose dusty planks rested a dozen or so dolls' heads. Nothing else. Just the heads: bisque, china and parian heads. All mottled, streaked and patterned, as if some mischievous child had marked them with a paint brush. He didn't notice the painting immediately, it all had been done in muted colors, all receding, all lifeless.

Lifeless, yes. Yet one of the doll heads was moving, rocking back and forth, her eyes peering out, then walling back into her head. What the hell made it move, he wondered. He glanced around nervously.

Finally, he had to make himself realize it was all of his own doing. His weight upon the floorboards had probably shifted the shelf slightly. The house was old, so were the shelves. Still he suddenly felt the urge to get out of the room into daylight.

He backed away guardedly, then turned away completely. The first few steps and he was still in shadows. Then, just as he stepped into the light, he saw it.

That quickly it flashed before his eyes. Kristy's doll. *Jennifer.*

There was no mistaking it. Jennifer's doll-face stood out among the others in stark contrast. A face he had seen so often peering at him from under the couch, or from behind a chair, or lying peacefully beside his sleeping daughter.

He picked the doll up. One of her hands touched her mouth. The other remained rigid at her side. Her eyes were sparkling and radiant.

As Ron gazed at the doll, he had the odd sensation that he too was being gazed at. He turned. A tall spectral shape stood palely before him. It might have been standing there for a long time, he thought. He stared past the small glow of the light, still motionless, not so much as the fluttering of an eyelid.

He waited in silence, more and more fearful, staring straight ahead. Finally the shape moved.

As the figure stepped beneath the light, he realized it was Nancy. He hesitated for an instant, unsure of what her reaction was going to be. Under the dim light, her eyes, the sparkling brown of mahogany, expressed a bewitching innocence. Her hair was drawn up onto her head, lending a strength to her features. She seemed easy and relaxed, with an air of grace about her.

Clearly, she was undisturbed by his presence.

A little sigh escaped her lips as she held out her hand. Automatically, without really understanding why, Ron handed her the doll. She looked at him gratefully before casting her eyes downward. She rubbed the tips of her fingers lightly over the network of lace at the bottom of the doll's dress.

"That's Kristy's doll, isn't it?" Ron said softly.

She nodded, then crossed to the far end of the room and placed the doll carefully with the others.

"Are these Mrs. Taylor's dolls, Nancy?"

She stood silent with her back to him. She gave no indication that she had heard his last remark. Her silence in that instant communicated a marvelous sense of relaxation and contentment. She was, Ron suddenly realized, completely at home here. He noticed how the dolls seemed to stand out with remarkable clarity against the pure whiteness of her dress; joined together as two spiritual forces of the cosmic mind. Mother and child. How beautiful it all seemed. Like children born of a perfect union they warmed in her presence.

The invisible force of her life manifesting itself in her children.

A sudden rush of peace enveloped him as he stood there. For a moment, it was like a great turquoise of blueness, then a rush of radiant yellow, and then a mysterious twilight in the softening folds of shadow. But always, all was sharp-cut and clear to his vision.

As if not to disturb even a single dust particle, he turned slowly, retraced his steps to the stairwell and softly descended the stairs, leaving Nancy alone in her own private sanctuary.

At the first floor newel post, not twenty feet from the living room, he found Kristy sitting on the lowest step, industriously fashioning a dress onto an ugly wooden puppet.

"Morning, sweetheart." He bent over and kissed her forehead.

"Morning, Daddy."

"And what do we have here," he began, but before Kristy could answer, he turned away, listening; he could hear low voices in the kitchen.

He pushed open the kitchen door and saw Mrs. Taylor sitting at the table. Chandal stood beside her.

"There you are! Come in, come in," Mrs. Taylor said, smiling the length of the table.

Ron started forward but was quickly intercepted by Chandal.

"Morning, Hon." She kissed him lightly on the cheek. She was wearing hoop earrings, her bright yellow cotton dress, and a touch of lip gloss. She looked startlingly alive.

"Good morning," he said, feeling a twinge of discomfort.

"Coffee?" she asked, reaching for the pot.

"Yes, please."

He noted that Mrs. Taylor served a good strong cup of coffee. Country coffee, made from freshly ground beans, served with real cream in china-thin and hand-painted cups. The breakfast was country style as well, plenty of homemade biscuits with honey, eggs, country-smoked ham, bacon and grits.

Ron felt self-conscious eating at the table alone. But neither of the women seemed the least bit disturbed by his tardiness. He watched Chandal move about the kitchen as though it were her own. He wondered what she was thinking.

He yearned to be alone with her, to discuss last night, but instantly, he knew he would not broach the subject unless she brought it up first.

While he watched Chandal, gauging her mood, she told Mrs. Taylor a story of her childhood that made the woman laugh. Tears gathered at the corners of her eyes which she wiped daintily away with her lace handkerchief. "Well, you know," she said, "it's nice to hear such memories. I mean it is sort of . . . comforting. Somehow the world has changed since then, don't you think? It has grown more aggressive, less gentle. Even here in Brackston, life has changed. Things move faster now," she went on. "Still, not fast enough for some, I imagine."

Chandal leaned closer. "Do you ever get bored? You know, doing the same things each day with the same people?"

Mrs. Taylor considered her thoughtfully a moment. "Only those who search for novelty are in the end bored. As for me, I have my own personal obsessions, my daily functions—and they never bore me—no matter how familiar to me they may become. It is always the beginning of things for me. Always the beginning." She smiled, her voice trailing off into a self-satisfied sigh.

Everything seemed to stop as her eyes sparked into a shining intentness.

"Besides," she added, "we here in Brackston believe in the principle of 'the common good.' I may be bored, but that does not mean Brackston is boring. The emotions we feel are not important in themselves. Their only value is how they affect the town as a whole. To sacrifice ourselves without a moment's thought for the common good. This is what we believe in."

Quietly Chandal came up beside her. Mrs. Taylor turned. Her eyes were smiling as she looked up at her. She slipped her hand into Chandal's and held on tightly.

Ron glanced away. He hadn't understood what she'd meant exactly, but from some recess of his mind leaped again the image of the huge stone that sat upon the hill. The image flickered, then faded. Nervously, he lifted his cup, allowing a few drops of coffee to spill on the table.

"Oh, my, my, look at that. Now, where's the dishcloth? We'll have that all cleaned up in no time."

"I'm sorry—"

"I've got it," Chandal said. She found the dishcloth and wiped up the spill with quick little swishes. Straightening, she gazed down at Ron as if she'd only now become aware of his presence.

There was something different about Chandal this morning, Ron reluctantly decided. He sensed a change, but wasn't quite sure what it was. She was behaving completely different —she even looked different—like a woman who has made a discovery. But of what?

"There, that should do it." Chandal moved back to the sink.

"So, what are your plans for the day?" Mrs. Taylor asked.

Ron's eyes narrowed as he pondered, and his answer was not exactly responsive. "Oh, I couldn't say."

Mrs. Taylor, a smile cemented to her lips, murmured, "Through the back gate of my garden, beyond the wall, is some of the most beautiful country you will ever see. A waterfall as majestic as life itself. And a swimming place. Just a small cove where the water runs deep and cool. Clayton and I would swim there often. So many days of our lives were spent there." Her face clouded as she concluded, "So many days . . ."

Ron nodded. "Would you like that, Del? To go for a swim?"

Shortly, perhaps unconsciously, Chandal said: "I can't."

"Come on. It'll be fun."

"I can't," she said again.

"Why not?"

"Because Mrs. Wheatley has invited us for lunch."

"Oh." Ron nodded.

"More coffee?" she asked.

"All right."

Mrs. Taylor started to say something, but she did not have a chance to finish. Kristy came bounding into the room consumed by frustration.

"Mom, this is awful! Just awful!" she cried, her shrillness a safety valve venting her agitation. She held up the puppet for all to see. "She looks terrible!"

Mrs. Taylor smiled, but weakly. "Kristy, you mustn't bristle. It causes frown lines around the mouth."

Kristy considered this seriously.

"Now, if you'll calm down, my dear, I'll be happy to help you."

"You will? How?"

Mrs. Taylor chuckled with glee. "Well, let's you and I adjourn to the sewing room, shall we? Clothing is everything to a young lady. You'll see, she'll look much better in satin. Yes, blue satin." She slipped Ron and Chandal a wink. "If you'll excuse us," she said and led Kristy from the room.

Ron dropped a sugar cube into his coffee and watched the bubbles rise. It wasn't his imagination; Chandal had definitely changed. For a second their glances locked. What was it that he saw in her eyes? Nothing he could understand, certainly. If anger over his getting drunk last night, it was well veiled—but there was something else, an expression he wasn't used to.

"I'm sorry about last night—" he began.

She shrugged. "No apologies."

"How'd I get home?"

"Sheriff Nash."

"Ah, the village constable. The enforcer of small-town law and order."

"Not a pretty thing for Kristy to see."

"What—Sheriff Nash?"

"Ron . . ."

He pushed on. "I tried looking for you."

"You did? When?"

"I don't remember," he said dubiously. "An hour or so after I left the dance. But when I got back the—"

"The dance was over."

"Yes."

"What happened then?"

"Then—then I must have passed out, I guess."

She nodded carefully as though debating her next words. "Well, I guess you were entitled." She put her hand over his and squeezed it. "Let's forget about it."

Ron had no idea what was passing through her mind. Conflicting expressions molded her eyes and mouth.

"Here, let me pour you some more coffee," she offered.

"I've had enough, thank you."

"Well, I haven't. I could drink it all day."

She chattered at random for several minutes, china cup in hand, running down the list of fascinating people she had met at the dance. Mrs. Taylor's aunt, Beatrice Wheatley, old Tyler Adam, Lou Harris, and, oh, yes—Cynthia Harris, his daughter. And then it came out, quite casually.

"Cynthia Harris. She's a very pretty girl, isn't she?" Chandal's voice seemed faraway, almost detached and not as friendly as Ron would have liked it to be.

"Who?"

"Lou Harris's daughter. You remember, we met them last night."

Ron paused. "You're mistaken. I didn't meet them."

"Oh, that's right. They came to the dance after you had gone. Still, Cindy mentioned meeting you at the beer tent."

"Oh, you mean the redhead?"

"Yes, the redhead."

"She came in looking for her father. Didn't stay long enough to actually meet her."

"Still, you must have looked at her."

"Yes, Del—I looked at her."

"Well, didn't you think she was pretty?" The question was loaded. And Chandal was watching him, he knew, even though she had moved away to gaze out the window, which was disconcerting, for he sensed that she was finely tuned to what he might say.

"Not really," he said and sipped the dregs of cold coffee. He was beginning to get that awful feeling, as if the situation were getting out of his control. To cover the slight pause that followed, he said quickly, "Where did you and Kristy run off to this morning?"

"Church."

"Church?"

"That's right. Church," she said. "The service was entirely in Latin. I didn't understand a word of it, but the ceremony was lovely."

They were silent for a moment. Ron had begun to perspire. The August heat was sweltering, even while sitting under the huge kitchen fan that fluttered lazily above. Chandal sat down in one of the two older side chairs near the doorway, fanning herself with a magazine. The air was heavy and still, the trees

125

beyond motionless, their leaves the deep, ripe green of midsummer.

"Del?"

"Humm?"

"Last night. The Punch and Judy show. It didn't seem to bother you."

"Why should it have bothered me?"

"It was brutal, that's why. Kristy shouldn't—"

"What? Oh, God, Ron. She watches worse than that on television every day."

"Then she shouldn't be watching television every day," Ron retorted. "And I don't want her going to the carnival again tonight."

"There isn't any carnival tonight."

"Oh?"

"Not tomorrow night either."

"Why's that?"

"I asked Mrs. Taylor. She said it was for religious reasons. Brackston . . . is a very religious town. For hundreds of years—" She paused, then rose to her feet.

"What?"

"Nothing."

She reached out and touched his hand with her own. The touch was brief and impersonal, lasting a mere few seconds, but he felt the chill after she had taken it away. Her blue eyes were dark, suddenly, and her expression inscrutable. For a throbbing moment of silence they looked at one another, then she turned and walked out of the room.

An hour later, the three women were dressed and ready to go. With a quick peck on the cheek, Chandal made her good-byes to Ron at the front door. Mrs. Taylor and Kristy waited by the gate.

"Are you sure you won't change your mind?"

"Honest, Del. I really feel lousy."

"Well, get some rest." She smiled. "And next time, don't drink so much. Promise?"

Ron smiled. "Promise."

Then slowly, reluctantly, he stepped back. He looked down at her face, haloed by the fierce rays of the sun, and in that instant, he thought she looked dismayed.

"Back soon," she said thickly, and turned and went down the steps.

Ron was much more relaxed that afternoon, calm and cool as he wandered around the house doing nothing in particular. Just wandering. If Chandal were going to make a direct accusation about his being with Cynthia Harris, she would have done so in that instant when her name had hung between them like a betrayal. Wouldn't she? Surely, she who knew him so well would have known how clearly vulnerable to attack he had been. But she had stopped short of asking the question. Did that mean she was saving it for some other time? Ron didn't think so. As far as he was concerned, the matter was forgotten.

He found a comfortable chair in the living room and sat listening to Bach. He hadn't the passion for Beethoven, or even the depth for Tchaikovsky's sadness. Brahms was out of the question. Yes, Bach. A clear and easy melody, pleasant to listen to. Strange though that Mrs. Taylor did not have any albums of Clayton Byron Taylor, her brother.

At one point he thought he saw Nancy walking in the shadows of the terrace, but he didn't call out her name, merely watched her from his vantage point until she had gone. Immediately he rose to look for her, suddenly wanting to speak to her about Kristy's doll. How stupid of him, he quickly realized; the girl was unable to speak. How would she answer any questions he might ask. In any case, Nancy was nowhere to be seen.

He returned to the living room and began to daydream. In his imagination he tried to recreate the room behind the pavilion Cynthia Harris had taken him to. Was it there that he had passed out? Was that where Sheriff Nash had found him? Or did Cindy bring the sheriff to the room after he had passed out?

The sudden and absolute silence of the room brought Ron back to the here and now. Back to the lushness of greenery, antique furniture, and the tiny click of the record player. He sighed, got to his feet, and began wandering again.

Around one, Isabelle Carroll stopped in for a chat. She was her usual cheerful self, chattering on incessantly. They had drinks on the terrace, and Isabelle joyfully described her work at the library, speaking of books as if she had personally discovered them. Ron was amused and found that he had begun to enjoy her company.

At two she looked at her watch and smiled, stretching as she stood up. "Ah, well—I'm off to do some gardening this afternoon," she said. "Such an enjoyable life. Books in the morning. Gardening afterwards."

Ron smiled. "It seems the perfect life."

"Well, it hasn't always been that way. Times were hard when I was a little girl. I know it's difficult to believe, but as a child I lived in a house with no running water and only a single fireplace for heat. We drew our water from a well. Oh, yes, indeed. Every drop of it. And we raised our own vegetables and made our own lard. Had to put it up in four gallon jars. We worked," she went on, "from sunup 'til sundown. Cleaning, spinning and sewing. The whole family did. It's a whole lot easier today. A whole sight easier. Amen."

Ron sat back chuckling and sipped his drink.

Isabelle regarded him tenderly. "You know, young man, I was mightily disappointed not to have been privileged to dance the 'Doll Dance' with you last evening. Mightily disappointed."

"The Doll Dance?"

"Yes. It is sort of a farewell to the first night of the carnival. It is very important who your partner is. I had hoped it to be you. It is during that particular dance that a person is supposed to be able to determine their future. A very special dance."

Ron almost laughed aloud, but suddenly realized how serious she was. "Well, I appreciate the compliment," he said. He watched as with a stifled sigh she turned away to gaze into the garden.

"Lovely here, isn't it?"

"Yes."

The garden was patched with sunlight and pitted with shadows from shrubs and trees. A tiny stream of clear water trickled from the mouth of the statue to splash over the mossy edge of a basin into the fern-bordered pool. An old-fashioned arbor, ramble rosed, arched the garden path that led to the steel gate. In this sanctuary of lush greenery and stillness, Ron regarded Isabelle in profile. Her lips were white, her eyes strained, and he wondered why all at once she seemed so nervous.

Suddenly into the apathetic afternoon, into its stillness, there came a loud, high-pitched shriek.

Howling and screaming, three young boys jumped onto the wall of the garden. Each was naked except for loincloths and moccasins. Their faces and bodies were covered with mud and daubs of white clay. Horribly grotesque, they dashed back and forth, screaming, then disappeared over the wall.

Isabelle moved quickly to the center of the terrace and stood hesitantly, her sharp eyes peering over her glasses. She seemed rather perplexed and said uncertainly, "Well, it just goes to show you. You can't make a silk purse out of a sow's ear. Hooligans, that's what they are. White trash!"

"Who are they?" Ron asked, and thought how strange it was that he had hardly reacted at all to their being there. It had scarcely occurred to him to even stir from his chair.

"Just a bunch of rowdies," Isabelle said, appearing sickened. "Carnival has them all stirred up."

"Seems to have everyone stirred up."

"Yes, well—" She glanced nervously at her watch. "Oh, dear, time to go. Time to go." She took a deep breath. "Please, don't get up," she said as Ron prepared to rise. "I'll just show myself out."

"No, please—allow me."

"How gentlemanly," she chirped.

Arm in arm they moved into the living room, then beyond to the front door.

"Now do try and enjoy yourself today," she said.

"I will."

"Good," she smiled. "I'll see you on Monday."

"Tomorrow."

"Yes. I'll see you tomorrow," she said, and as Ron shut the door behind her, he whispered: "No, you won't, I'm afraid." Tomorrow, God willing, Ron would be long gone from Brackston.

He looked around, waited a moment to make sure the woman had actually gone, then went out himself.

TWO

A DEADENING CALM TOOK HOLD—IT WAS A PLEASURABLE SENSA-
tion.

Ron found a well-worn path; it led to a group of trees not
far from the house, where five rough headstones marked the
five mounds placed side by side. A little apart from these was
another mound, alone.

He continued on over a firm and smooth carpet of pine
needles and followed the path south, up into the stark
openness and startling sunlight. Sharp jagged rocks surrounded him. He climbed higher, dropped over the hill, and started
his descent.

Not far below everything changed, the roughness of the
landscape ended, and again the pine trees were thick and
peaceful. The heat that had been oppressive in the openness
dropped away, and a cold breath came from the north, as
from an air-conditioner. Here the trees grew on escarpments
from the mountain slopes.

The waterfall, though not far away, could be seen only
from the edge of the trees where Ron stood. He moved
forward, the spectacle of it holding him captive. It was like a
living creature, a huge crystal serpent who ruled over the
countryside.

Halfway down, it broke on protruding rocks into three.
The top appeared motionless, but the three lower columns of
water veered sharply, each becoming independent of the
others, then righting themselves, they came together into a
final rush to the bottom.

Ron's path led him steeply down past a knot of young
aspens and pines, straight on to the rock and pebble below.
The swimming hole was small and sheltered, a sickle of
jagged rock encompassing the crystal clear water of the creek
that flowed down through the valley from the higher mountains to the east. He changed quickly in the shelter of a

nearby rock, and walked lazily out into the white hot blaze of the sun.

The surrounding area was deserted and perfectly still. He paused for a moment to stare up at the towering backdrop of cliff that hung just above him to the south. Squinting into the sun, he could see the soft glide of a hawk as it circled around, dipped, then floated like a cloud in the clear distance, before it disappeared completely from view.

Stepping over hot rock, he lowered himself into the calm water, and began to swim idly along the edge of the clearing, toward the northern arm of the stream. After the heat of the ground, the water felt cool and refreshing. Not being able to go any further in that direction, he pushed away and began swimming out to the center where the water deepened. He dove but could not touch bottom. It was deeper than he had imagined. After several more attempts to discover just how deep the water was, he decided to float lazily on his back, eyes shut against the brilliance of the sun.

A slight breeze moved over him, breathed, whispered; the tranquil water making no sound at all.

"Daddy . . ." the breeze whispered and Ron saw a picture of Kristy in his mind so vividly that it nearly startled him. It was Kristy in her party dress. Pink with white lace. She had just started school. Had made many friends. Kristy was good at that. Making friends. Barely turned five and already she had mastered the subtle art of charm.

Ron and Chandal had surprised her with a birthday party. Nothing elaborate. A cake, balloons, party hats and favors. The children were all off in the back yard playing Hide and Seek when Ron had suddenly realized that Kristy was not among them.

"Del, have you seen Kristy?"

"I think she's gone into the house."

"Humm."

Children don't retreat for no reason at all, and though Kristy did not follow any overt pattern of withdrawal, Ron had started to wonder about her. It wasn't the first time Kristy had just disappeared for no apparent reason.

"For what?" Ron asked.

131

"What?" Chandal stared at him in confusion.

"Did Kristy go into the house for?"

"I really don't know. The party is going well, don't you think?"

"Great. Great party. I'll be right back."

Ron found Kristy sitting motionless by her bedroom window. She had not heard him enter the room. Silhouetted by a flood of sunlight, she looked like a discarded doll, with shoulders limp, hands resting in her lap, palms cupped together as though they held something between them. Her thick black hair fell in damp, long strands across her cheeks and covered most of her profile. Still Ron could see that her soft blue eyes were large with excitement. Whatever she held in her hands seemed to please her enormously. She was leaning forward slightly, her thin frame resting against the window ledge, and she was looking, completely engrossed, at her hands. Her mouth was curved in a thin smile, and as Ron watched, her lashes flickered and she turned to gaze in his direction with a warm and loving smile.

"Kristy," Ron breathed. "What are you doing?"

"Playing."

"With what?"

"It's here. In my hands."

"What is, sweetheart?"

She smiled. "The darkness."

Ron laughed nervously. "What?"

"See." She turned her hands toward Ron and opened them.

"Kristy, your hands are . . . empty."

"Gone now. But it was there. The darkness."

"That's because your hands were closed. You were shutting out the light."

"But sometimes it's there when my hands are open."

Ron inched forward and knelt down beside her. "What's the matter, sweetheart? Don't you like the party?"

"Yes, Daddy."

"Your friends are looking for you. Don't you want to go out and be with them?"

"All right," she said and rose with her hands still cupped. "Here, you take the darkness for a while."

The simple gesture of her holding out her hand and offering

132

up her nonexisting treasure discouraged him. Was it just a phase she was going through? His hands trembled as he pretended to accept her gift.

"Daddy . . . " the wind whispered now as a sudden ripple of water rocked Ron, causing him to break from the floating position on his back. Treading water, he looked around, puzzled and a little shaken. The water remained calm, still.

"Daddy . . . Daddy . . ."

Ron looked up and there on the cliff, Kristy stood, the sun against her back, her hair blowing in a sudden breeze.

"Kristy?" Ron yelled.

"Daddy," she yelled back, her voice echoing down from the rocks, through the small inlet and beyond.

In the next instant something grabbed hold of Ron's legs, began to pull him under. In panic, he kicked, kicked hard, and at the same time plunged clumsily forward. Whatever it was took hold again, forcing him to tumble forward, so that his face was now under water, so that he was left helpless for a minute, his lungs choked for air; he struck out madly and tried to bring himself right side up.

"Daddy's funny. Playing with the darkness. Isn't Daddy funny?"

"Kristy!" Ron screamed, having lifted his head above water. Simultaneously Kristy's face loomed large before his eyes. She was smiling, then laughing.

"Funny, Daddy."

Panic-stricken, Ron screamed, "KRISTY!" Suddenly the water swirled and bubbled around him. Something below touched him—a cold, sharp graze along his thigh—as if a body had swum past him. He tried to turn, swim for shore, but the next thrust came fast, dragging him under. Fighting back, terrified, he groped his way back to the surface. He looked wildly around, gasping for air, his nose, chest and lungs full of water.

He thought he had freed himself. Instead, he felt himself being dragged under the water for what seemed like a lifetime. His lungs were bursting and his hunger for air was so primitive that although he was below the water, he screamed. Then he realized he had surfaced again. He held his head above water and tried to breathe. Kristy? Where was Kristy?

The sun nearly blinded him as he tried to find her. Still floundering, trying to catch his breath, he could feel the water calm around him. There was a gaspy puff of breath, his own. Another and another until he found himself cautiously feeling downward with his feet, with the tips of his toes. Whatever it was had gone.

Exhausted, he dragged himself onto the rocks and lay there for a moment. Everything was still. Perfectly still. From beyond the cliff the hawk came into view, floated above him momentarily, then disappeared. Gone. Kristy—gone. Hawk —gone. Ron's breath was still coming in short gulps. He wiped the last remains of water from his eyes and sat up. Gone. It was all gone. And with it a rush of relief.

Shielding his eyes against the sun, he looked at the empty sky. At the empty cliff where Kristy had been standing only a moment ago. Above him, all about him stretched a thin blue sac. Through it he could see wisps of clouds, an orange sun. His face slowly contorted with a sense of physical pain. Then a blank frozen stare. All gone.

THREE

THE CHURCH BELLS WERE RINGING AS HE FLUNG OPEN THE bedroom door. He found some solace in the deep throbbing bongs, but the sense of rushing water, his own voluble shivers pierced through the scrim of comfort. Teeth chattering outright, he faced himself in the dresser mirror and was not pleasantly surprised. His lips were white and his eyes had retreated into black caverns. He swung around to face the bathroom door as a voice shrilled:

"That you, Ron?"

"Yes."

Wrapped snugly in a terrycloth robe, her hair still wet from the shower, Chandal stepped into view. Her skin glowed from its recent contact with soap and cool water. Her feet were thrust into slippers.

"Where have you been?" she asked, tightening the belt around her waist. "We've been looking for you."

His low voice held a tinge of breathlessness as he said: "Swimming."

"Oh?"

"Where's Kristy?" Ron asked. Nervously, he reached for a cigarette and lighted it.

"In her room asleep."

"Are you sure?"

"Of course, I'm sure. She's taking a nap."

"Are you sure!" he snapped.

"Calm down, Ron."

"Check her room," he demanded. Chandal's face crimsoned at the surprise request. "Because I just saw her, Del. Just now, I saw Kristy standing alone on the cliffs."

Chandal knotted the cord of her robe tighter around her waist. "That's impossible," she murmured and disappeared into the bathroom.

Ron heard the connecting door open. Close. Chandal stepped back into the room shaking her head.

"Well?"

Chandal shrugged. "Sound asleep."

"Del, I'm telling you Kristy was standing right there at the edge of the cliff not thirty minutes ago!"

"That's impossible, Ron. She's been in her room asleep since we came back from Mrs. Wheatley's house."

"She may be there now. But she wasn't there thirty minutes ago."

"Ron, I've been right here . . ."

"While you were taking your shower. She could have gone out then."

"Why? Why would she do that? Ron, she never goes out by herself. You know that." Chandal shook her head. "Why am I standing here defending her? She doesn't need it. She's asleep, for God sakes. Go look for yourself."

Her face tightened in the backlash of Ron's suspicious gaze. "Ron, what is it? What's wrong?"

"Oh, Jesus, Del, I wish I knew." His fingers tightened on his cigarette until it snapped. Impatiently he snuffed it out in the ashtray. "What time is it?" he asked.

"...t?"
"Did you get some sleep?"
"No, Mrs. Carroll stopped by for a chat."
"Nice woman."
"Yes."
She stood beside him for a moment, took his hand, squeezed it. "Still bothered about last night?"
"A little."
"I told you to forget it."
He waited before he said dully, "Was Kristy upset?"
"Look," she said, and pressed his hand for emphasis. "You worry too much about her. She's doing what you should be doing. Resting. We've been through a couple of bad days. Nights too." She smiled. "Try and get some rest now."
He turned and slipped his hand around her waist. "I swear, Del, I don't understand what's happening to me. Maybe I passed out last night. I was drunk. Okay, it's understandable. But today—Jesus . . ."
"What happened?"
"That's just it. I *don't know*. One minute I was enjoying a swim, the next—the next thing I knew, I was going under. Being dragged under. Yet, there was nothing there. It was as though I was deliberately trying to drown myself. That was the most frightening part of it. I couldn't stop myself. I just kept going under."
"Maybe you had a sudden cramp."
"No, it wasn't like that."
"It could have been. You—"
"You weren't there, for Chrissake." He pulled away and stared from the window. He was silent for a long while, and so was Chandal, listening to the faint cries of birds drifting up from the terrace. Finally Ron asked, very quietly, "Did you have a nice time this afternoon?"
Chandal shrugged. "Mrs. Wheatley's a nice woman. She was disappointed you weren't there."
"And Kristy?"
"Bored," she said; "a little restless." She moved up behind him. "Come. Rest now." His back remained toward her.
"Will you lie down with me . . . ?" he asked quietly.
"Tonight. We'll be together tonight. All right?"

"Yes."

"I promise. Now rest."

"And you?"

"Kristy and I are going shopping with Mrs. Taylor. We won't be long."

Ron dropped wearily onto the bed and lay staring up at the ceiling. A small breeze came through the open doors leading onto the balcony, then died away, leaving the air so still that everything seemed suspended in time. The whole world was suddenly motionless, devoid of color, and hung from a slender thread that reached upward until it disappeared in the cloudless sky above.

He heard Chandal's murmur as clearly as though she had whispered into his own ear and yet she was rooms away: "Kristy, wake up, sweetheart. Time to go."

The world was a strange place, Ron mused. People, places—things. All strange. Now the great stone house moved beneath him. So slowly. Still he felt it. Moving. Everything moving.

"Will you join us later for dinner?" Chandal's voice drifted to him from the great arch leading to the hallway.

He did not answer. Did not look up. The light within the room grew dimmer still; Ron drifted into half-sleep, and his breath took on a slow even pattern. He held a strong image in his mind which repeated itself over and over again in an emphatic whisper: *"Daddy's funny. Playing with the darkness. Isn't Daddy funny?"*

Ron's tension eased gradually in the enveloping darkness, his mind swayed like a reed in a breeze, wavering now, now inclining under the force, toward a clear picture of Kristy, just a tiny thing—so tiny, so beautiful, with her hands cupped around . . . darkness. He had never forgotten that moment, not the faintest detail of it. And yet only today had the darkness seemed so vast, so impenetrable within those small white hands. Only . . . today.

He dozed off.

FOUR

Shadows began to lengthen as the sun dropped, and the town of Brackston settled into a cool dusk, followed quickly by night. The air was still and heavy and smelled intensely sweet.

In darkness Ron raised his blank face and, as though waking from a drugged sleep, peered around the room. In deepest folds of shadow, Chandal was kneeling at the foot of the bed. She gazed dreamily at him.

"Chandal?" he breathed.

"Yes. I'm here, sweetheart," she whispered softly.

He glanced around confused. "What time . . ."

"Nine-thirty."

"Nine-thirty?" Ron sat up, then stopped. He stared at Chandal, realizing she was naked. She remained still for a moment, then slowly began to slip the sheet away from his body. Dazed, he became aware that he was undressed, but surely . . . He had no remembrance of taking off his clothes, even of going to bed. Now he felt her hand moving hot against his thigh. Excitement flitted across her face.

She reached out, placed her hand between his legs. She caressed him a moment, then quickly withdrew her hand. Leaning back, head tilted, hair loose across her face, she covertly took in his nakedness, watched as his erection began to swell, rising, as if demonstrating that his desire was as genuine and urgent as her own.

He moved to bring her closer, but she squirmed away and slid off the bed. "I want to try something," she whispered.

He watched as she disappeared behind the translucent dressing screen. He could see from her silhouette that she had raised her arms above her, as if she were stretching, attempting to reach for something on the shelf above, and then her arms were lowered and the angle of her body narrowed, allowing only the outline of her breasts to be revealed.

Like a schoolboy, he stared at the shape, his desire drawing him forward, angling his body so that he could now see her waist, buttocks, and thighs. Suddenly the silhouette receded, and Chandal reappeared in front of the screen. She smiled at him and moved slowly to the bed, dangling two masks in her hand.

"Here," she said, "put it on." She placed one of the masks in his hand.

Ron stared at her in amazement.

"Do you remember them?" she asked.

He nodded.

"Put it on, Ron."

The mask was lighter than he thought, its narrow eyes and pushed-in nose creating depthless openings. An odd smell rose from it.

Chandal was looking at him anxiously, at the same time her hand explored the lower part of his body. He raised the mask slowly and brought it down over his head. Through the tiny eyeslits he saw an expression of longing on Chandal's face. She stepped away into the darkness for a moment. When she reappeared, she too was wearing a mask. So frighteningly perfect, Ron thought. The mask seemed a perfect blend of her body. A naked goddess whose slim body moved in quick gyrating motions, closer; she was on top of him now, straddling him. She had forced him into her and now swayed like a reed caught in the wind. With the mask covering his face he experienced a strange and profound rush of satisfaction.

"Oh, yes," she whispered. "Oh, my God of Spring. Xipe Totec, fill me. Renew me. You are Spring. You are the beginning of all things. You are my God," she whispered. "Fill me, fertilize me."

Through the eyeslits Chandal's eyes glinted with infinite pleasure. Animal eyes that glowed in the dark. He could hardly believe it was Chandal behind the mask. Then the mask leaned over him and spoke:

"The Goddess of Water—the God of Spring. Oh, fill me. Fill me good." He could just make out the shape of her lips moving behind the gaping hole of the mask. Her breathing had become a rush of short gasps, her tongue licking her lips, as she pumped harder, faster; he reached out and forced her down hard upon him. He met each thrust with a violent thrust of his own. Everything within the room seemed to expand, grow, reach out to become part of the ritual.

"So good. It is all so good," she cried.

The mask had come alive on her shoulders. The eyes, mouth, snake-plaited hair, all moved, sighed, breathed, too fast, everything was moving too fast.

The mask moved closer.

He wanted to stop. He had begun to feel a sudden pang of fear. "It's alive," he uttered in a long sickening cry and felt her flesh burn deeper into his own. "It's alive," he cried, yet he could not resist thrusting his body upward to meet hers. He believed then in his own lust, in the inevitable corruptness of his own soul.

Her breath felt hot and biting. He no longer had the urge or will to fight against his own baseness, wanting only that she should go on and on, that he could remain there, floating in the darkness, swinging back and forth, with the moon sending glimmers of flesh tones dancing before his eyes, breasts round and firm, her buttocks pink mounds of tenderness, polished brass doorknobs that moved, that opened and closed wanton doors.

"The stone around which moving is done," someone whispered and he pushed harder. Faster. Images flashed in his mind. The old woman from the brownstone screamed as flames licked at her wrinkled face, a door slammed shut and plunged a room into darkness . . . within the room eyes peered, dolls' eyes, all walled up in their heads, someone laughed, a star burst into flames and shot downward, people were running now, screaming, clawing to get out. Too late. Much too late. A knife was brought down—a child screamed, blood splashed against the wall, then like a waterfall, rushed downward, divided into three red spurts, then came together again to form a bloodstone pendant. The carriage house loomed up from the darkness. Like a hideously painted mask, its reddish brick front grimaced secrets, images sprang into miniature jet-black view between the cracks, crevices; someone laughed . . .

Suddenly it seemed as though all the rock and stone of the valley and its endless patches of dry earth filtered into the air, flowed into his mouth, creating a breath of life that perspired through the web-cracked fiber of his mask.

He clawed at his face, trying to rip the mask away.

Chandal's frantic image flashed again before his startled eyes. An ink-black image, twisting, turning, intensifying and expressing his own agony. He could feel his mind shrinking; it was as if the mask were vibrating the gray cells of his brain, shattering all things.

He tore at the mask, contorted, twisted—still Chandal forced him down. Black ants poured their way across his vision. The very form of fear danced in his eyes. "My face. Give me back my face!" he cried, clawing at the grotesque covering that all but suffocated him.

"Ron . . . Ron . . ." distant voices called to him, obscenely deceitful.

"Stay away. DON'T COME NEAR ME!" he cried out, and Chandal pounced on him. As she fell heavily upon him the masks on their faces came together, cracked sharply, then began to disintegrate. Someone laughed . . .

Ron screamed.

He awoke suddenly, in horror. He stared at Chandal's body lying limp next to him. A fine coat of sweat covered her body despite the chill in the room. He looked around uncertainly. His hand groped the side table for his watch. It was after four. But what had happened?

He pressed his fingers into the corners of his eyes, shook his head, trying to wake up. He realized now he was still half-asleep, caught in the wake of a dream, left to rock back and forth, paralyzed by a dreadful fear.

He managed to slip his legs from under the covers; he sat up. His heart beat in heavy painful thuds. Del, wake up. Don't go on sleeping. Please, Del.

He was still. He listened. He gazed into the maze of shadows that was his room. His eyes drifted to the canopy above. It seemed to shimmer in the glow of the moon. Then his eyes moved to the dressing screen. Were they alone? Was anyone else in the room with them?

He held his breath, and listened for the sound of breathing. The silence was a density, almost tangible. There was a gasp from someone. Then a murmur, almost inaudible. He spun around to gaze at Chandal. His eyes became steadier, more grave. He wondered if she were asleep. She might be pretending; there was something too steady in her every breath, as if she were regulating her breathing, anticipating his next move.

He studied her closely. The touch of evil had left no physical impression. She looked the same. She hadn't changed much in seven years. But now Ron perceived the world on two planes, where spirit, both good and bad, was everywhere. Waiting. Yes, there was the good. But there was also the evil waiting to crawl inside your flesh and dwell therein, as close to you as a Siamese twin. That was how close Elizabeth Krispin had been to Chandal. If Elizabeth's will had prevailed, they would have died as one person.

The heat pressed down on Ron like a wet cloth. His entire body was soaked in perspiration.

From the far horizon came a faint flicker of lightning, its sudden flash briefly wiping away the gloom of the bedroom, bringing out rich highlights on the dark rosewood desk.

Nothing would come of that heat lightning. It was another of the valley's deceptions—seeming to promise the nourishment of rain, never making good its promise.

To Ron, drenched in sweat, Brackston seemed made up of false heat lightnings. The lightning flashed again and Ron turned. All at once he realized there was someone else in the room with them. Someone hidden in the darkness, watching him. It looked like Chandal. But then? . . . His eyes darted back to Chandal who lay asleep beside him. The form in the darkness moved, dashed to the door. Ron jumped to his feet as the bedroom door slammed shut.

He turned back to look at Chandal, and there, lying at the foot of the bed, were the two masks. Their malevolent smiles glinted in the darkness. He was suddenly assaulted with a sickening sweet scent of perfume. It caught in his throat, in his nostrils, and even in his stomach. He went quickly into the bathroom and vomited.

FIVE

THE DOG TURNED IN ITS CIRCLE TWICE MORE, THEN LAY DOWN IN the shade. The hawk drifted in a lazy arc above the ridges. In the heat of the morning, the landscape had the appearance of bleached bone.

There was no rain again today. Oppressive and enervating, the heat enveloped the valley from one end to the other, elbowing westward into the desert and beyond to California. Now at 11:00 A.M. on a Monday in August, Brackston sweltered in temperatures close to a hundred degrees and still climbing.

Throughout the town, dozens of electrical pumps gulped water from deep wells, forcing it on its way to thirsty cattle and parched crops. Brackston had survived other heat waves. But none had ever been quite this severe.

Ron moved away from the terrace window and watched as Isabelle Carroll poured champagne punch graciously from a large, ornate crystal ladle. She was wearing pink lace and a hat with yellow roses. By design, the roses in her hat matched the roses in the center of the long, Duncan Phyfe table in the living room. She smiled as she filled small crystal cups with green froth and urged the guests to help themselves to the buffet.

The room was filled with the low hum of voices.

"Louis. How are you? Would you like some of Erica's delicious punch? Oh, coffee's at the other end. Certainly nice of you to have come."

Ron dropped into a chair and in a little while his nausea receded, leaving only a thick pasty taste and a slight vagueness. He still hadn't been able to speak to Chandal about last night. He had awakened that morning to a beehive of activity, all revolving around Mrs. Taylor's annual brunch in celebration of Mardi Gras tomorrow evening.

By the time he'd descended the stairs, the sun had turned the sky mint green and the house was bristling with activity.

Nancy, Chandal and Kristy were popping in and out of doors carrying large trays of food. Mrs. Taylor and Isabelle rushed about arranging flowers. In seconds the doorbell had rung and the first guests had arrived.

Now Ron wondered if the guests would ever stop arriving.

"How do you do!" Isabelle shrilled. "Would you care for some punch?"

The woman in green chiffon wandered over to Chandal with a glass of punch in her hand and began to chat. Ron let his eyes travel to the doorway. A sudden bevy of women moved into the room and Isabelle began to pour industriously. He sighed. He had traveled two thousand miles only to find himself right back where he had started. Sitting in the middle of people he neither knew nor cared about, feeling despondent.

A half hour passed. Maybe the tires for his car were ready. A pleasant thought. Half-heartedly, he sipped punch that Isabelle had foisted upon him. You've made a bad mistake, he thought; already he felt the liquid rumbling around in his stomach.

There was a gale of laughter, the laughter of a man who had just told a funny story and the shrieks of excited women.

Ron glanced quickly at Chandal. She seemed remote to him, distant. He set his glass down very slowly. I'm falling apart, he thought, at the same time his chest constricted slightly.

Rising to his feet, he self-consciously made his way through a press of bodies.

"I certainly do have charge of the punch bowl, don't I, Ron!" Isabelle said as he approached. "How's that pretty wife of yours? Her glass empty?" A glass changed hands. "And such a gathering. Our best ever."

Ron moved on, the champagne spilling slightly onto his hand. Around him men and women exchanged looks with each other, cocked their heads. Voices, bits of conversation filtered into his consciousness, slow, rhythmic words, unheeding.

"Hatred comes from necessity. It protects, insulates us from our enemies," someone said.

Singing. Somewhere there was the sound of children

singing. It should have been a welcome relief. But Ron frowned.

"Ah, yes. But every good has its evil. There are many ways of being."

Ron now made his way past Mrs. Taylor who, it appeared, was discussing her brother Clayton; the last sentence was still ringing in his ears. *There are many ways of being . . .*

"His work," said Mrs. Taylor, "was a union of mind and blood. A merging of instinct and spirituality. While writing here in Brackston—while creating his music, he found no barriers. His work became a marriage, not a war. In other words, he discovered his true self."

Ron passed her quickly, avoiding her smiling glance.

A small distance ahead, Chandal's image stood out, her fine hair shimmering in the sunlight, pouring golden shadows across her placid face. She looked so relaxed, Ron thought. So peaceful.

"How fascinating," Chandal said.

"Del?"

She looked up. "Oh, Ron, here you are." She took hold of his arm. "Mrs. Thomas, this is my husband Ron."

The woman in green chiffon studied him intently over the top of her bifocals. "Oh, how do you do. You're such a lucky young man. Your wife is so charming. And that daughter of yours. Delightful. Just delightful."

"Thank you." He glanced at Chandal.

The woman continued, "Well, if you'll excuse me, I must step over and say hello to Erica. So nice to have met you, Mr. Talon," she said and dissolved into the crowd.

"Del, I—"

"Well, stranger," she interrupted, "what brings you to this end of the room?"

Her gaze, he thought, was of studied casualness; too casual. Her hands were too busy for that gaze as they smoothed the front of her candy-striped skirt, working each pleat amidst all the stripes. She looked cool and light in the heat of the morning, but just a little antsy.

"I'm going to take a walk into town," he said. "See if the tires are in."

"I'll go with you."

"No, you don't . . ."

"Nonsense. I don't want you running off without me. Besides," she whispered, "I don't know how much more of this I can take."

"You too?"

"Uh-huh."

"Maybe if we're clever, nobody will notice we're gone."

They had barely reached the front door when they caught sight of Mrs. Taylor's blue eyes peering at them. She tapped long slender fingers over her lips to stifle a yawn before she said: "I don't blame you. These affairs tend to exhaust even the heartiest of souls."

"We're going into town," Chandal said. "Do you need anything?"

"New feet!"

The women laughed. Ron endeavored to look amused.

"I'll be sorry to see you go," said Mrs. Taylor. "There is a dinner planned for this evening. Oh, not a maddening cluster of people. Just a few close friends. Will you consider joining us?"

Ron's answer came too quickly. "I'm afraid we have to go." He softened his response with a gentle shrug.

Chandal remained silent.

From beneath her lashes the woman thoughtfully regarded Ron. "Not a chance of changing your mind, I suppose?"

"I'm afraid not."

Her face hardened for a moment, then for a reason which Ron hadn't the inclination to analyze, she smiled. "So you've had enough of Brackston," she said. "Well, if you haven't, mark my words, I have." Her laughter was brief. "Run along, enjoy yourselves. By this evening, you'll be on your way to San Francisco."

Her glance at Ron belied her words. It was oddly challenging. It was all he could do not to retort: "You bet your ass we'll be on our way to San Francisco."

Instead he turned and mutely followed Chandal down the path. She glanced back at the house for a moment. When she spoke there was a note of awe to her voice.

"Do you realize," she said, unlatching the gate, "that most of the people of Brackston have spent their entire lives on the same land that supported their fathers and grandfathers and heaps of generations before that even. Some have never been more than a few miles from their homes. Incredible." Smiling, she shook her head. "But it's good, though; good to see such a genuine commitment to tradition."

They strolled along the side path leisurely. Chandal continued to smile faintly. Glancing sideways at her, Ron was suddenly reminded of what a superb actress she used to be. Today, there was that something unique about her, larger than life, that had given her what he had considered to be star quality. Even in the way she moved now, her legs pushing forward with large brisk sweeps out into the stark sunlight. But there was also a quality he had never seen before. She was the same, but different; a woman going somewhere special.

Shaking his head, he said: "I don't quite see the people of Brackston as you do."

"Oh?"

"Most of them appear small-town, but . . ." He stopped himself.

"But?" she asked quickly.

"They are all different. As if they've come from different backgrounds. Different parts of the country."

"Ron, look at that house. Now tell me you don't expect to see Huck Finn running out the front door. All of them right out of the pen of Mark Twain."

Emphatically, he shook his head. "I don't think so. They give that appearance, but I don't think so."

Images merged, the town came into view as simultaneously the great stone atop the mountain leaped out from behind the trees. Wondrous, yet capable of arousing fear.

"Del?"

"Yes?"

"Last night—you and I . . ." Ron's words trailed off. He had a sense of shame about last night, whether he cared about admitting it or not. That's just how it was, because his actions, their actions, he knew, had magnified his worst hidden desires.

To his amazement, Chandal threw him a tremulous smile, her eyes glowing. "Last night," she whispered, "was wonderful. Just wonderful."

Her response was so unexpected, so disturbing, that he

could think of nothing to say in return. Instead he squeezed her hand and walked silently until suddenly she pulled him to a stop.

Just ahead was a small unpainted church with a steeple. It was a one-story building sitting back from the road. It was evidently newly built, for an accumulation of debris, left by the workman, still littered the ground in its vicinity.

Ron could feel the brilliance of her smile as she said to him, "Let's stop for a moment."

"All right."

They moved closer. Through the open doorway a chorus of children's voices rose soaring on the wings of organ music. The children, Ron realized, were singing in . . . Latin? He cocked his head. That's odd.

Chandal said, "Go on. Look inside."

He studied her face, shrugged. "Why?"

She laughed lightly. "A surprise. Go on, take a peek."

Moving to the door, he turned back, looking at Chandal searchingly. She coaxed him forward. Hesitantly, he peered in.

It was a small quite plain chapel with wooden pews to accommodate perhaps eighty people. The altar was made of carved stone. Above the altar was fixed a golden sunburst emblem of sorts. Nothing that Ron had ever seen before. There were none of the usual statues, nor was there a crucifix of any kind. What denomination, he wondered.

He moved further into the doorway, inch by inch, until he was far enough inside to see the entire room. Off to one side, almost to the front of the chapel, sat an organist. A small, wiry man with glasses, and next to him, three rows of children arranged according to their heights. Front row center stood Kristy. Her voice rang out in the room, rose on the still warm air; became absorbed in a chorus of other voices.

The music burst out triumphantly and then softened to a gentle harmony. Ron heard Kristy's voice above all the others.

"Isn't Kristy's voice beautiful?" Chandal whispered. Kristy stood relaxed, her hands at her sides, one clinging to her newly clothed puppet. Beneath the organist's feet a cat, paws curled under its chest, opened its eyes like steel gates, deliberately; closed them again.

Ron turned. "But . . . how can she know Latin?"

"She can't, silly. She's just faking it. Doesn't she look beautiful?"

"Faking it?" he repeated disbelievingly. "She's doing a damn good job of faking it."

He quickly backed out the door. "What is she doing here?" he asked sharply.

Chandal instantly sensed his harsh tone. "I don't understand?"

"Del, I thought she was at home. With us. With Mrs. Taylor."

"Mr. Gill came to the house earlier. He'll bring her back."

"Who is Mr. Gill?"

"The organist."

"A stranger for Chrissakes. You don't even know the man."

"Of course I do."

"I don't know, maybe it's me. Maybe I'm just so goddamn insecure all of a sudden. But I should know where my daughter is, don't you think? Or maybe you don't think I should."

"I don't understand."

"Ever since we've come to this town, you two are never around. I look up, where did everyone go? I looked for you Saturday night—the dance was over. Where were you and Kristy? Gone. Yesterday it was Mrs. Wheatley's—then shopping. I woke up last night and found you . . ." He broke off.

"Found me where, Ron? I was there for you last night, wasn't I?"

"Oh, for God's sakes, Del—I blacked out. Isn't that right? I blacked out. And before that, I didn't know what I was doing."

"And you don't know what you're saying now either. It's the same thing, isn't it? You seize on something, blow it out of proportion, then brood about it for days. Kristy is in there having the time of her life. She feels important. Let's not spoil that for her. Please, Ron." She touched his lips very lightly. "She's having a wonderful time and you've lost a little sleep. Let's leave it at that and not spend the rest of our vacation brooding. All right, sweetheart?"

She looked at him for a second in that warm, sad way, her

eyes very large in her little face. Fleetingly he wondered if her words were meant as a pacifier. He felt guilty now. His suspicions were killing him.

Relax. I must relax.

"Wait for Kristy," he said softly. "See that she gets home safely." He brought her head gently forward and pressed it to his shoulder. The smell of shampoo assailed his nostrils. But it was a good smell though; genuinely clean.

Smiling faintly, he left Chandal waiting outside the church door and moved away quickly. For the last time he told himself there was absolutely nothing to worry about.

SIX

THE TOWN WAS MORE THAN AWAKE. UNLIKE SATURDAY, THERE was a bustle of people everywhere. Ron hurried down the busy street, crossed the square and glanced swiftly at the Texaco sign ahead. He walked aways further, past small shops, decaying buildings and a single squat building topped with a large sign: HOMEMADE ICE CREAM.

Drained of energy, his stomach still a bit queasy, he stopped long enough to order a milk shake. It ran down to his stomach and dissolved as though it hadn't been, leaving a milky paste coating his parched lips. He was just turning to go when Cynthia Harris appeared in his peripheral vision. For a while he could not look at her. He was afraid to look at her. Finally, trembling a little, he glanced up. She had come to the doorway in a blue skirt with bare midriff—tall, sleek headed, crowned in flaming red; hand on her hip.

He watched her tall, lithe form hover for a moment in indecision, then disappear down the street.

"Now that's what I call tail!" shrilled the young boy from behind the counter.

In a thin, hesitant voice Ron said, "Yeah, she's nice looking." He paused, then added: "Do you have a pay phone around here?"

"In the back next to the restrooms."

"Thanks."

Ron dropped a dime into the slot, dialed 0, waited. A voice burst through for an instant, shrieked, then vanished. Turning slowly, peering, he saw Cynthia Harris approach the doorway again, her shoulder bones sharp, erect. After a few seconds she disappeared from view.

"Must be waiting for someone," the boy said with a smile.

Ron did not reply. A voice broke on the line. "Yes, operator, long distance call. Credit card." After accepting his card number, the operator rang him through to his office in Los Angeles. A distant rasp: a muted telephone. On the fourth ring, the answering service got it. Ron left Mrs. Taylor's number and instructions for Mimi to call him later in the day.

"She's back again!" the boy cried.

Ron turned and passed his hand across his brow, greased with sweat. Great and powerful, the earth moved beneath his feet.

The boy laughed, a low murmuring laugh, then asked: "She looking for you?"

"No," Ron said and ducked into the men's room. He paced the room for a moment, flushed the john to make it appear official, then slowly moved to the door. He closed his eyes for an instant and blew a loud sigh through his lips, as if to blow away the girl who now seemed to be stalking him.

When he emerged, Cynthia Harris was gone. He stepped cautiously out into the street. She was nowhere to be seen. Relieved, he moved on.

There were three cars parked in front of Matthew Todd's gas station. Yet, there was nobody sitting in them; nor were they being serviced.

For a moment Ron thought the station was closed. A tattered shade had been drawn down over the office window and the work area seemed deserted.

Ron went in at the front door and ducked into the office. Todd was there, behind his desk. Ron had a very distinct feeling Todd had heard him come in, although he had not raised his head.

"Has your man returned from Salt Lake City yet?" Ron asked.

Todd looked at him with blank eyes. "Oh, hi, Mr. Talon. Warm enough for you?"

"I guess," Ron said drily.

Todd slumped back in his chair and grinned up at him. "My man should be back any time now. He's been gone since six this morning."

"Oh." Ron nodded and felt the strain of disappointment. "It's after one now."

"Is it?"

"What time are you planning on closing?"

He shrugged. "Somewhere around five." He got up suddenly and stretched, rising stiffly on tiptoe. "How about a beer?"

"No, thanks. You are planning on getting those tires on my car before you close, aren't you?"

"Well, sure, sure," Todd said and snapped the shade up. Bemused, he looked toward the hills. "Look at it out there, Mr. Talon. Those mountains . . . It's magic, that's what it is. It's everything right on the edge of something, all the time," he murmured. "Always there, as if everything that's ever happened in the world can be seen in them. It's magic, that's what," he said.

Ron sensed that the man was stalling.

"How goes it at the Taylor place?" Todd asked suddenly.

"She's a nice woman."

"Hell, Erica's all right. She's invited me for dinner tonight. I kinda doubt if I'll go though." Raising his arms, he stretched once again, slowly, his neck cording against the light. He stopped, then, and glanced over Ron's shoulder.

Ron turned and saw Frank Hadley and his brother slipping out of the back door from the work area. Todd pulled back and gave them a solid looking-over. Ron could tell he was seriously appraising the situation, deciding whether to ignore them, or call them forward.

"Frank, Tim—you finished back there?" he called out.

"Hell, Matt, that engine is shot," Frank Hadley said and moved into the office. His brother Tim had taken but one hesitant step. "Well, Mr. Talon. I see you got to Brackston all right."

Ron could feel his heart banging away. He glanced again at

Tim Hadley. When their eyes met, he acknowledged Ron only by the slightest change in expression, the tiniest flicker of a smile and a sort of a nod, but nothing more. Yet he kept his gaze fixed on Ron.

"Tim, come in here, for Chrissakes. Say hello to Mr. Talon. Tell him how sorry you are for scaring his little girl like you did."

Tim merely shrugged, rebuked himself in silence.

"We were out hunting," Frank said. "The boy had too much to drink, didn't you, Tim? The beast and the spirits, that's all it was. Just drunken foolishness. Damn it all, Tim—apologize!"

"I didn't mean it," Tim said quietly. "I don't know why I did it. But I'm sorry. Real sorry for it."

He had walked the length of the work area slowly and now stood in the open doorway, his gray eyes fixed on Ron's face. He had a half-annoyed, half-hurt look on his face as he held out his hand.

Something, Ron found himself musing, was different about the man . . . then in a rush it came to him. He had considered Tim Hadley a simpleton. He wasn't, not in the typical sense. His eyes were too knowing, his expression too complex for your run-of-the-mill bumpkin.

Tim Hadley extended his hand further and said, "Friends?"

Ron hesitated. The other two men were silent, their eyes turned intently on his face. He felt like a museum specimen. Reluctantly, he accepted the handshake. Almost before their hands unlocked, he wished he hadn't.

"Well, now, what do you say? Let's all have a cold beer!" Todd flipped the lid on the cooler and ran his arm to the elbow in crushed ice. "Nothing better than a cold beer on a day like this."

Out of the graveled drive, leather heels crushed pebbles in a heavy rhythm; paused. Beyond the screen door a narrow figure stood, muted by the mesh.

"So this is where all the cocksuckers hang out! Oh, sorry, Matt; I didn't know you—"

"That's all right," Todd said. "Come on in, Lou. Like you to meet a friend."

The figure stepped into the office; the face sullen, stretched taut as parchment, sharp featured. The man's hair was a wild shock of gray, his skin a faded tan, yellowish.

"Ron Talon, this is Lou Harris," Todd said, gesturing. "Lou's a schoolteacher. The whole damn school actually." He handed Ron a beer. "Mr. Talon's in show business."

Lou Harris nodded, moved about the room, his eyes darting. "Nice to have variety in the town for a change. Hi, Tim, Frank."

They nodded.

"My God, I'm tired." Harris dropped clumsily into the chair closest to the desk. "You get that engine repaired yet?"

"Frank said it's shot."

"That's right, Lou, the Elders are just going to have to replace it."

"The bus is brand new."

"But the engine isn't."

"Fucking kids!"

"Looks to me like they poured sugar or honey into the gas tank."

"Fucking kids," he repeated.

Todd sat down on the edge of the desk. "Does the sheriff know who they were?"

"No, but we'll find out. Only a matter of time." He ran his hand over his face. "Carnival is going well," he said. "Thanks to the women. They've done a good job this year."

"Who do you think will be picked queen this year?" Frank Hadley asked.

"What?" He glanced away sharply, shifting his feet. "I don't know. Who can tell. It sure as hell won't be Cindy." He snorted, made a sudden gesture of irritation. "She's getting impossible to handle, damn her. Just impossible."

"Don't be too hard on her, Lou," Todd said. He sipped his beer carefully, gracefully, withdrawing his lips from the can with the utmost care.

"She's like all the young ones today. You have any children, Mr. Talon?"

Ron looked up startled. "What? Oh, yes. A daughter."

"God help you." He drew a cigarette from its pack and lighted it slowly. "Don't mind me," he said. "Those damn kids who fucked up the school bus. They've got me talking to

154

myself." He turned away from Ron, his face tight. "I don't like children. I suppose that's one terrible thing for a teacher to say, but there's nothing in the book that says I have to love them to do my job well. When I get done with them, they know what they should know. If I use odd methods, that's my business."

"Maybe that's why they screwed up the bus," Tim said dully. "Don't like your methods."

Harris nodded, then said: "Fuck off, Timmy."

Ron said: "Saturday, when we came into town, I saw a group of kids running in the hills above the town. Maybe it was them."

All the men laughed and started talking at once. Tim's voice boomed the loudest when he said: "Hell, they were probably getting ready for the Chase tomorrow, I reckon."

Frank and Matthew looked at him sternly.

"Chase?" asked Ron.

"Yes," Todd interjected. "Tomorrow there's a footrace near sundown. Just before Mardi Gras night."

"Are you staying for Mardi Gras, Mr. Talon?" asked Frank.

"I'm afraid not," Ron said flatly.

"Well, Lord, it's a shame. It's something to see all right. Fat Tuesday shouldn't be missed. Not for any reason."

Harris said: "Any carnival starts like ours did should be quite a carnival before it's all over."

Ron stood there speechless, feeling the hot wetness penetrating his shirt. Despite the closeness of the room, he had a hard time seeing the expression on Lou Harris's face. Cynthia Harris's father, for Chrissakes, seated not ten feet away from him. He wiped sweat from his neck; listened as the three men chatted. They talked about certain females, the bridge across the creek, the drought, the "Little Red House" at the edge of town, the North Fork, the auction, the upcoming election, taxes, crops and how Ned Peterson dug potatoes.

Suddenly Ron had the feeling that he was caught in a fraternity club. That hour after hour, day after day, men came to this grease-covered sanctuary to be buddies. To hang out, to talk talk that amounted to nothing, and yet talk that was vital to the kind of men who needed to gather together. The price of membership to the club: a man's face, nothing more or less. No women or children allowed. Just "The Boys." Ron almost laughed aloud. Chandal had always contended: Men are the gossipers of the world. Not you, Ron. But then you don't have a bunch of old maid men to hang out with.

Ron glanced nervously at his watch. It was nearly two o'clock.

"Don't worry, Mr. Talon. He'll be back soon." Todd flipped his beer can into the trash barrel. "You want me to drive you home?"

Ron shook his head. "No, I can walk. Thanks."

Lou Harris laughed. "Safe enough to go back now," he said. "I just saw Erica's tea gathering breaking up. Looked like a flock of geese caught in a spray of buckshot!"

Howls of laughter followed Ron out the screen door.

A few minutes later he crossed the square on his way home. From the bottom of his mind floated the image of himself clawing at a mask, swinging his fists in the air, trying to batter the horrid face . . .

But then came the opposite image of Chandal smiling, Chandal telling him not to worry about anything, that he had been brooding too much and causing problems when all he needed was a good night's sleep.

He had just stepped onto the sidewalk when Cynthia Harris stepped from an adjacent doorway. They came face to face and stopped. The sudden impact of seeing her again drove the breath from him. Her eyes clung to his and he could not turn away even as he cautioned himself: Here it is—trouble. You're looking at it. He managed to lower his eyes, but his other senses continued to send messages. A stir of air told him she had moved closer. A slight aroma of mint lingered in the heavy air.

"You've been sleepwalking for the last five minutes," she said. "I've been watching you."

"Have I?"

"It's not safe to wander about in the wilderness."

Ron chuckled.

"Mark my words," she said a little too seriously. "None of us are safe up against the wilderness, and this town comes pretty close to being that." She regarded him with meditative eyes.

Ron shrugged. "I don't know what you're talking about."

"Then I'd advise you to look out for consequences." Abruptly she turned and started off alone down a narrow street that ran south from the square.

He took several steps backwards, watched as she disappeared around the corner. It was maddening: Cynthia's concerned face had made it quite clear that he had better watch his ass. Yet, it had all been double-talk. The whole goddamn town seemed to talk in mumbo jumbo.

Suddenly from the distance he heard Cynthia Harris scream. The sound rose from the dusty earth, starting as an agitated whimper than rising slowly and steadily into a crescendo of terror.

His legs unlocked, and he ran down the street, following the screams that continued to fill the air. He turned the corner and stopped. The screams were coming from a small courtyard to the right. The sound was a horrible mess of contradictions: human and beastlike, high pitched and gutteral.

Inside the courtyard, he paused. With a frantic fluttering of wings, a cock streaked for the fence. A dog grabbed it between its teeth and tore its throat away. The cock died instantly. Its wings slashed the air violently at the moment of death. Then dropped limp on either side of the dog's mouth.

Almost before Ron could move, the dog dropped its prey and bared its teeth, prepared to defend or attack. Foaming at the mouth, the dog's yellow eyes moved wildly in its head.

"Cindy, don't move!" Cautiously, he reached down for a board. In his face rage was replacing confusion, as if he had just awakened to his surroundings. Body crouched, he glanced at Cindy, then back at the dog. He stepped forward; the dog growled warningly. He stamped his foot. For an instant, he thought the dog would leap at his throat. Instead the dog accepted a standoff, plainly indicating that he owned the territory between Cynthia and the only exit from the courtyard. Ron edged forward, found the razor-thin perimeter of that territory, the dog's growls guiding him. He inched toward Cynthia, extending his hand. "Come on," he breathed and she moved.

"No! Slower, slower," he coaxed.

She had begun to slide along the wall toward him. Ron positioned himself solidly, prepared to kill the dog if he had to. At the sight of the bloody cock lying on the ground Cynthia stopped; she burst into tears and fell limp against the wall.

Watching the dog's eyes, the saliva dripping from its teeth, the horrid shaking, Ron was startled by so much madness, and his fingers tightened around the board.

"Cynthia, please. Take my hand," he said.

Cynthia seemed to have given up, as if all was lost; that, being trapped, she was trapped forever. That there was no hope.

"Listen," Ron called to her; he had begun to shake violently himself. "Listen to me! Just move past me and run. Only a few steps."

Cynthia did not move. At least, not immediately. When she did, it was a sudden quick jerk.

And then, it happened.

Cynthia had almost reached Ron when a terrible snarl rent the day apart. The sound was so fierce, it could have been the sound of hell itself. Then the snarl was a sound no longer. It had lunged full blown, black and ravenous, with grinding teeth that gnashed at Cynthia's leg.

From that instant, each of Ron's movements were violent and quick. He smashed the board down hard. Again and again, beating wildly. He could hear the brittle cracking of bones. Screams mixed with howls. In sheer reflex action, Ron aimed the board for the dog's head and brought it down as hard as he could. The dog had begun to drag Cynthia across the ground, her leg in his mouth, his head shaking violently from side to side. Again and again, Ron smashed the dog, until every ounce of his strength was spent. But still the jaws wouldn't let go.

Now the horror struck Ron full force, stunning, leaving a black void, a smell, the sight of blood. Only the most rudimentary awareness managed to trickle through to his brain. The trickle became a rush. He reached out and picked up a large rock. Lifting it high over his head, he screamed:

"YOU SON OF A BITCH!"

With all the strength left in him, he brought the rock down. The rock crushed the dog's back, then fell to the ground.

Then something else fell, much heavier.

He stared down at the animal.

Cynthia lay a few feet away, paralyzed and stricken with fear. Exhausted, he knelt beside her body. For an endless time, it seemed to him, he could not bring himself to extend his hand. She was sweating and feverish, and when he lifted her in his arms, seeking to help her, he found himself caught up in a death struggle. She writhed in his arms, soaking wet.

"Oh, Jesus," he moaned.

Now he felt hands on his shoulder, heard voices and turned to see Matthew Todd drop to his knees beside him. The Hadley brothers peered over his shoulder.

"Get a doctor," Ron screamed. "Get a doctor!"

"No, that won't be necessary," Matthew Todd said calmly. "We'll take her to Beatrice Wheatley's house."

He lifted her clumsily into his arms. With a matter-of-factness that said he had performed such an act before, Tim Hadley stuck a stick in the girl's mouth. She bit it hard. Ron could see within her startled eyes that she was still screaming.

Todd pushed the others aside, and staggered forward with the girl limp in his arms. In the distance, from the far side of the ridges, there came a sound; slowly and steadily, a dog howled.

SEVEN

BEATRICE WHEATLEY LIVED NOT FAR FROM THE SQUARE. They came to her house via an obscure little right-of-way round a corner and down half a dozen very wide granite steps, past a flower shop, general store, then into a dirt road that narrowed to the width of a footpath. Suddenly before Ron's eyes there rose a stone wall ten feet high. It wound up the side of the mountain and stopped at the edge of the great stone.

The three men had already helped Cynthia up the walk that

led to the curved stone entrance steps and the massive oaken door.

Cynthia drew back, the blood dripping from her leg. "Please, I don't want to go in there!" she screamed.

Just then the oak door swung open to reveal an elderly woman. She looked to be in her mid-sixties at least, in spite of her hair, which was cut into a short bob of jet-black curls. Beneath this fantastic aureole her tightly pinched face was shrunken and wrinkled.

"You are safe now," she said, her white arms reaching out from the sleeves of her frock to comfort the girl. Her frock was made of a simple basic material that fluttered like rags against her bony limbs.

"Just relax," she coaxed.

Cynthia's face contorted into whispering terror, but then she reluctantly appeared to surrender to the comfort of the woman's sheltering arms. With a final sigh, she fell limply into the woman's embrace.

"There now," the woman murmured. "Rest."

There was some brief, awkward confusion as she ordered the men to bring Cynthia into the kitchen. She and Todd moved down the hallway, leaving the Hadley brothers to carry Cynthia, while Ron hesitated in the rear.

The inside of the house was dark and brooding and was a puzzle to Ron. He had expected a traditional large country home, furnished conventionally. Instead, there were only four small rooms.

Its small size was peculiar since Beatrice Wheatley was Mrs. Taylor's aunt. And instead of the expected antiques, Ron found old badly worn furniture, empty bookshelves and doors imperfectly hung, wavy with age.

The kitchen hadn't at all been modernized. There was a black iron range on which stood a giant kettle, a small yellowed icebox was opposite it. The porcelain sink had a wooden draining board. In one corner of the room, a rocking chair was drawn up in front of a television set. The cabinets, chairs and rough-edged table in the room appeared to be the originals.

"Put her on the table," Mrs. Wheatley ordered.

Cynthia whimpered: "No, no, please . . ."

The old woman took a damp rag and cooled her face. She

touched her forehead with her hand. "When did it happen?" she asked.

"About twenty minutes ago."

The old woman squinted at Cynthia's leg, then placed her hand on the girl's thigh. Despite Cynthia's disheveled condition, something of raw sex still emanated from her body. Her legs were spread wide, her skirt pulled up far enough so that the soft flesh of her upper legs appeared lush and inviting. Her blouse was partially open and Ron could see she was not wearing a bra.

"Oh, yes," Cynthia whimpered and opened her legs wider as the old woman ran her hand upward under her dress. Ron could hear the old woman saying something, heard the soft tone of her voice, saw her face lustfully screwed up, but he could not understand the woman's words.

The woman turned. "We'll have to hurry," she said. "Put the fire on under the kettle." Todd and Frank Hadley converged by the stove.

The woman moved to the cabinet beside the sink. It seemed as if she had not walked at all but had been lifted and transported to her distination like a bird caught in a sudden shifting of wind.

Her eyes were small and close set. Yet Ron imagined that they must at one time have been beautiful. Something about her eyes disturbed him, though he did not know why.

She did not speak, but turned back to face the room. Startlingly, her face had a different look, the look of a visionary, an exalted religieuse and for a moment the old woman seemed to be almost young. In her hand she held an oddly shaped stone.

"She's the only one in the community that has one," Tim Hadley whispered to Ron.

"What is it?"

"A madstone."

All watched as the old woman dropped the stone into the boiling water. Then something snapped. Abruptly Cynthia lurched forward like an animal out of control. She glared at the old woman. "No! You're not going to do that to me!" she challenged.

She was hysterical now. She jumped from the table and charged the woman. Tim and Frank grabbed hold of her.

Pinned her to the table. She kicked violently and screamed. "Oh, Christ! Oh, dear Jesus, forgive me, forgive me!"

Ron looked on in horror as the two men held her down, slapped large hands over her mouth, forcing her head down hard against the table. The old woman stepped forward, the hot blue stone steaming in her gloved hand.

"Don't ask Him to forgive you," whispered the old woman. "Ask me!" She slapped the smoldering stone on the blood-gushing wound. Cynthia's body rose from the table almost as if levitating. The men held fast. She screamed. Vapors of steam and burnt flesh rose in the musty air.

Her scream rose higher as her flesh became scorched by the hot stone; the sulfurous odor of her own burning flesh causing her to gag. In a final gasp, a final upward jerk of her body, a final dazed stare around the room, she passed out. Her body fell limp on the table. The room fell silent.

Now the old woman wrapped a piece of sack cloth around the stone, around her leg, carefully, tightly; Cynthia's leg had begun to turn a light blue.

"It will draw the poison out," Matthew Todd whispered.

Frank Hadley laughed. "She has more remedies than a drugstore."

The old woman dropped wearily into her rocker. She looked totally spent now, as if she had aged beyond recognition. She rocked in silence for a moment before saying: "She'll be all right. She'll sleep now. Take her to the bedroom."

Ron watched through the doorway as they laid her on the bed. She lay curled in a ball with her head thrown back, her cheeks sallow and drawn, breathing noisily through her mouth. A small shaft of sunlight cut across her partially exposed breasts, tinting them with yellow as if filtered through butter. After the bedroom door had been closed, Ron still maintained an image of her, a motionless form staring wide-eyed at the ceiling.

"Where is her father?" Mrs. Wheatley asked.

"In town."

"Do you want us to get him?" Tim asked.

The woman nodded.

"We'll see you later," Frank said.

Todd nodded as the two brothers left the kitchen. The front door closed. Todd bent over to whisper something to Mrs. Wheatley. She made no response. He straightened and turned to Ron. "I've got to get back to the station." He was at the door when he spoke again. "Stay with her for a while. She's not well," he said and disappeared into the hallway, his departure leaving a sizable void in the kitchen.

Ron stared after him, preoccupied once more with the meaning of Cynthia's words. He wandered the whole of the kitchen, peering disconsolately out of the window, seeing nothing but the huge stone atop the mountain.

"Are you all right?" The old woman's voice drifted over the back of her chair.

"Yes. Just getting my breath back."

"You didn't hurt yourself then?" She gazed curiously at him. It was not so much a gaze as a blood-stopping stare that riveted him.

"No," he murmured.

The old woman's lips parted. She laughed. There was no reason for her to laugh, but she did; there was no reason for him to think he was being laughed at, but he did. Her twitching lips widened, revealing a deep red line at the root of her front teeth.

Suddenly it seemed urgent that he stop her laughter, that she explain herself. Suddenly it seemed urgent that *he* understand what it was she had done to Cynthia.

"The stone you used," he said. "What exactly is it?" Conscious of the brief pause, he sensed the stone might be a subject to avoid. Still, he added: "It's called a madstone, isn't it?"

She looked up at him cautiously. "Calcium," she said.

Ron could only stare at her mutely.

"No great magic. Just a piece of calcium from a deer's stomach," she said. "Used to treat rabies. If the stone sticks, then rabies are present. When it no longer adheres, the person is cured." She paused. "Are you disappointed?"

"Cynthia will be all right then?"

She nodded. Then she turned quickly to look into the hallway. The dingy corridor was empty. No one was there. Ron looked back down at her, perplexed.

163

Without looking at him, she rose to her feet and moved slowly onto the back porch. "It's cooler out here now, thank goodness."

With her back to him, she remained motionless, staring into the yard. There, running straight to the foot of the hills, statues. A dozen or so brooding stone structures each more tortured in form than the next. Each resembling in some way a creature from another age. "Most people like the small form next to the larger form," she said. "Like mother and child. You relate to each through form."

"Has your husband done all of these?"

"Yes. Mainly to make me look at him more carefully," she chuckled. "I know more about him now. Through his work. There he is kneeling, crawling, lying . . . He looks soulful, mournful. He looks down, up, all ways. He creates from every point of view. From every mood." She strolled forward. "My husband, Thomas, is a fine sculptor. People refer to him as a stonecutter. But he is a sculptor."

They continued to wander through a vast graveyard of stone images. A hushed note crept into her voice as she took great pains in explaining the precise mood of each work. She spoke briefly of the mountains from which the stones were taken. How ancient and sacred they were. But always her eyes remained averted, wistfully gazing at the huge stone above all things.

With a nice sense of dramatic value, the slanting sun shot a spotlight on the stone's broad surface. It brought out the highlights of its brooding facade, tinting it purple. Softly the stone sent its purpleness down upon the valley.

Ron glanced at his watch. It was five minutes to five. "I'm sorry, I must be going," he said.

She stared at him mutely, doggedly, her eyes blinking steadily. "You have a lovely wife—daughter," she murmured.

"Thank you."

"We spent a lovely day together. Most enjoyable."

"They said they had a nice time."

"Your wife is an actress?"

"Used to be."

"Oh? I somehow was under the impression she still was."

Ron shrugged. "Now and then."

"I see. And your daughter. She's six?"

"Yes."

"Interesting child. So advanced for her age."

"Yes. Yes, she is." Ron's eyes darted to the window at the far end of the house, drawn there by an unanticipated movement. For a fleeting second, he saw an aged face that was nothing more than a loosely wrapped slither of bone, with pale and watery eyes, staring at him from behind the lace curtain. The old man's withered face loomed out at him, then vanished as long, red-veined fingers let the curtain fall back into place.

Mrs. Wheatley's voice droned on. She was saying something about Mardi Gras tomorrow night. Despite her ceaseless chatter, Ron began to move onto the porch. "I'm sorry. I'm late."

"I understand."

It was at that exact moment, just after five o'clock when the telephone rang in Beatrice Wheatley's kitchen. Quickly she held the receiver out to Ron. "It's for you."

"Me?" He was skeptical. "Hello?"

"Mr. Talon. Matt Todd here."

"Yes?"

"I'm afraid I have bad news for you. My man just called. His truck has broken down. He won't be able to get back to Brackston until tomorrow afternoon at the earliest." He hesitated. "I'm sorry."

Ron shook his head in disgust. "So am I."

Slowly he let the receiver drop into its cradle.

EIGHT

A CRUCIAL MOMENT, RON THOUGHT. SHOULD HE TELL CHANDAL about Cynthia Harris? What would she say? How would he be able to explain his being alone with the girl in a secluded courtyard? Then again, wouldn't someone else tell her if he didn't? More likely than not, the whole town knew about it by this time.

He allowed his gaze to move beyond the partially opened bathroom door. Chandal sat before the dressing table and dabbed her fingertips with perfume. She had put on her best dress, a white floating chiffon with silver sandals and her glittering bracelets. With her hair casually swept to one side and her skillful makeup, she looked sensational.

Ron hesitated for a moment, then moved into the bedroom and quickly began to dress. In a state of mingled confusion, he glanced at his watch. It was twenty past eight, almost time to go down to dinner. Outside it was already dark.

"Oh, damn!"

"What's the matter?" he asked.

"A run. Third time today. I'll have to change into another pair of hose."

He watched as she slipped out of her pantyhose and then donned a new pair, working her fingers skillfully to avoid a snag. Her legs seemed as firm as ever, but the curves were more pronounced, more blatantly sexual. As she let the soft material of the dress fall back into place, he had the odd impression that her entire figure had grown lusher, even fuller of breast and hips.

Chandal pirouetted, making the hem of her dress flare. Facing him, she stopped the spin so suddenly that it caused him to start.

"How do I look?" she asked.

"You look great," he said a little anxiously and kissed her cheek.

Her lips moved slightly to receive his. And they did. He made an all-out effort to make the kiss long and genuine. It fell a bit short. It was the best he could do to share her excitement and not leave her wondering what was wrong. She drew back and gazed at him.

"Ron . . ."

He pulled away from her, his eyes averted, burning with guilt. All at once he was crushed by a singular incident that had occurred two nights ago in that small room behind the pavilion.

"Is Kristy ready?" he asked nervously.

"She's gone down already."

"Oh."

166

"Ron, is something the matter?"

"No. Why?"

"I don't know. You seem different."

"Different? How?"

"I don't know." She shrugged. "It doesn't matter."

There was a long silence. He had begun noting that silences between them had become necessary to give meaning to their words. Timidly, he took her into his arms. She did not withdraw but lay her head against his shoulder. Since the night of the carnival, he had not once attempted to hold her like that. Strange, he thought, that she had allowed the Cynthia Harris incident to pass. She must have known, he realized now. Yet she rested so comfortably in his arms, the distance, if only for a moment, gone. Perhaps it was in friendship she now held him, and not love. No matter. It was a warming sensation.

Downstairs the whole house looked as if it had been turned completely around; large pieces of furniture had been removed, others brought in. The living room had been transformed into a concert hall of sorts, with bunches of flower arrangements adorning every table.

At eight-thirty sharp, punctual to the minute, the distinguished gathering assembled. Isabelle and Alister Carroll, Lou Harris, minus Cynthia who, thank God, must have recovered sufficiently to allow him to come, Matthew Todd, and Todd's wife, who turned out to be a stunning surprise. She was charming and beautiful, a tall brunette with a perfectly shaped face and green intelligent eyes. Sheriff Nash came in last with other guests whom Ron had never met.

When Nancy rang the dinner bell announcing that dinner was served, Mrs. Taylor slipped her arm into Ron's and allowed him to escort her onto the terrace. The rest followed without ceremony.

An elegantly set dining table was arranged in L-shaped fashion under trees illuminated by fairy lamps that touched them with a light and airy magic. There was the usual sweet scent of flowers; the fountain gently spewed water from its mouth.

Ron was seated across from Chandal, between Isabelle and

Alister Carroll. Kristy, oddly enough, was placed near the head of the table next to Mrs. Taylor. As Chandal smiled at Ron across the table he began to feel a bit more relaxed. The luxurious surroundings, the exhilaration provided by a fine wine, the nearness of his wife all combined into an intensely heady mixture.

After a brief lull, Mrs. Taylor, with an elegant manner, raised her glass and, nodding politely, said: "To our friends from beyond the ridges. May they find happiness."

"Hear, hear," murmured Alister.

All tipped their glasses toward Ron and Chandal and drank.

After an excellent dinner, more toasts were given and everyone sat back to enjoy coffee, brandy and a lavish array of desserts. Through the living room doorway, Ron could see that new guests kept arriving, and soon the living room was filled with people.

"Vous avez été splendide," shrilled Alister Carroll, kissing Mrs. Taylor, and the woman nodded with obvious satisfaction. Todd and Harris were gossiping. Todd's wife reached over and slapped his wrist. "Such talk. You men are awful!" Kristy stood alone by the statue tossing pebbles into the pool. She looked much older than her six years. Ron studied her for a moment. He had all but forgotten her presence this evening. Perhaps it was because she seemed so settled, hardly a bother, never complaining, never really making herself felt, as though someone had whispered in her ear, "Children should be seen but not heard," and she had willingly complied.

Everywhere voices hummed. The conversation was brisk and good-tempered. "Our library is overflowing with writings passed down by the town Elders," Isabelle was explaining.

"The stone is interesting," Chandal said.

"The stone represents the Sun Father," Isabelle beamed. "The canyon, the Goddess Mother of Creation."

Alister grunted. "The Elders are superstitious fools."

"I agree," Mrs. Taylor said with a dry cough. "However, we must respect their beliefs."

"Which are?" Chandal inquired.

"Well," Lou Harris said, "once upon a time . . ."

Everyone laughed as the man took a swallow of black coffee.

What an ass this man must be, Ron told himself. No wonder Cynthia was the way she was. He looked into the man's face and, in his mind's eye, saw the slight resemblance to his daughter. Without warning, Cynthia's face loomed before his eyes.

Harris cleared his throat softly when he realized that Chandal hadn't found him the slightest bit amusing. He laughed again but then cut it short; then, with an effort, he regained his composure and said: "In the beginning, it was believed that people lived in several worlds below. Successively, they emerged from them to a new world above. In the middle of this world, they erected a great stone."

"Utter nonsense," Alister insisted.

"Oh, I don't know," Isabelle said. "I have heard of stranger things. Why, whoever would have imagined that a Jew boy hanging on a cross could have changed the world. He's become a religious celebrity. Yet most people have never seen him. In a real sense . . ."

"Isabelle!" Alister barked. He stared critically, squinting at her.

All at once the terrace fell into a thoughtful silence, broken quickly when Kristy screamed: "A ghost! There's a ghost!"

All eyes followed her pointing finger. Off in the corner of the garden Tyler Adam stood silent, staring, his lank hair dampish looking, his eyes colorless and devoid of expression. As his empty gaze swept the guests, Ron saw Mrs. Taylor start, her fingers digging into the tablecloth to stop herself from crying out. Everyone sat motionless, waiting to see what the man would do.

"He looks lost," Chandal whispered, holding Kristy protectively.

"He was lost before he was born," Alister muttered.

White-faced and with a deep scowl, the man suddenly cried: "I greet you, Elders! I am Tyler Adam. I come to you seeking my portion."

A loud burst of laughter, nervous.

"Long ago we were one," he said coldly. "What are we now?" He paused, then added, "I cannot come in, is that it?"

169

"Yes—yes, you can come in," Alister said gently.

"No!" said Mrs. Taylor.

"He will behave himself. Won't you, Tyler?"

"No," voices repeated; others broke in, "Make him go away."

With his face filled with hatred and despair, he clenched his fists and raised them in the air. "Remember, Elders!" he cried, "All roads that lead down lead up as well. Behold the wonders of our town. The marvels carved by hand, the work of the stonecutter." He turned without warning to speak directly to Ron. "Beware," he said gravely. "They seek a prize," he whispered. "They seek a prize," he laughed.

The atmosphere within the small gathering suddenly descended to black. By their nervous mannerisms and clipped speech, many of the women, especially Isabelle Carroll, showed themselves to be quite shaken. Others simply sat in stunned silence.

In the next instant all was confusion. Lou Harris rose to his feet, shouting and waving his hands, Alister roared with laughter, while Isabelle began to hurl obscenities at the old man.

Tyler Adam straightened, spun around and shouted, "Let all who gather here be doomed forever in your Godless paradise!" He staggered back as a sudden shock seemed to run through his body and he stumbled against the wall, his hands clutching his throat as he gasped for air. Todd and Harris were on him now.

"Don't hurt him," Mrs. Taylor ordered.

"Scum!" Harris shouted. They lifted him to an upright position and had begun to drag him away into the darkness. That quickly, he was gone. Behind him, the terrace was in pandemonium.

"The fellow has no manners!" screamed Isabelle.

Alister roared with laughter, highly amused.

"Perhaps he's ill," Mrs. Taylor suggested nervously, her eyes trained on Ron.

"Ill, hell!" Alister was even more amused. "He spent half the day fishing, then talked up a blue streak all afternoon at the tavern. Does that sound like a sick man?"

"Why he should grow so grotesquely embittered, I'll never

know!" Isabelle feverishly dabbed her cheeks with her handkerchief.

"Because he is truly endowed with an incontestable misery of circumstance, perhaps that is why," Alister offered.

"Nonsense!" his wife shrieked with angry energy. "I'll be glad when the old fool is gone, damn him!"

Many of the guests in the living room had gotten up from their seats and were making motions to leave while Mrs. Taylor worked to restore calm. Kristy had begun to cry. In the distance, church bells began to peal.

This man, Tyler Adam, Ron thought, this is the same man who had trouble buttoning his shirt. This is the same man who had just sent Brackston's most respectable people scampering fearfully into the night. And the same man who, it seemed, was even now whispering a dull plaintive warning: *"Remember me."*

NINE

THINKING CHAOS, RON DROPPED WEARILY ONTO THE BED. YET there was no chaos in the room, no disorder of any kind. Just an unearthly calm that rested on the music which filtered up from the living room. Some of the guests had stayed out of respect. Mrs. Taylor needed an audience. Once a year, Mardi Gras eve, she would play her brother's music. It was an age-old tradition. It was a sacred happening.

For a moment, a very long moment, Ron froze there, *motor immotus*. The enveloping aroma of lilac was heavy, lingering, sweetening his universe. Was it the lingering aroma of Chandal's perfume? He wasn't sure. The room was full of thoughtful silence.

The music took away the silence now. It was a lilting up-tune with some sort of an undertone of sadness. The piano sounded off key. Or maybe it was Mrs. Taylor who was off key. Her voice, thin and breathless, had a curious monotony of tone.

Every now and then another silence. Was she turning pages looking for another selection or was she finished? Ron glanced at his hands. They were shaking. *I must get hold of myself.* He placed his hands on his knees and tried to fix his mind on something else. He studied the room. Clayton Byron Taylor's room. Where was he now, Ron wondered.

He was suddenly exhausted, almost to the point of feeling drugged.

"I don't feel well. Will you excuse me?" Ron had said.

Mrs. Taylor hadn't seemed to mind. As long as Kristy and Chandal remained, well . . .

"I want to thank you for helping my daughter today," Lou Harris had said to him privately.

"Is she all right?" Ron inquired.

"Fine." Lou Harris had stared at him thoughtfully. "I haven't told anyone. Mrs. Wheatley, Frank, Tim, Matt. We all agreed not to tell anyone."

Ron had watched the man join the others in the living room. The lights had been lowered. Mrs. Taylor had remained motionless for a moment, the small yellow lamp over the piano glowing placidly on her face. Ron had ascended the stairs to a concerto, offering, he had thought, Mrs. Taylor the opportunity to display her technical skills at the keyboard as well as announcing her complete understanding of her brother's composition. She played well. Toward the end of the first movement he had entered the bedroom and closed the door.

Now Ron moved into the bathroom, stripped, washed quickly, then put on his pajamas. It all seemed to take forever. He reached over to turn out the lamp beside the bed, stopped. He gazed from the balcony doors. There were two small lights flickering in the hills. Flickering lights like candle flames. He watched as they grew larger, then went out.

What was that sound? Another small tap against the window pane. He took a step forward. Then, pushing the glass doors open, he stepped onto the balcony. He peered out into the darkness. The night was quiet. Still.

He leaned over the railing and glanced around. A figure stealthily emerged from the shrubs. A bit of necklace glinted in the moonlight.

"Who is it?" Ron whispered.

"Cynthia," was whispered back. "I must speak with you."

"About what?"

"Please, meet me. Tomorrow morning."

"But—"

"At the stone atop the hill. Eleven o'clock."

"No, I won't be there . . ."

"Tomorrow. Eleven o'clock," she repeated.

He looked down at her; there in the moonlight, an exquisite molding, her face softly shaded from the darkness below, highlighted by the moonglow above.

How beautiful she was.

How incredibly beautiful. If it was loveliness, it was also an agony as well. He must protect himself against her, build a wall of abstinence, make himself look away.

Not daring to stand there any longer, he returned to the bed. For a moment he did not move. Some dread surrounded him, nameless and deep, something beyond the room, closing in on him.

He slowly drew back the sheets, slipped into bed, scornful of his desire. He knew there was no remedy for it. Sleep. He needed more than anything else to get a good night's sleep.

He stirred a little, turned on his side, saw breasts and thighs. Slowly he imagined Cynthia lying down beside him. In the distance Chandal watched; she was smiling. He turned away from Chandal into the awaiting arms of someone younger. He tried not to touch her. No, he would not touch her. He would fall asleep, forgetting she was there. Forgetting . . .

. . . she

. . . was

There.

TEN

TUESDAY MORNING THE HEADLINE ON THE FRONT PAGE OF THE Brackston *Sun* read: MARDI GRAS! Ron scanned the newspaper momentarily, then tossed it aside. Without forming a conscious decision, he had begun to keep track of time. The antique clock in the hallway chimed the hour. He glanced in its direction, then followed Chandal and Kristy into the kitchen. The small clock on the kitchen wall was a few minutes fast. At approximately one minute past nine, he sat and chatted with them as Nancy poached eggs and served them on toast with bacon, and added a stack of pancakes as a special treat for Kristy.

Nancy appeared edgy. Or was it he who seemed to rest on the brink of edginess. He was aware of the beating of his heart, a pervading sense of apprehension.

He still felt the same when, an hour later, he sat on the terrace watching Chandal clip roses from the rose bush. She moved with an easy air, picking and choosing which of the flowers to assassinate. He had never liked to cut flowers for that very reason. There was something so amputated about them. So doomed.

"Ron?"

"Humm?"

"Do you think it's possible for us to stay in Brackston a few more days? Until Friday?"

Ron could feel her looking at him, waiting for some kind of reaction to her question. "You promised me a week in San Francisco," he said calmly.

With no sign of being upset, she said: "Of course. You're absolutely right. I'd completely forgotten."

"Do you mind?" he asked.

"Not at all. You've been talking about Frisco for days now. I think we should spend some time there." She shielded her eyes against the sun for a moment. "God, wasn't that awful last night? I thought the man was having a heart attack or something," she said.

"Did you know that some of Mrs. Taylor's guests were town Elders?"

"No," she said with surprise. "Are you sure?"

"Didn't you hear Tyler Adam last night. He kept addressing them as Elders. Odd, don't you think?"

"What is?"

"That Alister would call the Elders superstitious fools right to their faces."

"Which ones, I wonder?"

Chandal's face had become flush with anxiety and a sudden rush of tension. She jabbed at the rose bush, thrusting the flowers into her basket haphazardly. "OW!" she shrieked.

"Get stuck?"

"Damn, that hurts."

"That'll teach you to pick on those poor defenseless flowers."

"Defenseless, hell!" she cried, sucking on the tip of her finger.

The door at the side of the house opened, creating a slight creaking sound. He turned to see who it was. It was Mrs. Taylor and Kristy.

"Mother, wait 'til you see! Wait 'til you see!" Kristy cried and ran to Chandal's side.

"My word, what's all the shouting about?"

"Look, look!"

Kristy held out her puppet with a great rush of pride and joy. Sweat dotted her cheeks and glistened like a hundred crystals. Carefully she handed the puppet to Chandal and then stood very still. Wonderingly, she awaited her mother's appraisal.

"I can't believe it. She's beautiful, Kristy. Just beautiful."

Mrs. Taylor moved up behind the child and placed her hands lovingly on her shoulders. "I believe Kristy's puppet has a chance of winning the contest tonight. Wouldn't that be wonderful?"

Chandal glanced at Ron. "Here, Kristy. Show it to your father."

Even before Kristy had reached him, he said: "I'm afraid we won't be here tonight, Mrs. Taylor."

Kristy stopped short.

"Oh? I thought—" Mrs. Taylor turned to glance at Chandal. "But . . . tonight is Mardi Gras."

"The car will be ready this afternoon," Ron said. "If we start out right away, I think we can make Nevada by nightfall."

"Oh, that's such a shame," Mrs. Taylor breathed.

Undaunted, Kristy smiled and handed Ron the puppet. "Look at her, Daddy. Mrs. Taylor did it all. She even has eyelashes. See?"

Ron looked at the puppet speculatively, seeing the symmetry in its unusual beauty. Across the puppet's face, a blue satin veil seeded with real-looking pearls. The shoes were also made of soft satin. The dress was empire waisted, full skirted. There was something pure and virginal about the cloth.

Unexpectedly, his thoughts turned inward, focused on the beguiling young lady who would wait for him in the hills. He tried to concentrate hard on his motives during the past few days. He came away with few answers, but he acknowledged to himself that he was going to meet with her. He had to find out if she knew anything. The only question left was how he was going to slip away from the house without drawing attention.

Kristy reached out now and lifted the puppet gently from his hands. Beauty on top of ugliness, Ron mused. Only yesterday, or was it the day before, the puppet had been a monstrosity. And now . . .

"But so pretty," Chandal said. "So very pretty."

Kristy smiled with a satisfied air.

"I will see to it that Kristy's puppet is entered tonight in the contest," Mrs. Taylor said. "Even if she can't be there." She gave Chandal a quick conspiratorial half-smile.

"Thank you," Chandal said. "It's very sweet of you."

"Oh, by the way," Mrs. Taylor began, turning to Ron. "Your assistant called yesterday."

"Oh?"

"With all the rush, I forgot to mention it. I'm sorry."

"It's all right. I'll get back to her."

"I'm surprised she called. Chandal had mentioned this was a nonworking vacation."

"It's important that I keep in touch with my office."

"Of course." She smiled. "Kristy?"

"Yes, ma'am?"

"Would you like to practice your singing for a while?"

"Oh, yes!"

"Come along then."

Hand in hand, they moved into the living room. Through the open doorway Ron watched Kristy flush deeply as she positioned herself beside the piano. When he next looked at her, the joy of the moment had crowded out her embarrassment. She sang beautifully, a thin voice that rode the still air like a bird heading south for the winter. She had no trouble following the complicated arrangement, as if she had sung to Mrs. Taylor's accompaniment for years.

In the midst of listening to his daughter's singing, the idea came to him. It rose up fully formed, a perfect excuse to leave the house, unlikely to arouse Chandal's suspicion. Still he sat there lazily until he heard the hall clock chime the half-hour. Abruptly he rose to his feet.

"Del, I'm going to slip out for a while."

"Where to?"

"A surprise." He grinned.

"For whom?"

"Mrs. Taylor. A gift. She's been so nice to us, I thought—"

"I think that's a wonderful idea," she said with surprising lack of curiosity. And something else. Eagerness? "Go on," she said, "I'll cover for you."

"And you?" he asked stupidly. As though he were now looking for an excuse not to go.

"I don't know, it's such a beautiful day, I'd like to . . ." She paused.

"It may take awhile."

She leaned in and kissed him. "We'll be here," she said, her voice trailing away into a lush whisper. Then she hurried away, flashing a smile back over her shoulder, walking as fast as she could.

ELEVEN

THE WHOLE SKY WAS COVERED WITH OPAQUE CLOUDS THAT HUNG like a soft white blanket above the valley; motionless, their stillness echoing the silence of the vastness as far as the eye could see.

As he climbed, the sun shone on his back and drew large beads of sweat from his body. He stopped for a moment, threw himself down on a rock, and sucked at the drops of sweat that covered his lips. His tongue came away with the taste of salt. He watched as a lizard, brown as the soil, slid jerkily past him and disappeared behind a rock.

Back on his feet again, he continued to climb but ten minutes later found that he was only halfway to the top. Every now and then he'd stop to rest and glance back toward the town. By now it resembled nothing more than a toy village laid out beside a child's train set. Each time he thought he'd reached the stone, he would find that he was only at the next ridge, the stone elusively wavering in the distance.

He stopped again to catch his breath. With his hands shielding his eyes from the sun, he stared at the huge stone atop the mountain. Its size defied all calculations of its distance from where he was. As the light changed the stone seemed to move further away into the distant shadows where the valley turned to the west farther still. The more he studied what lay ahead, the more skeptical he became about being there.

He pushed on, doggedly tracking the best paths, the little shortcuts through the rock that made the climb the least bit easier. At last, at the top of another ridge, his efforts were rewarded. The stone lay ahead only a hundred or so yards in front of him where the ground fell away into a plateau.

He walked a little ways to the edge of the cliff and stood staring, stunned at so much wide-open space. From horizon to horizon, wide as the rim of the world and so vast his eyes ached from an effort to encompass it, the sun poured a savage flood of heat onto the endless landscape as if hell-bent to beat into submission anyone foolish enough to be caught in its midst. Yet there was something more than heat and space which held his attention. A challenge of sorts emanated from the land itself, as if daring him to succumb to its power. Like an evil spirit, it beckoned and mocked him.

Hot and sweaty, he stood there. He tried to close his eyes. His eyelids flickered, trying to block out the light, but the strain became too great and he opened them again to relieve the pressure. The long climb from the valley had pushed him to his uttermost limits, and now he sat and leaned against the shaded side of the stone for support.

Eyes closed, he let the strain of the climb leave his body, melt away down through his legs. Little by little, his body relaxed and he felt the cool stone caressing his flesh. Oh, God, he felt so uncommonly good. Excited almost. His mind rang like a bell. He began to laugh. It suddenly dawned on him that it was one hell of a place to rendezvous. Still, people must come here. Frank Hadley had said the stone was famous. He almost got up to study it from a distance. No, too exhausted for that. Better just to sit there. Wait. He stopped laughing abruptly, partly because he hadn't the strength to continue, but mostly because he had suddenly found his laughter implausible. He stared at his watch. It was twenty minutes to twelve.

He glanced around. There was nobody. He could feel his aloneness, smell it. Had he gotten here too late? Had Cynthia come and gone? With effort, he rose to his feet. His eyes scanned the vast horizon which was stripped of all traces of contemporary civilization. He felt so helplessly alone, without ancestors or descendants, standing on the thin edge of existence—standing at the foot of . . .

"The stone around which moving is done," the wind whispered.

The thought took a long time to reach him. A very long time. Only after he had moved back to study the stone from a distance, after he had walked its perimeter several times, after he had heard the bells again, only this time he realized the sound was coming from the town below, only then did he realize he was staring at the stone he had dreamt about so often.

The realization did not stun him or even catch him by surprise. It was as though he had known all along, but only now had let himself acknowledge the fact.

His eyes fixedly stared down at the ground now. There, in the arid earth, a small red flower grew amongst the stones. One flower unlike any he had ever seen before. It was the only color visible to his eyes. Red, redder—the reddest of all flowers. Alone. *What have I gotten myself into?*

Instantly alert, as only someone pursued could be alert, he gazed up, down, around, in one quick, all encompassing glance.

He remained on guard for a long time. First standing, then sitting, always waiting. It was a few minutes past three when he came to his senses and realized Cynthia Harris was not going to show.

He halfway was glad she hadn't shown. Yet another part of him wished to hell she had. He wondered why his prior ignominious encounters with the girl had not completely dampered his zeal to be with her. She was trouble, he knew that. But she also seemed to hold the key to questions and answers that thus far had eluded him. No matter, she hadn't come and that, as they say, was that.

Moments later his slow disappointed strides carried him away down the first slope. A dangerous way to go, he thought, and veered to his left. In the distance he heard an odd sound: at first it put him in mind of chickens screeching; then he thought it must be the cry of a hawk, shrill and metallic; then he wondered if it might be the waterfall, its swift water creating thin echoes against the rock below.

The curious sound rose and fell, and went silent. But it soon was heard again from somewhere closer by. Breathing heavily, he edged along the rocks, then climbed the ridge; the sun shifted to his back. He wasn't sure of his direction now, only the smell of his own sweat and exhaustion. He stopped suddenly when he heard voices and laughter ahead.

And then—and then, just over the next ridge, he found himself staring down in astonishment at a group of children. They were huddled at the edge of the canyon. Rowdy and shrill, they waved sticks and clubs in the air while shrieking with laughter. Were they playing? he wondered. Then he flinched when he realized they had all come together, having trapped something within their tightly knit circle. An animal maybe. He wasn't sure. They each took turns striking the creature with their sticks; their cries disproportionately loud, each shrill note echoing in the vastness of stone above.

"Hey, you down there!" he shouted. "What are you doing?"

They laughed louder, squinted at him, their faces drawn into grotesque grimaces of mirth. Recklessly, Ron began to climb down the hill. All the children froze now, as if their facial muscles had locked into place—eyes peering menacingly up at him, ugly snarls possessing their lips. From beneath their feet a hand reached out, then another. In a moment the creature stood, naked and bloodied. Then screamed. Ron shuddered when he realized it was Cynthia Harris.

Instantly they swarmed all over her. They rode upon her back, driving her once more to the ground. Others had picked up stones and began hurling them at her.

Acting before he had time to think, Ron hurriedly dropped to the clearing below. No sooner had his feet touched bottom than the children were upon him. Like a pack of wolves, exactly like a pack of wolves, they seized him and drove him to the ground. They were all over him now, picking at his eyes, biting into his arms and legs. For a terrible instant he thought he was going to die. He tried to force his shoulders upward as far as possible, and then felt the blow of a heavy object across his forehead. In a rush of hot air he felt moist and knew he was bleeding. His head had begun to reel, his eyelids fluttered as he heard them wail with all the hysterical joy of warriors delighting in their fallen enemy.

Seeing idiots and monsters where only children should be, he looked around for Cynthia. He felt the last remains of his breakfast turn sour in the pit of his stomach as he watched her, arms wide, running toward him, past the flailing sticks, past the half-human specters that clawed at her body.

She howled like a mutilated animal as they slashed the tendons behind both her knees with a knife. Crazed, she spun around, ran toward the edge of the canyon. Ron had never felt so helpless in his life. He tried to rise but fell to the ground. He tried again. He screamed out in rage, falling to the ground again, his face and eyes buried in a swirl of dust.

And then there was silence. It confused him. There ought to have been sound. He rubbed his dust-filled eyes and peered beyond the rocks and saw Cynthia trying to climb to the next ridge, but there was no place to go. Other children waited for her above. They had her now—she was trapped. She glanced around, then froze. From all sides, they had begun to swarm in. Ron could see she had closed her eyes. He wondered if she even knew who she was.

Bizarrely, she laughed. It was as if she were suddenly playing a game she'd played back in school. Then with a long, shuddering cry, she leapt over the edge of the canyon, her young perfect body disappearing into the awaiting arms of the Goddess Mother of Creation.

A moment later the children were gone. In a paroxysm of excitement, they had fled, their laughter and jeers ringing in the air, their grotesque faces displaying ugly little grins as, one by one, they had disappeared into the stone, until all that remained was the settling of dust, a frozen panic, and then—silence.

TWELVE

THEY TOOK THE MAIN ROAD OUT OF TOWN AND HEADED NORTH. The houses along the road were mostly old. Many had log facings. Some had been deserted, others burnt out, leaving only the hearth, fireplace and chimney looming in the rubble.

"You all right?" the sheriff asked.

"Yes . . . it's just the heat."

"Put your head down. Better?"

"Yeah." Ron was sweating heavily. His upper arm moved like grease against his body where his shirt was torn. His cheeks and the back of his neck were wet. He opened his mouth and tried to breathe more deeply as his hand massaged the large bump on the side of his forehead.

"You say they chased her?" the sheriff asked and turned the car off the main road.

"Chased her, beat her . . ." Ron's voice broke.

"Go on. It's . . . quite a story," he said, biting down on his cigar.

"*Quite* a story! I know what I saw. I was there, wasn't I? Look, take my word for it. There were at least twenty of them. They chased her until finally she was driven over the cliff." Furious, he faced the sheriff, adamant, staring him down.

The sheriff appraised Ron for a moment, then said: "I'm trying very hard to understand . . . but it just doesn't make any sense. I mean, the children sometimes play in the hills. Strange games, yes. They play mountain games. But they are always harmless games."

"They attacked me, didn't they? I would hardly call that a harmless game."

"Maybe you frightened them. They got confused—"

"Oh, for Chrissakes! Cynthia Harris is dead, I'm telling you. And they killed her."

Nash sighed heavily. "Well, like I said—once we get to Lou's place, you let me do the talking." He turned again and aimed the car deeper into the woods. Just beyond was a row of tattered old houses. Shacks, actually, some of them painted an ugly red. Several of the houses had no trace of paint at all, just bare wood, weather-beaten and worm-holed.

But Nash wasn't looking at the houses. No, his eyes kept glancing through the windshield toward the great stone. When he realized Ron was watching him, he pretended to brush a fly away from his face. For a moment he held his bony white hand in front of his face for effect, then let it drop again to the steering wheel.

"The stone around which moving is done, right?" Ron asked.

"What?"

"Isn't that what it's called?"

The sheriff glanced at him quizzically. "Where did you hear that?"

"Is it true?" Ron pressed.

Nash shrugged. "I've never heard anyone call it that before."

In the small dim vehicle the man stared at Ron, one hand lowered at his side, his eyes narrowed. Ron steadied himself against the door as the car took a couple of rough bumps. The still air was heavy with the smells of sweat, stale cigar smoke, and another smell, less tangible—that of futility.

Ron leaned forward slightly. "Who are the Town Elders?"

Nash laughed. "Oh, hell, what can I say?"

"You can tell me who they are."

The man yawned. "No one knows for sure."

"They're elected, aren't they?"

"Not officially. People get together. Form a few committees—call themselves the Ruling Elders. But no one pays attention." He nodded his head. "That's Lou's house up ahead. Like I said—let me do the talking."

"Why?" Ron asked stubbornly.

Nash stopped the car suddenly, shut off the ignition, and jammed his foot down hard on the emergency brake. It took a little time for him to face Ron squarely. Even then, before he spoke, Ron could tell he was choosing his words carefully.

"You know," he said slowly, his words riding on a puff of cigar smoke, "when a fella travels far from home, he's gotta be prepared to forget the things he's learned. Habits, ideas, opinions . . . they just aren't any good to him in a new place. He's got to try real hard to understand new ways—get a feel for the landscape. He's got to adapt or . . ."

"Or what?"

"Mr. Talon, I don't want trouble. Lou Harris, he's a strange fella. Sometimes he's pleasant, sometimes he's not. If you're wise, you'll let me handle things." He ran his finger under his nose before he pointed. "That's him sitting on the porch over there."

Ron's eyes darted to a dilapidated white-washed dwelling surrounded by a rough-hewn fence the pickets of which resembled nothing so much as giant match sticks. The house stood lopsided and slanted to the lower side of the road. A stone path zigzagged drunkenly up the side of the mountain. Preoccupied, Lou Harris sat on the front stoop, his eyes fixed on a small fire that sent smoke rising into the air in a perfect cone.

Without saying a word, Nash swung himself out of the car

and hooked his thumb in his belt. Ron stepped from the car shakily. He still had a slight headache and his legs trembled against the weight of his body.

"Hey, pissweed!" the sheriff boomed. "You got a permit to burn on a dry day like this?"

"Hell, no," Lou Harris said. "Didn't know I needed one."

Nash grinned. "Let's go," he whispered to Ron.

"What brings you out here, Earl?" Harris squinted at Ron. "Hi."

"Hello, Lou." Ron suddenly felt panicked. He wasn't sure just why. Maybe the sheriff was right. His ways weren't their ways. Maybe he should have just shut his mouth and gotten the hell out of town.

"Thing is," Nash said, exhaling cigar smoke, "I've got to talk with Cindy."

Harris shook his head and broke into a shuddering laugh. "Shit," he mumbled. "You're a bit late."

Ron tensed, stared anxiously at the man who was still laughing. Only sadder now, a sudden confusion crossing his face.

Sheriff Nash chuckled. "Late? How's that, Lou?"

The man stopped laughing then, sniffled, his eyes blinking uncontrollably. He stared into Nash's face, then into Ron's. With an uncoordinated gesture of his hand, he said: "She's gone, Earl. Gone. Went off to Denver to visit her aunt."

"When?" Ron asked a little too hastily.

Harris stared at him, his face dropping into hard lines. "Yesterday. Soon as she got home from Beatrice Wheatley's place." He paused. "I thought I told you that last night over dinner?"

Ron shook his head. "No—no, you didn't."

"Trouble is, Lou, Mr. Talon seems to think something's happened to her."

"Like what?"

Nash shrugged. "Just worried, that's all. You sure she's in Denver?"

He sighed. "Yeah, I'm sure."

"Are you positive?" Ron asked.

"Well, hell!" Harris shouted angrily. "Of course, I'm sure. What the fuck is wrong with you?"

"Take it easy, Lou."

"Listen, son. You've got something to say—say it!"

Ron started to speak. Stopped. He looked nervously at the sheriff.

"Hell, you don't believe me, we'll call her!" Harris muttered.

"You don't have to do that, Lou."

"No, hell—let's call her!" he shrilled.

The sheriff rubbed his hand slowly across his face, his eyes displaying an annoyance good and proper. "I'm a damn fool, you know that?" he said in a low voice. "A goddamn fool."

"Well, you coming in or aren't you?"

He sighed and threw his cigar to the ground. "We're coming in, Lou. We're coming in."

Harris unlatched the screen door, led them inside and into the living room, where the faintly pungent smell of woodsmoke drifted through an open-screened window. The small room was a mess. Towels lay on the floor, stained and crimped by wet hands, and were exceedingly frayed and soiled. The woodsmoke smell gave way to the more penetrating, sweetish, acid odor of bourbon, gin and whiskey. Off to the side was a large railway stove with footrest covered with thick black soot.

In the corner was a small desk crammed with school books, old newspapers, tobacco tins and liquor bottles. A mirror hung crooked on the wall above it, its glass chipped from one corner and a crack running the full length across the surface, which was fly specked.

"Hello, Helen. Lou Harris. Put me through to my sister's house in Denver. Same number, yes."

Ron glanced nervously at his watch. It was going on seven o'clock. Looking up vaguely, he watched Lou Harris disappear behind a little roll of smoke from his cigarette; a small body, narrow shoulders tilted, phone held between his chin and his shoulder. His hands shoved papers around the desk.

"Margaret? This is Lou. No, no trouble. Listen, is Cindy there?" He moved to the end of the desk and glanced at Ron, his face drawn up tight. He smacked his hand over the mouthpiece. "Says Cindy's asleep on the couch. You want my sister to wake her?"

And now below him, below his feet, Ron could feel the

earth tremble. Shake, shake, in miniscule rhythms, sickly, remote. He knew it was his legs shaking, and not the earth.

"Well, go on," Nash said. "That's what you came out here to find out, wasn't it?"

Harris held the phone out to him. His face was cool, with that narrow set look in the eyes. Ron paused, contemplated them both, then breathing hard against his chest's constricting, he said: "No, don't wake her. That's not necessary."

It would not be Cynthia's voice, that much he knew. The rest was unclear, part of the enigma of mountain ways, not to be understood by him, not *ever* to be understood. The other thing was—caught between the two men's glances—he simply dared not take the goddamn phone. He could not.

Harris ran his hand through his thick gray hair quickly, frowning harder, his gray brows down low over his eyes. "Margaret? Just tell Cindy I was asking for her. No, don't wake her up, for Chrissakes, just tell her I called." He paused to listen. "Hu-ah. Well, soon as I get a chance, I'll write. Bye, Margaret. Oh, Margaret, tell Cindy . . ." He looked away at the two men, then lowered his voice, ". . . you tell her—hell, tell her I'm sorry. For everything. And that—" He ran his finger over his top lip as if to force out the words. ". . . Bye, Margaret," he said and replaced the receiver. He remained facing the wall, intensely still.

Nash removed his hat, wiped sweat from the band with his handkerchief. Then moving to the desk, he pressed his thigh against the rough wood, bracing himself. "I'll assume all responsibility for this, Lou."

"Earl," he whispered. "I've lost her."

"No, no, you haven't."

"She's gone," Harris said, shaking his head. With a swallow of smoke, he turned and began to speak in a low tone. It was barely intelligible, father talk about the problems of raising a daughter, and whether it wasn't better that Cynthia had decided to live with her aunt for a while. As he talked, his words became garbled, his meaning more abstruse, until he was unable to go on. He tried. He murmured. The words were blurred, like the mutterings of a beaten man, altogether unintelligible.

"Take it easy, Lou. She'll be fine. Why, in a couple of days she'll be begging to come back. You know how the young ones are. Anywhere is better than Brackston. That's what they say. Then—" he shrugged, "they realize what they have here. She'll be back."

"No," Harris said. He lifted his arm heavily and dropped it on Nash's shoulder. "She's gone this time for good." He pushed past the man and went to the window. The sun had vanished, and the thick clouds had turned the mountains a deep and remote purple. A weird light lay over the landscape, burying it rather than giving it life.

"It's going to rain, I think," he said in a far-off voice.

"Rain? Hell, it isn't going to rain today, Lou. It's Mardi Gras, remember?"

"Mardi Gras," Harris repeated in dead tones.

Ron was sure he was witnessing grief, that this was the very deadness of grief. And not just for a daughter who had decided to live with her aunt for a while.

The bells of the church, miles away, began to clang discordantly to Ron's ears.

"That's First Calling, Lou."

Harris nodded and started away from the window. He did not look at Ron. He was far away, remembering nothing, forgetting everything. He brushed by Ron as he went from the room.

"Well," the sheriff said. "I've got to be getting back."

Outside the sheriff's office the street was calm, silent, without humanity. Then suddenly it became clamorous with harsh and busy voices. Now the people of Brackston were everywhere—all in a rush, hurrying on toward the carnival grounds.

Ron turned his back on the sheriff and began to trudge the four streets home.

THIRTEEN

IT WAS NINE O'CLOCK WHEN HE FINALLY ARRIVED AT THE HOUSE.
Before he went inside, he stood on the porch and stared at his car parked in the drive. He had all but forgotten Todd's promise to have the new tire on the car by noon today. No matter. Todd had not made good his promise. The rear tire was still flat. It figured.

He let his gaze drift back toward the town. The clouds, which had been scattered throughout the day, had now settled into a solid and impenetrable mass. Far in the distance, he saw the illuminated Ferris wheel and roller coaster rising above the mist which had gathered over the valley, their hazy lights mingling with the changing hue of the night sky. Faintly he could hear the hum of voices and laughter. Other than that, the town was almost unnatural in its stillness.

When he entered the house, Nancy handed him a note. It was from Chandal. She wanted Ron to meet her and Kristy at the pavilion at ten. Kristy's puppet had been entered in the contest. Ron read the note again before he looked up. When he did, Nancy was gone.

He went immediately into the living room and helped himself to bourbon. Plenty of time, he reflected. He needed a drink. The house was oppressively quiet. It had the musty odor of withered flowers. He stared at the chandelier, the elegantly stuffed chairs and couches with their lavish floral patterns and immaculately placed doilies. Mrs. Taylor, he thought, had put her life, her very soul, into this house.

He had another drink. Yet he could not bring himself down. An overwhelming sense of doubt gripped him. He felt trapped and incapable of doing anything about it, as if he were an instrument reacting to a gravitational field set up by powers beyond his comprehension. He suddenly felt that he was heading to a destiny he was powerless to foresee or control.

He poured himself another bourbon and drank it down. Then he went upstairs and took off his clothes. Naked, he went to the window and opened the drapes. The night remained black before his eyes, the glass mirroring his own reflection. He noticed for the first time the teeth marks and bruises on his legs.

He took a long breath, drew the drapes, then ducked into the shower. He ran the water steaming hot. His flesh reddened. Yet he did not adjust the temperature. It was as though he wanted to burn away the memory of hideous little faces, purify his body, ridding it of the faint remains of any contact he had had with the children. He scrubbed himself vigorously with soap, rinsed off, then scrubbed again. Then for a long time, he just stood still and let the water pinch his flesh.

Suddenly he jerked his head around, thinking he'd seen a shadow move outside the shower curtain, the curtain itself moving slightly. It seemed incredible that someone had entered the room while he was showering, but the feeling was there.

The shower curtain moved again.

Slowly he reached out and shut off the water. He stood motionless, water and sweat coursing down his face. It was difficult to tell the difference.

And then it moved, billowing the shower curtain. He lurched forward, ripping the curtain aside. The bathroom was empty. Everything was quiet. He couldn't see into the bedroom, only its dim light filtering through the bathroom doorway. It contained no shadows.

Carefully he stepped from the tub and wrapped a towel around himself. He moved forward, stopped. Written in lipstick across the mirror:

"I WAS QUEEN. THEY"—

The message ended abruptly.

He cautioned himself to remain calm; he must not get caught in a sudden hysteria. He moved closer to the mirror and saw a lipstick tube lying in the sink. Whoever wrote the message had fled in a hurry. The letters on the mirror were childlike, the *e*'s and *a* appearing to have been written by a first-grader. He was sure a child had written the message, and

190

not a grownup. But why? What was the child trying to tell him? "I WAS QUEEN. THEY"—

"Mr. Talon?" a voice shrilled from below. "Are you up there?"

It was Mrs. Taylor's voice. Hurriedly Ron took a wet washcloth and rubbed away the message. It left the mirror streaked. He reached for a towel.

"Mr. Talon?" The voice was closer now.

"Yes, Mrs. Taylor. I'm in the bathroom."

"Oh, I'm sorry."

"I'll be right down." He ran the towel over the glass several times until all traces of lipstick were gone. He took the lipstick tube and dropped it into the wastebasket. Satisfied, he stepped into the bedroom and began to dress.

Something was radically different about Mrs. Taylor. In fact, nothing about her was similar to the way she had appeared. She sat alone at the dining table, her hair thrust under a turban. She had applied her makeup with a vengeance. Her lips were red and shiny, like an emergency light. Heavy eyeshadow put a strange and unfamiliar menace into her expression. Her eyes appeared dull and lifeless.

"Oh," she said with a start. "I didn't hear you come down."

"Sorry."

"I must apologize. I shouldn't have disturbed you."

"It's all right," Ron said. "I thought I'd freshen up before meeting Chandal."

"She's gone to the carnival."

"I know."

"Don't you look handsome this evening," she said, as though she had only first laid eyes on him. "Mardi Gras. Tonight is Mardi Gras. Can you feel it? Such an exciting time."

She paused to put her hand into her purse and produced a small silver box. Out of it she took three shiny green capsules. "I'd almost forgotten to take my medicine today," she said. "Mardi Gras does that to me. Makes me forgetful."

Something about the way she moved, the kind of listless energy with which she rose to her feet, her slow shuffle to the kitchen door, made Ron envision someone older, much older than the woman who now turned back to smile at him.

"Run along," she said. "You don't want to miss the contest. Kristy's puppet has been entered, you know. Exciting. Most exciting."

She smiled and disappeared from view.

Sweeping along the main street, Ron now approached Todd's gas station, when he saw a dark form wrapped in a cloak, standing back in the shadows. So still was the figure, and so dim was its outline, that it almost went unnoticed.

"Who is it?" Ron asked and as she moved, the overhead light fell full on her pale face as she fixed her eyes on Ron.

"Nancy?"

She moved forward, her face contorting under the strain of trying to speak. Tears had formed in her eyes and began to run down her cheeks. Pitifully, she reached out to him, as though beckoning him, as though telling him to come away with her into the shadows.

Ron did not move. Not even an eyelash.

Slowly, she backed deeper into the shadows. Her mouth moved painfully, trying to form words, trying to tell him something. Each whimper, each attempt appearing more painful than the last. Of course, Ron thought. She was the one who had left the message for him on the mirror. Not a child at all.

He started toward her.

"Mr. Talon!" a voice boomed and Ron spun around to face the gas station. Matthew Todd came toward him with quick strides. When Ron turned back, Nancy had disappeared into the darkness.

"Are you going to the carnival?" Todd asked.

"Yes."

"Good. I'll walk along with you." Almost before either man had taken a step, he added: "Sorry about those tires."

"What?"

"Didn't you get my message?"

"No."

"Spoke to your wife. The tires won't be here until tomorrow. I know you're getting edgy, but I won't let you down. Those tires will be on your car by noon tomorrow."

They passed under the glittering archway to the carnival. The crowd was twice as thick as it had been on Saturday night. Everyone seemed amassed together in convulsive knots.

Ron stared ahead into the flashes of light where everything moved, changed; where the Fat Woman on a platform sat in her chair with huge tears of laughter rolling down her cheeks. She toyed playfully with a dwarf who sat placidly upon her knee. Her howls of laughter continued uninterrupted as they moved on. Judy was off in the corner beating Punch half to death with her stick. In the distance, a chant:

> *"Judy had a baby boy.*
> *Judy had a child.*
> *Judy had a baby boy.*
> *By six—the boy was wild!"*

On another platform a hooded man uncoiled a long black thing, his bare arms and chest matted with clumps of red hair, his dirty pants tucked into his boots. A boy, no more than seven, sprang onto a stool, a cigarette stuck in his mouth. A crack of the whip and the cigarette flew from the child's mouth. The crowd roared its approval. "Again! Again!" they screamed. The boy laughed. Laughed. Those eyes. Those old eyes in a child's face.

Ron turned away as the whip cracked again. Shrill cheers rose and fell in an atmosphere of insanity. "Dumb," he muttered.

"But fun," Todd added. "Admit it, Mr. Talon. You probably haven't let loose like this in years."

Ron looked at him carefully; and when the man smiled, he said: "And I'm glad I haven't."

"You're just lying to yourself. We all like to see these things," Todd said.

Ron forced his way through the crowd, arms pushed and shoved him as he passed, and he followed a powder-dusty path past a line of tin fences and wire walls and with Todd still at his elbow, he halted.

"What's the matter?" Todd asked.

Glancing around, Ron said: "The pavilion? I don't see the pavilion."

"It's the other way," Todd said, all the time staring into Ron's eyes . . . a deep watch . . . and then he laughed and moved away. "It's the other way," he chuckled and vanished into the crowd.

In spite of his confusion, and in spite of a slight sense of panic, Ron wheeled around and, with vicious strides, fought his way back through the crowd until he had reached the pavilion.

Only a small group of people were clustered around the stage to the rear of the hall. Insects committed suicide above their heads, diving headlong into the yellow lights on the ceiling. The rest of the hall was dark. As Ron moved through a room piled high with folding chairs and tables and other unidentifiable objects hidden under sheets in the steamy darkness, he saw Chandal and Kristy sitting off to the side in the front row. He moved down the aisle as another puppet was held in the air. A soft applause followed. A child to the rear began to cry and let her head fall to her chest. "Shut up," the mother said and laughed. "You'll win next year."

"Del?"

Chandal turned. "Oh, Ron. Where have—"

"Del, I have to talk with you."

"Ssssh!" people hissed.

"Come outside. Bring Kristy."

"Please." A woman tugged on his arm. "I'm trying to see." Ron squatted.

"And the last puppet to be judged," the woman on the stage exclaimed, "belongs to Cynthia Harris." Ron's eyes darted to the platform. The woman held up an oddly shaped puppet. People were on their feet now, applauding loudly. A few children in the crowd whistled and stamped their feet. Ron looked at the puppet more closely and saw that it was two figures molded into one. A mother holding her baby to her breast.

Then all the people were together in front of the stage. "Cynthia Harris has won!" someone shouted. "She's the winner!"

Then he heard the low rumble and roll of wheels on wood in the darkness. From the front of the hall a huge wooden cart was pushed forward. Like a pair of blazing eyes, two storm lanterns that hung on ropes from a wobbly crossbeam overhead guided its way. Slowly it moved through the darkness, its large gaping slat-board front looking like a devouring mouth.

Ron waited in the corner, where the dark shadows met the harsh glare of stage light, and watched the mothers putting their children into the cart. He started when he saw Chandal lift Kristy up into the wooden enclosure.

"Del." He moved suddenly toward her. "What are you doing?"

Her face flashed with untroubled laughter. The heavy scent of burning timber filled the hall. "You don't know what the others know," she said. "You don't know at all."

"Kristy, get down from there!" he cried.

Chandal turned to stare directly into his eyes. With a start, he noticed her pupils were huge, dilated, her gaze hazy. Then suddenly she laughed and seemed to regain focus.

"Ron, take it easy. It's all part of the fun."

She took hold of his arm as the wooden cart began to move out the door. Around the cart flashed bright laughter, singing, people hugging each other, all in one action, one sound. Moans rang out. Voices shouted. "Rise! Rise!"

Out in the open air a stampede of voices. A chorus of joy released. The voices rose.

"Mardi Gras."

"Mardi Gras."

Chandal joined the second chorus. Her voice was high and hysterical as Ron tried to stop the cart from going any further. Everyone seemed to scream with unreasonable laughter as they observed his actions. Chandal's voice rang among the others.

"Mardi Gras."

"Mardi Gras."

Ron's eyes riveted to her face, the stern yet soft downturn of her lips, her mild frenzy. He trembled. Chandal held onto him. Her fingers tightened. People shouted, "Make way, make way," at the top of their voices. Ron's eyes darted to the cart. Kristy? Where was Kristy! Then he saw her, only her face, soft white with a shy stare downward beneath her lids and lashes. She was smiling. A shadowy cluster of faces cut into the light from one of the hanging lanterns . . . she was gone. From all around voices chanted.

"Rise! Rise!"

A full chorus of voices now as the chant grew louder . . . so many women's voices shrilling for the earth to come forth. On the peak, their voices trailed off. A small, wizened old woman leapt upon the cart. She goaded them on, her thin arms waving and pointing to the distant glow in the night sky. The chorus rose again, their voices seeming to sway in time to the old woman's movement.

Ron tried to see past the woman. A wave of heat crossed his face and flew down the channel of his throat, bypassing his mouth, on the way to his belly. He swayed. All swayed. Kristy? Where was she?

But he saw only the bright red glow of the lanterns swinging low. Now they were no longer lanterns. Stars. Shooting stars bursting and grinning . . . He was suddenly blinded by their fierce red glow. Without a shout or scream, without even an ounce of energy left, he allowed himself to be led. Chandal walked with infinite calm beside him.

The cart was drawn to a halt in front of a blazing fire. The air cracked with heat and excitement, and then a strange new chant began. Women's voices rose now as before. A child shrieked: "Look, mama, flames. FLAMES!" The crowd laughed. Then all focused on the fire which grew huger and huger with each passing moment.

The first child stepped to the edge of the cart, bowed her head slightly and, with a gesture of disdain, threw her puppet into the fire. Bewildered, Ron watched the flames leap higher toward the sky as people screamed and shouted praise for the mountains that were theirs. Another puppet went into the flames—ecstatic voices cried out to the earth below: "Rise! Rise!"

Chandal drew Ron close as the great fire lashed out . . .

. . . and he could feel her bones and flesh, and his insides melting, himself caught in a blazing, wooden-bodied holocaust. "Oh, God," he thought. "Oh, God," he moaned as he stood motionless among the hushed crowd—watching the puppets burn.

> *Fire is my blood.*
> *Fire is my life.*
> *When the sun fades,*
> *Fire is my home.*
>
> *Want is a fire.*
> *Desire is a stone.*
> *But life is the earth.*
> *Which belongs to me.*

FOUR

THE CROWNING

ONE

Father, the root of this dripping red flower
Among the stones has the taste of blood. And
Still I am hungry. This needful, never spent,
Nursing element—all mine for just a smile.
But do not run away, because . . .

HE WAS STILL HALF ASLEEP WHEN THE ENGINE OUTSIDE HIS window sputtered, coughed, sputtered again; he opened his eyes and listened as the car moved away down the drive until its choking sounds died away.

He slipped from the covers. As was usual these days, Chandal had long since risen, dressed and left the bedroom. She had wanted to make love last night. He could still feel Chandal's closeness, her legs wrapped around him, her face pressed desperately against his. And then, swiftly, rejected, she had rolled over to her side of the bed. He had the impression she was weeping.

You weren't cool last night, Ronald, he said to himself. No, not cool at all. He had taken Chandal by the shoulders and shaken her slightly. Anything to get that exalted look from her eyes, that look that said she was not quite normal. He had asked her—no, demanded of her: First, why in hell had she allowed Kristy to take part in that hideous spectacle and second, why had she herself gotten so fucking carried away like that.

"But how, Ron? I don't understand. Come on, give me a smile. A kiss."

Soft caresses mixed with harsher images in the darkness. Chandal fondled him while at the same time he saw Cynthia Harris going over the rim of the canyon.

He had told Chandal of Cynthia's death.

She had refused to believe him. "Surely Lou Harris knows where his daughter is. He offered to let you speak with her, didn't he?"

"Cynthia Harris is dead . . ." he breathed and inhaled close stagnant air.

"Don't worry, sweetheart, the girl is fine."

"As soon as the goddamn car is fixed tomorrow we're leaving."

"Of course. Anything you say."

Ron held himself aloof, just barely touching her. She laughed, exultant, moving cruelly. Her eyes were glazed and though she stared at him, she did not see him. Mindlessly she murmured over and over, "Make love to me. Make love to me . . ."

He pushed her away—saw Cynthia go over the edge. Saw a childlike message written on the mirror: *I Was Queen. They*—Saw Nancy's face in the shadows. Receding now. And then, as Chandal moved away, he saw Cynthia go over the edge.

Now the hall clock chimed the hour and Ron looked up. How long had he been sitting there? An hour? Two? It didn't matter. After a quick shower he made his way down the stairs. The only sound he heard was the low hum of the kitchen fan. He pushed open the door. The kitchen was empty.

The terrace, like the house, was also totally deserted, even by birds. The trees and the distant powdery mountains continued to shine with a kind of melancholy beauty, while he felt within him his own inner darkness and chill.

He had begun to think of Alister Carroll. The Ruling Elders are fools, the man had said. Isabelle Carroll had mentioned that the library contained literature on Brackston which the Ruling Elders had written. Ron continued to gaze vacantly out into the dusty stillness. A few clouds drifted in frenzied patterns beyond the ridges. Beyond the ridges, he mused. So close and yet so far.

"Oh, good morning, Mr. Talon!"

Ron turned to find Mrs. Taylor smiling and out of breath. "I'm so sorry," she breathed. "Have you been looking for me?"

Pointedly he refused to smile back. "Do you know where Chandal is? Kristy?"

"Poor you," she said consolingly. "Feeling neglected? I don't blame you."

Ron thought: Never mind poor me. Where the fuck is my wife? Instead, he said: "I guess I've overslept again."

"Mountain air. It does that to people. But once you get used to it . . . Have you eaten breakfast? Oh, of course you haven't. Nancy isn't here, is she?"

"I really don't know."

"No—no, she's sick again, I'm afraid. Poor girl. Never seems to be able to rise above her illness. Well, I'm afraid we'll just have to get along without her for a few days. If you like, I could prepare breakfast for you."

"My wife—"

"Oh, yes. She's gone over to my aunt's house. To help with the decorations. A new queen will be chosen tonight. Exciting. Most exciting."

He looked sharply at her. She appeared to be looking right through him. Her face retained a set smile, yet her eyes were swept with a kind of emptiness and vague disquiet; it was a face caught in conflict.

"Is something wrong?" she asked.

His vision blurred as he turned to study the mountains beyond. He knew silence was the best recourse for a man who distrusted himself.

"Poor Nancy," Mrs. Taylor prompted.

"Poor Nancy," he repeated obediently and thought: "I Was Queen. They"—

The shadows of the trees to the rear of the garden spread their long fingers across the horizon. With his back to Mrs. Taylor, he listened to her chat on for a moment. She talked about the large willows that had once been. Died, don't you know. And the river people who had lived for years just below the bend near the waterfall. Died, don't you know. Yet the river kept on. Something sad about a river, whereas there was nothing at all sad about a waterfall. Clayton had used to say write a tuneful frolic to a waterfall; write a dirge to a river.

And then, quite unexpectedly, he saw Cynthia Harris go over the edge.

TWO

TWENTY MINUTES LATER, WHEN RON ARRIVED AT THE LIBRARY, the tiny, red-bricked building looked gloomy and vacant, almost as though it hadn't been used in years. Upon trying the doorknob, he found it locked. The hot sun seemed to draw a strange heat from the building, casting off a foreboding light.

Pressing his face to the window pane, he knocked. There was no reply. Once again he pressed his face to the glass and let his eyes scan the room. It was a strange arrangement, to be sure. No tables or chairs, only a long wooden bench that ran the entire length of the room. On either wall, bookshelves—most empty. Only the two middle rows of each shelf contained books, and most of them seemed in terrible disarray. One section of books, the one closest to the door, seemed horribly dog eared, as if nervous fingers had turned their pages a million times.

A small desk was tucked into the far corner next to a pot-bellied stove. The surface of the desk was bare. There wasn't even a blotter. As far as Ron could tell, there was only one small overhead light, not sufficient to read by.

So this was the library Isabelle Carroll was so proud to work in.

He was just about to turn away when he noticed a small red flower lying on the floor beneath the bench. Its bright color loomed out, then receded into the rough flooring below. Now the library dropped into a pale gray, the color of dust.

Backing away slowly, then hurriedly, he walked with quick strides away from the building.

His route lay along Main Street, and in spite of his preoccupation he forced himself to observe various activities, tune his ear to snatches of conversation. All around him the town was fully alive. Women stood gossiping in doorways, two old men, leaning on sticks, chattered and gesticulated in a lively way. More people, men; four of them ambled slowly past, leaving the aromatic scents of farm life in their wake. As they passed, Ron imagined they had made a small gesture of respect. A slight nod of their heads. A lifting briefly of a hat.

Ron glanced after them, then stepped quickly into the ice cream parlor.

"The phone is to the rear next to the restrooms," the boy said smiling.

At first Ron didn't get it, and he guessed it showed. The boy answered his unspoken question: "You were in here the other day. Made a phone call, right?"

Ron hesitated. It was odd. For one split second, he had the strange feeling that all the people of Brackston knew exactly what his next move was to be.

The boy stood gazing from the window, looking thin, askew, frail, as if a great weight rested on his shoulders. Ron noticed age lines and a gauntness that had escaped him earlier. His face was immobile. So young, Ron thought, yet already so old.

He stepped slowly to the glass partition, dropped a dime into the slot. He dialed 0, waited. Heard an operator's voice. Then a click. He reinserted the dime. Different operator this time, a young feminine voice. Credit card number given, the operator rang him through. Mimi picked up on the second ring.

"Talon Agency. Hello."

Ron froze for a second; then, "Mimi?"

She knew the voice. "God!" she cried out. "Where have you been? I've been trying to reach you for days."

"I know," he said weakly.

"Where are you?"

"Brackston. A little town south of Salt Lake City."

"Brackston. Never heard of it."

"I know. That's why I'm calling—" He broke off and stared from the window. In a narrow alleyway beside the general store, he saw Tyler Adam rooting through a garbage can. Ron watched as the man worked his way along the side of the wall, picking and choosing with a sniff of his nose what his lunch was to be. Every third sniff he stuffed something into his mouth.

"Ron?" Mimi hissed.

"Mimi, hold on!" He dropped the receiver and moved. "That man?" he asked the boy. "Do you know him?"

"Everyone knows Tyler Adam."

Ron started for the door as Tyler ducked away behind the building.

"She sounds pissed."

"What?" Ron spun around. The receiver swung back and forth in the air, emanating Mimi's shrill voice.

"Yes, Mimi. I'm here."

"Jesus, what's going on?"

Ron turned his back on the boy, away from his curious gaze, and began speaking in a low whisper. "Mimi, I need information in a hurry. Brackston. Write it down."

"But—"

"Goddamn it, Mimi. Please, please write it down. B-R-A-C-K-S-T-O-N. Brackston."

"Got it."

"About two hundred miles south of Salt Lake City. There's a famous stone here."

"A what?"

"A stone monument. It's famous. Look up the town. It's not on the maps, but it should be listed somewhere."

"Ron, are you all right?"

Tyler Adam appeared again, but only for a moment. He held a shopping bag in his hand and was now dumping items into it which he had taken from the garbage can.

Ron glanced at his watch. "Mimi, I have to go. It's twelve o'clock now. I should be back at the other number around two. As soon as you have something, call me. If you don't get me at first, keep trying. Call every hour until you reach me. Call me!"

"Ron . . . ?"

"Brackston, Mimi. Look it up!" He smashed the receiver into the cradle and turned; Tyler Adam was gone. Ron stood there for a long moment. What was it—this deadly quiet that seemed to suddenly grip the town?

The sun had shifted to the west, creating a different mood, giving a new shape to the mountains. Earlier they had appeared bright and distant. Now, as the day progressed, shadows shifted and the reddish rock became the features of angry gods frowning down upon their intruders.

"Tyler Adam," Ron muttered. "You say you know him."

"Whole town does. He's lived here his whole life. Must be past sixty now, close to seventy. He's never been away from these parts, far as I know." The boy paused. "Want something?"

"What? Oh, milkshake."

"Vanilla?"

"Yes."

The boy seemed delighted with the order. "Hell, they say Tyler Adam knows these parts better than anyone. That there's nothing about these mountains he can't tell you. Animals, rocks, vegetation—he knows them upside down."

He looked at Ron, and his mouth made a wry grin. "Here you go. Hope you enjoy it."

"Thanks."

"Tyler used to be deputy sheriff. Still is, I guess. They say if anyone runs away into the mountains, the sheriff wouldn't think of going to look for them without Tyler. Not even a bird could get away from him, I reckon. That's just how well he knows the mountains. Guess he can see things in his mind nobody else can see."

Ron nodded and gazed fixedly at a large map framed in heavy oak above the cash register. The caption read: An Historical Map of Brackston. It looked as though it had been drawn by Whistler's Mother. Buildings appeared small in comparison to the overblown animals that grazed or stood in their vicinity. At the bottom left-hand corner of the map was a scroll. Etched in crude lettering: Brackston. The Gateway to the Mountains. A brief statement followed. "Between these ridges there is an independent challenging spirit characteristic of the first settlers." And who might they have been? Ron wondered.

He turned to look the boy straight in the eye and asked him directly: "The last few nights I've seen lights in the hills. Like candles. Do you know what they are?"

"Could be a lot of things. Last night was Mardi gras."

207

"But Monday wasn't. I saw them then too."

The boy thought over the matter. "Hard to say." He shrugged. "Could have been Corpse Candles."

Ron chuckled. "What?"

"Don't laugh," the boy said. "Folks around here take them seriously. They believe that when a candle is seen burning bright like that in the hills, it's a sign an adult will die. When the candle glows pale, it means a child will die. When more than one light is seen, different sizes, it means more than one person will die. It was the Widow Wheatley who first spotted the candles around these parts. Next morning she found her two sons lying dead in their beds."

"Widow? I thought she was married?"

"Oh, well—" The boy broke off. "Maybe she is."

"Cynthia Harris, do you know her?"

"Nope." The boy turned away.

"The girl who was outside the door here the other day. Remember? She was waiting for someone."

"No—no, I don't remember," he said and began rubbing down the counter.

"How about last year's queen. You must know her."

"Can't say as I do."

"Nancy. The young girl who works for Mrs. Taylor. She was last year's queen, wasn't she?"

"Shit—you sure ask a lot of questions."

"I'm curious."

"Why?" The boy's mouth had set in an unrelenting hard line.

"Aren't you curious?" Ron asked swiftly, hardly understanding the rush of anxiety that gripped him suddenly like a sense of self-preservation. "Surely you must be. Curious."

The boy looked up. "About what?"

"About—life beyond the ridges." Something in the boy's eyes leaped out. Intense aching curiosity, yes, then just as suddenly it was blotted out. By fear, Ron thought. He was sure the boy was afraid.

Very cold and steadily, the boy now answered: "Nope, I'm not curious. You—you remember that."

Ron felt the perspiration build around his collar. "I'm just a tourist," he said, managing a smile. "Just taking in local color."

"Ah-ha," he said without humor. "Look, I'm busy. If you don't mind . . ." Ron lifted his arms to allow the wet cloth to pass under his elbows. Relative silence, now.

Outside the ornate panes of glass and beyond the ridges, Ron could see the sun over the tops of mountains. His eyes followed intently the light of the sun down across the town, then across the rooftops where the street suddenly dropped away into deep shadows. High up in a tree, balancing gracefully, a bird. All at once its song broke the silence. Then another sound.

At first Ron hadn't noticed it. Then it thrust itself on his consciousness. The boy had his head pressed to an old box-type radio behind the counter and was mouthing words and phrases of a song—or so it seemed to Ron—in the air. The boy grew more intense, flicked the radio louder, developed a chant that grated terribly on Ron, a sort of "bump and grunt." He repeated words over and over with a little thrust of his crotch after it each time. "Teach me to cheat," he began. Then over and over and over: "Teach-uh! Me-uh! To cheat-uh! Teach-uh! Me-uh! . . ."

Soon Ron began to hear a new sound. He listened intently. He could hear the boy's voice clearly, but the other voices were garbled with laughter, as if the radio was picking up the voices of truckers talking over their CB radios.

As Ron strained to hear, the voices faded, replaced by a little girl's laughter. At least it sounded like a little girl. Finally, Ron screamed, "Shut up!"

"What?" The boy turned in confusion.

"Can't you hear that?"

"What?"

"On the radio. Other voices."

"That's singing."

Ron listened. Shadows fell across the boy's face. At that instant, looking up, Ron saw a group of children staring at him from outside the window. It was only a glimpse, and then they vanished, as though unwilling to let him know that they had been watching.

Everything seemed like that now. To move forward, then recede. Beneath him he felt an earth tremor. A gentle shaking, as though the town was in the throws of a mild earthquake hardly registering on the Richter scale. A tremor nonetheless. Then everything seemed to lessen, settle into a stillness.

For the first time he had the feeling of being beaten. He dropped a five dollar bill on the counter and made his way to the door. He did not know where to turn, what to do. Monday night—candles. Tuesday Cynthia Harris had died. Was it possible? But there had been two lights, not one. Of different sizes.

All at once he had the urge to get smashed. Cockeyed drunk. He needed something to relieve the anger and the budding hatred in his gut. Hatred? Hatred aimed at whom? Where was it coming from?

"Hey, you forgot your change," the boy yelled after him.

"Keep it," he muttered. When he glanced back over his shoulder, the boy was still looking at him, half smiling.

"But—"

"KEEP IT!" Ron shrilled. He waited around outside for a few minutes, not knowing exactly why he waited, and then he turned and walked slowly toward Matthew Todd's gas station.

THREE

HIS RELIEF WAS SO INTENSE, IT SWAMPED HIM. HE COULDN'T believe it. He just stood there staring at two new tires, grinning. Todd broke into a grin in return.

"How long will it take to get them on the car?" Ron asked.

"Well," he said rubbing his chin, "my man just went out for lunch. But as soon as he gets back, I'll send him right over. I'd say no later than three o'clock."

"Fine," Ron breathed.

"If you'll step inside, I'll write you out a bill. Save you some time that way. You pay my man after the job's done."

"All right."

Todd shifted the heavy gasoline can he held from one hand to the other and walked. He held the screen door open with his leg as he turned the heavier inner doorknob; the door disengaged and swung open. "Come on in."

Ron stood before the door, unable to move; a cot was now sprawled open in the center of the office, sheets and pillows were tossed sloppily on the floor; at the edge of a chair hung shirts and a pair of trousers; the office reeked of rotting flesh.

"Had a fight with my wife," Todd said. He put the gasoline can down beside the desk. "My new home for a while."

Ron bravely stepped inside and looked at the empty cot. The foul odor dissipated quickly, mixed with the pungent aroma of gasoline. He moved forward and hesitantly stood before the desk.

"Sit down, for Chrissakes!" Todd laughed.

Almost before Ron had settled into the chair, Todd handed him an ice cold beer. "Heard from Mimi today?"

"What?" Ron looked up.

"Helen Hager, she's got a tongue like a snake. Keeps wiggling. We thought about cutting her head off, but she'd probably keep on talking through her ass. You know how telephone operators are."

"Yeah."

"This Mimi sure seems anxious to reach you."

"I know."

"Bet that Girl Friday of yours has got you near bankruptcy by this time."

Ron shook his head. "Not really. She does a good job."

"Oh, bullshit!" Todd laughed. "Comes that time of the month when they get the curse, all women get crazy. You can't trust them. Any of them."

Both men paused to drink. The beer felt strange in Ron's throat and tasted like . . . what? He looked at Todd's smiling face.

"A little scotch never hurt no one. Adds to the flavor. Well, over the river and through the trees, as they say." He took a large swallow.

Ron merely sipped, then put the can down on the desk. "I, ah—it's late. I have to be getting back to the house."

"What's your hurry? Stick around for a while."

"I really can't. I still haven't packed."

Todd sighed heavily. "Well, if you can't, you can't."

"I'm sorry to be in such a rush."

"Ya," he said shortly.

Ron got the message. Todd was pissed that he was leaving

so soon. Bad etiquette, no doubt, something that good old boys did not do: sip a cold beer on the house and finish it on the run. He watched Todd drop into the chair behind the desk where he started scribbling on a pad, his head lowered.

"Your wife ever ask you about Cynthia Harris?" Todd mumbled without looking up.

"No, why should she?" Ron replied evenly without missing a beat.

"Well . . ." The man's lips broke into a tight grin. "Cynthia and you—it was pretty obvious."

"What was obvious?"

"That you two rolled in the hay a few times together. Oh, don't worry about it. Lou doesn't suspect anything. None of us thought we should tell him. Shit, if he can't keep track of his daughter, it's none of our business."

Ron, who was now really unable to sit still or to pretend any longer that he was unaffected by Todd's words sprang to his feet. "What are you?" he asked.

Todd stared at him blankly. "I don't understand."

"Oh, sure—you don't understand. No one in this goddamn town seems to understand anything when asked a question. What is it you want from me?"

"Funny," Todd said rising to his feet. "Funny how I never thought of that before, somehow. I thought you wanted something from me."

Without warning he jerked a small fishknife from the rack and, reaching into the cooler, lifted out a plastic bag of fish. Almost before Ron knew what Todd was doing, it was done. Todd had beheaded one of the fish and had ripped it open to the vent and had begun cleaning it with short, skillful strokes.

Now he cut off the tail and, drawing the blade toward him with little vicious strokes, severed the fins. "You like fish?" he asked.

"Look, I'm sorry. All I want to do is get on my way."

"I can understand that," he said, scraping the scales off the fish. "So, you've lost a few days' vacation. Not my fault, is it? People always taking their troubles out on other people." He turned and dropped the fish into the sink in the bathroom. "Your bill's on the desk. Like I said, pay the man when the job is done."

212

Ron couldn't resist asking, "What makes you so positive I was with Cynthia Harris?"

"Well," he said simply, "that's what the sheriff said. Now if you're calling Earl Nash a liar . . ."

"Just what is it he told you?"

"You want it word for word? Okay. He said Cynthia came and got him. Told him you were passed out in the small room behind the pavilion. When he got there, sure enough—you were out cold on the couch. Naked as a jaybird. When he asked Cynthia about it, she told him you two were . . . making love," he said with a cynical smile, "and then, right in the middle of it, you passed out."

Ron peered at him closely, at the leathery lines in his face. "How was that possible? I'd only gotten into town that night. I didn't even know Cynthia Harris then."

"Then? So you admit, at least, that you did get to know her."

"I didn't say that."

"You don't have to. It's plain to see." He shrugged. "Look, you don't have to defend yourself to me, Mr. Talon. All the rest of the world goes after things, hogwild and feverish. It's a disease—and everyone is sick with it, with generations of it. The trick is not to feel guilty about it . . . enjoy it. As long as you can still get it sweet and tender, why not enjoy it?"

Ron turned with a start when the screen door slammed sharply behind him.

"Oh, you're back," Todd said. "You bring me anything?"

"Burger," the boy answered, chewing. He was small boned, thin, no more than twelve. His jet black hair fell limp and greasy over his forehead. His eyes, a deep brown, fixedly stared at Ron.

"What are you eating?" Todd asked.

"Chilidog."

"You little prick. You know I like chilidogs!"

"Ahhh, I'm sorry; I forgot . . ."

"Well, don't forget it again. You're always forgetting."

"All right, all right." He slammed the paper bag down on the desk and dashed into the work area.

"Get those batteries charged!"

"Yeah, yeah . . ."

Todd shook his head. "Just like his goddamn mother. Hasn't got the sense he was born with." He tore the top page from the pad. "I didn't charge you for changing and mounting the tires. Only for the tires themselves."

"Thanks," Ron said, and eased himself out the door. "Thanks again."

FOUR

HE WALKED EAGERLY TOWARD MRS. WHEATLEY'S HOUSE. CON-fusion. Waves of it washed over him. It started with a general sense of numbness, then grew into a slight trembling of his hands and legs.

He had only one thought on his mind. To get his wife and daughter, pack, and get as far away from Brackston as possible. As soon as possible.

He turned onto a narrow dirt path, where the town fell away to smaller back streets and cottages. Through openings in the trees and fences he caught glimpses of the town square, in which he heard no sound, no busy hum of human activity. Amidst the stone crept lizards and grasshoppers, and here and there a solitary bird burst into sudden song, as suddenly stilled.

There was a deep calm around, but not the calm of night; the air still breathed the heat and life of day, if only for the hordes of insects that stirred beneath his feet.

He began to move more forcefully, his feet warming and the sweat starting to drench his shirt and the waistband of his trousers. Without conscious thought he realized he had entered a stand of pines from the sound of the pine needles crackling under his feet. Suddenly the area became thick with trees, too thick to see anything. He stopped. Everything was still. His breath came in short gasps.

He glanced over his shoulder. His wariness was habitual.

Like a blind man, he used his hands, feeling as much as

seeing his way through the trees, watching intently for any sign of life. The way was endless. All he could hear was the noise and commotion of his own body, still panting slightly, still blundering through the trees.

At first the noise seemed just part of the racket he made. But farther on he realized it was music. Chamber music: a violin, viola, cello and piano. A soft sound, restful and calm.

His breathing slackened as he rounded a turn; a large house came into view. He slowed his walk as he approached, wiping the sweat from his forehead with his handkerchief. He saw familiar sights now. The back of Beatrice Wheatley's house. Off in the distance, Mrs. Taylor's house. It was odd to look at the town from that angle. It all looked so different from where he stood now. Unbelievably different.

He had stopped outside the entranceway leading to a lush garden. The faded brass plate above the gate read: The Carrolls. He glanced around. Was this Alister and Isabelle's house? It had to be. Alister had said they only lived a few blocks over. That was about right. The music coming from inside the house was also right. The mood matched the couple perfectly.

Rising on tiptoe, Ron tried to peer over the wall beyond the garden. He was unable to see over the ledge. Without conscious thought, he entered the garden and followed the stone flagging that led to an arched doorway.

Hesitantly, he pushed open the door to reveal an expansive inner courtyard. The house was larger than he had imagined, neat and freshly painted, shadowed and root-embraced by three large trees. Anyone could tell at a glance it was a house well maintained, a house of a man who had done well in all his business dealings and was proud of it.

The shades were all up, as though to proclaim to the world that the Carrolls had nothing to hide, and through the large bay window, Ron could see the thin Alister Carroll sitting at the library table, reading. If anyone was honest enough to tell Ron what was going on, it was this man.

He had barely knocked when the music abruptly ceased. A slight creaking of sound said that perhaps someone had approached to study him from the small peephole below the knocker. If an eye had appeared, it was withdrawn before

Ron could decide it was there. He waited a moment before knocking again. Still no one came to the door. "Shit," he grumbled and turned.

Unexpectedly, the front door opened, and Alister Carroll stood peering out through the screen.

"Hello, Mr. Carroll. It's Ron Talon."

"Oh . . . hello. I hardly recognized you." He still made no move to open the screen door. "The women aren't here. They're down at Beatrice's house getting ready for tonight."

"I know."

"Oh." He opened the door apologetically. "Well, hell—come in! Don't mind me. You took me by surprise."

Nervously Ron moved into the hallway. Sweat beaded his brow. Instinctively, he wiped it with his handkerchief.

"It looks like you've been out running."

"No," Ron said. "Just a hot day."

"Nice to see you. Come inside here. The air conditioner is going full blast."

Without protest, Ron allowed himself to be led into the library. The room was immaculate and designed in good taste. Two brown leather chairs and a massive couch flanked the fireplace; solid oak bookshelves were lined with books bound in expensive red jackets. Plants were strategically placed. French doors, perfectly appointed, opened out to a glassed-in richly furnished patio.

Alister was behind the bar. There was a contentment, a grace about his movements, that suggested a man who enjoyed his home.

He passed a glass to Ron and settled on the couch, his body diminished by the large cushions that swallowed the heaviest part of his buttocks, making him tilt forward like a small hunched-over gnome. His eyes contained their usual clever sparkle over his long sharp nose that appeared to almost meet his chin. He was the same man Ron had come to know, except today he wore a tweed jacket and a cap of the sort that is associated with gents who frequent the race tracks.

Ron picked up his bourbon glass clumsily. He was unaccustomed to handling a drink this early in the day. He took a sip and grimaced.

"Too strong?" Alister chuckled.

"A little."

"Would you—"

"No, I think I can handle it. It's excellent bourbon. A little stiff going down, but smooth in the stomach."

"I appreciate fine liquor. I'm an Irishman. Perhaps that accounts for it. Haven't seen Dublin in forty years. Still like a strong drink though." He grinned. "You look a little tense today, Mr. Talon."

"I am, a little."

"How long have you been in . . ."

"Brackston? Five days."

He gave Ron a sidelong glance. "That'll do it to you."

"I don't understand," Ron said cautiously.

"Just a strange place. That is, until you get used to it."

"Oh."

"You know, not everything I say means something, son, as much as it feeds my ego to have you clinging onto my every word. It would be a horrible world if a man couldn't make a casual remark without drawing suspicion." Absently he sipped his drink, sighed appreciably, and settled back. "But then again, you probably haven't come here for casual conversation, have you?"

"No—no, I haven't."

"Then what is it you have come here for—a glass of decent bourbon?"

"I want to know about Brackston. What's going on."

He sighed profoundly, then sat up straighter. When he spoke, it was slow and easy. "It's a thankless business to interfere with the goings on here in Brackston. Perhaps you'd do well to remember that."

Ron opened his lips to speak, closed them as he met Alister's eyes. "The mountains," Alister added, "have their own ways. What you've learned in the city will do you no good here."

"Tyler Adam. Tell me why everyone at dinner the other night seemed so frightened of him."

"The man is an alcoholic. His behavior is erratic. He is capable of doing anything at any time. Hell, he's tried to solve his problems, but he suffers torments unimaginable to you or me."

"He didn't seem drunk. You yourself said he wasn't drunk."

"Only trying to cover for him. Anyone could see he was experiencing a fit of d.t.'s. Otherwise he wouldn't have come to the house like that."

"The Elders. He called everyone there Elders."

"Oh, maybe he thought there were Elders present. But there weren't."

"Then there is a group of people collectively known as the Ruling Elders."

Alister grinned. "Seems to me you're sure working up a powerful curiosity about this town, son."

"Is there anything wrong with that? Any reason why I shouldn't?"

Now Alister was frankly staring, his pale blue eyes studying Ron's face intently with no pretense of doing otherwise. And Ron had the sudden conviction that the man was learning a great deal about him, more than Ron knew himself.

"I believe," Ron said on sudden impulse, "that Cynthia Harris is dead. That she was forced over the edge of a cliff by children. Children that live in this town." Ron shot a keen glance at Alister's face; it was impassive as stone. He continued. "I also believe her death has something to do with the carnival."

Alister considered this for a moment or so. Then he chuckled—deprecatingly, as though he were about to tell a joke that wasn't very funny. "You know," he said casually, "we often get people who come to Brackston. Some by choice, others by accident. Like yourself. Some find our ways strange. Others do not. But none have ever called our children murderers. That's a pretty powerful statement—and one that might not go down too well with the citizens of Brackston. Children are what this town is all about. Brackston tradition passed on to its children. This—"

"Is that why children are allowed to run naked in the hills?" Ron interrupted. "Why they are encouraged to burn their toys, to watch brutal puppet shows . . . I was attacked the other day by Brackston children. Brutally attacked. Is this part of your tradition? They actually went—"

"You needn't give me a synopsis. The sheriff has already done that."

"And?"

"And—like him, I found it hard to believe. But when he told me Cynthia Harris was involved, I began to understand."

"Understand what?"

"Guilt is a funny thing."

"I don't follow."

"Almost everyone in town knows that you slept with her. All except her father, that is." He grinned. "I must admit that when I heard the news, I was a bit envious." He paused, then added, "Naturally, when the others heard the news, they responded with an odd sense of hatred toward the girl."

"Naturally."

"But that's irrelevant. What may help you is the fact—mark this—that Cynthia Harris knew she'd done wrong and decided, wisely, I might add, to leave town." He leaned back and assumed a comfortable position. The sunlight had deepened to bronze; on the patio shadows had begun to gather.

"Do you really expect me to believe that?" Ron asked sarcastically.

Alister laughed. An open full laugh without restrain. "If I were you, I would. Hell, let it go. Enjoy yourself. Forget Cynthia Harris. We all know redheads are a confusing lot."

In spite of the lightness in Alister's voice, Ron was conscious of an undercurrent of steady warning in his words. His eyes evaded the man's as he drawled: "The stone around which moving is done. The stone on the hill. Will you tell me about it?"

"Nothing to tell," he said. "There's always superstition in small towns. It's here. It's been here for ages. Christ Almighty, some of the old women in town still wear charms around their necks."

Ron looked up quickly, and was surprised to see Alister's face was affable as ever. Was it possible that the man wasn't hiding anything? That Ron was mistaken? But how the hell could that be? He'd seen Cynthia driven over the cliff. The children had attacked him, hadn't they?

"Charms," he mumbled. "What are they for?"

Alister shrugged his shoulders. "There's a hundred reasons. All just superstitious foolishness. That's no great mystery sitting up there on the hill, son. It's just what it appears to be. A big ugly stone. Nothing more. Oh, if you want, you can make it other things. But that's true of most things. That's why the Christians make pilgrimages to the Vatican, the Muslims to Mecca and the Jews to Jerusalem. All trying to make things what they want them to be. People here in Brackston aren't any different. Some call it religion. I call it plain foolishness."

"But you still haven't told me what that foolishness is," Ron pressed. "Just what is it the people of Brackston believe?"

"The issue is God and their hope of resurrection. Fear of death, son. All of them afraid of dying. Nothing unusual about that, now is there? Death scares the hell out of most people. Especially old people. So they begin doing things to make death a little more palatable."

"Like what?"

"Like worshipping that damn stone. Some call it the navel of the earth where all creation began. The umbilical cord, if you will. Some just call it the center or the cornerstone. Others believe it holds down the head of the snake. Don't ask me what snake. Without the stone, the snake would shake his head violently; if this occurred, it would shake the world to pieces. To some," he went on, "the stone represents all life. Oh, to you—you see it only from one side. Maybe, if you are curious, you take the time to glance at it from another angle. You see a different shape entirely, a different texture. You become confused; you may even forget you're still observing the same stone. But to the people of Brackston, ah, they see it as one complete whole. All sides at once, all textures as one texture, all shapes as one shape, all sides merging into one another: the present into the future, the future into the past, the past again into the future. There is no time then, you see. There is only the stone. If they have suffered in the past, it was because they did not have the stone to protect them. Some of the older generations of the valley suffered cruelly at the hands of others. Some were even tortured, I am told. Now they look to the stone for their protection. Perhaps even their salvation. It's sad, really."

For a moment Alister stopped speaking, his bony white fingers probing at his jowl and the grayed stubble under the bone of jaw. Then he lifted his eyes to meet Ron's gaze squarely.

Ron said, "And you? What do you believe?"

"Me. I believe in nothing," he said flatly.

"Corpse Lights. I've seen them in the hills."

Alister looked at him curiously. "That's odd."

"How so?"

"There haven't been Corpse Lights seen in these parts in years. Ever since—"

"The Widow Wheatley saw them right before her two sons died." Ron smiled now, sensing that he had finally caught Alister off guard. "That's right, isn't it? Widow Wheatley?"

"Widow? Where did you hear that?"

"Does it matter?"

He shrugged. "As far as I know, Thomas and she are married."

"Or they're brother and sister . . . living together."

A heavy silence hung in the air for a moment, before Ron went on. "And Mrs. Taylor. It's an odd coincidence that her brother's name is also Taylor. Unless, of course, she is married to Clayton Byron Taylor. Her brother. Then it would make sense."

"I'm not sure what you're getting at. Is there some way you can be more specific? Some word that you could, perhaps, use to . . ." Alister paused, smiling suggestively.

Ron's face reddened, but he said it nevertheless. "Incest."

"Dear boy." Alister's eyebrows rose.

"It's all around us, isn't it? Every marriage is a cousin to a cousin, or—"

"A cousin to a cousin, perhaps," he interrupted. "But, of course, you're suggesting something quite different. A brother to a sister . . . surely—"

"Clayton ran away, didn't he? Perhaps that's what he was running away from. That would have been a reason to run." Alister maintained a bemused silence. "Well, go on," Ron added, "deny it."

"Consider it denied," Alister said promptly.

Ron said, "It doesn't pay to ask questions around here, does it? The answers are scarcely answers, are they?"

"I've tried hard to be honest with you, son. Wouldn't you say?"

"The stone. What does the carnival have to do with the stone?"

"Nothing. Not a thing. The Carnival of Summer is just that—a silly once-a-year excuse to raise hell."

Ron looked at him, frowning, perplexed. "Why do I get the feeling there's something more to the carnival?"

"Well . . ." He smiled generously. "People are always particularly vulnerable on vacation. They become uneasy. They find themselves in a different world. Everything looks different. But are they really? I don't think so. Your ways are our ways . . . I believe it was Camus who said: 'The only value of travel is fear.'"

"Fear?"

"Yes, fear. Strange places, different people, not sleeping in your own bed. You have chosen to remove yourself from all familiar things. That is why people enjoy repetition—because they are not confronted with anything new."

He paused to massage his chin, fully embarked upon a lecture. "They like that. They like their little habits, their cozy ruts. It's safe there, you see. They know the territory. Ah, but to climb out of that rut, to venture into a new world—that can be quite frightening. It can also . . ."

Ron wasn't really listening now. In his mind he heard other words, words that Alister was probably saying to himself. *Look, son, don't give me a hard time, will you? I'm just passing on what I've been told to say by the Elders, and that is, relax. Sit back and let things happen because you won't be able to stop them from happening anyway. You know the old saying: "If you're going to get fucked, why not lie back and enjoy it?"*

And as time passed and as Alister kept on talking Ron began to compile all that had happened to him in the past five days, and that became his future, became all his future. If it were circumscribed, it was nonetheless his future, and days from now, even years from now, he knew if he were able to see himself clearly, he most certainly would see Brackston written in his eyes, across his forehead; he would even be able to smell it and taste it in his mouth.

Suddenly Ron glanced up and saw Alister looking at him indulgently. He must have given some indication he was leaving, because now Alister was on his feet, saying: "I'm sorry you have to leave so soon. I always enjoy talking to you."

The silence which followed served as a bridge upon which Ron and he could exchange a minuet of glances and innuendo, while a smile flickered on Alister's face. Rising to his feet, Ron had the opportunity to look at him closely. It was impossible to judge his sincerity; nevertheless, he was paranoid enough to favor slightly the hunch that Alister was lying through his false teeth.

Yet, it was obvious his surprise visit hadn't disturbed Alister at all. In fact, the man looked genuinely pleased.

"Thanks," Ron said, and thought, for nothing.

And with that, subtly yet unmistakably, Alister guided him to the door and shook hands, his eyes studying Ron in amusement.

FIVE

TWO LARGE SUITCASES AND ONE SMALLER ONE. KRISTY'S TOY box. His navy blazer and Chandal's trench coat. Ron surveyed these belongings which he had placed near the bedroom door. Without turning to look at Chandal, he could feel the air was full of nerve-shearing protest. "Did you check all the drawers?" he asked without looking up.

"Yes."

"Well, then—" He turned. "I guess we're all set." He watched as an indefinable sadness crept over her face.

"Do you want to eat dinner here before we leave?" she said. "Mrs. Taylor has offered—"

"I don't know." He glanced at his watch. It was almost eight o'clock. He had been shocked to discover, when he had returned to the house, that the tire on his station wagon was still flat. He had called Matthew Todd twice. First the man had said his helper had gotten drunk, but would be over soon. On the second call, which had been placed around six, Todd had said he would close the station soon and change the tire himself.

In the meantime Ron had taken a shower but had not felt completely clean when he'd stepped out of it. He had put on a pair of khakis, a short-sleeve dress shirt and had begun to pack. Though he'd become aware of massive hunger pangs, the desire to pack had been more pressing.

Now he moved to the window and peered out. The last rays of sun had begun to sink into the west. A single bell sounded a series of low plaintive tolls. Although he could barely see the town from the window, he held in his mind an image. He saw people drifting into the square, speaking rapidly, gesturing, completely absorbed in talk about tonight's crowning. Some would be carrying baskets of food or sandwich fixings in brown bags. Others would move around freely, hands and arms gesturing, bottles of whiskey sticking from their back pockets.

His eyes moved away from the town and drifted up to the hills. He stared at a landscape as desolate as any he could have invented. Mimi hadn't returned his call. Even if Mrs. Taylor had lied to him earlier when she had said no calls, the phone still hadn't rung in the past two hours.

"I don't understand why Mimi hasn't called back," he said, shaking his head in condemnation.

"Maybe she's busy."

"I told her it was important."

"Business matters?"

"What?"

"Is it something to do with business?"

"Yes, business."

"Something wrong?"

But Ron did not answer, not out of recalcitrance, but because he felt no desire to lie to her.

Listlessly, mindlessly, he leaned against the window frame. Thoughts came and went like someone had tossed a rock into a placid lake, sending ripples fanning out in all directions. Where was Nancy? Was she really sick as Mrs. Taylor had said, or had they done something to her? What actually did she know about the crowning? "I Was Queen. They"— Then again, maybe she hadn't written the message at all. Was Alister telling the truth when he'd said the carnival had nothing to do with the stone?

An amber light flickered in the hills, then went out. A Corpse Light? He wasn't sure. The more he thought about it, the more confusing and incoherent it all became; and that in itself frightened him most of all.

All at once he heard the bedroom door slam shut behind him and footsteps in the hallway. "Chandal!" he shouted, "Chandal!" The footsteps stopped. He threw open the door.

"What is it, Ron?" She turned to face him in the hallway.

"Please," he implored, "don't act like this."

"How am I acting?" she asked flatly.

"You seem so damn hostile about all this. As if I'm tearing you away from your home, for God's sakes."

"I'm not going to get into an argument with you. You want to leave, fine. You have made your decision. I'll abide by it. But I don't want to do any more yammering. I don't think I can take any more."

"Please, Del—I do not wish to stand here in the hallway discussing this."

"Nor do I."

Her stubbornness angered him, but he said quietly, "Then, please—at least come back into the room and let's discuss it calmly."

Chandal had turned pale. In a small voice she murmured, "All right, but I don't see what good it will do."

No sooner had she entered the bedroom than she began sobbing. "Okay," Ron said, "okay . . . You know I don't mean to hurt you." He brushed a few loose strands of hair away from her eyes. "Don't you?"

She raised her face to him. "Ron, what is wrong with us? Nothing seems right anymore. You and Kristy—that's all that means anything to me . . . But we don't seem to be able to talk to each other anymore. God, I looked at her today and thought—when we first had her all we could do was talk about how wonderful it was all going to be. But it hasn't turned out that way."

"That's not true—"

"Oh, God, Ron," Chandal said, drawing in a long shaky breath. "Don't you think I know what's going on? Practically the whole town knows."

"Knows what?"

"About you and Cynthia Harris. That you slept with her for Chrissakes!"

He breathed in sharply, on the verge of denying it. Images flooded his brain. Cynthia kneeling over him; murmurs of voices all around. Others had been there. Others had pinned him down. No, he had not slept with her. Not in the normal sense, and that was the issue. *That,* most of all, was the issue.

"Del, listen to me!" He grabbed hold of her hard. "Don't you see what's happening here? They're getting to you in the simplest possible way. With the simplest of all emotions. Jealousy, distrust. As long as you believe them, you'll never believe me. You'll always think I'm saying things to cover that up."

"Aren't you? Isn't that why you're so damned anxious to leave Brackston?"

Ron glared at her. "No, goddamn it, it isn't."

"Are you sure? Are you really sure it isn't your own guilt that's behind all this?"

Ron's reaction was quick and pained. "No, Del, it isn't."

She looked at him quietly, as if she were expecting him to continue. When no more was forthcoming, she shook her head. "Ron, I spoke with Cynthia Harris today. I talked with her in Denver."

Her words stunned him. "That's—that's impossible."

"Why, because you want it to be impossible? I wanted to hear it for myself. Cynthia Harris isn't dead, Ron. I spoke with her today."

"How? I mean . . ."

"I overheard the women talking today at Mrs. Wheatley's house. After everyone left, I had a talk with Beatrice. I told her what you told me. That Cynthia was dead. She laughed, Ron. Laughed." Speaking quietly, she kept her gaze on Ron's face. "One thing led to another. The next thing I knew she had dialed Cynthia in Denver."

Ron dropped wearily onto the bed. His entrapment was so clear and final that he moaned, "Oh, Del, Del . . ." He found it difficult to concentrate, and presently it became even harder, for he heard Chandal's voice saying: "I don't care about it, Ron. What's done is done. But to run away in the middle of the night only makes matters worse."

She slipped quietly to him, murmuring something he could not understand. Closer now, she whispered in an almost broken voice, "You still love me, don't you?"

"Yes," he said softly.

"Then it's enough. For me, it's enough. But we can't just sneak out of town like this. Let's show them we don't care what they think." She moved still closer and bent slightly from the waist. "I want to go to the crowning tonight," she said. "As if none of this has happened."

"No, Del—"

"Ron, we must. We must not run away." She kissed him lightly on the forehead. "I love you, Ron. You'll see. Everything will be all right between us now that this thing is out in the open. Everything. Years from now we'll laugh about all this. I know," she went on, "what you've been through. I know where I've failed you. Believe me, I know." Chandal's voice had changed. She was speaking to him from a reserve of tenderness and affection born of earlier years. And as he drifted with her soothing words, his body cooled and became numb, inert; and he was moved as deeply as he had been shocked just a moment previously.

Her voice trailed off as she moved to the door. She paused to smile at him, then left the room, the door closing softly behind her. Soon Ron could hear low voices filtering up from the kitchen and talking, amid the rattling of silverware and the clinking of china.

He touched the tips of his fingers to the corners of his eyes and noticed they were filled with tears. And he was ashamed. Even in the solitude of the bedroom he was ashamed. He began to talk inwardly to himself as though he were someone else, a friend trying to comfort him. *Stop it, for Chrissakes. You're going to be fine. Just fine,* and again he was ashamed, talking to himself that way.

The terrible silence of the world made his heart beat faster, and soon he saw, on the horizon, the blur of the moon. Not a moon, actually, but rather a bright smudge in an otherwise darkened sky.

Though the room was now dark, he could see the strange pattern of the wallpaper, and the glint of his reflection in the mirror. In the distance he heard the low hum of voices and laughter.

The night air was laden with other sounds; a faraway barking of a dog, the murmur of voices in the dining room below; a wail from Kristy as keenly heard as the ringing in his ears.

He rose slowly; though his head was light, he felt intensely sure of all his physical movements. There was no question in his mind about what he had to do. He must not wait until morning to leave Brackston; he had to leave tonight. But how? He glanced at his watch. It was twenty minutes to nine. He lifted his watch to his ear; its tick was rhythmic and soft. The numerals of the watch face glowed like tiny blue specks of dry ice. His chest began to tighten; he flicked on lights on either side of the bed. His eyes flickered at each burst of sudden light.

Unexpectedly there also came a sadness he could not overcome. He no longer felt any confidence in himself or in anything he thought. For it all seemed to be reduced to a situation without meaning, a pattern without sense, a game without rules that he could neither control nor comprehend. He was helpless.

Chandal is a person with a disturbed personality. Her actions last night speak for themselves. She is almost completely shattered now. Her ability to function is becoming more fitful. She has to work too hard to survive. We must . . . alleviate the pressure.

Ron tensed as he realized what it was he had just heard inside his head, and who had said those words. Dr. I. Luther, Chandal's former psychiatrist. Funny how when you remember you can't choose what it is you remember. Nowadays he forgot things from one day to the next. He even forgot people's names; yet he remembered some things . . . things that had happened years ago. Things that had been said. And he knew Brackston was a continuation of that past. Only now he wondered if it wasn't he who was going crazy.

He considered what the world looked like from inside a straitjacket. Not much different than it looked inside this room, he guessed. Just not as much furniture. His mind was wandering. He had to get hold of himself. After a breakdown comes the institutions, sometimes, not always. He remembered Chandal mentioning Lakewood Sanitarium once. Clean white sheets, clean white pillowcase, white-washed walls, Moorish style. And inside, light, bright, burning day and night, so that the attendants could see any change of expression . . .

Where was Dr. Luther, he wondered. What was he doing at that precise moment? I must write him when this is all over. Tell him what he probably already knows. That the first man who went crazy was Cain, and like all those who followed, he had good cause.

Laughter now in the hallway. The front door closed. The house fell silent. Stop them, he thought. Don't let them go to the carnival tonight. He remained frozen, isolated from all he ever was and all he ever hoped to be. He waited. Waited for Mimi to call. Waited for Matthew Todd to put the tire on the car. He waited, expecting, always listening.

His mind clouded.

The only thing he could do was to wait, to be made to wait, for something to happen.

SIX

DEATH CAME IN THE SMOG-GRAY LIGHT OF EARLY EVENING, cutting sharply through the suffocating air of Malibu Canyon.

The plum-colored Thunderbird rolled through empty streets for a while, then joined the commuters on the freeway and the tractor-trailers with their lights on.

Despite an overcast sky, Dwayne Clark insisted on running the T-Bird with the top down. Mimi Halpern sat relaxed, letting her hair and her Isadora Duncan scarf that trailed back from her throat blow freely in the breeze.

They had discussed everything of importance, and they were left with gossip and dreamy silences. Finally Dwayne leaned forward and fiddled with the radio, trying to separate static from music.

Somewhere between Malibu and Beverly Hills the highway narrowed, and automobiles darted nervously from lane to lane, avoiding the steel and double-wheeled monsters on either side. Mimi tensed a little and watched the other side of the highway and the trucks pouring out of Los Angeles. They looked more like animals than machines, angry animals, their drivers peering through the windshields with their expressionless eyes and their thin-lipped mouths.

When Dwayne turned off the highway, Mimi became aware again of the Thunderbird. She relaxed a bit and let herself sink into the richness of tufted leather.

"I hate expressways," she murmured.

Another turn and they were coming over the mountains, caught now behind a Cadillac that drifted over the double center white lines.

"Stupid bastard," Dwayne muttered. He tried to find a way around the car, but the road ahead was too narrow, the traffic coming in the opposite direction too thick.

"That's all right," Mimi said. "I'm in no hurry." She estimated that it would take at least another twenty minutes to reach home.

Dwayne ran his hand over his chin. "Cut myself all to hell shaving this morning," he said and continued to chat about how good business had been at the new nightspot he had opened in over the weekend. Not a big room, nevertheless . . . Mimi knew he was talking just for the sake of hearing himself talk and his chatter made her nervous. He really wasn't paying attention to his driving. She watched him turn dials again; a blues singer moaned in torch song style.

"How's Ron doing on his vacation?" he asked.

"Not so good. They're staying in a small town in Utah. Brackston. Ever hear of it?"

"No, but then I'm sure nobody else has either." Dwayne laughed, then frowned, still trying to get away from the Cadillac ahead of him.

Mimi sighed. "You really don't know how right you are. He called today. Asked me to check the town out."

"Oh? What's he thinking of doing? Opening a dinner theatre?"

"Very funny. He didn't say what he's thinking of doing. But I spent half the day checking all the available sources."

"And?"

"The big 0. There is no town of Brackston."

"Really? That's perfect for a dinner theatre . . ."

"At least I couldn't find it listed anywhere," she went on, pushing through Dwayne's patter. "Even Triple-A said they'd never heard of it."

"Well, maybe he gave you the wrong information."

"I don't think so. He was pretty specific. I'll know more when I call him tonight." She tensed. "I wish that guy ahead would make up his damn mind."

"Woman."

"Are you sure?"

"Have you ever seen a man drive like that?"

"Maybe he's drunk."

"Could be. Let's find out." Dwayne hit the accelerator.

From then on, things happened with terrifying speed. Mimi's eyes fluttered and she braced herself against the door. They came down a sharp grade and the car accelerated of its own momentum. She saw a straightaway ahead, and in the distance, a car waiting in a side road to the right.

"That woman had better stay put," said Dwayne, sounding his horn. The Cadillac moved closer to the right and slowed. Dwayne blasted the horn again and began to pass.

As he moved alongside of the Cadillac, the lady hit her horn. The horn blew and blew its warning.

"Up yours, sweetheart," Dwayne laughed.

"There's another car ahead!" Mimi shrilled.

"What?" Dwayne turned.

The driver ahead had stubbornly nosed his car onto the main road. His forward movement was imperceptible. Dwayne blasted the horn and swerved his T-Bird to the left, smashing his foot down on the brakes. The car's wheels found traction and suddenly skidded across the highway.

"We're going over!" he cried.

Mimi gasped and felt a tightness in her chest.

Dwayne tried to swing the wheel to the right, but it was too late. The car plunged down a steep slope, rolled over several times and crashed into the bottom of a deep ravine.

The universe exploded in a hideous, metallic shattering of jagged broken glass. A sharp pain ripped open Mimi's chest. She tried to move but she was pinned tight by the twisted metal around her. She knew she was about to die. Her pain gave way to numbness.

"Mimi . . ." Dwayne moaned weakly. "Oh, my God . . ."

His head dropped forward over the steering wheel, his mouth dripped blood, and then—his body went limp.

Mimi kept still, wondering for an instant where she was. Pain across her back and between her legs. Something . . . had happened. An accident.

Then reality came like a shock wave and she panicked. Through a windshield of shattered glass, she saw a mixture of smoke and flames, vicious flames that licked at the interior of the car. Moving her eyes, she saw Dwayne. His chest had been punctured by the broken steering wheel. He hung there, impaled on a sharp piece of broken metal.

"Oh, dear God . . ." she whimpered. She moved slowly, then quickly, trying to free herself. The flames roared higher. And then she heard it. The soft whispering of a child's voice.

"I hate you . . . hate you . . ." the voice whispered, then faded suddenly to mix with static over the radio.

Flames now, everywhere.

Tears sprang to her eyes. The flames crept nearer her face. She tried to force her body up, but she was pinned solidly. With her face drenched with blood and sweat, she screamed. Smoke bellowed and blurred her eyes. Her scream rose higher as the flames began to scorch her flesh.

"Blood turn to stone. Stone turn to fire. Burn, burn, burn . . ."

Horrified, Mimi stared at the radio. That was all she was capable of. Dumb amazement. It was impossible, she thought. Impossible, she screamed. Her scream rose high pitched and naked into the sky, a scream that was laced with unspeakable horror and intense physical pain.

"Oh, God!" she moaned. "Help me! PLEASE, GOD— HELP ME!"

The muscles in her face drew up into a knot, her body squirmed from side to side, fighting to free itself, fighting to keep away from the flames. Her fingers reached out, clawed at Dwayne's jacket. His head rolled over on its side to face her. His mouth fell agape.

"No! NO! NOOOOO!" she wailed.

Her scream rose in a single sustained note of agony, rose higher, more hysterical, until her scream, until the night sounds of the roadway, until the sound of crickets and the rustling of the leaves in the night wind all ceased.

Only the sound of roaring flames now.

And then, and then—the explosion.

SEVEN

NOW THE PRESSURE OF TIME BEGAN TO ASSERT ITSELF. MORE AND more stricken, glancing fearfully about, Ron continued to wait for Mimi to call. From time to time, he gazed from the window, looking out at the carnival lights illuminating the sky. From far off, he heard the jubilant voices and the sound of merrymaking. Fiddle strings exploded now, hung in the air like a rag doll, as if to say: Well, just because you're angry doesn't mean we can't enjoy a dance or two . . .

. . . Because the way things are going there ain't no hope for you.

Why? Why hadn't he stopped Chandal and Kristy from going to the carnival. It would have been so simple. Yet he had been unable to move. Unable to raise his voice in protest.

And still he remained frozen. Only his eyes moved from time to time in vacant madness.

That was all. Just his eyes.

The noise from the carnival rose higher, surrounded him, there was something happening to him, something *happening,* and he felt almost too exhausted to deal with it.

The hall clock chimed the half hour. It was very faint, so faint that he had almost missed it. This is crazy, he thought. He was insane to be sitting there waiting for Mimi to call. If he had any sense, he would get Chandal and Kristy out of Brackston. Now.

Then he realized he had made a mistake. *Stupid.* If it were going to be that easy . . .

The noise from the carnival was relentless. A terrific sound, and his ears rang with laughter carved from a gray-black space—what's happening, what—is—happening . . .

He flung himself away from the bed, clumsily reached for the telephone and dialed the operator. "Yes, yes—I'd like a Los Angeles number," he said and hurriedly gave the operator Mimi's number.

"Just a minute, please."

Ron stood with the receiver pressed hard against his ear. Come on, Mimi. Come on. He glanced nervously around the room. The light from the lamps on either side of the bed fell in odd shapes across the bedspread; as the rays crossed each other, each seemed to be challenging the other.

"Sorry," the operator said, "all the lines are busy."

"What?"

"All the lines to Los Angeles are busy."

"Please, this is urgent. Try again, would you?"

"Just a minute."

Ron turned suddenly, his attention drawn to the light footsteps in the hallway. "Del?"

There was no answer.

"Chandal, is that you?"

"They're connecting you now," said the operator.

"Chandal!"

"Just a minute, they're ringing the number."

"Damn it, Chandal!"

"There's no answer," said the operator.

"There must be an answer!" Ron snapped. "Keep ringing."

Every instant seemed an age while he waited. The carnival sounds came now in fierce bursts, and the glittering light in the distance flashed on and off, whirling around in the darkness. At times Ron could not seem to see an arm's length before him; but at others, as the carnival sounds grew louder, the room seemed to light up, as if the room itself had become part of the carnival atmosphere. A slight breeze came now through the room, fanning the curtains back.

In the midst of this Ron could hear footsteps retreating down the stairs.

"I'm sorry," the operator said, "but your party doesn't answer."

Ron paused for a moment, his eyes locked on the door. "Thanks," he said and lowered the receiver. With one quick lunge, he had reached the door and flung it open. Just as he stepped into the hallway, he heard someone move swiftly below. It was a soft step and upon it came the soft sound of a closing door. The front door.

He turned and charged down the stairs, stopped; at the living room window he saw the pale outline of a face materializing out of the darkness. Ghastly, the face hovered, its blue-white hue dripping with water, its eyes half dead with fear. The face seemed bathed in a blur of green light as if it were at the bottom of the ocean or in perpetual dusk. Startled though Ron was, he was absolutely certain he was staring into the face of Cynthia Harris.

All at once her eyes widened within the dark recesses of skin and bone, her lips cracked open, twisted into a demented grin, as yellow liquid erupted from the corners of her mouth.

She stood full-blown before him, like some ghoul risen from the dead.

Suddenly the doors leading from the terrace started to rattle and shake as if someone were desperately trying to get in. He tried to move, but something seemed to have him in a vise where he absolutely could not move any part of his body. He tried to cry out, but he was powerless to do so. Just when he thought he could not stand it any longer and was suffocating to death—something snapped.

Cynthia's shadow fell across his face as the whole house shook with destruction. He looked around quickly expecting to see pieces of china shattered, lamps or something, yet nothing was touched, nothing was disturbed, nothing was broken. Only a small red flower lay at his feet as though thrown there by unseen hands.

As he looked back toward the window, he felt the pressure around him releasing itself slowly. The face that had loomed so close, started to back away into the darkness like a lonely, tormented traveler. It moved further away still, until it vanished.

The house fell silent.

Hesitantly, Ron bent and picked up the flower.

EIGHT

DEAD OR ALIVE?

With fierce thrusts of his arms and hands, Ron pushed his way through the crowd. She had vanished as quickly as she had appeared. But he was sure of what he had seen. It had not been an hallucination, nor had it been a dream. Dreams don't cast shadows, and Cynthia had done just that.

Crowd roar rose soaring, screams of delight, hysterical.

Most of the crowd wore costumes this night. And masks. Some of the masks were actually head coverings, huge gaping things, eyes popping, teeth bared. Images darted in and out frenziedly, whirling in the cool-blue glare of the night as louder and louder came the sound of hissing, movement in rushes, here, gone; again here, crackling, hissing—then stilled.

Ron was instantly aware there was a different feeling about the carnival tonight. Less of the amusement park atmosphere. More of the . . . what?

He spun around as the crowd stilled; all became quiet. Perhaps that was why he had noticed it.

A huge wheel of fortune.

It stood out, its silver and gold symbols glittering against the subdued red velvet backdrop. It stood in place of the stage where the Punch and Judy Show had been on previous nights.

Ron watched fascinated for a moment. Then his eyes roamed the crowd restlessly. Why was it, all of a sudden, so deadly quiet? Everything seemed to have stopped, and the wheel, as it turned, seemed to creak and groan under the weight of its own immensity.

Now Ron smelled the stench. The oddly familiar, acrid, spicy smell of lilac. And another, more sickening odor he suddenly realized was that of fear. His own. And now he smelled nothing at all. It was almost impossible to breathe.

236

Sleep. Tonight . . . I must get some sleep.

For a long moment Ron thought he had spoken aloud. He turned to stare at the shadowy figures that loomed large and small, watching them shimmer in a thin veil of yellowish light, until finally they resolved themselves into other people, all involved in listening to the woman in black call out the number.

Ron fought back his drowsiness.

"Six," the woman in black called out.

A loud drone and roar from the multitude, raucous laughter which they kept up until the wheel was spun again, its silver and gold symbols glittering—only this time Christ's cruciform body was nailed to it, leaving bloodstains on the floor below. As the wheel turned, Christ's body spun around slowly . . . and then the wheel rolled to a stop with a rattling, smacking sound. Christ came to rest upside down.

"Sixty-six," the voice boomed.

Something inside of Ron surged and then came plummeting down. In his palm, dazzling him with facets of red fire, was the tiny flower left by the ghostly visitation. Confusion burst in his head, sweat on his face; he stared at the number sixty-six. It held him nearly hypnotized.

A lunatic impulse came to him, to call out suddenly, to scream: *"I've won! I've won!"* No, he warned himself. Move. Move as fast as possible away from here. He lurched forward, staggered slightly, then clutched the edge of the platform to prevent himself from toppling over.

"For heaven sakes!" Isabelle Carroll shrilled. "There you are. We've been waiting for you!"

Ron stared vacantly into her eyes. She looked wildly excited. He grinned. His mind had divided, it seemed, had become two separate camps. Part of it remained horror-struck. The other part marvelled that he was able to grin and calm down and think reasonably.

The expression of excitement on Isabelle's face had not changed. "The selecting of the queen is almost upon us," she said. "At the pavilion. You mustn't miss it. You do want to see it, don't you?"

Ron did not answer for a long time. He looked at Isabelle carefully, scrutinizing her. He held up the flower. "Do you know what type of flower this is?"

Isabelle glanced at it nervously. "Odd, isn't it? I believe . . . yes, it's some sort of poppy."

Poppy, poppy, Ron muttered to himself. Without apparent reason, his eyes had begun to film over.

"Are you all right?" asked Isabelle. Her eyes glowed, the pupils sharp black pinpoints.

"Yes. Why?"

"You look so tired. You're not sick, are you?"

"No," he said and whirled away, stuffing the flower into his shirt pocket, oblivious of the laughter shrilling about him in waves.

"Ron, wait!" Isabelle shouted after him.

He never looked back, never acknowledged the little lady who panted after him, who was much too sedate and genteel to keep up with his brisk pace.

Farther on, the green and red neon lights of the concession stands turned the darkness hazy with reflected light. He moved through the crowd faster now, Alister Carroll's words tolling in his head like a muffled bell. *"What you've learned in the city will do you no good here. The mountains have their own ways."* Perhaps that had been Ron's problem all along. Simple everyday logic wasn't any good here.

He stopped, frowned mentally, and looking at the glittering midway, the frantic bustling clutter of the throng, smelling the intermittent odors of sausages, steak and peppers, pizza in the stifling air, he thought: But if logic wasn't any good—then what the fuck was?

He turned, took a few more steps, and ducked into the pavilion. About ten feet inside the door where the massive rows of chairs began, he was stopped by a solid wall of jostling people. He started to push his way in, then stopped.

"Alone?" Sheriff Nash asked softly.

Ron turned to face him directly. The man seemed a bit edgy and appeared to be withering in the heat. Thank God, Ron thought; he'd finally found someone else in Brackston who sweated.

"Chandal and Kristy, have you seen them?" he asked.

Nash was about to say something when Ron felt a tug on his arm. A young boy stood alongside him. He wore a deep wine-red, one-piece coverall.

"Are you Mr. Talon?" the boy asked.

Ron nodded.

"Come with me," he said, and proceeded to push his way gently but firmly through the crowd, opening a path that enabled Ron to move with ease behind each step he took.

Twenty or so little children, each wearing the one-piece coverall, stood at various intervals, ogling each other, the crowd, and, Ron guessed, were acting as ushers. Here and there individual voices called out, "Marsha! We want Marsha!" Or, "Lucinda! Lucinda!" Other voices took up the cry, adding their own preference, until the great hall was shuddering with girls' names.

The noise inside the hall was loud now, almost deafening, a crescendo of ecstasy accompanied by faces that seemed possessed with happiness. The sound moved in huge waves between the walls of the hall, pulsating, and Ron could only follow the boy in dumb silence, watching, listening.

The lights began to lower slightly as the boy elbowed his way past the last cluster of people. Thereupon he indicated to Ron an empty seat in the front row. He raised his arm slowly, grandly. Your seat, sir, he conveyed proudly with large eyes. Ahead, on the stage, there was a great shower of white drops, pelting, sparkling splashes of light from a massive revolving crystal ball. It hung like a giant moon over all.

Ron wondered how the boy had been able to pick him out of the crowd, and then realized he had simply been told by someone. But who? He was about to ask him but the boy had vanished. Looking around, Ron wondered where Chandal and Kristy were. He stared into the crowd and saw the multitude lift their faces, smiling ecstatically. Confused, he sat.

He glanced around and saw Beatrice Wheatley. She was seated in the second row to his left, surrounded by a group of unknown figures who were all stockily built men with firm, square faces and dressed in work clothes. She wore a dark sackcloth dress and a red headband across her forehead. He had not seen her earlier because of the crowd that kept milling about in the aisles. She saw him now and broke into a smile. She greeted him with a wave of her bony-thin hand.

Ron turned and caught glimpses of Alister Carroll; he sat very still, gazing straight ahead, a thin smile on his face. Lou Harris was seated to Ron's right next to Matthew Todd.

Todd's heavy shoulders stood out quite sharply against the thinner men who surrounded him.

But where was Chandal? And Kristy? And Mrs. Taylor? There were two empty seats next to Alister Carroll. Perhaps . . .

Suddenly there was a roll of kettledrums. Above it the sound of flute pipes. The kettledrums reached an impossible crescendo as the hall was plunged into total darkness. Then someone close by said, "Ssssh!" loudly, once, and the hall was all at once silent.

A pink spotlight winked on. All stared upward, gazing in open-mouthed fascination like a crowd of spectators at an air show. A small woman came running onto the stage. There was a smile on her face and she nodded her head in acknowledgment of the hushed greeting uttered as she stepped into the spotlight.

Her eyes were luminous, blinding, as she welcomed everyone to the Forty-Fifth Crowning of the Carnival Queen. She looked thin and frail, but her voice boomed mightily from the loudspeakers on either side of the stage. Her speech was short, charming and before long, she began announcing each contestant. Various colored lights washed over the area as each child was led onto the stage.

The first child looked frightened, but she walked very straight alongside her mother, and the spokeswoman touched her gently as she went along to the other side of the stage. Behind her another mother and daughter, the child appearing a little dazed. Behind them there followed more than half a dozen mothers with children, all dressed in matching outfits, all trying to smile past the fear of the moment.

God, oh, God, Ron moaned inwardly, thunderstruck. Sweat burst out on his face again, nausea rose inside him, gripping his intestines, draining his face away to a milky-white pallor. The contestants—they were all children! Girls five to ten years of age. They stood like young adults, their faces heavily coated with rouge, lipstick and mascara. Their thin little-girl legs stood surprisingly steady in spiked high-heeled shoes. Some of their hands posed tantalizingly on outthrust hips. Good Christ! It wasn't possible.

"And last but not least," the woman said, "our final

entry . . . Ms. Kristy Talon. Our guest from beyond the ridges."

Ron started. Chandal looked straight ahead as she led Kristy onto the stage. Through startled eyes he saw Kristy give him a smile. Chandal stopped and positioned Kristy in front of her and he thought he could see her lips quiver. Kristy moved closer to her mother and reached out with her right hand and took hold of Chandal's hand. She held onto it for what seemed a very long time, and Ron saw Chandal nod in his direction and smile.

The selection process was brief and painful. "Ahhhhh" from the crowd as each child recited a poem. "Ohhhhh" . . . as each child paraded down a small runway, bowed gracefully, some not so gracefully, to the six judges who sat like statues off to the side regarding each child for a moment with vacant, heavy-lidded eyes. Smiles, good-naturedly, demurring; frowns slightly as each girl's description was read aloud.

Those who could dance, did. "Ahhhhh." Those who could not, sang. "Eeeeee." The crowd, leaping, roared its joy at the end of each performance. Finally Kristy stepped forward. A blue spotlight hit her full, held; the crowd waited, quiet, expectant.

Smiling distantly, she began to sing. Nodding its approval, the crowd listened, swayed. Ron could feel his legs trembling as she reached for the high notes. Perfect. She sang perfectly, confidently.

Fingers tapped Ron lightly on the shoulder. He turned. A thin finger pointed across the hall, leading Ron's gaze to Beatrice Wheatley who nodded to him with great satisfaction. Others around him spoke. "Oh, she's darling." "Such a delight." The words were picked up by others until they became an ecstatic whisper of sorts. A moment later there was silence once again from the crowd.

Everyone stared admiringly at Kristy.

As she finished her song, she bowed elegantly, and returned to her mother's side. High screams of delight from the crowd, ear shattering applause. Ron could only clap his hands twice, sharply, and then his arms fell limp at his sides.

". . . Well, folks, that was certainly a wonderful performance. But they've *all* been. It's been a terrific evening *all* the way, good and spirited with no exceptions. Over in the corner, our judges are working furiously now, trying to decide who our next queen will be. In just a moment, we, the people of Brackston, will have a new queen!"

A sudden high bloodroar from the crowd as everywhere people began to talk, scream, laugh; they began throwing confetti into the air, calling out to their neighbors. Hoots rose from behind masks, jeering—others crouched in the aisles, gnomelike, dressed in costumes and swilled liquor from flasks and bottles.

Ron shook loose from the crowd and shifted his attention to Chandal. She stood straight, looking at him. Her hands which rested on Kristy's shoulders were trembling. Kristy yawned, looked around calmly, and appeared bored.

From backstage a young boy dashed forward and swung into a locomotive of information. After handing the spokeswoman a slip of paper and after whispering into her ear, he dashed offstage again.

The great hall grew quiet.

The spokeswoman stepped forward and tapped the microphone to make sure it was working, or maybe she just did it for effect. Whatever the case, it had a startling impact on the crowd. Instantly there was a tremendous explosion of voices.

"Tell us! Tell us who will be queen!"

She looked over the crowd with calm austerity, nodded toward the judges. Then glancing down at the paper she held in her hand, she spoke:

"On behalf of myself, the judges, the Ruling Elders, we wish to thank you all for your kind and generous cooperation this evening. Our children are our future. They are our destiny. We place our trust and our hope in their hands. It goes without saying that the judges had a difficult time in making their selection this evening. Yes, very difficult. But they have reached their decision."

The crowd gasped in delight.

Around him Ron became aware of people staring at him and pointing in his vicinity. He crossed his legs painfully and stared straight ahead, perplexed, feeling impossibly conspicuous.

With suppressed elation, like a young girl who has just

been asked out on her first date, the spokeswoman said, "And the winner is . . ."

Ron held his breath.

"MS. KRISTY TALON!" the woman shrieked, her words echoing back and forth throughout the immeasurable length of the great hall, terrifyingly.

Oh, God, Ron thought. "Please, dear God, no," he moaned. In great pain, he looked up and saw Chandal kiss Kristy gently on the forehead. Kristy was smiling shyly, squirming a little.

Then Chandal nodded tightly in Ron's direction, smiling slightly, as gushes of tears streamed down her cheeks.

Around Ron people started to move forward, shuffling respectfully toward him. Beatrice Wheatley hesitated an instant, then started to move down the aisle with Lou Harris and Matthew Todd and many others. They were all coming his way.

As he stared about him with growing fear, Mrs. Taylor appeared, smiling, her starfish of diamonds winking in the multicolored haze of floodlights.

The noise and confusion was intense. Ron found it difficult to maintain his calm and kept glancing around at the crowd of people who all seemed to have their eyes fixed on him. Some peered jealously. Others with elation. All greatly involved in the moment.

"I know, I know . . ." Mrs. Taylor said. "Isn't it wonderful?"

"Wonderful! Just wonderful!" Beatrice Wheatley said in a low, husky voice.

Todd and Harris nodded their congratulations.

"Oh. They're going ahead with the ceremony," Mrs. Taylor said.

Everyone around Ron started down toward a small platform now, leaving Ron sitting by himself. At the far edge of the stage he suddenly saw Nancy, dressed in a long flowing white gown, moving into view.

"Nancy!" he called out.

She made a despairing gesture, then moved out of sight behind the black velvet curtain which had been lowered in front of the stage. The curtain rippled now as though there was a great flurry of activity taking place behind it.

The lights darkened a little. "Ahhhhh" from the crowd as again they peered up at the stage with oblique respect. Gradually some of the crowd began to sway with the slow rhythm of a chant, intoning the word more and more rapidly. "Kristy . . . Kristy . . . Kristy . . ." Other voices took up the cry until the hall was shuddering with the chant: "KRISTY!"

The lights dropped still lower, almost to darkness; slowly the curtain rose, its black folds lifting like the wings of a hawk, soaring into the archway above. A hot red spotlight beamed, focused on a huge stone that had been moved onto the stage.

The multitude fell hushed.

Slowly, ever so slowly, a tiny form began to appear atop the stone. The form rose as if being lifted by an escalator. Rose higher, until Kristy emerged full-blown, standing above all things. She was cloaked in gold, a wondrous mantle which flowed from her shoulders in huge, shimmering folds. In her hands she held a small bouquet of red flowers. Her fingers were jeweled, her features radiant; she looked about the hall with authority.

All at once Nancy appeared below. She hesitated before she started to climb the stone steps leading to the top. She moved slowly, ghostlike, her white gown catching fire as she appeared next to Kristy in the red spotlight. She was carrying a gold crown on a blue velvet pillow. With great ceremony, Kristy knelt.

"Ahhhhh" murmured the crowd, gaping, panting, watching Nancy place the crown carefully on the head of their new queen.

Then backing away, Nancy descended the steps and faded into the darkness, the last flickers of whiteness lingering in Ron's dazed eyes.

In the distance bells had begun to toll.

Instantly there was total darkness except for the searing spotlight, hard to look upon, which was now a shattering yellow. Kristy smiled in satisfaction; rose. Ushers rushed down the aisles, darted among the crowd and began handing them little snakes which they held wriggling in their hands.

Kristy slowly raised her hand in a gesture of benediction, her features serious and beautiful. Ron was stunned to see people falling to their knees in the aisles, bowing their heads, holding their snakes carefully.

The crystal ball above, suspended, began to revolve slowly, sending a million specks of light dancing in the darkness. Kristy peered out catlike. Voices like thunder shouted:

"Behold—the—QUEEN!"

There was a sudden roll of kettledrum, insistent, and above it Ron could hear the bells tolling jubilantly. The crowd grew quiet. Their silence was followed by a tremendous explosion and a fierce mass of flames rose from behind the stone; the crowd shrank back, but still gazed at the child standing in the burning light. All around her now, flames. She smiled upon her subjects in genial majesty. Then, one at a time, she began to toss the red flowers she held into the crowd.

They scrambled frantically for them as though they were gold, fighting among themselves like animals. Kristy gestured for silence. The crowd grew still. Just as suddenly the drums ceased, and a blood-red spotlight hit Kristy with full force.

Overcome, transfixed, Ron watched her bow. Suddenly the multitude rose. Those who were wearing hats or masks removed them. Others remained kneeling in the aisles with their heads bowed. A moment's hesitation and then Kristy was gone, having disappeared behind the great stone.

The crowd went wild.

"Marvelous, wasn't it? Just marvelous!" Alister leaned over the back of Ron's chair and smiled. "I'll tell you, I've never seen anything quite like it."

Mrs. Taylor rushed forward, shouting, "A masterpiece. A masterpiece!"

The lights began to come up slowly. Ron sat in awe-strickened silence for a long time. His cheeks burned with humiliation. He bowed his head, as though crushed by the weight of the entire experience.

People insisted on shaking his hand, their tongues wagging, their eyes popping, their smiles manic and distorted. Transported by joy, they milled about, until finally they began moving out the front door.

As the crowd dwindled, the stillness increased. Ron remained seated, staring straight ahead at the stage, at the papier-mâché stone, the red streamers which had been used to create the fire effect. The snakes, he now realized, were also fake. One lay at his feet. It was made of rubber.

Wearily he got to his feet. He sighed heavily and moved off to a side door marked: Backstage.

The small stairway led to an area crowded with equipment, cables, and lights. A door at the rear was propped open, revealing the carnival grounds lost in its own shadows. Some of the mothers stood near the doorway talking. Others were still coming down the stairs Ron had just used.

"Congratulations," a voice said.

"Thank you," Ron said flatly.

"She's so lovely," another voice said.

"Our best queen ever."

Ron nodded.

A few doors stood ajar, revealing small rooms, most being used as dressing rooms. People continued to stand around. Most stared at Ron with a heavy, grudging wonder, a sullen envy.

To the rear of the hallway was a door marked: Talon. A crown had already been hammered into place. In gold lettering was inscribed the word: Queen.

Ron was about to open the door when a large dog sprang from a darkened corner. It bared its teeth and began to growl, as if it had assumed personal responsibility as watchdog and had come across a dangerous trespasser. Ron drew back in confusion.

"Hey, keep that goddamn dog quiet," someone yelled.

A young boy moved beside the dog and fastened a leash to its collar. "Sorry," he said and led the dog away.

Almost before Ron had entered the room, Chandal was in his arms sobbing. She muttered over and over again, "Ron, she's queen. She won, can you believe it? She's queen. Queen."

Ron looked at Kristy over Chandal's shoulder. She looked terribly exhausted. Her eyes were swollen and her complexion was now a ghostly white.

"Come on," Ron said softly. "Let's go home."

They slipped out the back door and into the night. Ron stood for a moment uncertain as to which way to walk.

"Wasn't that fun?" Chandal whispered and Kristy nodded.

Ron glanced around nervously, still feeling a restless sense of anticipation, expectancy, that suddenly seemed out of place on such a calm night. It was like coming out of a movie after having been absorbed in the picture so that the outside world had ceased to exist for a while . . . And now, here it was. A cool night, waiting.

A breeze had sprung up and little swirls of dust raced along the ground scattering bits of paper and debris and a few programs that had been discarded. The word "queen" peered out at Ron from one of the programs. A reminder that on this day, Kristy Talon, age six, had been crowned Queen of the Carnival of Summer.

"Why, Chandal? Why?"

Chandal rolled over lazily in the bed. "Please, Ron. Not anymore tonight. They wanted Kristy. They begged me to enter her in the contest. What harm has been done? None that I can tell." The sound of her words died away gently like the most finalizing of final statements ending all discussion.

Ron could only shake his head. Moments later Chandal was asleep. For Ron, it took longer.

NINE

WHEN RON AWOKE, THE SUN WAS JUST BEGINNING TO SLANT into the room. He shifted his weight cautiously so that he would not disturb Chandal, and picked up his wristwatch from the side table. It was just after eight.

He left the bed. It was going to be another hot day. The room was already beginning to warm. He turned to stare at Chandal. For the first time in days she was not the first to rise.

He moved quietly to the chair and got into his trousers and shirt. He was just putting on his shoes when Chandal stirred. He looked at her; she turned over, but did not wake.

He crossed into the bathroom and splashed cold water on his face. After drying off, he looked into Kristy's room. This morning she was in bed, lying asleep with her arms around her puppet.

A queen, he thought, and shuddered.

The day was bright, not a cloud in the sky. Ron had moved back into his own bedroom and was now staring from the window. There was a gentle but rapid transformation as the sun rose. His body became motionless, as if held immobile by an unseen force. He was rooted to the spot, yet without any sensation of paralysis.

Minutes passed, and with the chiming of the hall clock, objects began to fade from his vision. There was nothing between him and the sun, not even a void, not even emptiness. Finally the balcony itself faded and what he was viewing was a giant screen on whose white surface images flashed. He saw Cynthia Harris go over the edge. Again; then, saw her face peering at him as a ghost of what she had once been. Her face melted quickly into Tyler Adam's face; the transformation was a gentle one, both having the same ghostly pallor. Tyler Adam appeared to have tears in his eyes.

"The Seeing Eyes," someone whispered.

Kristy appeared wearing her crown. For some strange reason, Ron found himself smiling. Perhaps because the crown she wore sat crooked atop her head and covered one eye. Her eyes grew larger as his smile diminished. Nancy's face loomed out, grew larger and larger in his mind's eye, but he himself seemed to be shrinking. Smaller. Smaller.

And that was the point, wasn't it? What he feared most. That he might disappear from his own consciousness, just as the others seemed to be disappearing and that he would be left drifting in his own insanity.

A sudden panic arose in him. He shook his head violently. Reality smacked him across the face.

Below, he watched Matthew Todd close the garden gate and begin to walk quite slowly away from the house. Dressed in a pair of greasy coveralls, he shifted his weight to one side, seeming to limp slightly on his left leg.

Ron backed away from the window and ran from the bedroom and down the stairs. He never took a breath, his legs moving almost as fast as his thoughts, until he'd thrown open the front door.

"Mr. Todd!" he shouted. His voice was harsher than he would have liked, hysterical and shrill.

Matthew Todd smiled pleasantly and kept on walking.

"Mr. Todd!" he yelled.

"Sorry about last night, Mr. Talon," he said mildly. "The crowning always gets me a little crazy. Congratulations again. A lovely queen. Prettiest ever." He swung his body into his pickup truck. "But you're all set now."

"What?"

"Your car is all set to go. I even fixed your tailpipe. Didn't charge you for it though. I left the keys and the bill with Mrs. Taylor. You can just leave her a check."

Ron turned and stared at his car. It was true. The right rear tire had been changed. Someone had even washed the car and had parked it in such a way as to show it off. He thrust his hands into the pockets of his perfectly fitted white trousers and pointed with his head.

"Someone's washed it," Ron noted.

"Tyler Adam. I gave him a few dollars."

"Is he still around?"

"Went back into the hills, I think. The trouble with Tyler," he said confidentially, "is he still thinks it's 1929. Ask him, he'll tell you straightaway—Hoover is president of these United States." He shut the door to his pickup. "Well, you be careful driving over those hills. And if I don't get to see you again, well . . ."

Ron was still looking at his car when Todd started his engine. "Yes, sir," he said and let loose the emergency brake. "The hardest thing in Tyler's life," he said with a chuckle, "is that he doesn't know prohibition's been repealed."

Laughter and engine noise roared, mixed, then faded away down the drive.

By eleven o'clock Ron had taken most of the luggage down to the car. As he put the largest of the suitcases into the luggage space, he glanced up. Chandal stood poised at the window watching him. There was a strange glow to the glass which made it appear as though she were standing in a freshly watered garden, yet her face remained dead white.

Ron felt suddenly impaled by her gaze. Whatever she was thinking, whatever she was feeling, he had never seen such a look on a human face as on Chandal's. And as she watched, she moved her lips, quickly and jerkily, waited a moment, then disappeared from view.

It might have been a moment, or it might have been an hour. He wasn't really sure how long it was before he finally climbed the stairs for the last suitcase.

When he opened the bedroom door Chandal was lying face down across the bed. The floorboard creaked as he stepped into the room. Chandal turned with a start to face him. She did not say anything, but he could see abject pleading in her eyes.

Slowly, quietly, he moved across the room to the window and looked out. From the corner of his eye he saw her lie back again, her forehead deeply furrowed.

Ron sighed. "Is Kristy ready to go?"

"She's with Mrs. Taylor saying good-bye."

"I'll just go take a look," he said and turned.

"For Chrissakes, Ron. Have we been brought to this? Spying on people?"

Ron held back his anger. "Ah, I just want to make sure she's all right." He stole a quick look at her and added hastily, "You still don't believe me, do you?"

Chandal cleared her throat. "I've listened very carefully to what you've had to say."

"Then what makes you hesitate?"

"I didn't think I had. I merely—"

"Then you had better take a good look inside yourself." He reached for the last suitcase.

She thought for a moment. "I guess I feel there's a reasonable explanation for all that you've said."

Ron stared at her across the small space between them. "These people are using us, Del. Don't you understand that?"

Her eyes dropped for a moment. "I don't know," she said softly. "They've been nothing but kind to Kristy and me. My God, they took a complete stranger outside their own community and made her queen."

"Why, Del? Why do you think they did that?"

She looked up at him. "Because, in all honesty, she was the prettiest."

Ron sighed. "Yeah, right," he said and turned to face the window again. He did not move. He heard her coming toward him. Soft steps that weren't in any hurry. She was wearing a perfume today he could not identify; an odd scent. She slid in front of the balcony doors gracefully, facing him, away from the sun. Her hair haloed in the stark light. "She is special, you know."

"What?"

She'd said it so softly that even this close he had not heard her. She repeated what she had said.

"In what way?" he wanted to know.

Chandal shrugged. "Many ways." She gave him a little conspiratorial smile. "Looks, intelligence . . ."

"I don't believe this!" he said excitedly. "For the last six days we've been trapped here, and you're—"

"Trapped?"

"That's right. Trapped." He looked into her eyes pleadingly. "Please, Del—don't you understand? It's all beginning again. The past—it's all here. I can feel it. Why can't you?"

Abruptly she turned away. "Because that was seven years ago. Oh, Christ! Seven years," she cried. "Can't we get past all that? Once and for all—forget it?"

"Del, I'm pleading with you—let's not argue. Let's just get Kristy and leave here now, before it's too late."

"No—no, I can't." She shook her head. "I can't leave here now."

"What do you mean, you can't?"

"How?" she shrilled.

"How? Just get in the goddamn car and leave. That's how." He reached for her.

Chandal drew back, her face tense, her eyes riveted on him.

"Kristy has been crowned queen," she said slowly. "These people have given her that honor. Tomorrow is the last day of the carnival. Kristy must be there. We must be there. We can't let these people down. Oh, Ron—they would hate us. Always hate us."

Ron became quite calm now. The feeling seeped through him gradually, each part of his body touched by a local anesthetic, deadening his emotions and sharpening his senses. He was all at once possessed by the power of cool-headed logic. "All right, Del. But hear me out. Seven years ago—"

"Don't, Ron—"

"We're responsible for something, Del. No matter how grim the situation."

"We agreed—no explanations."

"The old lady in the brownstone, Elizabeth Krispin—"

"She has nothing to do with me! She's gone. Stop trying to push me into a thumb-sucking, analysis-ridden category."

"It was you who was in the clinic!"

Chandal turned away in desperation.

Ron hesitated. "I'm sorry. I—I shouldn't have said that."

She wheeled around to face him. "The last of all human freedoms—the ability to choose one's attitude in any given circumstance. I choose to be free of her. Free of that woman. Just as I choose to be free of the past."

Ron looked at her sharply. "No, Del . . . we're not free. Not of her, not from the past."

"I think we are," she said flatly.

He could see she was visibly shaken. Sweat had begun to cover her forehead. She rubbed her arms instinctively, shivering as if caught by a sudden chill.

"All right, then." He sat. "I'll make you a deal. I'll ask you to do something that anyone ought to be able to do. If you can do it, I'll stay in Brackston until Saturday. And if you can't, we'll get in the car now and leave. Is it a deal?"

"Name it," she said.

"Tell me about your past," he said. "The old woman in the brownstone."

Chandal laughed. "Tell you about her? I can write a book."

"Good. You sit down on the bed. I'll stay seated here."

Chandal dropped on the bed. "This is all quite silly, you know."

"Maybe yes. Maybe no. Describe her. Tell me what she was like. Looks, personality, you know? Give me an image. Did she look like a Duncan Phyfe chair—a Victorian couch, an armadillo?" He paused. "If you're free of her, then you should be able to tell me what she was like."

Chandal let loose a ventilating breath. Her hands began to shake, and she quickly folded them together. Ron lighted a cigarette and held out the pack. She shook her head.

Several minutes later he glanced at his watch. He flexed his legs and pressed the soles of his shoes solid to the floor. Chandal's fingernails had begun to dig into the flesh of her hands.

She smiled nervously. "What's the reward for prolonged observation?"

He stared at her without smiling.

Chandal said, "She was . . . interesting looking."

"She was nice looking. Beautiful eyes."

"Nice, beautiful—I didn't say that!"

"No, I did." He paused. "Did you enjoy her company?"

"She was irritating."

"Why?"

"She just was, that's all."

"Everyone is irritating at times."

Chandal sneered. "Is that supposed to make me feel better?"

"Better, worse, it's a simple statement of fact."

"Simple statement of fact—I like that. The fact is, that when I was with her I got this gnawing kind of pain in my stomach. It was like having a rat in my belly which was methodically eating through my diaphragm trying to get to my heart. But it wasn't a rat at all—it was her with that insipid smile of hers." She paused. "She was horrible."

"Then why did you let her . . . possess you?"

"Possess," she said in a faraway tone.

"Yes, Del. Have you forgotten? You were—"

"So now you want us to start calling each other names. Neurotic, schizophrenic, hebephrenic, obsessive and so on. All right, it sounds like fun. My turn."

Ron shook his head. "I didn't mean that."

"GOD!" Chandal burst into tears. "I'm sick to death of you! Of always forcing me into the past. Leave it alone. For Chrissakes, leave it alone. It hurts . . . it really hurts." She tried desperately to wipe the tears away. "But you don't seem to know or care. I'm tired of the past. I want it ended. Now!"

He took hold of her. "Del, don't you understand? *Can't* you understand?"

"Understand what!" she screamed.

"That you're obsessed with this goddamn town! Can't you see that? Or maybe you do see it. Why, Del? Why are you accepting this?" He stopped suddenly, his eyes riveted on her face. "You're part of it, aren't you? Del?" He shook her violently. "Tell me what is going on. You know, don't you! Tell me what you know!"

She stood silent, her eyes brimming with tears. And something else. A dazed look. A vacant stare as wide as the canyons beyond. A stare that was impossible to fill.

He nodded. He understood. He had hoped that what he had said would have meant something, but of course it hadn't. He understood. For the first time he fully realized she no longer wanted anything but to remain in Brackston. She was obsessed with the town as she'd been possessed with the old woman in the brownstone years ago. The inevitable somehow had a way of being . . . inevitable.

Moments later, Chandal followed him out to the car. She stood motionless by the car door. "Do you really need to get away?"

"For a while. I'll be back soon. I just need time to clear my head." He slipped the key into the ignition. He tried to suppress the sob which rose in his throat, desperately tightening the muscles of his larynx.

"Kiss me once more," she said.

He leaned out the window and kissed her. There was a moment's hesitation. Neither one knew quite what to do. What to say. Finally he started the car, shifted into drive. There were still a few tears on Chandal's cheeks. They caught the sun. Glistened.

"I'll see you later," he said. He aimed the car out the drive. He drove slowly at first, easing away from the house.

When he looked into the rearview mirror, Chandal was gone.

He hit the accelerator hard.

TEN

THROUGH THIN-LASHED WATERY EYES THE OLD MAN, UNCOMPRE-hendingly, searched his wife's face for a clue as to how far his illness had progressed.

"Rest now," the old woman said and placed his hand on his chest so that he could feel his heart beating. Unwanted truths would not be spoken. Not by her. She sighed and looked away.

"He—he will be gone soon," the nurse whispered, and the whisper itself was a prayer of sorts. She stared sympathetically at the old woman, who stared as sympathetically back. Yet it seemed to the nurse that this curiously small woman was actually taking relish in her husband's dying.

The old woman laughed softly. "You will see," she said, "he will get better. Much better. His illness will not exhaust him. He is inexhaustible."

The woman paused for a moment to stare at the vase resting on the dresser which contained one red flower of monstrous size and beauty. "Like his flower," she breathed. "Just like his flower. Inexhaustible."

Something quickened within the old woman's chest walls, like the spitting and crackling of fire. It was challenge. How often in life, she wondered, had she come to this point. Many times. She smiled, the room's dazzling array of sunlight evoking tiny flickers of yellow from the draperies upon her face. Still the old woman's face remained ghostly and without texture under the soft, dull waves of her hair. Only her eyes moved about the room with vibrance. She glanced at the hypodermic syringe, wrapped in cotton, on the nightstand.

The old man turned his head suddenly, moaned almost inaudibly. His wife nodded.

"He's in pain," she said without looking at the nurse. Instead she quickly moved to the bed, bent over her husband, watching intently. She studied his thin, aging face, with the deep furrows of purple under the eyes, the purplish glow of his mouth and cheeks. He appeared to be hardly breathing now. No, hardly breathing at all.

The nurse took up the syringe, shot a few drops from the tip, then plunged the needle firmly into the old man's arm. A slight trickle of blood gushed forth as she withdrew the needle.

The old woman nodded with satisfaction as her husband seemed to instantly begin to rally; his body gave a quick jerk, his chest heaved in and out suddenly, as if in haste. Then his breathing evened out, grew more steady, more determined, as if by a hidden command from his wife. He moved his head to gaze at the nurse. Caught in the fragmented half-world between life and death, he stared in puzzlement now at the strange woman dressed in white, who hovered at his bedside.

"There!" said his wife proudly. "I told you. He'll be just fine now, won't you, dear heart? Just fine. Why, in a couple of hours he'll be sitting up. Won't you, dear? Won't you?" she coaxed.

The nurse dabbed the blood away with alcohol and cotton, after which, she placed a flesh-colored bandaid over the puncture. This done, she quickly retreated to take up a position beside the door.

The room fell silent, muffled; there was not a sound to be heard. Not even the thin voices of the children who at that hour usually played along the wall and in the vast empty field out back.

When the woman turned her gaze from her husband to the great outdoors, the white-hot scene lay spread before her: to the right the ancient wall wound its way upward to the top of the mountain, its steps long since having fallen into ruin, leaving only a faint hint of their existence; to the left the deserted play field and the roofs of the houses beyond.

"The room will be too hot soon," the old woman murmured. "He won't be able to rest this afternoon. We'll have to take him below."

The old man's mouth relaxed now and lost that pursed-up expression of pain it wore both day and night. His breathing was easy, quiet, the covers over his chest rose and fell gently. When he raised his eyes, he gazed peacefully at his wife. She had become the center of his existence. His only hope. She knew that, of course. She knew only too well that it was her turn now. She must be the one.

ELEVEN

RON DROVE DANGEROUSLY FAST THROUGH THE BLAZING LAND-
scape. The hilly, winding roads were narrow and, in most
places, dropped suddenly into deep gorges. For mile after
mile, he sat forward in the seat, peering through the windshield, straining his eyes to make out the next sharp curve of
the road ahead.

The strain of vision became a brutal headache.

He drove fast, as fast as he dared.

The town fell away and he drove the car swiftly through the
pass and on to the road high above. He accelerated until the
speedometer needle hit the 70 mark. From time to time he
glanced into the rearview mirror, imagining that any moment
he would see them. The road back and front was totally
deserted.

Eighty now as the wind rushed through the window and
swept beads of sweat from his forehead. He had known
immediately—when the oddness had started—that the past
had come alive again and was stalking him. Even now he
could feel the horrible sensation of those moments years ago
in the carriage house. Could see lines of the old woman's face
superimposed upon the younger, smoother face of Chandal.

"*But the old woman is dead . . .*" a voice whispered.

And Ron laughed hysterically.

He took the next curve at sixty, coming dangerously close
to the edge, then slowed and began his descent. He knew he
was on the brink of something beyond his control, plunging
into whatever it was they had planned for him.

Only he didn't know who *they* were. He'd seen them in his
dreams, heard their voices soft upon the wind, but hadn't
been able to make out what they were saying.

He glanced into the rearview mirror, became aware that he
had just passed Frank Hadley's General Store. Something
was wrong. Definitely wrong.

Without conscious thought, he jammed on the brakes.

257

What was it? He lowered his head to the steering wheel and closed his eyes. His shoulders hunched forward and his whole body ached. *What was wrong?*

He slammed the car into reverse.

For a while he stood perfectly still, allowing the experience to make some sort of sense. Frank Hadley's store was closed. No, more than closed. It was completely vacant and had been boarded up.

It took only a few quick moments, a few quick jerks on the boards to the rear of the store, before he watched the door swing open. He peered into the darkness.

After a minute or two, he unhurriedly moved inside. His steps were slow and deliberate. He paused for a short while taking in the calm and the dense darkness. Nothing remained. It all had been removed. Counter, cash register, shelves, all gone. Only emptiness.

As always when you make a mistake, you begin to sense it vaguely. Had he made a mistake in coming here? As the shadows thickened noiselessly beneath the dilapidated tin roof, he became conscious of another element in himself. It was a tiny spark of instinct, a primal part of him still alive and vibrant. Survival. He knew that he was in mortal danger and that to return to Brackston would surely be a mistake. He was now free of the town. They had let him go. Chandal had let him go.

Oh, God. He was positive that in some way she had become part of the conspiracy. NO, he thought, remembering the tears that had glistened on her checks. But, yes. Yes, they had her. Another agony. Kristy. Was she . . . Yes, he whispered helplessly. Both of them a part of it. The question was—*what* . . . what in the name of God did it mean to be queen?

I WAS QUEEN. THEY—

Beneath the roof there was suddenly only darkness. His eyes fell away from the store and focused on a prior conversation.

He remembered what Alister had said to him. *"It's a thankless business to interfere with the goings on here in Brackston. Perhaps you'd do well to remember that."* The thought now made him feel vulnerable, almost possessed.

He turned quickly and tried to find a source of light. Any source of light. His mind was blank, his eyes, unseeing. The last thing he wanted was to go back to Brackston. Yet he could not think of not returning.

Oh, God—he hadn't the courage to return. The will. "Oh, Jesus—please help me," he thought helplessly. Then, as though teaching himself a lesson he could not quite grasp, he repeated again and again: "Something. I must do something. I must do something . . ."

He was certain of what was going on. He knew that he was not helpless, although he hadn't a clue as to what the next appropriate action should be. He must get outside help. But where? The closest town was a hundred and fifty miles away. What would he tell them? What could he say to convince them? He felt tears coming to his eyes.

He was not shaking, but very quiet and still.

Yet he knew he was crying. Nothing could console him and stop his tears. Someone once said: "When a man cries, either he cries on his mother's shoulder, or he cries alone." Ron was alone.

Suddenly he turned and stared into the darkness. Something had moved. He waited. There! It had moved again. His thoughts started to go awry. The darkness, the sudden noise were becoming too much to handle.

"The devil's greatest trick is to make you believe he does not exist," whispered a voice. Whose voice? Ron began desperately to say the word again and again: Devil. Devil. Devil. Then he ran the sound together like a chant— DevilDevilDevilDevil.

Now he found the sound taunted him, ridiculed and mocked him. The chanting, his chanting, subsided. His tears flowed more easily, more as a relief than the pain of suffering.

Moisture blurred everything as he turned to stare at the small shaft of light filtering in from the back door. It came as a great relief.

As he stepped into his car, the sun torched the dashboard. Everything around him was still. To his left, the road led away from Brackston. To his right, the road led back. As he started the car, he was still undecided.

TWELVE

THE TAVERN SAT BACK FROM THE MAIN STREET, CRUSHED BE-
tween a large rock formation and a clump of aspen trees;
most of its customers were sitting at wooden tables in the
courtyard out back. The radio competed with the dice game,
in which wooden cups were smashed down hard on the tables,
accompanied by raucous cries from the players.

Ron found his way across the room and sat in the far
corner, his back against the wall. Tim Hadley peered at him
from across the table. It was almost as if Ron had expected to
find Tim Hadley sitting there.

Tim greeted him warmly and without surprise. "It's good to
see you. How are things going?"

"All right. How are you doing?"

Tim nodded. "Can I buy you a beer?"

"Why not?"

Beers in hand, both men leaned back and talked with
studied casualness for a while before Ron got down to what
was on his mind.

"I notice your store is closed," Ron said.

Tim laughed. "Shoot, what store?"

Ron was silent. He could see that the man was drunk. He
knew if he took his time, he might be able to get the truth out
of him. He leaned in, studying the coarse, brutal face of the
man seated before him, noting that his chin had come forward
slightly, and that a cold, hard glitter had come into his eyes.

"You've been to the store?" Tim asked.

"Yes. But like you've said. What store?"

"Business was bad. We had to close."

"That isn't what your brother told me."

"Oh?"

"The last time I was there he said you did your best
business around carnival time."

"Well, not this year." He emphasized the statement with a
twisted smile.

260

Ron took a deep breath and attempted to put aside his annoyance. "Everything inside has been removed."

"Has it?"

"Just like that. Gone."

"That's right. Just like that."

"Whatever you say," Ron muttered, too tense really to understand what he was saying.

An angry flash came into Tim's eyes, but he turned away and lifted his chin haughtily. "Hey, two beers here. And a bottle of . . ." He looked at Ron. "Jack Daniels all right?"

Ron nodded.

"Bottle of Daniels," he hollered.

"I didn't see you at the crowning last night," Ron said. "Why's that?"

"Don't like it, that's why."

"I found it pretty sickening myself."

Tim sniffed. "You let your daughter take part in it, didn't you?"

"I had no choice."

"Most of us never do." His face clouded as he said this.

"No, I guess we don't."

Tim looked up and ran a measuring, speculative eye over him. "You're a good man. I know that. A good man." He stared at Ron admiringly. "Here's to you." He lifted his mug and polished off the last of his beer.

The next round arrived on cue. He put down his empty mug, picked up the full one without so much as a pause, and began to drain it.

A sudden strained silence. Ron glanced at his wristwatch. Almost two-thirty. Tim took a toothpick from his vest pocket and stuck it into his mouth. Then swilled some more beer.

It was the damndest thing Ron had ever seen. A man drinking beer with a toothpick in his mouth.

"Going to storm," Tim said. "Cool in here though." The toothpick between his tobacco-stained teeth wig-wagged continuously from one side of his mouth to the other as he spoke. "Tomorrow night is Last Friday. The ladies are probably over at Beatrice Wheatley's house getting things ready, I imagine. She's head of the committee, don't you know."

"No—no, I didn't know," Ron said.

The man sniffed. "To give blood and so a new life."

Ron hesitated. "I don't understand."

"Hummm." A sudden thought seemed to strain his white face with color.

"You just said something," Ron pressed. "Something I didn't quite understand."

Tim remained silent, preferring to pour two glasses of Jack Daniels. He shoved the glass beside Ron's elbow. Then sat back and regarded him thoughtfully. "Matthew said he'd got that car of yours fixed. I'd thought you'd be out of town by now."

"As a matter of fact—" He stopped himself and paused.

"What?" Tim Hadley asked anxiously.

"As a matter of fact," Ron repeated, "I had all but left town. But when I passed your store, well . . . I just found it interesting that it was closed all of a sudden."

Tim began to speak. Stopped when he saw Ron's eyes locked on his toothpick. He smiled and took it out of his mouth. "Coon dick," he said.

"What?"

"It's made from a coon's dick," he said proudly. "Daniel Boone used to have one just like it. I saw it once in a museum in Harrodsburg, Kentucky. Long glass case with all them other do-hickies in it. Never wears out."

While Tim Hadley's eyes stayed glued to his face, Ron struggled for the next question. "The carnival," he said, "it isn't like a regular carnival, is it?"

Tim gnawed at his toothpick and, looking down at his fingers, he slowly and with difficulty flexed them. "Nope, it isn't."

"What's it all about anyway?"

He looked at Ron for a moment, then stared past him as if looking for someone.

"You expecting someone?" Ron asked nervously.

"You know," he said slowly, "the only reason rabbits ain't extinct is because of their smartness. A rabbit is plumb clever. If I was telling children how to hunt rabbit, I'd say look right under your nose. But you have to take your time and look real close. And sure enough, you'll find a smart rabbit trying to fool you. But if you see him, you've got him. Just move in on him, then stand there and wait. He can't stand that. He'll make a break and then—then you shoot the little son of a bitch."

He poured more bourbon into each glass, then added: "Now another thing to remember is.that rabbits are like strangers." He raised his glass. "Here's to you."

"Yeah," Ron said and turned away to survey the room. He hated the place. He hated Brackston, he hated Tim and Frank Hadley, he hated Mrs. Taylor and the Wheatleys and the Carrolls. His eyes scanned over the haggard faces of the few patrons that dotted the room. Which ones, he wondered, knew what was going on? All. He was under no illusions—he was sure he was being observed from all sides.

He swallowed the bourbon before turning back to face Tim Hadley, who wasted no time pouring another drink for each of them.

"Our blood sometimes bears the seed of our destruction," he said and gulped down more bourbon. Church bells tolled in the distance. Three times.

Ron was really feeling the effect of drink when it tolled an hour later. Four times. Tim had been talking about rabbits again, about hunting and fishing, and Ron found that Tim's speech so tickled him that he laughed aloud, sharing Tim Hadley's pleasure; he laughed at the extraordinary experience the man talked of, the perceiving of a wilderness which heretofore had seemed a malevolent world, poisonous and stagnated.

Finally, Tim whispered: "Blood is necessary to save the world and the people in it." He giggled, the liquor spilling from the sides of his mouth. "Ask the Widow Wheatley, she'll tell you."

Through a haze of bourbon, Ron said: "Widow? Then she and . . ."

"Thomas . . ."

"Thomas, that's right, Thomas." Ron found pleasure in repeating the name. It was a wall to lean against.

"Thomas Wheatley," Tim said, "died." He studied Ron's stunned reaction with private glee.

"When?" Ron asked, struggling desperately to sober. "When did he die?"

"Very recently," whispered Tim, leaning in toward Ron

until Ron could feel light drops of spittle as Tim spoke. "You see, Beatrice, she's the Keeper . . ."

"TIM!" Frank Hadley appeared suddenly beside the booth.

Through a great drunkenness, Ron stared up at him. The man appeared to have just stepped out of a jungle. Sweat poured from his forehead and ran in a steady stream down his face. He wore a solid green jump suit and boots. He was carrying his rifle cocked under his arm.

"Tim, we had best be going."

"Shoot, Frank, we was . . ."

"Get to your goddamn feet, boy!"

"What the fuck is wrong with you?"

"You were foolish to come back," Frank Hadley said, frowning at Ron.

"I see I was," Ron snapped, his speech slurred.

"Get up, Tim. Now!" When Frank took his arm, Tim stumbled up, giggling, and with his hand roughed his brother's hair affectionately, much as he might have greeted a long-forgotten son.

"Let's go home, boy."

Tim chuckled. "Shit, where'd that be?"

"You're goddamned lucky I came along," Frank said. "No telling where you'd have wound up." He held his brother steady. "You know people around here don't like drunks. No telling what they'd of done to you."

Vaguely, it seemed, Tim realized the wisdom of his brother's words. He shrugged his brother off and smiled at Ron. "Nice talking with you, Mr. Talon. Nice." He laughed. "You poor dumb suffering brute . . ."

When his brother touched his shoulder, he made no effort to resist, and allowed himself to be escorted from the tavern. "Good-bye, you poor dumb . . ."

Frank Hadley wasted no time pushing him the rest of the way out the door. He watched as the two brothers passed in front of the window and then vanished.

Ron let his eyes drop to his empty glass. He reached out for the bottle, nearly knocking it from the table. He steadied his hand and poured. Bull's eye. He drank.

Then panic rose. What if it were all delusion? A mocking hideous delusion? His brain started to unravel. Lousy goddamn world, he thought with unusual bitterness. What was the world but insanity? Christ died—for what? So towns like Brackston could . . .

In his daze, clinging to his glass, he still hadn't noticed the figure standing outside the window. "Help me. Mother of Jesus . . ."

His head began to sag.

The withered face of the old woman smiled. "Let's keep an open mind," she whispered.

As if the darkness and pain behind him had been merely a little transitory test, the horizons of life and existence now began to grow darker, more painful. He tried to breathe, but found no air.

Now he began to feel a great distant space closing in on him. Noise dwindled, light grew dimmer, sucked, forcing him into uncharted space where he felt cold, frozen. The last faint echoes of sound died. All was quiet.

The old woman moved. A slow smile of recognition touched the corners of Ron's mouth as he heard her say: "It's me. The same spirit. Come."

Elizabeth Krispin, he started to say obediently, but her smile gave her away and he saw through the trick.

No, just another old woman with a warped soul, with the smell of death about her, darkness in her eyes.

(Funny, Daddy, playing with the darkness.)

The old woman's head drew back; her toothless gums showed through a widespread grimace of gaiety. She was laughing.

Her face branded his consciousness. He could see her still smiling—ear to ear—hysterical—even as his body escaped his control.

He fell then with a dull thud across the table.

Into darkness.

THIRTEEN

CLOUDS DRIFTED ACROSS THE HALF MOON; IT WAS AS THOUGH the world was all at once covered in a shroud. Ron tried to move. He ached. Hesitantly, almost timidly, he struggled slowly to his feet.

He was stark naked.

In his great drunkenness, he stepped through the reddish glow shimmering ahead of him; beyond that was darkness, the immeasurable. He concentrated hard on each step taken. He felt a rush of wind, saw half-glimpses of eyes, heard vast mutterings . . .

Two scavenger dogs slinking silently through the dark night, moving past him down the narrow path. The pair walked at an unhurried pace on soft paws.

Now he moved with the dogs, past houses, through gardens, behind small buildings, the noise of the town soft in the background. Still he followed the dogs because they seemed to move through the darkness with purpose. They were familiar, comprehensible things to his primitive instincts.

The moon was out again, and in the milky light he saw the dogs come to an alleyway. They swung into it; he was not far behind. The darkness in the alley was thick and syrupy, and entering it was like being dropped into a jar of molasses. Under bare feet he felt wads of newspaper, broken glass, tin cans. He pressed his hands to the wall, letting them guide him through the maze of damp brick that seemed endless.

He came suddenly into a large yard, where the moonlight seemed frosted and brittle. Beyond, past a rotted wooden fence, loomed the cold peaks of mountains.

The dogs were on the other side of the fence now, heading for the hills. He leaped, pulled, and with both knees managed to force himself up over the fence.

As he hit the ground, he quickly looked around. He was standing in an immense junkyard. There was a small light on the second floor of the building to his left. Perhaps someone was in the building, or perhaps the light was merely a precaution.

He started to make his way between bits and pieces of dead metal. Stealthily, he crept along. He had never felt so alive. Nobody around but him. King of the junkyard.

He laughed out loud. Then laughed again. Fuck it. He knew he was drunk. Yet his thoughts seemed sharper than ever. Here he was, hungry, lean—a silent, lonely hunter—a dangerous animal.

The dogs cleared the junkyard and moved upward into the hills. He followed along some thirty yards behind, surprised at his physical stamina. Also surprised at the suddenly strange, savage, surreal landscape.

"Where are the dogs?"

Even here in the open air, the stench of garbage assailed his nostrils. It was the odor of a modern civilization gone amuck. Heaps and heaps of garbage loomed out at him, an ocean of dead yesterdays. He felt suddenly tired, very tired. He glanced around.

"Where the hell am I?"

He tried not to panic.

Not that he was frightened. He wasn't. Just tired all of a sudden. But he was sure he could make it. His eyes darted feverishly through the garbage, looking for the dogs. He wasn't sure of anything now. He tried to move each of his limbs. His legs and arms felt leadened. A sharp pain pressed his bowels, gut, and chest.

Ignoring the pain, he rushed through the rubble, until he had reached the fence. He scaled the fence and dropped back into the junkyard. He was running now, scraping his arms and legs against sharp protruding metal. He reached the mouth of the alley and paused, his breath coming in sharp gasps. Behind his eyelids panic ensued. It was the wrong alley. He didn't know how he knew this, he just did. He turned and was sure he was certain of going crazy.

At first all he heard was his own harsh breathing, then came the muffled voices. In the darkness women stood aside, naked, holding smoking torches. The reddish flames lit the air and the ground around him.

"Hold them higher!" a voice shouted. The women obeyed. He raised both hands against his eyes to block out the sudden harsh light. The wind blew chilled around him, the flames fluttering and flapping like bird's wings. His body began to quiver, then to jerk a little. The current of time had stopped, only the whispering grew and grew until he was caught up in the sound, swept away into the hills and dropped to the ground.

He looked up. He saw that he was in a dark cave. He saw carvings upon the walls. Grotesque distorted pictures that no man could possibly dream of. "Look, see. See!" shouted seductive figures, their eyes glittering with hatred. The pictures upon the wall came alive now—a putrid smell seeped up from rock. It was as though he had been dropped into the mouth of a scavenger bird.

Gagging, he tried to struggle to his feet. They leapt upon him, held him down. "You came back. You wanted to know! You wanted to see! See!"

He could feel himself drawing hatred and death to him from all sides, like a sponge absorbing water until it lies bloated and full. With a strange and distorted vision, he stared at his own face carved in stone. Against his will, he closed his eyes and leaned toward death.

Still they shouted as a great spectacle of primitive images flooded his vision. He saw snakes slithering through the sockets of dead men's eyes, people hung in cruciform positions, others boiled in oil or quartered by horses. A body snapped suddenly into four parts—blood splattered against the wall; dark wrinkled hands reached out and took him by the throat, fingers began to squeeze, his vision blurred . . .

Other faces appeared, many faces, thousands and thousands, tortured, twisted, harrowing masks of humanity, all coming and going and yet all seeming to be there at the same time, peering up from the mud, smiling in agony through stone, changing and renewing themselves, until they were all there, all one . . . all Ron.

With the last flicker of images he saw withered faces, saw broken fragments of torment, saw . . .

Himself buried alive.

FIVE

LAST FRIDAY

ONE

Father, the root of this little dead flower
Among the stones has the taste of blood. And
Our hungry world feeds on itself. Ssssh. Can
You hear it? A sweet sound; the sound of things
To come. But do not run away, because—why,
Because then you shall miss all the fun.

HE DIDN'T KNOW WHERE HE WAS, RON DECIDED, BUT WHEREVER
it was, he did not like it.

The back of his head materialized first. A sharp ache. One
quick stab of pain that passed quickly into the back of his
neck. Then suddenly it vanished, and his jaw came to life. For
a while nothing existed except his jaw. He pointed it in the
direction of the ceiling and tried to open his mouth. His lips
were dry and cracked. He opened one eye just enough to
discover the dim outline of black shapes, long and thin, and
closed it again.

For a while he was satisfied to lie there and suffer. Then it
began to come back to him. Something vague about someone
carrying him—he couldn't recall who—down a narrow hallway, and the banging of steel. Something equally vague, the
terrible sensation of being lost in a maze of stone that twisted
and turned and confused him. There his memory stopped.

Suddenly the air seemed more smoke than oxygen. He

opened his eyes and saw Sheriff Nash's smug face, cigar stuffed into the corner of his mouth, peering at him. The sheriff was wiping sweat from his forehead with a handkerchief.

"Don't worry," Nash said. "You're not dead."

Ron shut his eyes again. "Then how come I feel dead?"

Nash let a chuckle roll from his lips. "Are you hungry?"

Ron experienced another sharp pain in the center of his forehead and an odd queasy sensation in the pit of his stomach. He decided he was too sick to be dead, and opened his eyes again. "What time is it?"

"A little after ten."

Ron did not respond for a second. Ten? It hadn't reached him yet. Hadn't connected. He sat up with a blinding, crashing headache that effectively stampeded any consecutive thought. The only reality was dry thirst and pain and the queasiness rumbling in the pit of his stomach, and until they were relieved, he could think of nothing in concrete terms.

He managed to lower his legs to the floor by degrees. He glanced around miserably.

The sheriff went on chattering animatedly as if nothing untoward had happened, smoking his cigar, casually drifting from topic to topic, until finally he unlocked the door and stepped inside the cell.

Suddenly it dawned on Ron. He was in jail for Chrissakes. "What . . . what am I doing here?"

"You look sick," the sheriff chuckled. "The john's through that door."

Ron's bare feet smacked the cool slab floor as he stumbled forward. The bathroom stank of cheap soap and urine. He held onto the sink and drew a glass of water. The water made a U-turn in his stomach and came back up. He retched violently. Body still shaking, he gazed at his image in the mirror.

"You all right in there?" the sheriff hollered in.

"Yeah."

His face looked sunken and in need of a shave. His shirt and trousers were dirty and disheveled. It wasn't until he leaned closer to the mirror that he discovered his jaw was swollen and bruised. He shook his head. Someone had removed his jacket, shoes and socks. They had also taken his wallet, the loose change from his pocket, and his wristwatch.

The door opened and Sheriff Nash appeared behind him in the mirror. He snorted. "Well," he said in a tight voice, "how does all this strike you?"

"How did I get here?"

"I brought you, naturally."

"Why?"

"Well," he said noncommittally. He paused, watching him. "Drunk and disorderly."

Ron stared, his full brows drawn down against his eyes; he leaned against the sink, one hand straying to his jaw.

"Go ahead," the sheriff went on quickly, "say your piece. I mean it. Say anything that comes into your head, the first thing that hits you. Go ahead."

Ron started to speak, checked himself. In bewilderment he glanced at the door, the walls, the sheriff's face grinning, his lips partly open.

"Come on," the sheriff said. "I'll fix coffee." His voice trailed off.

In the little low-ceilinged room out front he snapped on the bulb suspended from the ceiling, seized it to keep it from swinging, then turned to Ron and pointed to his desk. "Your belongings are in the envelope."

"Where's my shoes and jacket?"

"Over there."

Ron's jacket was hanging neatly over a chair, his shoes with socks in them were placed just as neatly below. He sat and put them on.

"Do you remember what happened?" the sheriff asked.

He shook his head dumbly.

"Well—" Nash laughed. "It'll come to you. It always takes a while." He fingered his newly shaven chin and faced the crouched, intent figure near him. "You know what it is I hate about being sheriff?" he asked. Sunlight, vicious yellow, poured into the room through angular steel bars the instant he had reached out and snapped up the front shade. "Making coffee. I just don't like making coffee."

Ron could not get hold of it yet. Morning. It was ten o'clock in the *morning*. What day? he thought.

"What day is this?" he asked.

"Friday." The man's eyes drifted to the calendar which hung on the wall, between numerous plaques and citations, and the gun rack whose mahogany frame held a large display of vicious-looking weapons. "Last Friday," he added with a sigh.

"I've been here all night?"

"All night."

"And I never woke up?"

"Guess you needed the rest," he said. He fumbled around for a while, pouring water over instant coffee, dropping sugar cubes and instant cream into his cup. "How do you take yours?"

"Black. One sugar. Does my wife know I'm here?"

"Had to tell her. She didn't seem too upset."

Ron went to the desk, ripped open the envelope, and looked at his wristwatch. It had stopped at six minutes to seven. He shoved loose change into his pocket, his wallet into his jacket, and peered into the envelope. "I don't see the keys to my car anywhere."

"That's cause they aren't there. Matt Todd drove your car back to Mrs. Taylor's house last night. It's against the law to park on the streets of Brackston after dark." He paused. "You want me to drive you home?"

"No."

"I don't mind—"

"I need the air."

"Probably do you some good. Here's your coffee."

"Thanks."

"You hungry? I can order something."

"No," Ron said and felt the first comforting drops of coffee pass his lips. He was starting to feel a little better, but not much.

"It's no trouble."

Ron shook his head, glanced around anxious to leave, stepped back, then said: "What exactly happened last night?"

"It seems you caused quite a disturbance in the tavern. You had a run-in with Frank Hadley."

"I don't remember."

"You'd been drinking pretty heavy for almost four hours."

"Frank Hadley—he wasn't even there. He'd left with his brother."

"Came back, he said. To apologize."

"For what?"

"He didn't say."

"Did he say what started the fight?"

"The truth is, Mr. Talon, he hadn't the vaguest idea why you struck him that way. Nobody else did either. It's a knotty problem, I'll tell you."

Ron rubbed his jaw. "Is that how I got this?"

"Frank said he had to protect himself. You got pretty mean. I figured it was best to let you sleep it off."

Ron stood perfectly still for some moments. There was a numbness inside him as if someone had anesthetized him, dulling his senses. Yet he knew that this man, this soft-lipped hick standing in front of him was a lying son of a bitch. That he was as false as the chunks of instant cream that floated in his coffee.

"Am I free to go?" Ron asked.

"Sure. Hell, we got no complaint. Just wanted to keep peace in the town last night, that's all."

Ron put his blue porcelain cup down on the desk; a few drops of coffee spilled on the floor. "You really must think I'm a child," he murmured. "A frigging child. Handing me that bullshit about last night. What do you take me for? You're lying. All of you are a pack of goddamn liars!"

"I think," said Nash, unperturbed by the outburst, "that you should go home now."

Ron jerked his jacket from off the back of the chair, his face red with rage. "If you had the balls you were born with, you'd tell me the real reason for locking me up last night."

"Why would I lie to you?"

"I don't know." Ron stared at him. "I really don't know. But I'll tell you one thing. I'm sure as hell going to find out."

"What is it?" the sheriff said matter-of-factly. "What are you afraid of? Is it me? Are you afraid of me?"

Ron did not answer.

He laughed. "Hell, I don't mean you any harm. You say I lied to you. That I locked you up for other reasons. What other reason could there be?"

"Well, for one thing," Ron said flatly, "I'm still in town, aren't I? I'm still here." He turned away. The door slammed behind him on the way out like an exclamation mark.

The sun was high and a warm breeze swept the sky clean of clouds. There was a freshness, a buoyancy in the town; a surge of festivity. Shopkeepers stood in doorways shouting to passersby—soon all businesses in Brackston would be closed for the Sabbath. The excitement spread quickly through the town.

Sabbath, Ron wondered and watched crowds gathering in the square. Women in head scarves with arms folded, swarms of children tugging at their skirts, teenage boys dressed in tee shirts and dungarees, teenage girls in halter tops, short skirts and thick platform shoes assembled at the corners or near the mouth of the carnival grounds. More children dressed in ragged clothing hurried through the streets with handfuls of stones and rushed to be the first up the mountain.

A snatch of dialogue here, a whisper there. Old men with long unkempt hair and whiskers exchanging pieces of information about crops, the bewildering idiocies of the younger generation and fond memories of previous Last Fridays. They talked and nodded their heads; stopped suddenly to peer at Ron as he passed.

"We have gathered to witness," a voice murmured, but halted in midsentence.

Ron had been warned. Now, he realized, there would be no more warnings. No authority to appeal to; this was Brackston, where the only authority was the Ruling Elders. They, he knew, would administer their own justice.

As he moved awkwardly through the square, he saw new faces he had never seen before. Families of them, all chattering about Last Friday. All gleefully discussing the new queen. The new queen. The phrase ran through Ron's mind, leaving him sickened.

On the far side of town, smoke from the chimneys of the houses trailed across the dilapidated rooftops, marring the clear sky that stretched like a green sac over endless mountain ranges. Fires? Ron mused. On a hot day like this?

A woman came to her gate as he passed. She leaned over and said in a low voice, "Your daughter is lovely. A queen."

Ron did not stop but, glancing at her briefly, walked slower up the road. Some of the woman's neighbors came to their doors and windows. Eyes moved from side to side. Mouths open, laughing, whispering. His steps were heavy; his face weary with fatigue. He opened his mouth a little to make breathing easier. It didn't help.

Short of breath, he trudged on, until at last he'd reached the house. The steeple bell began striking the hour. He entered the front door as the final stroke rang.

TWO

RON TALON WAS ON THE COUCH, SITTING STRAIGHT BACKED, facing the windows, the terrace and the sun, when the phone rang. His eyes were closed, a glass of bourbon sweat in front of him.

He had found the house empty. His station wagon was gone, so were Chandal and Kristy. All the suitcases were also gone. Though he had prepared himself for this since the very beginning, it all seemed unreal to him.

He let the phone ring.

He kept his eyes closed.

He knew that there was one thing in life that was absolutely certain. You must pay, in some way, for everything you are, for everything you have been. There were no exceptions. And it had been foolish to think for one moment that there would be no payment due for that time spent in the carriage house in New York City. For possessing the bloodstone.

Evil begets evil. He felt a pressure climaxing inside his body. He felt the past in his mind and stomach and chest loosening and flowing, the scabs giving way, and a fresh separation of bone, flesh and tissue.

Chandal had been possessed. In order to rid herself of evil, she had inadvertently committed evil. Not intentionally. But people had died. Doreen Hammer had died. Billy Deats had died. Eric Savage, Ron had discovered later, had died. None of it had been Chandal's doing. Still, people had died.

The past was more than a darkness of mind, it was a nudity of soul. It was a place of deep sorrows and hopelessness.

His vision blurred. The sins of the mother visited upon the daughter. Was that it? Was that what the carnival was all about? The crowning, Last Friday, Mardi gras? Yes, he was sure that it was. Yet he was helpless to know what to do.

The telephone rang again.

He lifted the receiver. "Hello?"

"Mr. Talon?" asked the operator.

"Yes. This is he."

"Go ahead, California, your party is on the line."

The voice on the other end belonged to the receptionist at his office. A shy girl in her early twenties. Sometimes Ron had had the idea she wouldn't mind being in show business. Now the voice had an odd, choked, rather breathless quality to it. The girl spoke slowly at first, then told him almost in a rush that Mimi Halpern was dead. That she, along with Dwayne Clark, had been killed in an automobile accident Wednesday evening. "It's such a tragedy, really . . ." Words of sympathy and regret etched their way into his eardrum and he could see Mimi smiling, her saggy-haired, gray cat-eyed beauty beaming at him across his desk.

"We've tried to reach you for several days now. We closed your office . . . there was only the bookkeeper and me, so . . ."

"You did the right thing," Ron said, testing his voice. It was remarkably steady.

Ron knew Mimi's death was no accident. Dr. Luther had suffered a similar accident in New York while treating Chandal. Only the doctor had been fortunate enough to escape with his life.

". . . We're still quite stunned."

"Yes. I understand," Ron said and felt tears brim in his eyes. "Please, I—I must hang up now . . ." Slowly he lowered the receiver, then let it drop into its cradle. All at once he felt a kind of shattering inside and wondered if he wasn't going under, right here, right now—sinking to the bottom of life, drowning in his own misery and despair.

The pain turned to sudden anger which materialized in his physical self. He vowed war on Brackston. He vowed to destroy every last one of its people. He would topple their mountains, poison their rivers, burn down their houses. "Do you hear me, old woman? I swear as God is my judge—I shall destroy you! ALL OF YOU!"

He heard the last rumbling traces of his words die away; replaced in the silence by a little graveled whisper, deliberate and slow.

"Come . . . get . . . me . . . if . . . you . . . can."

Then silence. He steadied himself. His vision blurred again, reminding him he was falling into repetitive patterns. He waited. His pain waited with him.

And then he heard it. A light tread on the creaking stairs. He sat very still and quiet. As the footsteps descended the stairs he realized they were moving beneath him and not above as was the usual pattern. He knew it would have been better not to have heard them.

He staggered to his feet. His face was peaked, pale. He moved into the hallway and saw that a door leading to the basement stood ajar. He inched through the doorway and down the narrow stairs toward the awaiting darkness.

The silence below was more nerve shattering than the previous clamoring in the streets, more frightening. As he came to the bottom step, he paused. Something was radically different. In fact, nothing about his surroundings was similar to substitute images. There was something awesome, even terrifying, in the glacial chill that rushed at him from the open-mouthed archway ahead. Yet there was no movement of air. And no sound; no sound at all.

He knew he was waiting for their next move. They would move, he knew. They hadn't summoned him below for nothing. His instinct told him that he was in the midst of an occurrence, not the beginning, and that the moment was upon him.

Yet, he didn't regret it. He couldn't understand why he didn't. The thought astounded him. And, in a half-crazed sort of a way, elated him. Perhaps he realized he could not live with this kind of tension, not any longer. He could not live in constant fear. He had to do something soon.

It didn't seem quite so dark now; Ron's eyes were beginning to adjust. He could feel sweat roll down from the back of his neck, struck suddenly by the cold air.

He moved; something moved with him. Beyond the massive archway a wan, watery light glittered, shifted, as though something or someone had moved a light source. A candle? A flashlight? He wasn't sure.

He weaved through the passageway ahead and stopped to gaze at the large room circling him. Softly lit, its shadows crawled away to cluster in the corners. The room's low slung ceiling was supported by pillars carved with lozenges and croziers. The floor was covered with rough broken stones and in the far corner the gapes of a naked opening of a well. Above the well a hemp rope dangled, swayed, disappearing into the depths below. A small lantern was resting on the well's ledge, its yellowish light fanning out, softer, until it dissolved into blackness.

Something moved beyond the light.

Ron twisted around, startled. For a moment he could not see anything. Just darkness. And from within the darkness: scratching. The harsh, grating scraping of fingernails.

Someone moved again, laughed. A childlike giggle. A few seconds later Kristy stepped into the light and stood still, utterly motionless. Her thin shoulders drooped, allowing her arms to dangle freely at her sides, the palms of her hands turned upward toward the ceiling as if she were about to receive something of importance. Her pink tongue slowly licked her dark red lips. Then she hissed.

Ron's mouth felt dry. He tried to work up some saliva, but there was none. Sweat broke on his forehead, ran down over his brows, into the corners of his eyes. He blinked away stinging fluid.

"Kristy?" he murmured and moved closer.

The child backed deeper into the corner, until her face became almost lost to the shadows. Only her large eyes peered out.

"Kristy? Are you all right?"

"Jennifer is dead, Daddy. She's dead." She stared speculatively into the well. Her face was twisted, uneven. Her mouth turned down on the right side. Her left eye seemed lower than the other. Her black hair hung limp over her white forehead and cheeks.

"Is Jennifer down there, Kristy?"

She did not answer.

The make-believe took Ron by surprise and drew him

closer to the well. He reached out and took hold of the rope. Slowly, he began to pull.

Kristy responded at frequent intervals with nervous little bursts of laughter, little screeches of enthusiasm and pleasure.

"I did it, Daddy," Kristy explained anxiously. "I killed her."

When the last of the rope appeared in the weak light, Ron saw it was wound around Jennifer's doll neck. He had hardly lifted the doll from the well when Kristy screamed: "She's dead! Look at her, Daddy! She's dead, she's dead!"

Kristy's face was very flushed. For the first time there was color in her skin. Her features were twisted and disturbed.

"What have you done?" Ron's voice sounded to him detached, remarkably so.

"I made her bleed first," she hissed. "Then I killed her."

The doll's china-face had been bashed in. Her eyes had been removed. Both arms and legs had been slashed with a knife.

Kristy giggled. "You are having a bad dream, Daddy. A nightmare. But do not run away, because . . ."

She moved now; the air moved with her, a warm breeze that carried with it the slightly unpleasant odor of dead flowers. Swiftly, she ran to a small door, not as tall as an ordinary door, but as wide. Opening the door, she laughed: "But do not run away, because . . ."

"Kristy!" he screamed.

She was gone.

He reached for the lantern. "Kristy, please . . ." He spun around; the door swung open completely and smacked the wall. "KRISTY!"

That gripping sensation in his stomach now as he inched through the doorway. The passageway ahead was narrow, choked on either side by a bizarre lattice-work of limestone, roots, and parasitic vines. There was room enough for one person, but no more.

If this was a trap, it would be over within the next few seconds.

He straightened, holding his breath, and stared into the darkness. There was a silence which he felt reluctant to break. How still it was, how absolutely unmoving—not a ruffle.

"Kristy?" he breathed. "Where are you?"

He raised his eyes, as if to try them out. The light from his lantern shone only a few feet in front of him, fading suddenly into thick shadows and impenetrable vegetation.

Now he moved without sound, one careful step at a time, the pale light guiding his way. He found a small opening and took a route that was neither direct nor circuitous. It was merely there, as if he were being guided along a path made just for him. He moved effortlessly, soundlessly, with such fluidity that there was no sensation of movement, merely a gliding forward into the bowels of the earth. The way grew thicker and more choked with foliage and vines, yet his speed had actually increased. He was totally alone, or so it seemed to him. The cavern was quite still, just an occasional fluttering of wings overhead. A flapping sound.

Before him, the walk was barely visible, only a shade lighter than the surrounding darkness, but still sufficiently lighted to enable him to find the next opening.

Once more, there was a flapping of wings.

He stared upward. He could see nothing in the darkness. Yet he felt air move against his face, and something came to rest above him. From the impact, he knew that it was something immense.

He turned quickly and held out his light. He had arrived at a broad and spacious portico, its columns spiraling upward to support an elaborately carved roof. To Ron, it was astonishing. Like an archaeologist who has just stumbled upon some great hidden treasure, he was rooted to the spot, his mouth agape.

As he paused to recover himself, a light emerged from a passageway ahead and shone full upon the walls of the cavern. A dark vine cluster appeared far and wide in front of him, and behind it rose a copse of lofty forest trees, sleeping in the melancholy half-glow of azure light.

Something moved, flashed in the distance.

"Kristy!"

The shadowy figure in a drab yellow cloak vanished.

There was another flapping of wings and another sound behind him. He turned and felt a hard object brush against his neck. He screamed, beating his hand wildly about his head. The hawk screamed.

Light flashed as he turned and started to run. His body became unfamiliar and awkward. He dashed through the arching vines, slipped. Breathless, he regained his balance and began running again, his eyes darting upward. The hawk was gone.

"Kristy? KRISTY!"

He touched stone, dismayed anew by the dark twisting amphitheaters, the hanging stalactite, the quaking rot of bone beneath his feet that reeked its smell with every step. Strange shapes caught his eye; putrescent smells choked his nostrils.

He rushed aimlessly through the dark subbasement tunnels below the earth. "Kristy?" he cried. "Where are you?" His voice echoed, enlarged, came back to slap him across the face.

Abruptly he was propelled downward into instant hallucination. The little clearing in which he stood expanded before him, opened like a huge jagged slit. Swiftly animals rose from their graves; bears, pumas, jackal and hyenas. They leapt enormous before his eyes. Just as swiftly a large lizard emerged, opened its huge jaws and began to devour its prey.

Everything before Ron had gone into action, thrashing violently, echoing, bones cracking, splintering and still the hallucination persisted—the air was rent with sickening screams. The ceiling became alive with the massive fluttering of wings; bats, guacharos and swifts, their breasts, in the half-glow, resembling flecks of fire; prehistoric cave dwellers began emerging from beneath the stone. Blind groping creatures with withered flesh and fungi hair; their eyes sightless sockets devoid of life, their screams impotent wails, soundless, yet their lips were twisted with unspeakable sounds of terror.

"Noooo!" Ron screamed. He ran. Sharp light speared his eyes. He veered to his left, running, always running, trying to find his way. Voices now. Human voices. He paused breathless to force his senses to try and separate the sounds around him, what was real from what wasn't.

In front of him the space widened, revealing an endless expanse of soft golden light. Everything felt suddenly warm and cozy. Too cozy. Yet he could not move away. He swallowed dryness in his throat and then saw her. He stared into the soft light at Kristy. And Kristy stared back with eyes that were wide and shiny like a quiet night.

"The darkness," she whimpered. "The darkness. I can't get out of the darkness. Help me, Daddy."

For an instant he was startled, not expecting to see her so suddenly, so clearly. As his eyes adjusted, he recognized the figure before him. It was not his daughter at all, but the little girl he had seen in his own garden weeks ago.

He caught a glimpse of movement, a quick flash as Kristy moved from the shadows and darted behind the little girl. Their images merged.

"Kristy?"

The little girl smiled. "Help me, Daddy. Help me."

"Kristy, come to Daddy."

The little girl hissed vehemently, in irritation, puffing her lips out; then she moved away into the darkness. Kristy, like the other child, had simply vanished before his eyes.

"Daddy . . . don't leave me. Don't leave me!"

The high quivering voice, pitched almost to a scream, droned on and on, growing fainter until abruptly it ceased.

Ron looked dazedly around. Moved. He wasn't sure where Kristy's voice had been coming from.

On either side of the passageway the earth's crust suddenly turned to igneous rock, throwing off large amounts of heat. Yet, further on, the passageway was ice cold. Suspended from the roof, incrustations, like icicles. A sizzle as fire and ice mingled.

He stopped for a moment as an overwhelming panic seemed to strain and shift the organs of his body. In the blanket gloom, his strength began to deteriorate. From great depths of weariness he heard his daughter's pleading voice: *Daddy, help me. Please, help me.*

Her voice grew louder, nearer. He moved quickly, following her voice that echoed along the gigantic corridor. A curious yellow light filtered into the passageway ahead, and the passageway became other passageways, cold and hot passageways, endlessly multiplying, and thronged with great rock formations, which appeared to move as he thrust between their jagged edges.

Yes, Daddy—come to me. . . .

He held the meager light out in front of him. Ahead was a small opening. He moved swiftly through the narrow space. He turned suddenly and saw he was caught between two walls. Now the lantern dimmed. It came back again, but only to flare for a moment. Then it flickered to a tiny speck until it went out.

Without allowing himself to think about his situation, he rummaged through his pockets until he found a book of matches. He struck a match. It wasn't much, but enough to get him to the other side.

The match burned evenly for a second, then quickly flickered and died. He struck another, moved. Struck another, moved. With only three matches left, he did not want to think about what was to come . . . about how lost he was and how little oxygen there seemed to be. He paused to curse the darkness. He struck another match and carefully approached the opening ahead.

It took him several moments before he realized that his match had gone out. Yet the space ahead was aglow with light. Candles. Yes, there was definitely candlelight ahead.

When he emerged from the darkness, he found himself in a dim and half-lighted chamber which he realized was some sort of a crypt. Around him, chiseled from solid stone, eagles and jaguars and dancing jackals. Visages of gods graced the ceiling and a break in the roof far above let a bolt of sunshine fall to a carved sandstone floor. Upon the floor were sprinkled hundreds of tiny red flowers.

The wide chamber was lighted by lofty candelabra of elaborate bronze, and around the walls were wrought vast hieroglyphics, in dark and solemn colors.

At the extremity of the crypt, a solid gold casket. A small tripod stood at a little distance, from the incense in which the smoke slowly rose. Near this was a statue of a winged goat-headed god with serpent's tail and cloven hooves, and the soft light gave an additional and yet solemn calm to its large, harmonious, passionless features.

With a flush of awe and ghostly fear, Ron moved and longed for an echo to his noiseless steps. He moved to the end of the chamber quietly, without taking his eyes off the casket.

And now he knew where he was. Kristy had described it only too clearly. A place where they have dancing jackals, she had said. And flower wars. Kristy had known all along.

He hesitated before peering into the casket. The sunken, withered features, the purple lips and flowing white hair were instantly recognizable to him. It was Thomas Wheatley. The stonecutter.

All at once a thin bony hand placed itself lovingly on the old man's cheek. Ron spun around with a start, seizing the edge of the casket for support.

The Widow Wheatley smiled. She fixed her gaze on him unwaveringly. "Brackston, Utah. Grandeur above, secrets below. If you are looking for a scenic drive, take any road out of town."

Her voice echoed about the chamber, metallic and jangling, bouncing airily above the gods, swirling about the great goat-headed statue which stood silently confronting him like a mad tribunal of one.

But in a moment there were more than one. Many more. From out of the shadows stepped the townspeople. Matthew Todd, the Hadley brothers, Lou Harris, Sheriff Nash, Mrs. Taylor and Isabelle Carroll. Scattered among them, children.

At first, Ron did not recognize Kristy. She stood back in the shadows, flanked by the boy and girl who had been part of the happening from the beginning. She wore rags, a tattered brown sack dress—and, around her waist, a pelt. Upon seeing her, Ron didn't know what he felt. Relief? Confusion? Anger?

He looked at the other faces—at Matthew Todd's, which seemed to reflect arrogant power; at Isabelle Carroll's which shone with unbridled pleasure; and at Kristy's—relaxed, totally at ease, her eyes smiling.

"Kristy?" The word caught in Ron's throat.

Kristy laughed, hissed at him, saliva forming at the corners of her mouth. Then she stood motionless, her eyes vacant.

Blankly, he stared at her, unable to believe, unable even to absorb what he saw. "What have you done to her?" he breathed.

"Done? We have done nothing to her," Widow Wheatley said.

Ron could not take his eyes from his daughter. She looked

so unnatural. Almost—drugged, hypnotized. Odd that the association should come into his mind. Yet he had seen that look before. Mrs. Taylor as she popped green pills into her mouth. Chandal as she lifted Kristy into the cart. Lou Harris as he spoke of his daughter.

Drugs?

The word raced through Ron's mind. It would certainly explain a lot. Chandal's lack of concern. His sudden lapses of time, his extended periods of sleep.

"Let me speak to my daughter," he said.

"Speak of what?" Matthew Todd demanded.

"I'm her father!"

Frank Hadley raised his gun. Laughed. "Oh, I'm not going to kill you now," he said. "Unless I have to."

All eyes sparkled at the thought.

Without thinking, Ron snapped. "What the fuck is wrong with you people? She's my daughter. I just want to talk to her."

Widow Wheatley hesitated. She spoke, tightly, to Sheriff Nash. "Control him. Or kill him now. The choice is yours."

"Why?" Ron screamed. "Why are you doing this?"

She wheeled around and glowered at him. "You want to know? For your wife's sins, Mr. Talon. For the mockery and shame and death she has leveled on our people. It's all here—our revenge, our hatred. Can't you feel it. See it? Thousands of years of hatred sculpted into the stone, buried beneath the earth, jammed into the cracks and crevices. It's all here. Buried . . . alive. This valley bears the hatred of the world. Yea, though I walk through the valley of the shadow of death . . ." She smiled. "We are the Ruling Elders. And these," she indicated the children, "are the Keepers of the Hate."

The others moved closer, their eyes animallike, shining with the purity of vision and purpose, moving in harmony with their fellow men, a pageant of human hatred, personified. And now the hungry smile to go with it . . .

"We have not forgotten," she hissed. All hissed with her.

Ron suddenly felt himself seized by violent hands. Widow Wheatley's lips were still moving. "Your wife has taken something from us. Now it is our turn to take something from her."

She poked her bony white finger into his face. Sweat poured down each side of her long nose in a thick stream, soaking her dry cracked lips. Behind her, heavy figures, tiny figures lusted for blood—silent, waiting.

"Life is the only substance we have. We are truth. God is fiction! Our hatred—that is real! That is substance! That is the only truth there is!"

She nodded to the others.

Matthew Todd and Frank Hadley forced Ron quickly to the ground. Tim Hadley and Sheriff Nash came behind him carrying ropes. They pushed him against the cold stone, pinning his arms back. They tied his hands roughly; when they let go, he slid down and fell on his side. He lay there, his face bent toward cold stone. Sweat suddenly froze on his face from the cold air, then just as suddenly exploded and rolled down his face, coating his cheeks, flooding his eyes. He opened his mouth and tried to breathe, but sweat bubbled in his nostrils, flowed in his mouth until he had begun to choke.

Then from all sides children came smashing; like little gnomes, each having a whiplike tree branch, small heads and flat round eyes, they began to beat him savagely. Ron threw himself into a fetal position in a paroxysm of fear. He struggled feebly to protect himself, but was unable to escape their lashes.

"HATE . . . HATE . . . HATE . . . HATE . . ."

They repeated the phrase again and again in vicious tones, brilliantly enunciated, and gradually everyone in the crypt had begun to sway with the slow rhythm of the chant, intoning the word more and more rapidly. As the sound increased, each Elder stepped forward and spat at him furiously. The children smiled, laughed gleefully. Kristy's laughter seemed the loudest.

"Kristy," Ron cried.

Kristy moved closer and raised her stick. "Ahhhhh" from the Elders. She brought the branch down hard across his face. Instantly dark blood streamed greasily from the side of his mouth. She brought the stick down again. Again. And again. Panting, she stepped back and smiled with satisfaction; nodded.

The Widow Wheatley took the child lovingly into her embrace. She peered down at Ron. "Nothing can change the laws of creation. The power of light and darkness. These are the stuff we are carved from. So it will remain. Must remain. Our children, what they have seen, what they have heard, they will remember. They . . ." She nodded her head profoundly. "They, most of all, are the best Keepers of the Hate."

Now the assembly began to disperse. They drifted away imperceptibly into deep crevices from whence they came. The Widow Wheatley was the last to depart.

"Revenge is our justice," she said. "Hatred is our supper."

She paused an instant longer. Her features sun-tipped, radiant. "What is there to eat?" she whispered. "What is the real food? I have meat to eat that you know not of; for flesh is meat indeed." She sighed heavily. "Oh, passing stranger—sleep well. For your days are numbered."

She laughed then, at first with some restraint, then more and more raucously, finally guffawing. Abruptly laughter and footsteps receded into the darkness.

Ron's head sagged on his neck. He lay like a corpse, motionless and alone.

THREE

IN THE DARKNESS OF THE CRYPT, HE HEARD THE SCURRYING OF lizards. Then felt the soft angular body of a snake slither across his leg, slowly, in frightening dalliance.

As the snake slid over his body, Ron neither moved nor thought. Sequences of notions, possible actions, insights, ideas drifted from his mind like birds in the sky, as happened so often in the past week.

The snake slithered smoothly across his chest.

Still he did not move, breathe, blink an eye. Such a motionless suspended state brought with it a dark, indistinct feeling of death, preparedness for death, a preparedness as if he had died twenty times, and had come back countless more times, and had accumulated a knowledge that everything he felt and did was exactly in line with death.

Like a silky leaf in a warm, windy rain, the snake grazed his cheek, its long body slithering up the side of the rock. Then more lazily, like heavily rising cream, then fanning and spreading its tail, the snake slid from his body and disappeared into the rocks above.

After releasing his breath, Ron tried to raise himself but found he was incapable of standing, and let his body fall again to the ground. And he wondered whether it was dusk or dawn.

Only a pale half-glow shone through the opening in the roof far above. He had lost all track of time. The candles within the crypt had all gone out, leaving the chamber almost in darkness. He had drifted off a few times; either he had passed out, or he had fallen asleep—he wasn't sure. It was as though his exhaustion had taken the form of a dangerous illness. He had dreamed of hot summer days and scorching raging fires and had awoken drenched in sweat.

Now the chamber was cool, and the blood on his face felt more scablike than liquid. He thought of his family, but so tormented was he that one anxiety pushed another aside, each more painful than the last, until finally he felt alien to his own thoughts, unable to live within their tortured dimensions.

The uncertainty was unbearable.

He moved his hands passively behind his back. The rope had cut off most of the circulation and coldness seemed to be seeping into his bones. He remained still, staring ahead at the goatlike image that stared back at him with piercing intensity.

Almost without his being aware of it, his attention had shifted from the malevolent face to a small clearing beyond. Something was moving. A shadow—small, hunched—a silhouette; then it faded into the darkness.

For a few long moments, the space ahead was lifeless, then—from within deep shadows emerged Tyler Adam. His steps faltered, but it seemed not out of cowardice. Rather he moved with innate caution, intelligence.

Ron stared at him, and he felt a sudden rush of paralysis. There was blood on Tyler's face, and he held in his hand a long knife as though he were out to avenge whomever it was that had struck him.

What little light there was came through the small opening

above, and filtered down across Tyler's haggard face as he moved closer. He opened his mouth to speak, and more blood came from his mouth. Ron gazed into his eyes, and drew back from what he saw. A maniacal glee. Urgent. Yet somehow lifeless.

"Look at me good," said Tyler Adam, softly. "Remember me."

"Tyler," Ron whispered. "Help me."

He moved quickly to Ron's side and dropped to his knees. He pressed his face close. "So they got you, boy. They got you good, did they?" His breath stank of cheap liquor.

A chill passed through Ron, far deeper than anything the cold bowels of the earth could produce.

"The Elders," Tyler whispered. His face had contorted into a lustful grimace. "Blood is what they seek. Blood is the prize."

"Tyler. Cut the rope." Ron thrust his body sidewards and forced his hands away from his back. "Cut the ropes."

Tyler hesitated, staring at him. His breathing was heavy, even. "Huh? Oh." He smiled, but his eyes narrowed. If eyes were the windows of the soul, Tyler Adam had no soul. His grin faded. Like an awkward child, he groped and pulled at Ron's hands. "They've got you good, boy."

"Please, hurry."

His voice more serious, Tyler said, "I don't want to hurt anyone—" Then, firmly, "But now I must."

Ron felt the thrust of the knife between the ropes, the back side of the blade a cold piece of steel against his wrists. The knife moved twice, quickly. A cold burning pain in his wrists. Ron gasped. "Tyler! You're cutting me. You're cutting my—"

Confused, Tyler turned to face him. "I am sorry. I didn't mean to hurt you . . . I am sorry."

A stream of light flashed above the shadows of Tyler's head . . . above him, above Ron . . . and music. Carnival music loud and raucous. Tyler's eyes shot upward and he laughed. "So it is finally here—Last Friday." His eyes darted quickly back to Ron's face. "Yes, my friend," he said with a leer. "So sorry."

He thrust the knife under Ron's chin, pressed the blade into the flesh of his throat. He laughed and forced the knife deeper. "Look at me good," he said. "Remember me . . ."

His face twisted as his hand tightened around the knife's handle. "For my hatred is the last thing you will see . . .' "

"TYLER!" boomed a voice.

Stroking the handle of the knife with his thumb distractedly, Tyler hesitated. He looked at Ron and grinned. Then, slowly, gently, he lowered the blade.

"That's right, Tyler. Not yet."

Alister Carroll materialized from the shadows, and moved, with stealthy silence, to the casket. He was silent for a second. "Tyler," he said, "Mr. Talon is not your responsibility. Please, go back to the others. I will come up soon."

Tyler scrambled to his feet and, pausing at the archway, sheathed his knife. The crypt thrust its massive shadows over his face. He hesitated a moment longer, then bolted away into the darkness.

Alister stared at Ron in silence. Finally, he sighed and said, "Life is difficult when one looks like Tyler. I'm afraid he is suffering from a sort of male menopause."

Ron twisted uneasily and could feel blood seeping from his wrists. He adjusted his hands and realized that Tyler had, after all, cut a portion of the rope, for now his hands moved freer. He carefully kept his eyes riveted on Alister.

In the distance, a universe away, carnival sounds rose suddenly, grew louder.

With a certain amount of hesitation, Alister moved to the goat-headed statue, opened a small compartment within the goat's stomach, and brought forth a scroll. "They say curiosity killed the cat. But that satisfaction brought him back. I wish you such satisfaction."

He held out the parchment scroll before Ron's eyes. Its faded yellow surface made it difficult to read. Ron leaned forward and squinted.

"Herein let it be stated," the doctrine began, "that we are of one mind, of one spirit, bound toward one common destiny, to avenge all crimes committed against our people. And we swear to our Lord Ahriman to live by the doctrine, under the laws set forth in each declaration below."

The declarations followed:

1

Every man, woman and child shall obey the Grand

Ruling Elder, or in the Grand Ruling Elder's absence, the Keeper of the Hate.

2

Those who shall depart, attempt to depart, or help others to depart, shall be subjected to the Chase. Departure is a major offense.

3

Those who divulge secrets of the Doctrine, the Carnival of Summer, those who do not live in accordance with laws governing the Doctrine, the Carnival of Summer, shall have their tongues removed.

4

Those who shall commit mayhem upon their neighbors, upon the Ruling Elders, without prior warning, shall receive punishment commensurate with the offense committed.

5

Those who seek to marry outside the conclave, those who willfully commit unauthorized adultery with outsiders, shall be put to death. Offspring from such an unholy union shall also be put to death.

6

Those who worship any Lord or God other than Lord Ahriman, shall die by fire. Worshipping any Lord or God other than Lord Ahriman is a major offense.

7

Those who obey the Doctrine, those who spill the blood of an enemy, shall be rewarded with everlasting life.

KNOW YOU and YOUR NEIGHBOR by these declarations, and go in peace.

Ron's eyes moved to the top of the parchment, fixedly stared at the words: the Grand Ruling Elder. His mind raced. Who was it who was this powerful in Brackston, fit to rule a people whose only laws were to control themselves from killing "off-season" or being killed themselves? Laws that went a step further. Towards keeping them, restraining them from ever showing a drop of human decency . . .

Ron's eyes moved from the parchment and stared at Alister with an intensity so great that he turned away when their eyes met.

"The Grand Ruling Elder. Who—" Ron broke off.

Alister had begun to smile.

Ron stared at him in dumb amazement. "You," he breathed. "It's you."

A pause. Then Alister nodded.

"And the Widow Wheatley . . ."

"The Keeper of the Hate. All children—her children."

Ron glanced at the parchment. "Cynthia Harris . . ."

"She was going to help you depart. A major offense. We even believed she may have wanted to leave with you. An even greater offense. It sets such a bad example for our other young people who have certain curiosities. Lou understood. We had no choice. Regrettable, actually. I liked Cynthia, I really did." He shrugged. "As for Nancy, well—she really became a problem after she was crowned queen last year. She was not quite up to the demands of the throne. We had no choice but to remove her tongue."

"Tyler Adam?"

"Well, poor Tyler has broken 'Declaration Four,' I don't know how many times. An eye for an eye. Perhaps you've noticed?"

Ron shook his head.

"The man is blind. Totally blind. Strange, I thought you knew that. He committed mayhem upon Matthew Todd's oldest boy. Then he was suspected of killing Widow Wheatley's two sons. The vote was: An eye for each son." He paused. "Some say he was blinded by his own hatred. Others, well—"

Ron now saw the age-old shrewdness in Alister's eyes. There was the fear, the helplessness, the longing, but most of all there was a pool of knowledge that goes with the territory, that goes with living all those years.

Alister smiled. "It's all here. The masks. The dolls. Ah, a doll collection is most important when educating the young ones. The child makes the doll by hand, naturally. That's very important. Their first born must not be store bought like your Kristy's Jennifer. No. It must be fashioned to the child's own distinct personality. She plays with the doll first, but soon—a strange thing happens. She begins treating the doll as though it were a human. She argues with it, scolds it, until one day an arm disappears, then a leg—and the child is happy. Happy to see her playmate punished, crippled. It all gets easy—real people next." He sighed heavily. "I'm afraid, son, you've opened one of the great black boxes of life, and no one can help you now."

"Why? Why, for Chrissakes!"

Alister clicked his tongue. "A man like you would never understand our ways. It isn't in you."

"Just as it wasn't in Clayton Byron Taylor?" hazarded Ron. "Was that why he escaped?"

Alister tilted his head back and allowed himself a genteel chuckle. "Clayton Byron Taylor fascinates you, doesn't he, Mr. Talon? Well, perhaps that curiosity should be satisfied as well. No, Clayton never escaped. And Clayton was not the brother of Erica Taylor. Are you even more intrigued?"

For some inexplicable reason, Ron found himself dreading Alister's next words. "You don't have to—"

"Clayton Byron Taylor," continued Alister inexorably, smiling, "never existed."

"Never existed . . ." repeated Ron dumbly. "But . . ."

"We of the valley have dreams. We are born of flesh, Mr. Talon. We have normal desires, normal ambitions. But it is the rule of the valley that our destiny lies here, never beyond the ridges. We are in the world, but not of it. Mrs. Taylor has another side, an almost separate personality. It is out of this other identity, highly creative, but of very weak character, that the music comes. We allow this music. Hell, we even enjoy it. And we have filtered it to the world. But always under a pseudonym."

"Clayton Byron Taylor," breathed Ron. "Then—"

"Mrs. Taylor wrote the music, yes."

"But I saw his picture. At least, I thought it was his picture."

"What you in the business would call a publicity shot," Alister replied. "The music was composed by Mrs. Taylor and dedicated to the memory of a much younger brother who died many years ago trying to escape the valley." Alister smiled gently. "If you have any other questions, Mr. Talon, merely ask me. Don't make a further fool of yourself with your ridiculous speculations."

Unhurriedly, he rolled the scroll up, placed it back into the goat's stomach, and turned to face Ron. "I like you," he went on. "I really do. I made the Elders take a vote. I saw to it that you'd go free. Not an easy matter. The voting was split. It caused Matt Todd and his wife to fight bitterly. The poor bastard sleeps in his gas station now because of you." He shook his head sadly. "It was I who cast the deciding vote. I let you drive out of here. It isn't often a person gets a chance to do that. Why did you come back, son? Why didn't you just keep going?"

"It's something you wouldn't understand, Mr. Carroll."

Alister had taken out his pipe and was scooping tobacco into it from a pouch. "It's rare," he said casually, "when a man is willing to sacrifice himself for others. I guess that's why I liked you right from the beginning."

"Will you tell me one thing?"

Alister cleared his throat. "If I can."

"If I had gone for help. If I'd of brought them back here to Brackston. What then?"

"What would they have found?" Alister puffed leisurely on his pipe. "Tidy little streets, tidy little houses. Lots of flowers. The scent of lilac permeating the air. A nice, quiet, safe little town nestled in the mountains, now aglow in the rising moon. Or—" He broke off.

"Or?"

"Or perhaps," he said with a smile, "they'd have found no town at all. Just a stone. A stone around which moving is done. But does it matter now?"

Ron's cheeks had reddened. "What's going to happen tonight?"

"To tell you the truth, I don't really know." He removed the pipestem and began to blow through it. "What happens on the hill tonight is up to the Widow Wheatley. She never lets the men in on her little secrets."

Ron knew Alister was lying. They all knew; every last person in Brackston knew but him.

Alister suddenly looked bored. "Only thing now," he said, "is to pray for rain."

"Why's that?"

"If the rain comes . . . but it won't . . ." Grimacing, he folded his arms to indicate that he was finished.

"What then?" Ron asked.

"Then—then you may have a chance."

This said, Alister Carroll walked the length of the crypt slowly and paused in the open archway, the deep blue shadows and a light mist swirling around his ankles.

"Tim?" he called out.

Tim Hadley edged his way into the chamber. He held a double-barrelled shotgun waist-high, carrying the rifle in the crook of his arm.

FOUR

HE WAITED UNTIL HIS BREATHING FADED, SLOWED TO A STEADY unbroken rhythm. And then, to be certain, he waited a while longer. Tim Hadley's head finally dropped to his chest.

Ron felt along the rope. His fingers found the frayed portion. He wished Tyler had made a deeper cut. The rope was thick, and it wasn't going to give way easily. He scooted back a few inches on his buttocks and pressed the rope against the rock. He began to work his hands up and down slowly.

Tim murmured something and Ron could feel his pulse quicken. He took his hands away from the rock, straightened. Tim remained in a stupor.

He began the wrist movement again. Rubbing the rope against the rock, blood seeped into his palms in a steady trickle.

In the dead light of the crypt everything looked barren and unreal. Now and then a sudden flare of light from above. With it, an explosive sound and a bloodroar from the multitude. "Ahhhh." He timed his movements with the sounds that were coming more frequently now.

"Ahhhh"; he rubbed. "Ehhhh"; he rubbed harder.

Suddenly the rope snapped. Ron's hand automatically shot out in front of him. Tim looked up, startled. Quickly Ron put his hand behind his back.

Tim stared upward, wiped a yawn away with the back of his ruddy hand. Then sniffed the air as the smell of cooking wafted up.

"They're cooking the meat," he said. "Roasting it. Stinks, doesn't it? That stench will get into your clothes and hair if you're not careful. Takes weeks to get rid of it."

"What kind of meat?" Ron felt himself sickening.

Tim Hadley smiled and pulled a flask of liquor from his pocket. He gulped feverishly and held the flask out to him.

Ron shook his head. His gaze drifted to Tim's shotgun propped by his side. The distance between them was too great. He knew he'd never be able to get to the weapon unless Tim moved away.

Another splash of light, followed by a small explosion. "Ahhhh."

"What's that noise?" Ron asked.

"Fireworks. The Elders always like to make a big show of things on Last Friday. To get the young ones all stirred up. Me, all that noise rattles my guts."

"I don't suppose there's water down here."

"Not fit to drink."

"How far below are we?"

"Depends on which direction you take. Fifty feet— hundred, hard to say."

Ron reached down with his hand and touched the ground, and suddenly his hand froze. The stone behind him was ice-cold. He groped, trying to find a rock to use as a weapon.

He heard Tim say, "You're a goddamn fool!"

He jerked his hand up into position as if it were still tied. "What?"

"Coming back the way you did. A goddamn fool." Tim drank again, emptying his flask. With a gesture of disgust, he flung the flask across the chamber.

Another flash; explosion. "Ahhhh."

Ron tried to speak, but his mind was a blank. A heavy mist crept its way along the chamber floor, truncating Tim's torso at the waist.

"You were warned," Tim mumbled. "You should

have . . ." His voice faded. He straightened and shook his head. "Piss on you!" he cried.

Ron flexed his fingers, trying to work out the numbness. The thumb on his right hand ached. "I really need a drink of water," he said.

"Shut the fuck up!"

"I need—"

"I said shut up!" Tim rose in the mist like a great bear and stared down at Ron. He swayed slightly, reaching out to brace himself. Stiff with anger, he looked away, stared at his flask. Snorting and grumbling and spitting, he said, "Do you know how many lives are buried here? Do you? This fucking mountain is covered with the dead." He glimpsed the casket. "But the stonecutter—he has her. Widow Wheatley. Every year he dies—every year he comes back!" A surge of outrage strained his eyes.

Ron slid his left leg under his right, pulling himself up into a more solid position. He shifted his body weight closer to the rock, until he was set in a coiled position ready to spring. "How long have you been part of this?" he asked.

Tim's eyes lowered. "Twenty-five years. Just a boy I joined. Just a . . ."

"It bothers you, doesn't it?"

"What's another life? Here one minute, gone the next."

"But still, it does bother you."

"Guilt is weakness. And I told you to shut up!"

Tim stood above Ron, clenching his fists. His eyes were glazed, his skin white. Sweat ran in a steady stream down his face.

A sudden flash of light; an explosion. "Ehhhh."

Ron prepared to strike.

Again Tim Hadley's eyes shifted to his flask, and this time his eyes locked on it; a glitter of silver shroud by a yellow mist. He moved toward it.

Ron moved too. He rose and dashed in a single movement for the shotgun. He never stopped to look at the man to his right. He reached out and jerked up the weapon, bringing it around like a club, striking Tim Hadley above the collarbone. A rush of air burst from his mouth as he fell forward, striking his head on the edge of rock, and collapsed into stillness.

Ron stood for a moment, frozen. Waiting for Tim to move.

He had the shotgun aimed at his head and his finger readied on the trigger.

He drew a breath, waited. Then let his eyes scan the crypt. In the moonglow darkness all he could see were half-faces of statues leering at him. The muscles in his back and shoulders felt cramped. He shook off the sensation. He knew he had to move. But where? He'd never be able to find his way back through the maze of tunnels and passageways. He also knew he would not be given another chance. The next time they'd kill him.

But he wasn't concerned with his death now. It was Chandal and Kristy he worried about. What had become of them? How in the hell was he going to reach them? Even if he did, what then? His options were nil.

Move, goddamn it. Move!

He backed to the center of the crypt and turned. Alister had gone off in that direction. No, there. He swirled in three directions at one time. He wasn't sure.

A sudden flash of light. A small pop. "Ehhhh."

He glanced up, debating another alternative. It was worth a try. There were ledges all the way to the top. At least he knew where he was going. A knot formed in his stomach. It was his only real chance.

He moved. It was too late.

The rush came from the side, out of the shadows of the far wall. Tim Hadley threw himself at his legs, and Ron thrust his hands out to prevent his head from smashing into the rocks. They rolled, Ron punching and Tim Hadley clutching, the air reverberating with grunts and groans. Dust, clots of earth, sticks snapped. Ron smashed his fist into the man's face; his head jerked back, his nose busted open like a ketchup bottle. Tim yelled and released him, and Ron stumbled to his feet.

But the man had already regained his balance and charged again.

Ron turned to meet it, but before he could lift the shotgun he was hit by the full weight of Tim Hadley. He stumbled and fell backwards onto the ground. Tim's body fell on top of him. He shoved the shotgun out with both hands to protect himself, but he didn't have the strength to lift against that massive body. Quickly, Tim pressed the shotgun down against Ron's chest, then forced it forward until it was pressed across his throat.

As Ron struggled, he felt the cold metal cut the air from his windpipe, until finally he began to gag for air. He could feel his lungs about to burst as the dead weight of the man on top of him pressed harder. He jerked his arm free and jammed his hand into Tim's face. Bracing his foot against the rocks, he tried to jerk his body up, trying to throw Tim over on his side. There was no moving him.

For a moment Ron thought about giving up his struggle. Letting go. The palm of his hand fell back, reached out, groped, fashioning itself around a stone. With his last ounce of strength he smashed the stone into the back of Tim's head. Hatred and revenge and power oozed out of him as he struck him again and again and again, until finally Tim Hadley stopped moving.

Ron staggered to his feet, his chest heaving, and stared down at the man. He lay perfectly still with his face lying in a pool of his own blood. Jesus Christ! Ron hoped he wasn't dead. He stood for a moment in frightened awe, rooted to the spot. Then his senses burned again and the numbness left him. He had to move, and move quickly.

He removed his shirt, then his tee shirt; tore two small strips from the bottom, and bandaged his wrists. With the remainder of the tee shirt, he fashioned a strap and tied it to either end of the shotgun. Donning his shirt, he slung the weapon over his shoulder and tested the makeshift strap. This done, he began to climb.

FIVE

THE ROCK GAVE WAY BENEATH HIS FEET. HE REACHED OUT AND clung to the vine cluster above his head; one leg remained dangling in midair. Shaking, he glanced down. He heard the rock hit with a deafening crash on the ground below. It had taken a long time getting there.

Quickly he pulled his leg up and stood cramped on a narrow ledge. His outstretched arms were starting to strain. He inched closer to the wall. Held for a moment.

Turning around slowly, he saw evidence that the walls around him were partially caved in. Above him was a small niche. In slow motion, he lifted his foot to the next crevice. He pushed against it. It held.

He paused to catch his breath. A slight wind whistled among the rocks, adding to the feeling of desolation. From where he stood, he could see the moon. It hung in the sky like a bent spoon.

He waited and listened. All he could hear was the wind on stone and the occasional mutterings and carryings-on of the carnival.

With a light step, he moved a notch higher. One more step, another, then he dropped to his knees, trembling uncontrollably. A feeling of death rose within him, chilling his body. He unslung the shotgun and sat. He knew he was lucky to still be alive. He closed his eyes briefly, giving thanks to God, then took several deep breaths in preparation to move. Hands splayed by his buttocks, he opened his eyes and scanned his surroundings. With an effort, he stood.

Slowly he realized that there was an opening in the rocks behind him. No, more than an opening. A carved arch. He moved closer. A maze of catacombs lay ahead. A labyrinth of tunnels . . . and steep narrow steps that spiraled up.

He waited a few minutes for his eyes to adjust. He saw no movement on the steps. They had probably been used years ago when the crypt was first built. Satisfied that it was all clear, he slung his weapon over his shoulder and started up the steps.

When he emerged into the light again, he was no more than twenty feet from the opening at the top. He felt a small amount of relief, but noticed there was no way to get to the opening except through a narrow tunnel.

"Shit," he muttered. If there was one thing he'd learned during his stay at Brackston, it was that narrow openings were not safe places.

With a sense of uncertainty, he felt along the rock inside the tunnel wall. He came away with a handful of wet sandstone. It was obvious the tunnel wasn't very safe. The surface of stone was loose. Water seeped between its many layers. He slapped the inside wall with his open hand, harder; small pieces of rock fell from the opening.

He stepped back. The opening was no more than two feet in diameter. The opening of the average doorway was three feet. He studied the tunnel a moment longer. A crack ran along the wall before arching back to join the mouth of the tunnel.

Ron concentrated hard, then made his decision.

He crawled the first few yards with ease, dragging the shotgun with him. He could feel the slimy surface of stone against his skin. Reaching up with his palm, he felt the ceiling. Solid rock.

With enthusiasm, he glided like a water snake another five yards and then abruptly stopped. Ahead the tunnel narrowed. He tried forcing himself forward. It was no go. Trapped in darkness, he debated what he should do. Goddamn it! He forced his body backwards until his feet touched the ridge and then dropped.

His breath came in sharp gasps. He reminded himself not to panic. He waited until he felt the tension leave his body. If he could remain calm, remain relaxed, it should be possible to crawl through that space. He was sure of it. All he had to do was to remain calm, to breathe slowly.

He began to climb again, forcing himself to rest at various intervals. Then he burrowed with both hands in the wet stone. Rested. Moved a few inches. Burrowed some more. He was almost to the top when he saw a bright burst of light ahead. It came back again, but only for a moment. Then total blackness.

Now he could feel a steady stream of air as another piece of stone broke loose in his hand. Just a little more and he could get through. Just a little more. Then it happened. The earth around him began to move. He saw the earth give way first and then heard it, *woosh* followed by silence. He could not breathe. God, he was buried, imprisoned and suffocating in a large mound of earth; paralyzed by the heavy earth and stone that had collapsed around him.

He attempted to take small breaths. He continued to do

this for several long moments, but the weight on his chest became impossible to bear. He grew dizzy. And he knew, absolutely knew, that he was about to die.

The children knew better than to ask questions. They sat shivering with expectation.

Now a tide of people squeezed through the back gate of the carnival ground and followed a well-worn path leading up the side of the mountain. The horseman sat astride his animal and ordered the people to clear the way. People grumbled.

"Stand aside!" he ordered, forcing the huge sweating side of the animal against the crowd. "Citizens of Brackston. Stand aside!"

"Crucify her!" someone shouted. A chant quickly began. "Crucify her! CRUCIFY HER!" Behind the cries, meat roasted, wanton fingers probed lustfully between the whore's legs and dirty faces smiled while greeting their neighbors. "How are you, Abigail? Beautiful night, isn't it?"

"Jack . . . Russell . . . good to see you. You both know Michael?"

"How are you, Michael? This is his first Last Friday, isn't it?"

Michael nodded, hanging onto his father's hand.

Then suddenly they came. Out of the vast wilderness, out of legend and myth, out of the depths of human hatred itself.

They came first into the town square, shaking their death-rattles, uttering strange lamentations. Part man, part beast, part bird. Wearing ceremonial dress adorned with jackal heads, bear heads, bird feathers and grotesque wooden masks, they danced on hooves, claws and on bare feet. With eyes peering through long bird beaks and gaping goat mouths, through bull nostrils and ram horns, they flashed symbols of fire and stone.

They moved on, dancing for the smiling children. No longer men, but embodied forces of earth and sky swirling through the dust of the hills, shaking that remote noise of hatred, stirring and entreating the children to awaken to the wonder and mystery of their role in the cosmic order of things.

Suddenly it was over.

The mountainside fell hushed.

With great frenzy and excitement, all eyes turned to face the stone. The time had come.

Huge birds of many colors were hovering overhead. A faint breeze was stirring through the trees with a whispered sound indescribably smooth and soothing. The bright moonglow—pure, dazzling yet soft—illuminated a scene of paradisiacal splendor. Pure whiteness glimmered on either side of him, the soft glow a warming sensation.

So this was death.

The thought trickled through his consciousness like a faint reflection of something glimpsed in a steamed-over mirror. Abruptly something roared in his ears. Fireworks—thunder?

Just as Ron's lungs were about to explode, the earth slipped away from his face. He forced his body forward enough so that his head was now resting in a small pocket which enabled him to breathe. Above him he could see the glimmer of moon and stars.

Christ, he was alive. Alive! He felt a slight breeze caress his face. He endeavored to raise his right arm and he laughed like a person emerging from ether with aches and painful stiffness in every part of his body. His arms were all but immovable.

Alive, he whimpered inwardly. Was it possible?

With great effort, he pulled his right arm free, then digging frantically, he freed his left arm. Stretching out both arms, he pulled himself up until he had freed himself.

The ground beneath him began to tremble. He froze. All his terror returned. His slightest movement could disturb the balance of things, sending him down again in an avalanche of dirt and rock that would bury him forever. He could almost envision his fears liquified, ice-blue in color, oozing from the stone above, the earth below.

But the shotgun was still lodged in the earth below. He could see it. He dropped to his stomach and reached down with his hand. His fingertips just grazed the nose. The earth started to sink, the shotgun with it. He reached farther, straining, groping. Taking hold of the weapon, he pulled. The shotgun came up as the earth slid away, leaving the chamber below completely sealed off.

He rolled over on his back and hugged the shotgun like a long lost lover. His breath came in short gasps, eventually slowly and steadying.

Finally he managed to stand up. He switched the shotgun from his right hand to his left and stripped off the makeshift sling. Both of his wrists were still bleeding, the exertion having pumped the blood more violently through his veins. The bandages on his wrists were soaked in blood.

He paused only long enough to wrap another layer of tee shirt around each wrist. Then turning slowly, he saw he was standing some ten feet from the mouth of a cave. He inched forward along the wall until he had reached the opening. His whereabouts, his next actions, and his approaching destiny were merely links in an endless chain of things unknown.

SIX

THE STARS WERE FADING ONE BY ONE, SMUDGED BY BILLOWING smoke that rose lazily before his eyes. The night was slowly turning a slate gray. Far below a dark group stood motionless before the gates of the town. High and slender torches cast their light over various faceless countenances, hushed for the moment in one solemn and intent expression. Now there rose a slow and dismal music that floated far along the desolate ridges; while a chorus of voices accompanied the woodwind sound.

First came the musicians, playing a slow march—next the women, chanting their strange melodious dirges. The female voices mingled with those of children, whose light and airy voices made a striking contrast of life and death—the fresh flower and the withered one.

Ron leaned against the edge of the cave, feeling the cold stone prickle through his shirt. It didn't seem quite so dark now; his eyes were beginning to adjust. He could see the shapes of houses far below and the menacing bulk of stone leading up the side of the mountain.

Now a sudden burst of flames on a plateau above the gate

on higher ground. Children dashed madly about torching a huge stack of wood. The fire flashed luminously across the gloomy valley—it shot above the massive walls of the neighboring cliffs; and Ron started to behold the blaze reddening on the creatures' faces who danced around it.

They were circling the fire now, dancing in a madman's frenzy, delirium, their huge animal heads weaving in and out of shadows. The fire blazed up with a roar, sending a column of red flames soaring. They moaned and wailed and shouted. Even though the words were unintelligible, Ron felt that their hideous shrieks were like a hand held toward him, a handshake with death.

While the voices swelled, mounting to a climax, the procession from below rose; they shuffled in single file along the narrow path. One by one they came, stepping in rhythm to the solemn, dark tune. The musicians led the way, fanning out; then the old women arrived at the plateau followed by the children. Hundreds more remained below, stood in monumental silence, and stared up at the spectacle.

Squatting on his heels, Ron transferred the shotgun from his left hand to his right. He was suddenly aware that the singing had changed to chanting and had increased in volume. The air was thick with pungent odors, with the smell of meat burning and woodsmoke and a strange aromatic overtone that seeped into his nostrils and eyes. But it was the chanting that clouded his mind. Momentarily the night vanished, and his anger, even his presence in the town were no longer important. The monotonous chant had found its way into his blood . . . He jerked himself to his feet, shivering, and could feel his arms and legs trembling.

He froze when she appeared. No one on the plateau turned in her direction, yet beneath their apparent disinterest, they were aware of the group's precise placement to her ever-growing presence.

The Widow Wheatley came in her black garments, barefooted, and held a red flower in her right hand. Her head bare, her locks disheveled, her face paler than marble, but composed and still, she hesitated. Swiftly she cast the flower into the fire.

"Let this flower," she wailed, "the roots of which are covered with the blood of our slain brethren, let its pedals burn, let its smoke rise in the air, let the stone breathe in its bloody fragrance. Flower to smoke! Smoke to stone! Burn!"

"Ahhhh" from the crowd on the plateau.

"Ehhhh" from the multitude below.

Then all fell silent. Their eyes seemed to be fixed on something holy and invisible to normal sight. Their faces greased with grins of lust.

The Widow Wheatley spoke quietly for several minutes, her tone tender, her even flow of words leveled at the children who huddled at the feet of animal-headed humans. Her voice rose then in a shrill cry.

Ron became aware of a flurry of movement at the town gate. He stepped farther out of the cave to get a better view. Instantly he realized where he stood. Good Christ! He was standing in the mouth of the stone. The stone around which moving was done. A mouth as it had appeared from below was actually a cave. The realization came quite suddenly, with startling effect: He felt himself weakening; his wrists were bleeding profusely. His legs started to give way. He stepped back slightly and held onto the stone for support.

Widow Wheatley's screech penetrated his consciousness. The cry of hunger demanding to be fed. The scream of a hyena in the madness of the quarter moon.

She screamed.

The crowd roared back.

At the peak of pandemonium, she chose to signal for silence. Instantaneously it was granted so completely that all seemed to hold their breath. This silence screamed worse than any human voice Ron had ever heard. He could feel fear wash through his blood, chemicalize his mouth with raw acid.

And still they were silent, caught in the throes of some emotion that was so ugly he could read it in the twisted postures of their bodies silhouetted against the light.

It grew. He could feel them willing it to grow.

Praying, reaching, begging to feel more of that ugliness, that substance of evil he could not quite identify.

Widow Wheatley moaned now, then shrieked again and again, body writhing as the crowd watched until suddenly she seemed to have reached a climax and could now proceed with some sanity until her need would build again. She motioned.

308

Suddenly the gate to the town was flung open once again and the masses parted to permit a small figure to pass. A child in royal cloak and crown, a torch held high in her right hand. As she proceeded, most of the crowd fell to their knees in adoration; reached out to kiss the hem of her cloak.

Ron's vision seemed to have strengthened to permit him to see what he loathed to see. By the time the child had reached the plateau, the sight of her had burned an image into his brain that could never be forgotten. Kristy, his beautiful baby; his bright-eyed child; his piece of the future.

Kristy, the queen.

She had stepped onto the plateau now and dropped a graceful curtsy to the Widow Wheatley. It was a sweet gesture, well done. Even Ron could read its meaning. It plainly gave the message of a queen humbling herself before the Queen Mother. It was not only a respectful thing to do; it was tradition.

The Widow Wheatley put out a deprecating hand and drew Kristy to her feet. First she kissed her on either cheek and then the old lady did the kind thing, the thing hardest for a proud old lady to do. She gathered her skirts and began to lower herself to the ground. First to her knees, then lower; still lower, until she lay face downward at Kristy's feet, hands outstretched, groveling.

The crowd went wild.

The noise actually seemed to rock the ground under Ron's feet.

Kristy had helped the Widow Wheatley to her feet and now gestured that the gate to the town be opened once again. Four men stepped forward, their shoulders bent under the immense weight of a platform upon which was affixed a gleaming white sedan chair. Upon the chair sat a veiled woman.

The four men advanced forward slowly, heads bent, proud to carry their burden.

Ron kept his eyes fixed on the woman. Something about the way she was dressed prodded his memory. Her gown was empire-waisted, full-skirted. The veil was seeded with white pearls. He could see her startlingly clearly; the entire platform blazed with torches, dozens of torches whose flames fanned out in the gypsy breeze until they seemed likely to spark onto the woman's dress, to devour fabric like kindling wood; to make for themselves a torch. A human torch. And still the woman sat unmoved in her veil, her empire-waisted gown, pure, virginal.

Kristy's puppet.

The realization hit Ron unkindly. It was an agony. Something too horrible about it to endure. He wailed aloud.

Oh, God, oh, sweet Jesus. Oh, how could it possibly be that the woman was dressed *exactly like Kristy's puppet?* He could not decide why this was the most horrible thing; he was afraid to think about it; but he did think about it in spite of himself and just when he almost had the connection—

—The woman's veil blew back.

His heart shuddered. Stopped momentarily.

Chandal, he wept. Oh, God, no, not Chandal.

Under torchlight, Chandal's eyes were brilliant, her face reposed and flowerlike. Too peaceful. She was too peaceful.

His obsession with time now began to pay him back with a skill. He seemed to be able to grab hold of every second and make it last just a little longer. Each second was freeze-frame: his wife. Click. His daughter. Click. His wife.

"The idea of life as sacrifice."

Click. Sheriff Nash.

"Blood is necessary to save the world and the people in it."

Click. Tim Hadley.

"To sacrifice ourselves without a moment's thought for the common good."

Click. Mrs. Taylor.

Suddenly, with speed that makes understanding violent, Ron knew what was about to happen. Just as the Cretans sacrificed their loveliest daughters to the Minoan bull, and the Carthaginians burned their living babies to placate the great god, Moloch, so too was Chandal about to sacrifice Kristy to the God of Stone. The God of all Hatred.

The thought sent Ron's body into a spasm.

All at once his legs gave way. He was falling. Drawn too close to the brink of the ledge he was on. He could have been, should have been, killed.

A vast bottomless hole yawned all around him into the fiery bowels of the earth. Instead he had all but impaled himself upon the V-spread prongs of an outreaching rock. Shuddering, he held on, arms aching, and began to climb backwards.

He refused to look toward the black hole, refused to even acknowledge its presence. And yet he knew it was there.

His feet connected with earth. He had reached a new level to the cave. At once he struggled to find a new vantage point.

The procession, he noted, had progressed from the plateau to a second higher clearing of ground. As he watched, Kristy and the Widow Wheatley, the first to arrive at this level, turned to welcome the rest of the royal party. It was a rugged path. The men carrying Chandal struggled to keep going. They were dressed in short tunics; their bare chests dripped sweat. One of the men staggered and fell to one knee.

The crowd moaned and pressed forward, threatening to break the gate to the city, as the sedan chair nearly slid to the ground.

"Rise, fool!" shrieked Beatrice Wheatley, plainly indicating that, if necessary, she herself would descend and labor to carry Chandal forth.

The man had managed to get his foot under the weight of his body, even as his massive arms struggled to press his side of the platform higher.

A relieved sigh as he straightened. A cheer as the platform began once again to progress.

Ron's eyes burned. He could scarcely endure the sight of his wife's calm, yet exalted, countenance. He glanced away and focused instead on the small party who trailed behind the sedan chair. They were much closer to him now, a brief climb away once they would have all attained the third level where Kristy and the Widow Wheatley stood waiting. Directly behind the sedan chair was another woman who cried aloud as she walked; moaned; seemed to be praying or begging. Her clothes were fine but had been torn. Her hair was in wild disarray and as torch light illumined her face, maddened from her fright, Ron saw that blood ran down from her hair to cover her cheeks.

She stumbled forward. Upon her shoulders she carried a massive cord of timberwood.

Behind her strode Tyler Adam. Tyler's head was up, his face gleamed with joy. He also carried a cord of timberwood, effortlessly, as though it weighed nothing. High expectation was in the way he stepped forward impatiently, prodding the woman ahead of him to go faster.

Last of all came Matthew Todd and Lou Harris.

As Todd stepped onto the knoll high above the town, a tumultuous cry rang out, a thundering of feet stamping the ground, a blare of musical instruments.

And then the chant.

"Crucify them! Crucify them!"

Ron's breath came out in a grunt as though he had been kicked in the stomach.

He had almost forgotten the shotgun he had held between arm and body for so long it seemed a part of him, welded into place. He found it almost impossible to raise his arm to release the weapon. He sighed as his finger experimentally reached for the trigger.

Sometimes, a voice seemed to say, *death comes as an answer. The only answer.*

He looked down now at the base of the stone that sheltered him. The stone around which moving is done. The stone around which people gather to worship a dark god. A god of hatred and death. As though he knew he would see it, he nodded at the immense stone cross at his feet. At its four points were wood so that nails might connect with a carpentry surface. To either side were straight cords of timber.

Grimly Ron nodded at these also. These two were crosses, as well, he realized. Their crossbows were carried by those who were chosen to be crucified. His gaze shifted down the hill and he eased into position for the leap he was going to have to make. No matter what, he was never going to let it happen, was not going to let Chandal sacrifice her daughter, his daughter. Their daughter.

Soon he could see the bustle of activity under him. The woman let loose a piercing scream of terror. Two men held her; another ripped her dress from her body. The act was swift and violent. Hammer blows rang out. The woman screamed repeatedly as the square-cut iron nails were driven into her wrists. Todd wiped a splattering of blood from his face, then moved to her feet.

Rivulets of blood flowed freely over the rocks now, making their serpentine way into the dark crevices of stone.

Ron's eyes moistened. His body trembled, shook—the hammer was brought down again, twice more. And it had been done. Nail at a time. The crowd roared. Now the woman's body hung shuddering upon the cross.

Tyler Adam took the first nail without a whimper, his eyes shining; he seemed ready to assist in his own crucifixion if they would have permitted it. And the crowd roared even louder.

The second nail was driven cleanly through the major vein in Tyler Adam's wrist. A startled look came into his eyes. He hesitated. His mouth trembled. He looked puzzled.

Then Ron realized that Tyler Adam did not hate himself so perfectly after all. That death, this kind of death, was not as he had imagined.

Tyler screamed and begged to be taken down. He screamed as loud as the woman had screamed. He promised to do anything if they would only take him off of his cross.

His screams made the blood run quicker.

He died too quickly and that was a shame, for it was a highly effective crucifixion.

Ron's body had trembled so violently that he had fallen limp, still shaking. Yet he contemplated his leap. Impossible odds. He could perhaps overpower Lou Harris and Matthew Todd, but that left the remaining four men. Even with the shotgun, he could never hope to take down all of them before he himself would be seized.

Still he could hear the eerie howling like demons as the woman upon the cross droned on in pain. Her moans seemed to complete the terror of the carriage house in New York that had somehow been left undone. It swirled in his brain like a fan gone berserk.

The Widow Wheatley turned, lifted her arms; and the four men wailed with wild screams of devotion. Bowing, they leapt over rocks and descended into the darkness below.

The music stopped; abruptly. The crowd below grew still. Matthew Todd emerged from the shadows, but his features were not his own. There was a snout, and a wiry mass of brown hair, and sharp ears like those of a goat.

He turned with great majesty and surveyed the multitude below. A second face appeared. A two-headed creature. The Goddess of Water—the God of Spring. The two-headed monster looked doubly horrifying atop Lou Harris's slender, poised body.

The multitude far below was moving again; no music now, only wild shrieks of adoration.

The Widow Wheatley's hands reached out and drew the veil away from Chandal's face. Chandal's eyes remained fixedly ahead, dull and transfixed.

"We bid Thee, O Mother, rise!"

"Rise!" howled the multitude.

"Climb . . ."

"Climb . . ."

"Wind go into blood . . ."

"Wind go into blood . . ."

"Blood go into stone . . ."

"Blood go into stone . . ."

"Oh, spirit as true as stone, guide her hand. For a child without desire is a stone without a place to rest. Hear me, Ahriman, guide her."

"Guide her . . ."

"Who is stone . . ."

"Who is stone . . ."

"O Mother . . ."

"O Mother . . ."

"You are . . ."

"You are . . ."

Thus the chant continued as Matthew Todd and Lou Harris took hold of Chandal and removed her cloak. She was left to stand motionless beside the massive stone cross.

The Widow Wheatley turned suddenly to Kristy. "I adjure you, child! By the mountains, and by the Deathstone that stands above all things, that you awaken not, nor stir—until it pleases me."

It was the sight of Kristy's eyes that gave Ron his first clue, and he felt his mouth twisted in that same incredulous horror that still held Tyler Adam's mouth rigid. Kristy's eyes were as empty of life as was the rest of her face, and her lips barely moved when she spoke.

"I hear you," she whispered. "I obey."

"Sacrifice is all!" The Widow Wheatley's hoarse voice graveled. "Let hatred and fire cover your desire!"

The Widow Wheatley laid her lips first on Kristy's forehead, then her left eye and then her right eye and then on each breast.

"Thou art ready, child," the Widow Wheatley screamed. "Thou art our future. Thou art our queen. Let us make the womb prepared!"

The multitude fell hushed as Kristy moved away to the foot of the stone. She knelt, uttered a brief chant; then, slowly, she drew back a large black cloth that covered an altar which had been carved into the base of the stone. Resting atop the altar was a huge slab of stone. Inscribed were the words: Chandal Talon.

And Ron knew what was to come. It was not Kristy who was to give up her life. It was Chandal.

"Motion is being!" cried Widow Wheatley.

And Kristy moved toward Chandal. The child's eyes were suddenly alive, bright and intelligent.

"To be is to move . . ."

Matthew Todd placed a knife lovingly in Kristy's hand. Lou Harris anoited her with ointment.

"Sight is this and gone now." The Widow Wheatley drew back.

Kristy turned, lifted the knife in the air; and the multitude leaned forward in the darkness, panting for blood.

Thirst. Thirst. Thirst.

". . . Mother, make your bed soon," Kristy hissed. "For I am full with hatred and revenge, and I look now to sacrifice you in order that this revenge be put to sleep. First, blood to drink, then to bed upon your cross." Thus spoken, she pressed the knife into Chandal's flesh.

"Nooo!" Ron cried out, going mad. Waves of revulsion and nausea swept him as he dropped to the first level of rock below. A total interior explosion surged through his blood. Now he moved out away from the rock against which he had landed, his muscles bulging, arms flailing, and in a rush of agony leapt to the ground.

His roar became a wild moan as his eyes darted frantically about him.

"Kill him!" the Widow Wheatley cried and moved.

Lou Harris and Matthew Todd moved with her.

What followed took only seconds. There was a quick flash of torchlight as Matthew Todd sprang forward. He advanced one step—it was his last on earth. Ron pulled the trigger. Matthew Todd's chest opened in a single gush of bone and tissue. He fell to the ground with a wild bellow, his arms reaching toward Ron as he twisted from side to side without moving his legs.

Ron brought the shotgun around like a club and caught the Widow Wheatley across the chest. She fell to the ground like a loose bundle of rags. Almost at once he leveled the shotgun and caught Lou Harris in midleap. His left hand was a fist, his right held a knife. His blood splattered across Kristy's face as he went down. With a sharp intake of breath, his body drew up into a knot next to the Widow Wheatley.

Perhaps it was the blood of a dead thing on her living child that brought Chandal from her trance. Whatever the case, she screamed and dashed to her daughter with wild hysteria. Her scream—the shock, stunned Ron for several seconds. When he recovered, he felt the earth tremble beneath his feet. Bodies were strewn lifeless on the ground; but he saw them not—his eyes were fixed upon the ghastly white face of his daughter—a face of unutterable pain, agony and despair. Her eyes opened and shut rapidly, as if sense were not yet whole—then suddenly she opened her eyes and began to sob. "Mommy . . . Mommy . . ."

Ron moved quickly to her side. Chandal screamed. "Ron, we must save her!"

"We will," he muttered. "We will."

Fiercely, he grappled Kristy in his arms with a half-caressing motion to still her wails. He turned wildly, dazedly, not knowing what to do next, and felt the quiver of Kristy's body in his arms. He had forgotten how small and helpless she could feel in his arms.

Suddenly a piercing cry shattered the night, laden with anger, protesting an outrage that was too sharp to bear in silence. The single voice was quickly joined by another. Figures began climbing the rocks toward them. Heads lifted all along the path. Men ran to the edge of ridges and called questions from torch to torch. A rush of voices now that pulsated and collided with excitement. Every head was turned, listening, eyes searching the area of the stone. Outrage quickly spread. Ritual was suddenly thrust aside.

Other sounds broke upon the hill. Wails, sharp commands,

cautionings. The whole town was suddenly, angrily alive and on the move.

Ron tensed with indecision. Then, moving at last, he hugged Kristy closer into his arms, grabbed Chandal by the hand, and rushed into the awaiting darkness.

SEVEN

THE DESCENT BECAME EXCEEDINGLY DIFFICULT. THEY MOVED IN deep shadows along the ridge that was faintly lighted by a phosphorescent glow. Ron turned abruptly and headed east, still descending. Chandal was close to panic. In the confused dimensions of night, they had lost all sense of how far they were from Mrs. Taylor's house. There were steep drops and ridges in the side of the mountain, and as they reached each new level, they expected to see the house, but it was never there. With each disappointment, their fear increased. Kristy had begun to cry again, and Ron finally could not carry her any further.

Chandal fell exhausted to the ground and began to cry. "I can't go on," she shrilled. "I can't. You go on. Take Kristy."

"For God's sakes," Ron pleaded. "We have to get to the car."

"I can't. I can't move."

"Please, Del. We're almost there."

"No, you go . . . leave me."

But Ron would not leave her. Eventually he brought her to her feet, and they ran a bit farther, to the crest of another hill. Still the house was not in sight.

"How much farther?" breathed Chandal.

"Just a little more . . . a little more."

Cries rose from a dozen places on the mountain, lifting from the rocks on the opposite sides of the ridge, from the shadows of trees, echoing back and forth until the whole landscape seemed to be afire with anger.

"Del, get down." Ron shoved Chandal onto the ground and knelt beside her, still holding Kristy in his arms. Three figures appeared above them at the top of the cliffs, halted in torchlight for a moment in quick consultation, and then disappeared over the rocks.

The searchers made no effort to be silent, hollering back and forth to each other, cutting through the underbrush with long blades. They moved in waves, leaving no stone unturned. As they combed a section of hillside, they moved on, but always one or two stayed behind to make sure no backtracking could be accomplished.

They sent jackals running into the night, flushed birds and lizards from their hiding places, drove anything alive out into the open.

Torchlight flickered here—there, almost everywhere. Now alert voices, speaking in low tones had moved closer. They were close. Damn close.

"Del, we have to move."

He helped her to her feet. Exhausted, they pushed on. A small path lay ahead. They traveled it for a while, saw torchlight ahead, and quickly dropped over the side and into the underbrush.

A little further on, Chandal again collapsed. She was crying helplessly now, her cheeks glistening with tears.

Ron lowered Kristy to the ground beside her mother. He turned to stare into the darkness. Fragments of voices were everywhere, the shrill cries of people involved in a hunt.

After a moment he glanced down at Kristy's ashen face resting on Chandal's breast. She appeared to be in a coma. Chandal lifted her harrowed face to the opaque moonlight and asked mutely for forgiveness.

"We'll be all right," Ron murmured softly. "All right."

He climbed quickly over the next rise of rock. Paused. A moment later, he dropped down beside Chandal. "Del, listen to me. We're at the road leading from town. Do you understand me?"

She nodded.

"I want you and Kristy to wait here." Chandal's eyes widened. "No, no—don't be frightened. Just listen to me. It's our only chance. If I can get to the car, get back here—then we have a chance of making it. If I'm not back in an hour, take Kristy. Follow the road. Keep moving."

"No, Ron—"

"Del, you must. Kristy can't go any further. Neither can you. After a while, you'll be stronger." He glanced around. "I've got to hurry. They're starting to work their way down the mountain." He looked at her. "I love you, Del." He kissed her quickly. "As I come up the road, I'll blink the lights on and off three times. Be ready to leave then. But—but don't come into the open unless you see me blink the lights. Got it? Three times."

He kissed her again. With that, after a brief pause, he rose; his expression was composed and rigid. With trembling hand, he touched Chandal's cheek. She leaned her face upon his hand. And as Ron lingered, she said, "Hurry. We'll be all right."

When he was well away from the underbrush, he began to run, paying no attention to the snapping dry branches beneath his feet.

Reaching the next ridge, he paused to catch his breath. From where he stood, he could see into the dark deserted town below.

Raising his eyes slightly, he could see his goal. Mrs. Taylor's house stood out clearly on its hilly perch. Seeing it encouraged him, and he dropped down the sharp embankment careful to avoid sending loose stones tumbling below. All he could hear was the wind and the occasional flutter of bird wings. Off in the distance, torches lighted the night sky.

He didn't know how long it took him to reach the edge of town. His legs trembled from the exertion of keeping his balance along the route, and he felt an extraordinary relief on coming onto level ground. For a moment his body strained to recover its normal equilibrium.

The town was quiet. The streets were deserted and reposed in dark velvet; only the roofs of houses and stores caught the glow of the moon.

He approached Mrs. Taylor's house from the south, taking a recently discovered path, a narrow track that wandered in back of the town. Coming this way after stopping at Alister Carroll's house, he had noticed relatively large fences and walls and property which seemed to have been abandoned.

The path was steeper than the normal route and also safer. His legs and arms brushed stone and rotted timber on either side; the air was so dense with heat that he could hear his own labored breathing. This appeared to be the only sound.

He emerged out of the shadows in the far corner of Mrs. Taylor's garden and his eyes moved slowly across the front wall. Three figures were hunched in the darkness by his car.

Children. They were all children. The oldest boy was standing apart from the other two, leaning against the house. His arm rested negligently against the railing, yet there was nothing relaxed in his stance.

Bending to pick up a stone, Ron realized there was a fourth boy seated behind the steering wheel of his car. He stood by the wall watching the slow and almost hypnotic movements of these figures. He knew they had been expecting his return.

Still Ron hesitated no longer. He moved over the wall, stumbling a little on the soft, uneven soil, and started for the car. No one had seen him yet. The three figures were less than twenty yards ahead of him and he had walked half the distance before the boy in the car threw on the headlights.

Ron had no plans now that the inevitable moment had arrived.

He squinted into the light and carefully tried to weigh the personalities of each of the three boys who faced him. He tried to move with an appearance of easy confidence, but he was trembling, and not with cold. He stopped a few feet away from them. No one moved.

The tableau remained unbroken for a moment.

The oldest boy smiled. He was quite relaxed, his face untroubled.

Ron said sharply, "I've come for my car."

He waited for a reply. There was none. He shouted, "Get out of my car!"

And then, like a platoon of deranged dwarfs, they charged; two at his legs, one at his throat.

Things dimmed and wavered before him and twice he found himself stretched on the ground. He did not recall how he'd gotten there. The second time he staggered to his feet, his hand was covered with blood. Whose blood? He wasn't sure.

And then suddenly he was raging out of control. He hurled himself against the nearest boy, the oldest, and drove his knee hard into his groin. He turned as something glinted before his eyes. The knife flashed.

Ron lifted the stone quickly and smashed it into the boy's skull. The boy's body fell forward against him. He withdrew, letting his body fall to the ground, and moved back as close as possible to the car. He tasted blood on his lips and felt it flow from the corner of his eye. His vision blurred.

A body suddenly sprang over the hood of the car, landing on his back. He felt a set of sharp teeth at his throat. He reached up, flipped the boy over his shoulder onto the ground, and brought his shoe down into the boy's face. Then he saw the oldest boy leap at him from amid the headlights of the car.

Ron swung his arm around, jammed his elbow in the boy's face. He fell backward, blood spewing from his mouth and nose.

The car started up. Through the violence of his own pain, he realized he was about to be run over. He looked at the boy's face twisted in hatred behind the steering wheel.

It was then that some furious kind of terror seized him, because there was no reason to kill the boy. Yet, when he dragged him from the car, he could not stop himself.

He brought the stone down again and again and again. When he finally stood, blood was splattered over his entire body, and the boy was dead. Relief rushed hideously through his brain, flooded his body. He turned. All appeared either dead or unconscious. He closed his eyes. He wasn't really sure he actually knew who he was. It was like wearing the skin of a stranger. And then he heard it.

The car sat still, its motor running.

EIGHT

ALL HE COULD SEE WAS ONE DEEP BLOOD-RED HUE OF FIRE, which lighted up the whole mountain far and wide; but below, the nether part of the mountain was dark and shrouded.

Once more recovering himself, he nosed the car slowly onto the main street of Brackston. He kept the headlights off. It was late, near midnight as he inched the car through the deserted square. He felt completely alone.

At the edge of town the spired blackness of trees stood in monumental silence, and on either side dwellings watched over the empty street. A gray haze dusted the trees, shimmered between branches and splashed shadows across the hood of the car.

Ron had just turned the corner when he heard the low rumble of thunder. He sucked in his breath. He was suddenly aware that the sound increased in volume. Drew nearer. Overhead, thick clouds had begun to gather over the valley. He felt the first stirrings of curious panic, a fear that if he relaxed his attention for so much as a moment he'd be swallowed alive. At the same time the possibility of rain seemed immensely attractive. Alister Carroll had said, *"If it rains—you may have a chance."*

It was this thought that held in check his feeling of desolation and doom. It was too still. Too damn quiet all of a sudden. Were Chandal and Kristy all right? Would he find them safe, waiting for him?

A brief flash of lightning shot through the hills, followed by a low roll of thunder. The sound, the light engulfed him, bearing him with it beyond the ridges into the empty spaces of the revolving universe.

He hit the gas pedal and started to climb. He had to remember to flash the headlights three times. But not too soon. No, not too soon.

With one knee jammed against the door, he fixed his eyes

on the fire, now no more than a rosy glow under a veil of sparks and ash. It glowed like a jewel at the bottom of the ocean. High above rose the stone; and the death image seemed a glowing plane of faces made of bizarre cubistic compositions; shadows flickered wildly in the changing light.

At that moment, as the stone dissolved in total darkness, Ron could see the path up ahead and the underbrush where he'd left his wife and daughter. He was unutterably tired, chilled by the wind and vaguely disturbed by the inexplicable stillness of the entire area. His gaze wandered the hills. Where were the torches? He was both hunted and hunter. He positioned his hand by the light switch on the dashboard. He checked in the rearview mirror. A gaping black void fell away behind him.

Reluctantly he flashed the lights. Once, twice, three times. He eased the car over to the side of the road and stopped.

Unexpectedly he panicked when he saw a discarded torch, set upright in the ground, to which had been tied a pelt. At its base lay two masks, and on a bush several feet away, a piece of material from Chandal's dress.

Oh, dear God—no, no . . .

Leaving the motor running, he stepped quickly from the car. "Chandal?" he whispered. "Kristy?"

He turned with a start as lightning flashed in the sky behind him. In the seconds that he hung there, straining to see through the muted underbrush, a thunder rumbled through the hills, stirring the leaves and echoing dully in the canyon and somber valley. When it passed, there came a silence so complete that a faint snapping of twigs fifty feet ahead was clearly audible.

The sound came quite suddenly, with startling and dramatic effect, followed by the sound of a child's voice. "Daddy, help me. Help me."

Almost at once there was again a general drop in the level of noise around him, a hush that seemed to foreshadow something yet to come.

"Kristy?"

"Help me, Daddy. Help me."

An almost complete silence had descended on the area. And then Ron saw her. Kristy stood immobile under the trees, her pale complexion glowing white against the night, her eyes piercing and huge. But where was Chandal?

Once or twice more Kristy's voice pleaded for help, the mournfulness of her tone seeming to screen an impatient readiness for action.

Get back into the car, Ron warned himself. This is a trap. Get away now before it's too late. He hesitated.

"Please, Daddy. Help me. Mommy is hurt."

The struggle within Ron only lasted a few seconds, but during that period of intensity, he realized he had no choice. He had to go to his daughter's side no matter what the consequences. Like a disease spread by panic, the violence of the emotions in the struggling swept over him, drawing him into the darkness toward his daughter.

NINE

SHOULDER TO SHOULDER, HOLDING HER BY THE WAIST, RON helped Chandal up the embankment. He would not let her rest until they had reached the car. Rocking back a little, teetering, she gripped the edge of the car door.

"Daddy, Mom is bleeding. She's bleeding."

"I know, sweetheart," Ron breathed.

"She fell when they came. All the way down there."

"I know, I know. Get in the car, Kristy."

Kristy opened the back door and slid in first. Ron felt Chandal starting to sink to her knees. "Hang on, Del." He clenched his teeth, moved his hand slowly over her cheek and nose, felt the puffy flesh, bruised and raw under his fingers. He moved her body forward until she dropped wearily onto the seat.

Ron was panting when he climbed in, panting and soaked with sweat. He could feel his heart pounding. He locked the doors and rolled up the windows.

The car had only moved a few yards when a shadowy figure stepped into the roadway ahead. The girl stood motionless, her face almost hidden in the shadows, ten yards off.

His heart pounding, Ron hit the headlights. The girl's face remained immobile.

"Ron, it's Nancy!" Chandal moaned.

"I know."

"Stop, Ron. Help her."

"Please, Daddy—it's Nancy," Kristy cried.

Ron slowed the car. Nancy held out her hands pleadingly, begging him to stop. He let her image slide past him, though he kept the white blur in the corner of his eyes; her face stayed where it was. Abruptly he hit the brakes.

"Kristy, open the door," Ron said.

"All right, Daddy."

Kristy opened the door as Nancy moved to the car.

"Hurry, Nancy," Ron said. "Get in."

Nancy gazed into the back seat, and not a sound was heard; there was something terrible, yet softening, also, in the silence; and when it broke, it broke suddenly and abruptly—it broke with a shrill and bloodcurdling cry from Kristy—the vent of the final despair as Nancy lunged for her.

Still screaming, Kristy fell back across Chandal's lap, too late for her mother to protect her.

Fingernails raked her face, gouging the corner of her eye; fingernails tore at her neck, pulled at her hair; violently Nancy tore into Kristy's shoulder and began dragging her from the car.

Ron spun around and grabbed for her throat. She opened her mouth and snapped at his arm with her teeth. He brought his fist around and drove it into her face. Her eyes walled back. Spittle spewed from her mouth. With one vicious thrust, he threw her body from the car. Her scream was instantly drowned out by the confusion of closing and locking the door.

Kristy screamed again as the first human hit the windshield with a hammer and sent showers of glass into the back seat. They were all over the car now, clawing and scratching and trying to pry their way in. One of them was Mrs. Taylor.

Ron jammed the car into reverse and pressed down on the accelerator. The car shot back and he could see bodies thrown into the dust. Jamming the car into drive, he pressed down again on the gas pedal. The car darted forward.

"Dad, Mom is . . . blood!" Kristy screamed and threw

herself forward grabbing hold of her father's neck. The car swerved, almost colliding into a tree. Ron shifted his foot from the gas pedal to the brake.

"Kristy, stop it. STOP IT!"

"I'm scared!"

Ron held tightly to the steering wheel. The car slid down an incline, but he knew he had it in control. Quickly he brought it up onto the main road, but instantly his back tires locked into the soft earth. He smashed his foot on the accelerator; the back tires dug deeper.

Ahead, like a group of frenzied animals, their ranks reeled and reformed, lurching forward under the momentum of recovery. There was no concern for their lives, but the anger on their faces indicated a deeper perplexity of hurt, a muted questioning of what was happening.

Then there rose the high shrieks of women; the men stared at each other, but were dumb. At that moment Ron felt the earth shake beneath the car; the cliffs above trembled; and, beyond in the distance, he heard the loud crash of stone; an instant more and a mountainous cloud seemed to roll toward him, dark and rapid.

Lightning flashed violently as the first large drops of rain splattered on the windshield.

No longer did the crowd think of justice and Ron and Chandal and Kristy; safety for themselves was their sole thought. Each turned to run—each dashing, pressing, crushing—amidst shrieks, and groans, the crowd vomited itself over the rocks and through the numerous crevices.

"Ron, help us!" Chandal pleaded. "Don't let us die."

Ron hit the accelerator again. The tires spun in their tracks.

Huge stones began to slide down the mountain, striking against each other as they fell, breaking into countless fragments, emitting sparks of fire, which caught whatever was combustible within their reach.

Below, the town had been set on fire, and at various intervals, the flames rose sullenly and fiercely against the solid gloom of night and rain.

Above, wild, haggard, ghastly with fear, small groups encountered each other in the momentary flickering of torch-light, but without leisure to speak, to consult, to advise; for the rocks fell more frequently now, extinguishing their lights, and all hurried to seek refuge beneath the nearest shelter. Never on earth had the faces of men seemed so haggard—never had there been a race of people so stamped with horror and sublimity of dread.

Quickly Ron threw the car in reverse. The car hesitated a moment, the tires spinning, then lurched backward. That's when the creature threw itself across the windshield so that its body lay directly across Ron's line of vision. For an instant, he stared into its eyes, its blue eyes. Mirrors of hatred.

In that moment Ron paused, then smashed his foot down on the gas pedal. The car shot back; the creature rolled forward across the hood and landed in front of the car. Violently Ron threw the car into drive and hit the accelerator. He felt a slight thud as the tires crushed the body. The body, Ron knew, of Alister Carroll.

The groans of the dying were broken by wild shrieks of terror—now near—now distant. In a universe of pouring rain and falling stone was heard the rumbling of the earth below, and the horrible grinding and hissing murmur of the escaping gases through the chasms of the mountains.

And then, in a sudden illumination, a burst of flames as the stone erupted, hurling a massive heap of rock and fire down upon the town, and the whole of Brackston's civilization began to break apart.

Even after reaching the main highway miles away, Ron imagined he heard screams, an echo of screams, in the flickering destruction in the ultimate darkness, not quite screams perhaps, rather the roar of rage, the furious rage of trapped animals.

And then, and then—it was over, swiftly, abruptly over. The din, the lunacy of Brackston, the whole shattering experience, was done.

They drove through the night without stopping, without looking back, until finally they watched the changing landscape as it grew somehow less intense. Since the whole area was still covered with deep shadows, it was hard to tell, but it seemed to Ron that the earth had now become greener, softer.

And he knew, finally knew, that morning would come.

EPILOGUE

HE ASSUMED THAT THE CHANGE IN HIMSELF WOULD BE AUTOMATIC. That he would be better or worse, but at least different. But like other travelers to different places, he soon decided that what belonged to Brackston must forever belong to Brackston and even his memory of the whole thing would have faded like a summer tan had Chandal let it. It became too easy to say "that time in the mountains." Ron actually found himself starting to tell the story to friends one night. It was in a tiny silence between words that he felt drawn to look toward Chandal. Her huge eyes met his in a kind of shock. He stammered, lost his place and trailed off.

Later at home he found her standing by the bedroom window staring out at the pool where the lights had first appeared so long ago, and wordlessly he went and put his arms around her.

"About tonight," she said after some time.

Still he said nothing, knowing she could feel him nod against the top of her head.

"I don't like talking about it to people. It's a kind of pretending that the whole thing was, oh, an adventure rather than—the way it was. Just pure black hate. Just looking into the eyes of pure black hatred. And I won't forget it. Not again. I keep telling myself, Ron, that maybe the whole thing couldn't have happened if—if I hadn't let myself forget the way it was back in the brownstone. And again in the carriage house."

"Del—"

"Maybe," she said. "Maybe it wouldn't have happened this time."

He met her gaze. "Maybe."

"I keep watching Kristy's face. Sometimes I can't take my eyes off her for hours at a time. I watch the way she plays with her dolls. I look for signs that she's—" Her voice broke.

"She isn't, Del. She got through it okay. I know she did." Gently, he added, "I watch her too, you know."

"I wasn't sure. But I'm glad." She took a deep breath. "There were always things you wanted to know. Things I never wanted to talk about. I can't tell anyone else. But now I want to tell you. Tonight."

He tasted fear, the familiar dry acid taste of it on his tongue, but he managed a bit of a laugh.

"What's funny?"

He hugged her tighter. "It's the second half of our wedding ceremony, Del. The half I always felt got left out. I guess I'm ready. But you know that if you share this part of yourself with me, you'll never get rid of me. You've got me for life."

"I'm counting on it," she said.

As she began to talk, he could feel the light coil of amazement inside of him that bounced up a slight smile to his lips. And he thought, even I. Even after all this, I have to fight to believe.

In that moment he understood how private is the destiny of each man and so amazing that words can barely pass the lips to describe it. He gazed at his wife and felt privileged to understand her halting words, her pain.

And around them were their own silent promises. To themselves and to each other. We will remember this time. We will remember.

And in the stillness of night, it was peaceful in its own special way.